WEAPON

BY

CHRIS A JACKSON

ILLUSTRATIONS

BY

NOAH STACEY

This one is for Anne
As are they all

A special thanks to *The Elfwooders*
Best damn editorial staff money can't buy

WEAPON OF FLESH

A NOVEL

BY

CHRIS A JACKSON

ISBN 1-4196-0795-2

First edition: June 2005

www.jaxbooks.com

PRELUDE

She stirred in the impenetrable darkness. Heavy links of chain clattered with her every movement, awakening her to the misery of the iron collar that chafed her neck, the sodden rag of a dress she wore, and the fetid odor of old blood. Torchlight flickered through the cracks beneath the massive door to her cell, the faint rattle of iron keys snapping her attention from the bundle she clutched so tightly.

Was someone coming?

They visited twice a day with food and water, but she'd been fed only hours before. Perhaps they came with fresh clothes, or simply to clean her filthy cell. She longed for clean skirts, or even a blanket.

The clatter of a key in the lock stiffened her like the crack of a whip. Yes, someone was coming.

Hinges squealed in protest and torchlight blinded her, but the figure silhouetted in the open portal bore no food, no clothes, and no water. It bore nothing save an iron-shod staff of crooked and gnarled wood. The shape of the staff struck a chord through the numbness of her suffering. She remembered it clearly. She remembered the one who bore it. And, worst of all, she remembered that day, weeks ago, when he stole her away from home, husband, and family.

She opened her mouth to scream, to deny, to plead, but even that small act was stolen from her with a mumble of guttural

1

syllables and a wave of his hand. She sat paralyzed, unable to move, speak, or even blink as he strode forward and stole from her the only thing she had left. Prying her numb fingers away from the bundle of bloodied skirts she clutched to her breast, he lifted the protesting babe in one careful but unyielding hand. Another flow of words stilled the babe's cries and the man, if man he was, smiled down at his prize.

"Perfect!" was the only word he uttered that she understood. He turned and walked away, having taken the only thing she had that was of any value to him. As the door closed, and the light faded, never to return, the magic that held her waned, and her piteous wail rent the dank air of her cell. She lay sobbing and empty, forgotten by the creature that had stolen her baby boy.

 CHAPTER I

In the forever midnight of a deep cavern, the pat-pat of unshod feet echoed as a wiry boy of six sprinted unerringly along. His eyes glowed faintly in the darkness, the magic within him drawing in the surrounding heat that emanated from the very womb of the earth; it allowed him to see, after a fashion, even when those born to utter darkness were blind. He ran tirelessly through the darkness, unfeeling and uncaring, absorbed with the task of navigating the underground and seeking the goal he had been assigned.

A chasm opened before him, heat billowing from its depths, brightening his vision. Without slowing his pace, he gauged the gap and chose which points of stone he would use to launch himself across. Without pause, for fear was unknown to his mind, he leapt to the sheer wall, bounding off a tiny crag of stone in a spinning flip that brought him to the other side. He landed in a roll that brought him to his feet at a run. The cavern continued on, twisting and turning as if wrought by the passing of a great worm. And though miles had passed under his feet, his pace didn't slow.

Finally, the place he had been told to seek loomed out of the darkness. The cavern ended in a steep shaft, the thick, acrid scents of sweat, rotting food, and excrement wafting up to assail his sensitive nostrils. Ears that could hear the heartbeat of a

3

mouse picked out the clink of chains, the grinding of bone between teeth, and the restless click-clack of iron-shod feet pacing on stone.

Briefly, the boy gauged the steep incline of the shaft. It was too wide for his arms to stretch across in an attempt to slow his descent, but a solution clicked into his mind even as he dived into the blackness. His bounding roll alternated in skidding contact with ceiling and floor, slowing his plummeting descent minutely with each impact. As a result, when he tumbled into the room at the shaft's end, he had only scrapes and bruises.

Battered and disoriented from the tumultuous descent, he still rolled to his feet, squinting at the glaring torchlight and taking in his new surroundings at a glance. The room was hewn out of living rock, a perfect half-sphere, the walls set at intervals with iron rings and manacles. Only two of the sets of restraints were occupied, and the two slavering orcs glared at the intrusion into their captivity. Their disgruntlement was only brief, however, for with the boy's arrival their manacles clicked open and fell from their chafed wrists.

The boy stood poised, his breath coming in deep, readying gasps, for he knew his task was not at an end. He knew this type of foe, for he had faced them before. He knew they would attack, and he knew he must kill them. That was his purpose. That was the master's wish and the only reason for his existence.

True to expectations, the two orcs scooped up their long, curved knives, formerly out of reach, and snarled in preparation. Their curved tusks clacked and gnashed in challenge. They grunted to one another words in their own crude language, words the boy didn't know, yet could interpret readily enough by their obviously aggressive movements. They were fighting over him, over which would get to kill him.

He waited, analyzing their movements and attention until they were paying much more interest to one another than to him. Then he moved.

The smaller one raised its knife reflexively, as he knew it would. His hands clamped around the thing's meaty wrist, fingers digging into the nerves near the long bones as he drove a kick into its throat. The knife dropped away, so he released his grip and let the choking creature fall, lunging for the weapon. But the second orc was already there, its huge, hobnailed boot clamping down on the knife before the boy could scoop it up. He rolled out of its reach and regained his feet, then stopped to reassess the situation.

Everything had changed.

The two orcs were now talking in tones that suggested cooperation instead of competition. When the larger one finally handed back the other's lost weapon, the boy knew he was in for the fight of his short life. He had never faced two before, let alone two who fought cooperatively. He readied himself and lunged.

The small one was still his target, but until he could get a weapon, the boy would be woefully outmatched. The thing snatched its knife out of reach, but that was predictable enough, so when his tiny foot smashed into its knee with enough force to snap the joint, the boy gained the element of surprise. Its howl of pain shook the air, but ended in a strangled gasp as the boy's claw-like fingers dug into its neck, collapsing the fragile bones around the trachea. As soon as the damage was dealt, he released the orc's throat and tumbled away, evading his dying victim's thrashing limbs.

Unfortunately, in his attempt to escape the creature's grasp, he had also left its weapon behind. The other orc scooped it up even before its former ally's dying throes had fully stilled. As the strangled gasps faded to silence, the boy faced the larger of his two opponents. The orc brandished its two curved knives with a snarl of confidence, stretching its features into a tusky grin of glee.

The boy stood and waited.

The attack would come, he knew. *Sometimes it is better to react than to act. Remember!* The words echoed in his mind, a memory of the countless hours he had spent under the master's care. Now he heeded those words and waited.

Even before the creature attacked, he knew it would be a feint.

He dropped under the false attack, swept a foot to trip the creature, then twisted over the other knife, which was meant to disembowel him. His hands clenched the huge wrist, thumbs digging in while he pulled it to close enough to bite. His teeth clamped onto the prominent tendons, snapping them like over-taut bowstrings. The dagger fell away and, even before he rolled to his feet, he was lunging for it. He did not see the backstroke of the other dagger as its pommel met firmly with his temple, darkening his vision and knocking him into a sprawling roll.

As he rolled to his feet, the boy realized he was in trouble. There was no pain; the magic prevented it. But he couldn't see clearly, and his balance was askew. His hearing and other senses were as acute as ever, and he reverted to them as if by a command of his absent master's voice: *If your senses flee or choose to deceive you, do not trust them. Seek that which is true. Remember!*

The scrape of an iron-shod boot on stone rang in his ears, and he dodged away from the lunge that he knew it accompanied. Air whisked past his cheek, and he reached out to grasp the arm that bore the knife that would have taken his life. Fingers pressed into the pressure points, and he heard the howl of pain, then the dagger hitting the floor. He let the weapon go, knowing he couldn't find it with his vision so awry.

The large artery in the pit of the arm will bleed freely if severed, weakening your opponent quickly. Remember!

He heeded the words in his mind, plunging his teeth into the noisome armpit and clamping them around the pulsing artery and the nerves surrounding it. Claws raked his back as the beast thrashed to pull its assailant free. Warm saltiness gushed over his face as he was torn free by his own momentum. Once again he rolled to his feet, but this time he knew he had won.

His vision cleared to reveal his lone opponent, one hand clamped onto the wound in a vain attempt to staunch the pulsing flow of blood that gushed from the pit of its arm. The orc was bleeding to death, unable to stop the red spray that painted its side and the floor at its feet. He had won, all he had to do was wait for the thing to die.

It collapsed to the floor in its own puddle of gore after trying in vain to staunch the flow. The boy watched patiently, unfeeling, as the crimson pool spread to eventually wet his toes, and the creature finally stopped twitching. His eyes left his victim as the hidden door finally opened.

"Your first attack was clumsy," the master said without preamble, waving the other servants forward to take away the dead orcs. "The first blow should have been a killing stroke, but was ill-timed and weak. Focus is the key when surprise is your ally. *Remember!*"

"Yes, Master," he said, committing the phrase to memory.

"You did not assess your second opponent's reaction to the failed attack and gave away the weapon you attempted to attain. Predicting your opponent's reaction is essential to survival. *Remember!*"

"Yes, Master."

"You spend too much effort trying to attain your opponents' weapons. This is dangerous and can distract from your goal. What is your goal?"

"My goal is to kill my opponent before he can kill me, Master."

"Yes! So, do not endanger yourself in attempts to get your hands on a weapon. You *are* a weapon. *Remember!*"

"Yes, Master."

"Good." The master fished something out of one of the pockets of his robes and handed it to the boy. "Here. Eat."

The boy snatched the piece of dried jerky and devoured it instantly, the saltiness of the meat mingling with the pungent tang of the orc blood that smeared his lips.

"Now, follow me." The master's words were more than a simple command; they wound themselves around the very core of the boy's will and forced him to comply. The magic impelled him to obey. Serving the master was his only purpose; that and to kill when the master bade him. He followed the master through the keep's winding passages until he finally recognized his surroundings. A few moments later he knew their destination and relaxed. They were going to the needle room.

"Clean yourself, then lie upon the table and hold still," the master commanded, turning to his pots and bowls as the boy complied. After a quick sponge bath from the bucket of cold water, the boy removed the filthy cloth that girded his skinny loins and climbed onto the thick stone table. He lay utterly still as the dyes were mixed, heated, ground, and infused with the magic that would, in turn, infuse him. Then the master drew out the needles, dipped the first into the glowing dye, and began the tattooing, a process the boy had endured every day of his short life. The magic prevented any pain; all he felt was the press of the needle as the ink seeped invisibly into his skin and the tingle of magic as it flowed into the core of his being.

It was the magic that made him strong, the magic that made him fast, and it was the magic that made him follow the master's orders. The master had never told him all the things the magic did or why. It was not in the boy to question, but he did wonder what purpose his magic and his life would serve.

Hours later, when the master had finished and was near exhaustion, he sent the boy to his room, a tiny nook that adjoined the master's laboratory. The boy sat on the narrow straw pallet and listened to the only man he had ever known as the dyes were put away, the mortars and pestles cleaned and stored. He wondered what the master wanted of him, what his next command would be. He didn't sleep, because he hadn't been ordered to, but sat and listened to all the sounds of his environment, all the clicks and groans of Krakengul Keep that he had listened to every day of his life. He sat and wondered what or whom he would kill next when the morning came.

 **CHAPTER II**

Fingers scrabbled for purchase upon the rain-slicked stone, finding none. The boy shifted his stance, moving his feet upon the tiny ledge that supported him a thousand feet above the rocky shore of the Bitter Sea. Rain lashed at his back as the wind tried to peel him away from the cliff face. He clung tightly and stretched his twelve-year-old frame, feeling for his next handhold. His fingers met a narrow crack; he jammed them in and twisted, testing the hold before committing his weight to it. It held, so he lifted his weight easily with the three-fingered purchase and held himself up until his other hand found a similar grip further up the crack.

Thus he ascended the cliff another thousand feet before he reached the plateau. He heaved himself up, quickly assessing the damage to his hands and feet. One finger was bent unnaturally, so he straightened it with a crunch. The other scrapes, cuts, and bruises were already healed. Clearing the rain from his eyes, he could see Krakengul Keep only a mile or so to his left. The Bitter Sea lay behind him, whipped into waves by the storm and stretching beyond the limits of his sight. Before him, the plateau sloped down and, miles into the distance through the slackening rain, he could see the edge of the forest. Beyond that, faint lights flickered among the trees. He wondered briefly what those lights were—fires perhaps? Orcs? Or elves or men, maybe? A distant

9

horn-call touched his ears, and he dashed off immediately for the keep, banishing his curiosity.

Entering the outer courtyard, the boy was greeted by an unusual sight. Five horses stood there, heads bowed against the rain, their reins looped loosely over the hitching post. All bore harnesses and saddles, and one was garbed in light chain barding with ornate tooling in the leather. They towered above him as he walked past, their plate-sized hooves clack-clacking nervously on the flagstones. A servant exited the keep and approached the horses, glancing at the boy in passing. He took the reins of two of the mounts and led them to the stables. Apparently, whoever owned these horses would be staying for a while. The boy ascended the steps eagerly, curiosity once again tickling at the back of his mind.

He didn't have long to wonder who these visitors were. As he entered the great hall, he beheld the master and five tall figures standing around the long table nearest the cavernous fireplace, four men and one woman. All the newcomers bore weapons—bows, swords, knives, and many other types he had never seen before. They stood like warriors, too, for as they all turned to watch him approach he could see the balance and strength in their movements. The master bade him come closer, and he felt the scrutiny of the five.

"This is Master Xhang," the master informed him, gesturing toward one of the five. "He and his assistants will be teaching you the use of weapons and the proper defenses against them. You will not kill them."

"Yes, Master," he responded, noting the light chuckle from one of the tall figures. The sound was unfamiliar, strumming cords of curiosity in his mind and tensing his muscles.

The one called Master Xhang also noted the chuckle and snapped a curt order to the man in a language that the boy didn't understand. He understood well enough, however, when the one who had laughed unclasped his heavy cloak, stood his longbow against a chair, and drew a long, curved sword. The boy's mind clicked with a possible correlation: perhaps laughter was a prelude to combat.

"This is Cho Thang. He is skilled in the use of the katana, which you will learn presently. Now, defend yourself."

The boy immediately moved away from the group, sidestepping into the open area between the long tables while keeping his eyes on the tall warrior's sword. He noted the man's movements, finding no flaw or obvious weakness. He stopped and waited, assessing his situation. The man was much taller than he, and the sword gave him an even longer reach. He bore another short sword at his hip, curved like the one he wielded, and a small dagger. These the boy could use if he could get his hands on them, which was not likely. What was more, he had the distinct disadvantage of being told not to kill the man. Well, there was not much he could do but wait for the attack, so the boy prepared himself and settled into the focused relaxation that readied him for any opportunity.

The series of attacks came in a flurry so quick and precise that the boy barely evaded the killing strokes, and received two shallow cuts on his shoulder and stomach. He hadn't been able to penetrate the man's guard in the slightest, his grasping fingers and lashing feet meeting only air. The two paused for a moment, assessing one another anew. The man's features showed slight surprise at the boy's quickness, and his narrow eyes widened as the shallow cuts he'd inflicted closed and vanished without a trace. The boy showed nothing, but his mind was working full speed. This was no orc or bandit that he could easily outwit and outfight; this was a trained warrior, and all he could hope for was to stay alive and exploit any openings that presented themselves.

The next flurry of attacks was longer and even more furious. The boy's hands and feet slapped aside killing strokes more than a dozen times before one cut finally passed his guard, slicing deeply into the muscle of his chest.

"Stop!"

Both combatants froze at the master's command, the boy because it was ingrained in his soul to do so, and the warrior because he was simply trained to obey. Both stood poised as the master and the other warriors approached. The steady pat-pat of blood dripping from the boy's heaving chest was loud to his ears. The wound was closing, but he had lost a good amount of blood and felt its loss in the slight weakness in his limbs.

"Master Xhang, your assessment."

"The boy is quick and trained well for his age, but lacks focus and knowledge of combat. He missed several opportunities to grasp Cho Thang's sword and exploit the opportunities that this would have presented." His eyes raked the boy from head to foot, a thin smile tugging at the corners of his long mustache. "I believe he was holding back, constrained by the order not to kill and your additional order to defend himself. His tactics were primarily those of survival, not aggression. We must break him of this flaw."

"I give you one year to do so, minus one hour per day during which I require his presence in my laboratory. At the end of that year, you will receive your payment."

"Very well," Master Xhang agreed with a bow, then a sidelong glance at his apprentice Cho Thang. "But may I suggest that you rescind your order for the boy not to use lethal force. He'll learn nothing by holding back."

"Your people will be at risk, Master Xhang. I won't be responsible for their welfare if I rescind that order."

"I won't hold you responsible for their welfare. We are warriors, after all. Risk is our life, and I wouldn't have my people become soft with a year of sitting on their backsides risking nothing worse than a bruise or two." He snapped a short phrase to Cho Thang, who cleaned his sword on a cloth from his belt and sheathed it, bowing low to his master and then to the boy.

"Rescind the order," Xhang said with a nod and another thin smile.

"Very well," said the master, facing the boy. "You will be training with Master Xhang and his men for one year, beginning today. You will fight each of them many times. You will fight as you are taught to fight and kill if the opportunity presents itself, but only when the order to fight has been given by Master Xhang or myself."

"Yes, Master."

"Good." The master turned to Xhang and said, "He is yours for one year. At the end of that year, I'll assess his training. If any of you survive, you'll receive the agreed-upon sum."

"Very well." Xhang spoke to his people at length, received nods of obedience from each, then bowed to the master. "It is agreed." His narrow eyes snapped to the boy. "Go and clean yourself, eat your fill, and return here in one hour."

The boy simply looked at the master questioningly; having never received an order from anyone else, he didn't know if he should obey.

"You will follow Master Xhang's orders. Go."

The boy sprinted out of the room, heading for the baths. He had never had a whole hour to eat and bathe before and intended to make the most of it.

One year later, six figures stood in the great hall of Krakengul Keep. Four warriors stood at rigid attention. Cho Thang was missing the last joint of the two smallest fingers of his left hand and bore a wide scar from his left ear to the nape of his neck. The other warriors also bore marks and scars; even Master Xhang had felt steel part his flesh under the boy's hand. One of the warriors was dead.

The boy also stood at attention, a stance he had learned from his trainer. The master stood at ease, a thin smile tugging at the corners of his mouth as he looked upon the boy with a scrutinizing eye. He'd spent an hour every day reinforcing the magic that had forged the boy into a weapon, but until now he hadn't noticed the added height, broader frame, and surer stance. His pupil had learned the use of every weapon the warriors bore, and how to defend against each, both with weapons and without, just as Xhang had promised.

"You've performed admirably, Master Xhang, and your payment awaits you." He nodded to two servants who entered

Weapon of Flesh

the room bearing a heavy coffer.

"You have kept your end of the bargain, and my people have also learned a great deal in this last year." Xhang bowed deeply to the master, and then again to the boy. "Your pupil is skilled. He'll serve you well."

With that, the four surviving warriors turned and left, taking their well-earned pay with them. The master simply watched them go, a faint smile on his lips. The boy stood stock still before him, awaiting his next order, firm and confident in his newly acquired skills. When the outer door boomed closed, and the sound of hoof beats dwindled to silence, the master finally turned to his pupil.

"Your next instructor will train you in the skills of stealth and intrusion. You will not kill him, for his expertise is in evasion and the art of silence, not combat." He nodded once, a gesture that the boy found strange, until the light tap on his shoulder from behind.

The boy leapt like a cat standing on hot coals, clearing the master's head by a foot and landing in a dodging roll. He had heard nothing, smelled nothing, and felt nothing until the finger tapped his shoulder. It could have easily been a knife severing his spine. The last year had taught him skills with weapons, and to be confident in his abilities. The last two seconds had taught him that all his skills were useless if he was unaware of an enemy.

The diminutive man who had been standing behind him chuckled with amusement, twirling a dagger in his left hand and smoothing his immaculate goatee with the other. He wore dark leathers, supple with use. Many pockets and pouches dangled from his belt, and a number of tools rode in specialized sheaths sewn into the thighs of his trousers. When the man's mirth subsided, the master continued.

"This is Master Votris. You will learn from him all that he can teach you of stealth and intrusion. Follow his instructions."

"Yes, Master." The boy regained his composure and approached his new instructor.

14

"He's as clumsy as a three-legged ox," the man said flatly, shaking his head. "But he's quick and agile enough. We'll see what he can learn."

"You have one year. He will report to my laboratory for one hour every day at sunset. The rest of his time belongs to you." The master turned his back and walked away.

"Humph," Votris scoffed, eying the boy critically. "Well, the first thing, I suppose, is to teach you how to stand without fidgeting like a stallion with a mare in his sights."

Votris moved to the boy's side, and it was like watching a ghost. He walked with such grace and fluidity that the boy thought his mind was playing tricks on him. Not a scuff of leather on stone, no squeak of buckle nor brush of cloth could be heard, even by the boy's enhanced ears. He realized that he had much to learn in the next year.

 CHAPTER III

The boy's feet padded through the patch of loose shale without disturbing a single stone. Rain pelted him, slicking every surface, but each time his foot landed, his step was sure and silent. When the shale gave way to sandy soil he ran on, just as he had for the last ten miles, as he had for every morning of the last year. Each day he ran a new course, and nowhere on the plateau was there a single footprint to mark his passage. His trainers had taught him well.

His age was now somewhere in the middle of his sixteenth year, though he wouldn't have known it if asked. He was still slim, but muscle rippled under his well-tanned skin. His height was that of most men, though he wouldn't have been called tall by anyone but a dwarf. The last two years had added discipline and focus to the previous training. One instructor had been a defrocked monk of some distant and obscure order who had taught him the value of focusing his body's energy. His last instructor had taught mental discipline and the importance of a still and ordered mind. But all of his trainers, however varied in their abilities and strengths, taught him to apply their teachings for only one purpose: to kill.

He had learned his lessons well.

And still, every day for one hour after sunset, he lay on the master's table in the needle room and the ink vanished into his skin. The magic was part of him now; it would never fade, would never diminish. He was one with it. He could not always feel the power within him, but power there was, he knew, for he saw in the eyes of his trainers their astonishment at the feats he could accomplish.

But today was different.

Yesterday his last trainer had departed, so today he expected a new one. He wasn't particularly surprised when he entered the courtyard of the keep to find a stout, two-wheeled cart attached to a pair of sturdy horses. What puzzled him was that the servants were putting baggage into the cart, not taking it out. Bedrolls, food, and equipment were being piled in carefully and lashed down. He'd never been in the stables, so he didn't know that this cart belonged to the master.

He stilled his curiosity as he'd been taught and entered the keep, prepared for anything, or so he thought.

"There you are!" The master snatched him aside as soon as he entered the great hall, now in much disarray with scurrying servants. "Here," he snapped, handing the boy an armful of soft clothing. "Clean yourself, then put these on. Return as quickly as you are able. Go."

"Yes, Master," he said, scurrying off to the baths, unsure of the command, yet forced to comply by the magic that coursed through his veins. He placed the strange clothing on a chair in the bathing room and quickly stripped out of his loincloth. Soap and water was applied judiciously, though he was again unsure why he would need to bathe after only a ten-mile run in the rain. But bathe he did, and thoroughly; he could *not* disobey.

The real dilemma was the master's order to put on the clothing he'd been given. He'd seen others wearing such things, and these weren't any different than what the servants wore, but he'd never worn pants or a tunic, and he'd never watched anyone dress. It took him a while. He put the pants on back-to-front once and struggled briefly with the tunic, unsure of the lacings, which he eventually decided to leave hanging loose. The cloth belt he wrapped double around his waist and cinched tightly in a knot he knew wouldn't slip. The last he did as he sprinted back to the great hall, which was now slightly less chaotic, though still strange.

Every servant he had ever seen in the keep stood in a straight row, all facing the hall's entrance, and all fidgeting nervously. Something was definitely amiss.

The boy stilled his mind and took his place, exactly where the master bade him return to, for he could do naught else. He stood and waited, enduring the itching clothing, calming his hammering heart, and stilling his tumultuous thoughts.

"Good!" The master's bellow echoed through the hall, surprising everyone except the boy. Now the master approached him and his face changed. It stretched into a smile, something the boy had never seen. His eyes raked the boy from toe to brow, and his staff rapped the floor smartly. "Very good! We're ready to leave."

"Leave, Master?" The boy didn't understand; leaving was something other people did. The trainers, the people who brought food and other things, they left. How could the master leave? How could *he* leave? He'd been here in the keep, on the plateau, his entire life. Where else was there? His agile mind briefly flashed with memories of lights in the distant forest. Maybe they would go there.

"Yes, boy, it's time to leave. Your training is complete, as are the spells I have woven into your flesh. It's time to fulfill your destiny."

"Destiny? *My* destiny, Master?"

"Yes. Now, go stand by the cart and wait for me."

"Yes, Master." The boy sprinted out of the great hall and stood by the sturdy two-wheeled cart, questions whirling around his mind like leaves on the wind. What was a *destiny*? He'd heard the word before, of course, but never really understood its meaning. If they had to leave for him to fulfill his, perhaps it meant something people did when they left. If the master was leaving with him, would they find the master's destiny as well? He forced the questions down, knowing that he wouldn't get answers until the master gave them. Two cleansing breaths brought calm and shifted his mind into the enforced quiescence of a light meditation.

He took in his surroundings—the keep, the courtyard, the sights, sounds, and smells that he had known throughout his entire life. The thought that he wouldn't ever see any of it again came to him, and he mulled it over, finding the concept difficult to grasp. He could find no remorse in leaving his lifelong home, though he may not have been capable of such an emotion. He had no desire to leave, and he had no desire to stay. His desires had never been a significant issue in his creation, so he didn't consider them. All he considered was what lay beyond the plateau, what they might encounter, and what his destiny would hold. For curiosity was an emotion inseparable from every human psyche. The master had deemed it necessary for survival, and it hadn't been suppressed by the magic like many of his other emotions. The magic hadn't taken everything human away from him—not quite.

The groan of bronze hinges stirred the boy from his calming meditation. The master stood at the great doors of the keep, drawing them closed with a dull boom of finality. Then his hands moved in graceful arcs, and words that the boy couldn't understand pulsed through the air with power. When the words ended, a subsonic tremor shook the castle to its very foundations, and a fine spider web of white light traced every seam in wood, metal, glass, and stone. The master turned and descended the steps to the courtyard, dusting his spotless hands upon his robes.

"There we are, safe and sound."

This didn't make sense to the boy, but his comprehension wasn't required, only his obedience. The master climbed into the seat of the wagon and released the creaky brake, then turned to his silent minion.

"We're going on a journey. At the end of that journey, your destiny awaits. You will walk beside the wagon and remain wary, for the world beyond the plateau is dangerous. If there is trouble upon our path, you'll use all the skills you've been taught to combat it. Is that clear?"

"Yes Master," the boy said, tensing and relaxing muscles in the rhythmic patterns that brought him to a state of calm preparedness.

"Good."

The whip cracked over the backs of the two stout horses, and the wagon lurched forward. The boy followed without a word, too many unanswered questions whirling in his mind as he walked away from the only home he had ever known.

In the city of Twailin, a tower rose in the midst of a grand estate. It loomed above the tile roofs and ornate balconies of the homes of the richest nobles and merchants who populated Barleycorn Heights. But the master of that estate, while wealthier than the vast majority of his neighbors, was not a highborn noble or a merchant, as many thought, at least, not in any commodity that anyone wanted for their own.

The master of the estate stood upon his tower this evening, looking disdainfully down on his wealthy neighbors. His name was Saliez, though none of his associates used that name. They called him only "Grandfather," though he had sired no children, nor taken any under his care. He was the Grandfather of Assassins, the headmaster of their guild, a merchant in death. Terror and killing were the only commodities in which he dealt.

Business was good.

Business was so good, in fact, that not a facet of commerce, government, or graft within the city of Twailin was beyond his grasp. He wielded more power than that sniveling Duke Mir, sitting so smugly in his walled keep high on the bluff that overlooked the city, and surely garnered more respect from his guild members. Why, not even the city constabulary, half of whom were on the Grandfather's payroll, respected that doddering old fool. Only the Royal Guard remained steadfastly loyal to Duke Mir, but the Grandfather had spies aplenty among them. They were no threat.

The Grandfather's minions, the entire Guild of Assassins,

respected him utterly. They had learned to respect him. They had learned that disrespect resulted in death…or worse. And there *was* worse. They had all witnessed worse first hand. They had witnessed it from the Grandfather's own hand, for he was not only their guildmaster, he was their foremost practitioner.

But this night, despite the disdain he expressed toward his highborn neighbors, the Grandfather of Assassins was elated. He had come to this, the highest point in all the city save for the spires of the duke's palace, not to gaze down at those who were nothing but contracts or clients to him, but to take delivery of a message that his eyrie-master had just received. He held that message now in his triumphantly clenched fist, for his life was soon to become much easier, and his business tenfold as lucrative. The message he clenched so tightly bore only two lines, lines that only his eye would ever read and understand. He flattened the crumpled parchment once again, though he had read it many times already.

Your weapon is ready.
I will arrive with it in seven days.

~ Corillian ~

"Arrogant bastard," he muttered under his breath, crumpling the parchment again. "Sixteen years, and he makes me wait another week! Ha!"

He turned and stalked back into the tower, casting the crumpled note into one of the glowing braziers that lit and warmed the eyrie. He could wait one more week. After all, he'd been waiting almost two decades for this. What were seven more days?

By the beginning of their third day on the road, the boy was beginning to think that the only true danger in the world beyond the plateau was boredom. They'd been plodding along at a pace that could be challenged by any tortoise in good health, and the most dangerous thing they'd encountered had been a nasty patch of poison sumac. Every night they ate their stew and he watched while the master slept; then in the morning they would eat their porridge and the boy would pack their gear. The master allowed the boy the few hours of sleep he required in the back of the wagon during the early part of their daily travels. He would wake him around mid-morning and order him to once again resume his plodding pace beside the wagon. The boy's keen senses attended to their surroundings as the master studied his books and scrolls, lounging in the driver's seat.

The trip would have been endurable, even pleasant, if not for the boy's nagging curiosity. So many questions rattled around inside his head that he began to be distracted by them. *Where were they going? How long would it take to get there? What was a destiny, and was his different than anyone else's?* He had even tried to ask the master for some answers to these questions, but had just been told to be quiet and vigilant.

After three days, he was bored with being vigilant. Oh, he was still watching and listening as best he could; the spells of obedience required him to do exactly as he was told. Yet, while his eyes and ears were tuned finely to their surroundings, his mind wound through complex trails of thought, surmising this and imagining that, all concerning his destiny. It was undoubtedly the distraction of his own tumultuous thoughts that allowed him to be so caught unaware.

The snort of a horse snapped his attention back to his razor-sharp senses in a heartbeat, and he immediately knew that there were at least six people on horseback hidden in the brush on either side of the road. They were still a stone's throw away, three on each side of the muddy track. The boy could hear their breath, their mounts shifting, the creak of leather on harness and belt, and the click of an arrow being nocked onto a bowstring. This did not bode well.

"Master," he said in his usual calm tone.

"Yes, boy. What is it?"

"Men with horses and weapons are hidden on either side of

the road fifty paces ahead." He heard the rustle of paper and the thump of one of the master's books landing in the bed of the wagon.

"Well, now." The master's voice held a waver of interest, perhaps anticipation. "Well, well, then. Keep walking, boy, but be ready. They mean to rob us, and we'll have to kill them."

"Yes, Master." Some of the master's words were unfamiliar, but the last were clear enough. The boy relaxed, slipping into the pre-fight meditation that prepared his body and mind. He cataloged his opponents, their number—seven, not six as he'd previously thought—their weapons, and their positions. From this, he estimated the order in which they would attack and whom his first target would be.

As he predicted, the bandits crashed from the woods when they were about ten paces away, startling the carthorses, and bringing their bows to bear.

"Ho there, old man!" the burliest of them said, leveling a heavily-built crossbow at the master and bringing his fidgety black mount abreast of the two cart horses. "This here's a toll road, and you're only allowed to pass if you pay up."

"Toll road?" the master said, a quirk of amusement in his voice. "I wasn't aware of that. This is open land, sir, unless I miss my guess. And you are nothing but a thief. I'll not pay, and you'll let us pass."

The boy could hear the falseness in the master's voice and quickly reassessed their foes. Six men and one woman sat astride well-kept mounts. They all had bows: three crossbows, three hunting bows, and the woman bore a short horn bow. Her eyes flickered nervously between the boy and his master. The crossbows were cocked and loaded, which meant they could be fired readily. Those would be his first targets. The others would have to draw and take aim first, which would take at least two seconds; plenty of time. He shifted his feet upon the rocky road, readying himself.

"That's where you're wrong, old man," the burly man said, shifting his aim from the master to the boy. "I own this road, and you'll pay up, or I'll put a quarrel in your young son's eye."

"Very well, you brigand!" the master snapped, reaching to his belt and plucking out a bulging pouch. "This is all the real money we have. The rest is just goods, things we'd planned on selling. Take the money and go, but leave us the goods to barter in town for something to eat this winter." He tossed the jingling pouch at the leader, forcing him to lower his weapon to catch it. The others relaxed visibly as their leader laughed and hung his crossbow over the saddlebow. He loosened the strings and drew the bag open, but instead of coins pouring out, a skeletal hand much too large for the bag to hold lunged from the dark interior.

"Kill them all, boy," the master said in a whisper as the long, clawed fingers plunged into the man's throat. As the bandit fell from the saddle, screaming through the blood flooding his throat, the boy blurred into action.

He leapt into the air, tossing up the stone that was clenched between his feet and catching it as he spun. Before his feet hit the ground, he sent the stone whistling at the nearest bowman, scattering bits of skull and brains among the bandits. A crossbow cracked, but the boy had already calculated the bolt's trajectory and intercepted the shaft in flight. Spinning again, he flung the heavy crossbow bolt into the eye of the next bowman, and then bounded past their dying leader, his foot snapping the bow of another before his fist smashed the astonished man's throat.

A bow twanged—the horn bow from the sound—but the master had erected a shield of shimmering energy, and the arrow glanced off. The boy snatched a dagger from the man choking at his feet and flung it into the chest of the bandit who had not yet fired his weapon. As he turned to the other crossbowman, he saw that the man had dropped his weapon and drawn a long saber. The bandit's sturdy mount bore down on the boy, the curved sword cocked back to take his head. The boy simply ducked under the blow, grabbed the saddle, and swung up behind his attacker. His hands grasped the man's head and twisted sharply. As he stared into the man's dying eyes and thrust him out of the saddle, hoofbeats rang in his ears; the woman was fleeing.

He was untrained in horsemanship, so chasing her was out of the question. He hopped out of the saddle beside the dead man, pulled a bolt from his quiver, and retrieved the discarded crossbow. There was a crank for cocking the thing, but the boy simply placed the stock against his chest and pulled the string back until it clicked. He placed the quarrel in the notch, took aim, adjusted for windage, and fired at his fleeing foe.

She toppled from the saddle, the bolt lodged squarely between her shoulder blades.

"Well done!" He turned to the master's voice, but stopped in shocked surprise.

"Mast—"

He leapt, but it was too late.

Another crossbow cracked, and the thick shaft plunged through the back of the master's neck before the boy's fingers could intercept it. The last bandit, who had been hiding behind them in the trees, spurred his mount into the deep forest. The boy wrenched the heavy bolt free and considered his chances of knocking the fleeing bandit from the saddle; they were minuscule, so he dropped the bloody shaft and surveyed the scene.

Seven bandits lay dead, their mounts scattered, some still running. The master lay slumped over his knees in the seat of the wagon. One bandit had escaped.

He had failed.

"Master," he said, doubting that he would receive an answer. The bolt had severed the spine. The master was dead.

The boy's head cocked to the side as his eyes took in the details that his mind was ill-prepared to handle. He had seen death. But this was the *master*.

The boy stood on the wagon for some time, wondering what he should do. He had failed to do as he had been instructed, which troubled him. But the master was dead, which made him feel strange. There would be no repercussions for his failure, but there would also be no instruction from the master as to what to do next. Should he dispose of the bodies as he'd seen the servants do? He didn't know how. Should he stay here? He doubted that anything would change if he did. The master would stay dead, and he'd be no closer to his destiny.

"Destiny," he muttered, wondering why he said the word aloud. He looked down the road in the direction that they had been traveling. The dead brigand still lay there; her mount had returned and was nosing the corpse.

Midday arrived, so the boy ate an apple and a piece of jerky from the cart's stores, thinking only that this had been his instructions at midday the previous two days, so he should do the same today. When the shreds of core and stem dropped from his fingers, he had made a decision.

"Destiny," he said clearly, dropping from the wagon to the road.

How far?

There was only one way to find out.

What is my destiny?

The answer was the same.

For the first time in his life, the boy initiated an act of his own volition: He placed one foot in front of the other in the direction that he knew his destiny lay. He then repeated that act, then again, until he was walking. He did not look back, did not regret and did not mourn the loss of the only man he'd ever known. Such things were not part of his makeup. There was only a burning curiosity about his destiny, what it was, and where it lay. And would he know it when he found it?

He walked away from the wagon without taking a single thing with him. The two sturdy draft horses stood in their traces, the wagon sat there full of their supplies and equipment, the master still slumped dead in the seat.

He had been trained to kill, not to survive.

The boy walked through the rest of the afternoon, his pace somewhat faster than the plodding gait of the master's wagon. When darkness began to descend, he slowed, thinking for the first time about food.

His steps faltered, the weight of his very first decision crashing down like a stumbling block. There would be no stew tonight. The master had made the stew, and the master was dead. He looked back in the direction of the wagon. There was food in the wagon, he knew, and he could be there easily before dawn. He would miss dinner, but he might yet have breakfast.

His head turned in the other direction; his destiny lay somewhere down this road. How far could it be? He was hungry, but not starving, and at this particular time, his curiosity burned more urgently than the empty pit of his stomach. He estimated how far he could travel without food, but the information gained him little. He didn't know how far he had to go, or even how much road there was. Surely it couldn't go on forever.

He walked on.

The night descended, and his eyes took on the faint glow of the magic, illuminating the road for him to see. His mind mulled over the decisions he had made, wondering how he could have improved them as his feet trod on, tirelessly eating up the miles between him and his goal.

CHAPTER IV

When darkness began to descend the following day, hunger started to vie with his curiosity much more urgently. Thirst was less of a problem. Water from any of the roadside puddles quenched his thirst adequately, but hunger, he found, was a type of pain to which he was not immune. It was a frustrating dilemma. He tried eating some of the grass and leaves growing beside his path, but they tasted foul and offered him little energy. He saw many a squirrel and bird and knew he could knock one out of a tree easily with a stone, but he also knew the meat had to be cooked before he could eat it. He knew nothing about cooking except that it required fire, and he knew nothing about building a fire.

His pace slowed to a more conservative gait; he was not truly tired, not yet, but he had decided that he wanted to find his destiny before starvation found him. This was the pace that traded miles for energy at the most economical rate.

As the night deepened, a sound that didn't blend into the usual nighttime noises of the forest pricked his ears, snapping his attention into focus. The sound had come from far ahead, beyond a low hill where a faint glow could be seen against the darkening sky. He heard another sound, metal against crockery, and the lilt of a woman's voice. He moved forward warily, remembering the master's words about the dangers of the lands off the plateau.

He topped a small rise and moved into the forest for better concealment, then crept through the undergrowth for a better view of what lay beyond the hill. The tidy little collection of buildings that would barely merit the description of "village" didn't look threatening, but he had learned from his instructors that appearances could deceive. He moved forward cautiously, his steps disturbing not a leaf nor making a sound.

Unfortunately, the road passed directly through the little village. There were nine small buildings made of wood and one made of stone on its lower half, which was the only one to boast a second floor. They weren't built for defense and didn't look at all formidable. When the woods gave way to pasture and stone fences girded the road, the boy was forced to either walk in the open or take a wide detour that would cost him unknown miles and hours.

He made a decision—he was getting good at making decisions, this being his third—and stepped into the open. He paused, listened, deemed it safe enough, and strode cautiously down the road. His intention was to simply walk through the little town, but even before he reached the first building, a tidy little house with a pen of milling swine and a white painted porch, he smelled food.

It wasn't so easy to make out through the pungent odor of the swine-yard, but he definitely smelled freshly baked bread, roasted potatoes, and braised pork. His mouth began to water and his stomach growled loudly. He cinched his cloth belt more tightly around his slim middle, trying to stifle the sound. He didn't want to be betrayed by the noise; it might provoke some kind of attack from the people who lived here.

He was hearing many noises now: clinks and clatters of metal, pottery, and glass; the dull thud of metal biting into wood; the murmur of voices; and the occasional higher pitch of laughter. He walked on, his gaze flickering among the faint movements behind windows, the shifting light of candles and lanterns; even the flitter of an owl gliding silently overhead caught his eye. The bird settled to a perch on the gable of the tallest building, its head swiveling to scan the twilight road.

The tall building was set back from the road further than the others, its front yard lined with hitching posts. A large turning yard and a tidy stable were framed by split-rail fences to the left of the main building. He could see someone in the stable pitching hay into the stalls and quickened his pace. When his steps brought him to where the wind carried the scents of the inn's kitchen across his path, his mind virtually exploded with the fabulous aromas of cooking meats, baking bread and pastries, stewed and spiced vegetables, and the pungent scent of ale.

His feet stopped walking as if he'd received an order from the master, his mind overwhelmed by the aromas of well-cooked food. He peered through the windows at the shadows moving within, catching glimpses of a woman carrying a huge tray of meats, cheeses, and bread. His stomach made his next decision for him, and he approached the door.

The boy paused there for a moment to listen, cataloging the voices he heard. There were at least seven people inside, probably more. He'd have to be cautious. He gripped the brass handle and turned it carefully. It wasn't locked. He pushed it slowly open and stepped into the noisy interior.

The noise abated somewhat as he swept the room with his gaze. He noted six men seated at two tables; each wore a belt knife, and all four at the larger table wore swords. There was an unstrung longbow propped in the corner behind that table. The two women wore no obvious weapons, but their skirts could easily conceal several, though nothing could be hidden in the tightly laced corsets. Another man stood behind a long counter that occupied one entire end of the room, a pewter mug in one hand and a rag in the other, the two working against one another, though it was doubtful that either would become cleaner or dirtier by the contact.

The boy saw their eyes on him and wondered what was so interesting about him.

In their eyes, he was a stranger, unarmed and alone, which was unusual enough. He was a bit travel-worn, but no dirtier than several of the men sitting at the tables. His lack of a pack, belt pouch, or any kind of a weapon marked him as highly strange. His clothes were those of a peasant and he wore no shoes, which might mean he was a slave.

"You want somethin', lad, or are you just gonna sit there and stare at us all night?"

That brought laughter from four of the six men and one of the women, as well as the man who had spoken, the large one polishing the mug. The boy tensed, knowing that laughter was often a prelude to attack.

When the laughter subsided and no one tried to kill him, he wondered if there might be other reasons for laughter. He approached the long counter where the big man still stood polishing the dirty mug and said, "I'm standing."

"What?" the man snapped, ceasing his polishing and putting the mug aside. "Yer what?"

"I'm standing." Everyone was looking at him strangely, so he elaborated. "You asked me if I was going to sit and stare at you. I'm not sitting. I'm standing."

This heralded more laughter from the four men at the table, but not from the woman or the man behind the bar.

"Listen, lad, don't try to get wise with me!" the man growled, tucking his rag away and narrowing his broadly set eyes. "You come in here wantin' somethin'. What do you want?"

"I want food."

"Well, you'll be showin' me some money first then," the innkeeper said, cocking his brow skeptically.

"Money? What is that?" The boy had heard the word before, but was unsure of its meaning and didn't want to make another mistake. Unfortunately, he'd already made one, and the room burst into laughter once again. He was beginning to think that the four men at the larger table would laugh at anything he said.

"You know, gold, silver, even a copper or two. Money." The innkeeper shook his head sadly.

"Oh, coins. No, I have no coins. The master had all the coins, and I didn't take any of them when I left."

"Left?" The innkeeper and several of the others were staring at him more intently now. "You mean you ran away?"

"No. I walked."

More laughter broke out all around the room now, even the quieter of the two women chuckled behind her hand. The boy was

31

dumbfounded at the meaning of all this laughter, so he thought it best if he tried to explain.

"The master was dead." The laughter stopped short. "I saw no reason to stay."

"Did you kill him, lad?" the large man asked, his voice slightly different than before.

"No, the other men did that." They stared at him again, so he elaborated.

"Seven bandits came from the woods and tried to take things from the master. We killed them, but an eighth was hidden and shot the master in the throat, then rode away. The master was dead, and I knew that my destiny was down the road, so I walked away. Now can I have some food?"

The room erupted into laughter, several comments regarding his destiny and what an unlikely story it was ringing around all at once. Finally, the large man behind the bar banged a tankard hard on the wooden surface and the uproar subsided.

"Sorry, lad, but no money, no food. Now get out before you stink up the place permanently."

The boy sniffed the air, detecting a wide range of scents mingling with that of the food. His own odor was only that of a bit of sweat and four days on the road. Surely the man didn't mean that.

"No money, no food?" he asked.

"That's right!" the innkeeper retorted hotly.

"Give me some money, then."

This brought a loud snort from the man. His round face reddened, and his voice came out harsh. "Listen, kid, I don't know if yer stupid or just wrong in the head, and I really don't care, but yer not gettin' anythin' from me, so beat it!" With the last words, the man's huge hand reached over the bar to grip the boy's tunic.

The boy snatched the man's fingers in a grip of steel, twisting backward until they popped out of joint. He pulled hard, using the man's heavier weight to splay him over the bar, and brought his elbow down on the extended arm. Bones cracked like kindling and the man screamed in pain. Other shouts rang out around him, so he thought it best if he finished the man quickly. He cocked back his hand for the killing blow.

"NOOO!"

The boy stopped. He looked at the woman who had screamed, simply because he had never heard such a bloodcurdling plea. He didn't release the man's mangled arm, but his curiosity burning to know why the woman was so distraught.

"Why not?" he asked, cocking his head at her quizzically.

"Just don't hurt him anymore!" she pleaded, but the boy was noticing that the other men were finally getting to their feet. And their hands were on their weapons. He released the bartender's arm and balanced himself.

"I don't know who you are, boy, and I don't know what you want, but you'd best leave or yer gonna regret it." The most formidable of the men stepped away from the larger table, his hand resting on his sword hilt.

"Why?" was all that the boy could think to ask. He had done nothing wrong. The innkeeper had attacked him, and he had retaliated. Those were the rules of combat.

"This is why," the other man drew his sword, a well-kept longsword of medium-hard temper and keen edge. "Now you'll be off, or I'll—"

The boy moved like a stroke of lightning.

As the sword came free and pointed toward him, his feet left the floor. His palms clapped onto the flat of the blade near the tip while his foot swept in a short arc to impact upon the weapon's midpoint. The finely tempered steel snapped and the hilt spun out of the other's grasp. Continuing the spinning motion, the boy's other foot crashed into the man's chest. His opponent's feet left the floor and didn't touch again until the wall behind the large table stopped his trajectory. The man lay there stunned, clutching his broken ribs and struggling to breathe.

The boy now stood where the man had. He was poised in a crouch, the two-foot piece of the man's broken sword clasped between his palms near the broken end and held over his head perfectly parallel to the floor. His eyes scanned his remaining opponents, gauging their nerves and skills and the weapons that still rested in their sheaths.

"We can take 'im, Lem," the youngest of the three whispered, fingering the hilts of a dagger and shortsword.

"Not me," his friend answered, eying the crumpled form that lay wheezing against the wall behind them. He moved his hands away from his own weapons. "Jorry was a better blade than me, and the kid took him like a cheap whore with a butter knife. I say give him some food, Marra, and send him on his way."

"Sure, sure," the barmaid prattled, moving from where she was tending the injured innkeeper to a cold box. She retrieved a heavy burlap sack and stuffed cheese, bread, and a cold leg of mutton into it, then thrust it over the bar at the boy. "Just take it and go..."

The boy relaxed his stance somewhat, yet remained vigilant, wondering if this was some sort of feint or ruse. They were all looking at him worriedly, some still fingering weapons, but most trying to look as non-threatening as possible.

"Here, here. It's food." The barmaid placed the laden bag on the bar and backed away. "Take it and leave. We don't want no more trouble!"

Trouble? What trouble was there? They had attacked him, and he had defended himself. He didn't understand their behavior at all.

The boy relaxed his stance fully and walked cautiously to the bar. He felt like he should say something, but it seemed that every time he opened his mouth, someone laughed and then attacked him. Perhaps silence was more prudent at this point.

He carefully placed the broken length of sword onto the bar and picked up the bag. He moved to the door, but once again felt as if he needed to say something.

"I only wanted food, not trouble." He watched for some response—laughter, another attack, anything—but they all just stared at him. He pulled the door open and stepped into the night, quickly continuing his journey.

Reaching into the bag, the boy retrieved the loaf of bread and bit off a large hunk, chewing as he walked. He could hear the voices of the people in the inn for some time as he lengthened his stride and continued his meal. Many of their words were strange to him; he had no idea what a "hangin'" or "constable" were, and didn't know why they would need to have the former and get the latter. He simply walked on, eating and thinking as he traveled. In the future, he would try to remember: no money, no food. Perhaps he would be able to avoid trouble that way.

The midmorning sun was halfway to its zenith when the faint tremor of galloping horses stopped the boy in his tracks. He stood still, eyes closed, feeling the cadence through the soles of his feet. There were six of them, he could tell from the pattern of hoof beats; they were running flat out and were still far enough away that he had time to make a careful decision about what to do. The decision was simple: stand or hide.

He opened his eyes and studied his surroundings. To his right was thinning forest with little undergrowth, to his left a stone fence with jagged topping stones and a rolling green field dotted with sheep. The fence was higher than he could reach standing flatfooted. It offered little in the way of an obstacle, but there was always the chance that something lay beyond that he couldn't see. There was little choice. The boy tossed his food bag over the fence, took a three-step running start, and executed a perfect rolling jump that cleared the sharp topping stones by a hand span. Thickly thatched grass met his feet on the other side, which was a pleasant surprise. He recovered his bag and stood quietly with his back against the stone wall and waited for the horses to pass.

When the sound of the thundering hooves reached its height, curiosity won out over caution. He needed to know who these horsemen were. Were they after him, or was his caution misplaced?

He gripped the highest protruding stone that he could reach and lifted himself up, gained purchase on the topping stones, and chinned himself to peek over. The glimpse he got of the receding horsemen yielded a wealth of information. Three of the six were men from the inn, the three whose friend he had injured. The other three he didn't recognize. All wore weapons, and their bows were strung and close at hand. The leader, or so he seemed, wore a helm of bronze and rode a horse both taller and stronger than those of the others. Their mounts were all lathered as if they had run a fair distance, and some quick calculations lent credence to the theory that they had come from the village. That they sought him wasn't a far stretch of his somewhat limited imagination; the trouble he had inadvertently created had followed him. He would have to be more careful from now on.

The sun had moved to its highest point when the boy reached the crossroads. He approached cautiously, moving along the edge of the road where the concealing underbrush was only a step away. If those who sought him lay in wait, he could vanish into the undergrowth in the blink of an eye.

He'd never seen a crossroads before and didn't know what to expect. Would someone live here, tend the well and the simple structure that served as a shelter for any traveler who felt the need to stop for the night? He listened for several minutes and knew that no one hid in wait, so he moved into the open to better assess the choices that lay before him. The well yielded enough cold, sweet water to sate his thirst, but the crossing roads left him with another decision.

Life since the master had been killed seemed to be nothing but one decision after another, and he felt that each one he made hung over his head like a great weight, ready to crush him if he chose poorly. This decision wasn't without some information to guide him at least, and he stood quietly for some time, weighing his three options. The tracks from the six horsemen were plain, and it took no skill to see that his pursuers had stopped for water, then continued west. If they sought him, which seemed likely, they would return by the same road. To the west, the road was no longer girded by stone walls, but rather split-rail fences and open fields that would offer him no cover if he encountered the horsemen. That made the northern and southern roads more attractive simply in the interest of avoiding his pursuers. He looked to the north where the road rose into hilly, forested country. To the south lay low, rolling hills and empty pastures. If the horsemen returned to the crossroads and took the same track as he, either by design or chance, he would rather be in rougher country that offered cover.

The boy took a bit of bread and a hunk of cheese from his dwindling bag of supplies and turned to the north, eating as he walked and wondering if he'd made the right decision.

Chapter V

So, what do they call ya, then?" the portly man asked, shoving a wheelbarrow of coal onto the pile that fed the forge. He dumped the load and let the wheelbarrow drop, turning to the boy and dusting off his hands.

"They call me Lad," the boy answered, not knowing how else to reply. The master had only ever called him boy, but the people at the inn had called him lad, and he thought the latter sounded more like a name.

"Well, Lad then, is it?" The man rubbed his beard with a hand blackened with soot and coal dust, his broadly set eyes narrowing with scrutiny. "Well, I guess a man's name's his own business, ain't it? And ya need money, do ya?"

"Yes. I need money for food."

"Well, yer skinny enough, that's plain to see, and half the blokes in this gods-forsaken hole give some phony name, don't they? No matter to me, is it?" The man's gaze raked up and down the boy appraisingly. "I can't see what you can do for me, though, can I? Yer too skinny to heft a load of coal, and I doubt you could even swing a hammer." He looked around the small smithy dubiously then shrugged. "Sorry, Lad."

The boy didn't understand. All he had told the man was that he needed money. Now he was talking about things he could and could not do for him. Did the man mean that if he did these things, he would give him money? There was only one way to discover the truth. "I can swing a hammer, and I can lift that cart loaded with coal."

"Oh, ya can, can ya? Well, you'll just have to show me then, won't ya?" He pointed to the wheelbarrow, then to the wagon he'd been unloading. "Shovel that cart full and bring it over here to the pile near the forge then."

"Yes, M—" The boy stopped; this was not his master. The master was dead. He didn't know what to call the man, but he'd heard others use another term that was respectful and used that now. "Yes, sir."

He retrieved the wheelbarrow and, though he had never seen a contraption like it, easily mastered the simple balance of it. At the wagon, he hopped up and took the broad-bladed shovel. This was another implement he was unaccustomed to wielding, but it wasn't difficult. In short order, the wheelbarrow was brimming full. He hopped down and took the two handles.

"Careful now, Lad," the man warned. "I don't want ya hurtin' yerself."

"How could I hurt myself?" he asked, lifting the load easily and wheeling it over to the large pile.

"Well, I, uh—" The man stared as Lad emptied the cart and set it aside exactly where he had picked it up. "Well, I guess yer stronger than ya look, aren't ya?"

"I don't look strong?"

"Well, I didn't mean to— I mean, you're kind of skinny, so I thought—" The man gave a snort of laugher, which clicked as a warning in Lad's mind. "Well I guess you're just wiry strong, not beefy strong like me." He flexed his huge shoulders.

"I guess," Lad said, still not really understanding, but feeling that it was best to agree. He didn't want trouble.

"Fine then, I'll pay you two pennies a day and feed ya. You can sleep behind the forge; it'll be warm enough for ya there, won't it?" The man looked at Lad as if there would be an answer forthcoming, but Lad hadn't the slightest idea what to say. He didn't know if he was supposed to agree, disagree, name a different amount, or stand mute.

"Will that be acceptable?" The man finally finished.

"Yes," Lad said immediately.

"Good! You can start by unloadin' the rest of that coal and shovelin' the dung heap there into the wagon. If you finish that before supper, you can muck out the stables."

"Yes, sir." Lad got right to work.

He grabbed the cart and brought it back to the wagon, while the man attended his forge and the huge horseshoes that he was beating into shapes more likely to fit the plate-footed draft horse waiting patiently in the stall. Lad took a moment to wonder how long he would have to work to afford enough food to make it back to the crossroads. Just one glance around the logging camp where this branch of the road ended told him that this was not where his destiny lay. His long-belabored decision at the crossroads had been wrong, and the mistake had cost him time, but there was no way he could have known which of the three choices led to his destiny. Now he needed more food, for his supplies were gone, which would cost him more days. The concept of working for money with which he could buy food to continue his journey settled well with him. He hadn't caused any trouble here, and the smith seemed pleased with his work. He could work here for a few days, buy food, and continue his journey without worries about having to evade the clumsy pursuit that had dogged him out of the first town.

His only worry was about his destiny.

He'd already been on the road for five days since the master was killed; he hoped his destiny would wait for him. It was another day and a half back to the crossroads, then who knew how far to his destiny, if he even would know it when he saw it.

"Grandfather." The young apprentice's voice cut through the silence of the vast chamber that was the guildmaster's private suite. The apprentice stood at the open door, his toes half a step back from the aperture. The door had been open, as it often was, but woe to the lowly apprentice who broke that intangible barrier without consent. There were no guards at the door to the suite; there didn't need to be. And a lock would have been even more superfluous. This was the abode of the most deadly assassin in the city of Twailin. Guards and locks would have been ridiculous.

Shadows fluttered within the blackness of the balcony, and the Grandfather of Assassins strode through the open arched doors, his stride fluid, his countenance assured. This was his domain; no one was foolish enough to attack him here.

"What news, Sereth?" he snapped, striding across the priceless rugs toward the uncomfortable apprentice. "Has anyone spotted Corillian?"

"There's no news from the east road, Grandfather." The youth bowed low, presenting an easy and hopefully painless target to his master. If the lack of news enraged his lord, it was better to be killed quickly than to survive to endure the master's torments. "A three-wagon caravan of wool arrived from Melfey this evening, but brought no news at all of anything unusual."

"Blast!" The guildmaster whirled and strode back across the room to his broad desk. "If Corillian has one trait, it is punctuality. If he can calculate the exact time required to complete a sixteen-year project, I grant he has the faculties to estimate the travel time from Krakengul Keep!"

Sereth risked a glance, then straightened. The master was not in a homicidal mood, as was evidenced by his own continued heartbeat, but Sereth didn't want to push his luck. He stood silently while the Grandfather scratched a lengthy note upon a sheet of parchment. "I want you to hand-deliver this to Master Targus. He's doing some hunting, so he may be difficult to find. Check the taverns down by the wharves first, but don't come back without putting this in his hand." He sanded the scroll dry, then rolled it, sealed it with wax, and pressed his signet into the seal. He crossed the space from the desk to his apprentice in seven long strides, his black robes fluttering to reveal the glitter of steel, silver, and gold within the ebony folds.

"Go!" the guildmaster said flatly, handing over the scroll.

"At once, Grandfather!" Sereth tucked the scroll into his tunic and turned to go, grateful for having been given a task without enduring any punishment for bringing bad news. He had no idea where to find Master Targus, but at least he knew where to start looking.

"Here we are!" Flindle pushed open the heavy bark-plank door and ushered Lad into the long, low structure of the mess hall. "The rewards of a hard day's labor!" The aromas of the long line of tables heavily laden with food and the sound of sixty hungry men and women all eating and talking at once washed over them in a palpable wave.

Lad froze in his tracks.

He had never seen so many people crowded into one room, and his combat-honed reaction was to assess the danger of the situation before proceeding. These men were the same he'd seen come in upon the three huge wagons less than an hour ago. Flindle had called them the "jacks," and their arrival had heralded the official end of the workday. At the time, Lad had noticed with professional concern that half of the men carried dangerous-looking double-bitted axes of a type he'd not seen before. They looked lighter and quicker than battle axes, and Lad had wondered if they were weapons or tools. Now the men all sat unarmed, shoveling food into their bearded faces with a frenzied intensity.

He evaluated the noisy room with one long, sweeping stare, cataloging the exits, the layout of the tables, and the array of potential weaponry that littered the serving table and the kitchen behind.

"You all right, Lad? You look like—"

A heavy hand landed on his shoulder and was slapped away before Lad could even think of his reaction to the unexpected physical contact. He was in a fighting stance before Flindle's yelp of astonishment told him that he had overreacted. By that time, the rumble of conversation had stilled, and the eyes of every man at the nearest table were on him.

"Ayee! Damn it, Lad!" Flindle gripped his wrist in pained shock, his eyes staring in wonder at the diminutive boy. "Sorry I startled ya! Holy Horatio, you're quick!"

"I didn't intend to hurt you, Flindle" Lad said, relaxing his stance. "I wasn't aware that you were going to touch me and reacted without thinking."

"Oh, you didn't hurt me none!" Flindle said with a smile, raising his injured hand and flexing his tingling fingers easily. "Just surprised me is all, ain't it?" He stepped up to Lad and slowly placed his hand once again on the boy's shoulder, turning him toward the table of staring lumberjacks.

"This here's Lad," he told them all, patting the boy's shoulder carefully. "He's workin' for me and doin' a fine job, he is. He's been on the road for a while, and he's a bit jumpy is all. Ain't it, Lad?"

"Yes," Lad responded, uncomfortable under the scrutiny of the men, as well as Flindle's hand on his shoulder. He had never in his life been touched in a capacity other than combat by anyone other than the master. He was grateful when the smith's hand finally lifted and swept in an arc, indicating the table of staring men.

"These louts are jacks, Lad. And if any of 'em gives you trouble, you just tell me!"

This brought a rout of laughter from the room and several derisive comments regarding what Flindle could do with his threats *and* his new laborer. Several of the suggestions made little sense to Lad, but he decided to stand mute rather than respond.

"Just you ignore that bunch, Lad, and come on over here." Flindle led the way to the serving table where a few men and women were dishing out huge slabs of braised beef, mounds of potatoes, steaming biscuits, and greens onto large wooden platters, then dousing it all with heavy brown gravy.

"You eat hearty, Lad," Flindle instructed, pointing out where to retrieve a fork and knife. "Seconds, thirds, whatever you want! You put in a man's work today, and you should eat like one!"

This, at least, was one task at which Lad needed no instruction. When he placed his laden tray down and took his seat beside Flindle, the noise and motion surrounding him faded into the background of mouthful after mouthful of wonderful, delicious, and life-giving food.

"Well, the way you eat, we'll be puttin' some weight on you right enough, that's for sure, ain't it, Lad?"

"Yes." Lad walked slowly from the mess hall back toward the forge, both to match Flindle's pace and to ease the discomfort of an overfull stomach. The heavy-set blacksmith was strong as an ox, but walked at the pace of one, as well. Lad was growing accustomed to the man's ceaseless questions, realizing that most of them were rhetorical.

"I gotta say, you're a right good worker, I do." The blacksmith snorted in laughter and fished a small flask from his apron pocket. He tilted it back to his lips and swallowed. Lad didn't know what was in the flask, but Flindle sipped from it constantly. "You did more work in half a day than anyone else I've hired could have done from sunrise to sunset, didn't ya?"

Lad just walked along, not knowing what to say, which was often the case with Flindle's questions. He had discovered that staying mute was often an answer in and of itself.

"Ah, here we are now." Flindle stepped into his forge and sat on one of the low stools. He propped his feet up on the edge of the banked coal fire and let out a sigh of contentment, his eyes squinting up at the deepening night sky. "Aye, this is the life, ain't it? Why, look at all them stars, would ya!" He took another swallow from his flask and held it out to Lad. "You want a snort?"

"What's a snort?" Lad asked, looking dubiously at the flask. He'd been curious about its contents; now was his chance to find out. He took it from the blacksmith's wavering grasp.

"A drink! You know, a li'l bit of the dragon's breath!"

Lad sniffed the open container carefully, his nose wrinkling at the astringent odor. He had been schooled in the use and detection of more than a hundred different poisons and potions, but had never smelled anything like this.

"What's dragon's breath, Flindle?" he asked, deciding that he'd rather not taste something so foul-smelling. He gave the flask back to his employer.

"Why, it's whiskey, ain't it?" The flask tilted to the man's lips again, a stream of the liquid escaping to trickle into his bushy beard. "Good stuff, too! None of that rot-gut potato squeezin's that the dwarves make. Good corn whiskey!" He sipped again. "Sure you don't want some?"

"Yes, I'm sure." Flindle seemed to be acting strangely since he'd eaten, and Lad was beginning to think that it had something to do with this whiskey he was drinking. Perhaps it was poison after all.

"Well, that's okay." Flindle tilted his stool back on two legs until his back thudded against the anvil, then stretched his broad frame in an expansive yawn. "So, what's your story, Lad? Here you come, walkin' in out of nowhere, no shoes, not a penny to your name, and skinny as a half-starved rat. On top of that, you're jumpy as an unshod colt! Gotta be somethin' to that, ain't there?"

"My story?" Lad was once again unsure of what to say. Flindle wanted something from him, but Lad had no idea what a story was. He was curious again, however, and forged ahead. "What's a story?"

"Boy, you're an odd one, ain't ya? You know! Where are you from? Where's your family? How come you're on the road all alone?" Flindle tilted the flask again, then leveled a bleary-eyed stare into Lad's eyes. He squinted slightly as if he were seeing something he didn't understand, and then shook his head. He glared at the flask in his hand, jammed in the cork, and stuffed it into his pocket.

"Damned cheap booze got me seein' things. Oh, to hell with it, Lad! You don't have to tell me nothin' about yourself, do ya? I'm just tryin' to make conversation is all, ain't I?" Flindle levered himself up to a slightly wobbly stance and nodded to Lad once more.

"It's late, and I'm fer bed." He glanced again at the boy and shook his head in confusion. "You put more coal on the fire if you get cold now, hear? I'll see you in the mornin'."

"Yes, sir," Lad said, his curiosity blazing like a forest fire in his mind. What was Flindle talking about? Was the whiskey really making him see things, or had the man seen something in him that he didn't understand? The thought worried him slightly, but not overly so. He was safe here, at least for the time being. He had food and a warm place to sleep, and would get money for the work he had done this day. He wrapped himself in the moldy old blanket Flindle had given him and sat down with his back to the fire box. The bricks were pleasantly warm from the banked fire, and the night was cool and alive with the sounds of the forest.

Not really tired, Lad sat up for some time, staring out at the quiet logging camp, listening and thinking about the decisions he'd made, the paths he'd traveled, and, of course, his destiny. The night dwindled on, and the moon settled behind the lofty pines, deepening the darkness and heightening the faint magical glow from Lad's eyes.

CHAPTER VI

Don't stir up trouble, Targus," the Grandfather of Assassins ordered his Master Hunter. The half-elven chap had been hunting people for the guild for decades and could follow a ten-day-old trail over rock, snow, sand, or even ice. Whatever he hunted, he brought back, be it animal, man, or elf, dead or alive. "It's two days past the appointed time of their arrival. Corillian wouldn't be late for this; he knows what's at stake. Something has happened to them and kept him from sending word. There may be rumor of it somewhere on the road, and more can be learned from a wagging tongue than a slit throat."

"Of course, Grandfather." The slim man leapt into the saddle, snapping his fingers at his two apprentices, who followed suit. He squinted up at the faint blush of the early morning sky. "The weather has been good and will remain so. The tracks will be easy to read. I'll find the weapon and bring it back to you."

"Remember, Corillian could look like anyone if he so wished—old or young, man or woman—but the weapon should be about the age of your younger apprentice. He should look like a normal boy, but he may act strangely. He's dangerous. If he's run away, don't try to capture him. Just track him." He handed up a heavy pouch. "If you don't find them on the road from here to Krakengul Keep, send word, but keep looking. Spend whatever you must to loosen tongues, but find me that weapon."

"Consider it done!"

Targus lashed the money to his saddle and dug one spur into his mount's wither, spinning the gelding on its hocks. He and his apprentices clattered out of the courtyard and through the streets of Twailin. The hunt had begun.

"Leavin'?" Flindle turned from the forge to face Lad with a scowl that would have curdled milk. "Why, you only been here three days, haven't ya? Six pennies ain't gonna buy you enough food to get you anywhere, Lad."

"Six pennies will buy four loaves of hard tack and one measure of jerky, Flindle." He inclined his head quizzically at the blacksmith. "I have eaten much more than I usually do for the past three days. This should be enough."

"But, I... Well, dammit Lad, I was just gettin' used to seein' your face around, wasn't I?" He scowled again and spat into the forge fire. "I'll double your pay if you stay another two days."

"I can't stay longer, Flindle."

"You got someone chasin' you?" the smith asked, his eyes narrowing. "If you're runnin' from somethin', Lad, this is a far safer place than the road."

"I am not running from something," he assured the man with a quizzical look. "I am *walking to* something, but I'm not sure what it is."

"Ha, well, you keep that sense of humor, Lad. And, here." Flindle went to the back of the forge and dug into a pile of junk that littered the bench. He returned with a short knife in a moldy leather sheath. "A man oughtn't to be without some kind of weapon, even if it's just an old belt knife." He held the sheathed blade out to Lad hilt first.

"I don't need a weapon, Flindle," he said, his mind clicking onto a magically reinforced memory. "I am a—"

"Nonsense! Take it!" Flindle grasped Lad's hand and pressed the hilt into it. "The world's not a safe place, is it?"

"No, Flindle. It's not a safe place." Lad looked at the knife and drew the short blade, which was sharp and clean despite the bedraggled sheath. It wasn't balanced for throwing, but would part flesh readily enough. He sheathed it and tucked it into his rope belt.

"Good!" Flindle extended his huge scarred hand.

Lad stared at it, then at the man's face, misunderstanding written plainly on his features. Did Flindle want the knife back now? Was this some test? The palm was held vertically, not flat as if he were expecting to be handed something. Then a memory surfaced; he had seen many of the burly lumberjacks clasp hands in a short ceremonial greeting. But this was not a greeting, rather a parting. Could it be that the same ritual served two purposes? Lad slowly extended his own hand in the same manner, and Flindle snatched it and squeezed so hard that Lad had to return the pressure.

"Take care, then, Lad." The big man turned away then and began pumping the huge bellows that fed air to the forge.

Lad felt an odd tugging in the pit of his stomach, watching the man tend his forge alone. Though it felt like hunger, he knew it couldn't be, for he had eaten a large breakfast. He turned to go, but glanced back again, his hand drifting to the twisting in his stomach. He felt like he should say something, but he knew not what. He felt that maybe he should stay and work longer for Flindle, but he couldn't. There was one word he had heard others say many times when parting, though he didn't know if it was appropriate now.

"Goodbye, Flindle."

The big man's head snapped up from his work, and a stiff smile stretched his features. "Goodbye, Lad."

Lad attempted to mimic the smile, but it felt strange. He had never smiled before. He turned away and let his feet carry him toward the mess hall where he knew he could buy the bread and jerky that would sustain him back to the crossroads and beyond.

"The boy leavin'?" One of the teamsters led two heavy draft horses up to Flindle's stall.

"Yep." The smith thrust four pieces of bar stock into the glowing forge fire, glancing in the direction in which Lad had left. "He's a strange one, ain't he? All fired up about workin' for me, he was. Does a better job than anyone else I've hired in the past two years, then decides it's time to leave when he ain't even got enough saved up to feed a starved dog for two days."

"Sounds like he's on the run," the teamster said, hitching the two horses to the rail.

"That's what I thought, but I dunno." Flindle looked down at his hand, the one he'd clasped with Lad's. It ached a little. He was a blacksmith, and there was a blacksmith's strength in his hands, but shaking hands with Lad had been like matching grips with a hand of stone. "I don't know what to think about that boy."

Three dark horses thundered up to the crossroads, the riders reining in to bring the lathered mounts to a halt. Almost thirty hours hard ride from Twailin had left the horses near exhaustion and the riders sore and tired; so far, they had seen nothing resembling their quarry. Targus slipped down from the saddle, his eyes scanning the ground even before his feet came in contact with it.

"Walk the mounts out while I have a look at this, Mya. Jax, draw some water for them." Targus knelt to the hard-packed dirt while his apprentices moved wordlessly to comply. His eyes read the ground like a scholar's would read a text, and the history of the last few days unfolded before him.

Six horses with riders had passed from east to west in a hurry five days ago; they had stopped long enough to water their mounts and then continued on. The same six had returned a day later, traveling in the opposite direction, more slowly. A wagon had passed from east to west the previous day as well, but Targus and his apprentices had passed that one on the road, and it wasn't the one they were looking for. The six horses going first one way then the other bothered him. They hadn't ridden as far as Twailin, for there hadn't been enough time between their two passages to reach the city.

"They were searching for something," Targus muttered quietly, mulling over his explanation of the behavior of the six mounts. "Or someone..." This didn't bode well.

There was other wagon traffic evident upon the rutted track; one heavily laden wagon with a team of four draft horses had come from Twailin and turned up the logging camp road five days ago, and several had gone the other way, laden with timber, no doubt, and returned less laden, probably with supplies for the men who worked the camp. Other traffic had taken the southern track toward Melfey, but they had all come from Twailin. There were no tracks from the east that turned off the main road.

"A lot of traffic," his elder apprentice said, stepping up beside his master. "Someone was in a hurry."

"Yes, Jax." Targus felt the crease along the edge of one of the hoof prints. "In a hurry going west, but not so much of a hurry going back east. And equally laden in both directions. They didn't find what they were looking for."

"A search party?" The apprentice knelt beside his master, studying the tracks with an experienced hand. "Not from Twailin. There must be trouble up ahead."

"There *was* trouble, and it escaped them." Targus stood and walked a slow, careful circle around the crossroads, stopping at the watering trough to wet his face beside the slurping horses. As his soft leather boots scuffed the earth around the northeast corner of the two crossing roads, he stopped. Something here wasn't right.

There were no tracks, but a few grains of dirt were pressed down into the hard soil more deeply than they should have been. Something had stood here, or been placed here and then picked up. Targus walked a slow circle around the spot. There were no tracks around it. He looked up, but there were no overhanging tree limbs from which something could have been dropped or picked up. The undergrowth beside the road was undisturbed. A squirrel chittered at him from a nearby tree, snapping his attention. Targus frowned down at the mystery written in the dirt; he didn't like mysteries that he was unable to unravel.

"Something?" Jax asked, tracing a wide circle around the spot that Targus was studying.

"Less than something, but more than nothing. A riddle without an answer." He outlined the spot where something had stood with his finger. "Something stood on this spot without leaving a scuff or print, and didn't leave a track while coming or going. What possibilities are there to explain this, apprentice?"

"Something that flew, or a wizard using a transposition spell." Jax also looked up at the lack of overhanging branches.

"Or something that doesn't leave tracks or doesn't walk, but has weight enough to leave an impression when it stands in one place long enough." Targus' younger apprentice walked up to the scene and cocked one eyebrow, one slim finger running along her shapely jaw as she knelt to examine the spot.

"And what might do that, Mya?" Targus' voice was flat, unreadable, but his face was alight with his youngest apprentice's audacity.

She shrugged and stood. "I have no idea, Master Targus. You've told me that there are people trained in stealth who can walk without leaving a track. The Grandfather, for one, doesn't leave a mark when he walks across the courtyard, not even in the dirt of the stable yard."

"True, but I doubt there are any master assassins roaming the countryside. We search for a wizard and a boy your age who has been magically enhanced as a killing weapon." Targus stepped right into the middle of the spot he had been examining, then walked past his two apprentices. Both looked down reflexively, and each could see the clear scuff of their master's boot. Their eyes met and an infinitesimal shrug of Jax's shoulders was answered by an equally minute nod from his younger peer. They moved to the horses and mounted. By late that night they should be in the village of Thistledown.

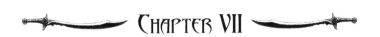

Chapter VII

"Stableboy!" Targus snapped, stepping out of the saddle as his mount came to a halt in front of Thistledown's one and only inn.

"Yessir!" The boy came running up and eagerly took the reins from Targus.

"Walk them out, groom them, and give them a mash. They've been running hard, so take your time." A silver crown arced through the darkness, and the boy snatched it out of the air like a bat picking off a stray moth.

"Yessir! Right away, sir!"

"Jax. Mya. With me."

The two apprentices handed over their mounts and mumbled acquiescence, following him up the steps to the inn's door. Their knees wobbled after so long in the saddle, and a night's sleep loomed at the top of the stairs like a proverbial pot of gold. That treasure vanished as readily as any leprechaun's secret stash as soon as they entered the inn's common room, however, for they could all see that something unusual had happened here. There was information to be gleaned from this place before any of them got a single wink of sleep.

The bartender stood with his arm in a sling and bound in splints, his free hand lazily polishing a mug while he talked with a man wearing the garb and odor of a swineherd. Two barmaids scurried to and from the tables, all of which were seated to capacity; all of the occupants looked like locals. Mya also noticed that several planks in the main room's back wall had been recently replaced. Either they'd been broken in some kind of disturbance, or their replacement was a coincidence.

Targus didn't believe in coincidence.

"Innkeeper!" He moved to the bar, his face open, his smile friendly. "I would purchase a meal and a room for myself and my friends, but I see that your inn is full to bursting. Have we happened into Thistledown in the midst of the spring festival?"

Mya almost smiled at her master's manner; having seen it dozens of times, she knew the magic he worked on such people as these. This, even more than his ability to track any living creature anywhere in the world, was Targus' most valuable skill. He could blend into any surroundings like a native and often talked the locals out of everything up to and including their daughters' virginity. But right now there was no time for fun; he was working, and his only goal was their quarry. She marveled at his skill, memorizing every movement, every nuance of his voice, learning his skill of persuasion with every move he made.

"'Tis no festival that put my arm in splints, good sir," the innkeeper stated, lifting his injured limb for all to see, as evidence to his claim.

"I thought it may have been a simple scuffle, as often breaks out when spirits are high, that resulted in your injury, good innkeeper." Targus placed a gold crown on the bar. "We'd have a sip of your ale before dinner and listen to the tale of what happened to put you, such a capable man, into such a state."

"A madman came through here not a week ago and did this damage you see, good sir," the innkeeper said, motioning his nearest barmaid to fill three tankards for the new arrivals. "Or mad *boy* I should say, for no older than your young lass there was he."

"Oh, now I'll not believe a mere boy could lay a hand on you, much less deal such a blow as to put your arm in splints!" Targus quaffed a swallow of ale and smiled winningly. "The fellow must have been wielding a fair length of stout oak to mark you thus."

"Nay! And that's the weird of it, sir, for 'twas naught but a boy, and dressed like a slave, he was. No boot on his foot, nor knife on his belt, I say." The entire common room had gone silent, all of the locals listening intently to the tale that they had all undoubtedly heard before. "It was well into the night, and myself and the two girls were seein' to the needs of six good customers when in comes a boy no older, as I've said, than your own girl here. He just walks in and stands at the door, dirty and smellin' like he'd rolled in one of Master Fensford's sties. I asks him what he's about, and he says he needs food. Well, I figured him for a common beggar and told him that, without money, he wasn't gettin' nothin' from me!"

"A fair assumption, I say," Targus said with a nod and another swallow of ale.

"And so I thought, but it wasn't so, for it was like he didn't even know what money was, and asked me outright 'What's money?' Well, that got a laugh from the customers, it did, along with the rest of his cock-and-bull story, and I was beginnin' to think that the poor lad was wrong in the head. Then he comes out and says 'Then give me some money'!"

"The audacity!" Targus had them in his pocket now, and Mya could see that the entire room was rapt with the retelling of the tale.

"Exactly what I said!" the innkeeper agreed, thumping his good hand upon the bar. "I would have offered him work if he'd asked for it, but to come right out and *tell* me to give him money, well, I made to throw him out like I would any good-for-nothin' beggar, but that was what set him off."

"Set him off? How do you mean?"

"Well, I made to push the lad, but he grabbed my hand and pulled it near right off, I tell ya!" Murmurs raked the crowd as the scene was replayed by the innkeeper's clumsy movements. "Then, barehanded, he snaps my arm like a stick of kindling, clean as you please! Just *crack*! And my arm's bent like a horseshoe from elbow to wrist!" Some of the patrons made comments of disbelief at this, but both of the maids corroborated the story to the letter, silencing the crowd.

"And he'd have done worse, but for Marra pleading with him to hold," the innkeeper continued, nodding to the blushing maid. "I don't mind sayin' that I was worried that I'd drawn my last breath right there, but then Jorry McAllen and his three brothers stood up from their table and he told the lad to be off or else."

"So the boy released you and left?" Targus was playing the innkeeper well, egging him on at just the right moment.

"Oh, he released my arm then, sure enough, but as far as leavin'... Facin' four well-grown men all totin' steel and well acquainted in its use, the boy just stood there and asked why, like he didn't understand. Well, Jorry drew steel then, tellin' the boy that he'd use it if he didn't leave, but the words weren't even out of his mouth before the boy took him."

"Took him. An armed man?"

"Aye, armed with this." The innkeeper reached below the bar and retrieved two pieces of a broken sword. He dropped them on the bar for all to see. "I was starin' right at the boy, I was, and he moved so fast I couldn't see it, nor tell you exactly what happened. One moment he's standin' right where you are, the next Jorry's slammed up against that wall there with broken ribs, and his sword is snapped like a twig. Not only that, but the boy has this long piece here clapped between his hands, and he's crouched down like a wildcat ready to pounce. Well, Vik, the youngest, wanted to fight him, but Lem said he'd not draw steel on someone who could take Jorry so easily, and I gotta say, I think he made the right decision."

"So what did you do?"

"Well, Marra here put some leftovers in a sack and told the boy to just take the food and go. And, believe it or no, that's exactly what he did. He picks up the bag and goes to the door, then turns and says that he never wanted any trouble, just food. That was the last we saw of him, and I'm thankful for that."

"So you just let him go?"

"Let him go, indeed! Should we have tried to stop him and all been killed?" The innkeeper made a rude noise and put the broken pieces of sword back beneath the bar. "The constable took a few men to search the road for him. They rode almost as far as Twailin, and found no sign of him. They left this morning up the dwarf road to the east, but I don't think they'll have any better luck."

"A strange tale indeed, innkeeper!" Targus finished his ale and waved at the full common room. "As to our own needs, if you're full to capacity this evening..."

"Oh, we've a few private rooms where you and your friends can have a meal, and there's no shortage of beds. All these folk live hereabouts and they'll be headin' home soon enough."

"Very good!" Targus motioned his two apprentices to follow, and they were soon seated comfortably in a small room set in the back of the inn. When the maid left them, Targus lowered his voice. "This mysterious boy is undoubtedly our quarry. The innkeeper's story may be exaggerated somewhat, but there's no doubt that they were lucky. The boy could have easily killed them all." He fixed his apprentices' eyes with his own, driving home the gravity of the situation.

"We must inform the Grandfather of what's happened. Somehow, the weapon has escaped Corillian and is roaming free. Mya, take all that we've learned here back to Twailin and relate it all to the Grandfather. Talk to no one but him about this."

"Yes, Master. I'll need a fresh horse." Her voice was thick with lack of sleep and the thought of days ahead that would offer no rest.

"Here." Targus pushed a small pouch across the table to her. "Buy the best horse this place has to offer and leave as soon as we eat. And take this." He handed her a small glass vial full of amber liquid. "Drink half of that after you eat. It'll keep you awake and alert for a full day. As you feel it start to wear off, drink the other half. That should get you to Twailin. Jax and I will take your horse as a spare and head east. I doubt the weapon is in that direction, but my instructions were to travel all the way to Krakengul Keep unless we found what we were looking for."

The door creaked, and the maid entered with a huge platter of food and a pitcher of ale. An hour later, Mya rode out of town to the west astride a leggy gelding, her senses sharp as a needle and her ears ringing from the effect of the potion. Targus and Jax would leave Thistledown to the east in the morning.

Lad bent to the watering trough and drank deeply. The downhill slope had allowed him to make good time from the logging camp. He'd left that morning, and the night was at its deepest now, perhaps a quarter day before sunrise. He tore off a hand-sized piece of hardtack and chewed one corner, looking down first the road to the west, then the road to the south. He chewed and thought.

When the piece of bread was gone and he'd had another drink, he turned to the west. There was no solid reason that west was better than south, but there seemed to be a few more rutted tracks in that direction, coming from both the southern and the logging camp roads. Traffic meant people, and he knew that his destiny had something to do with people. It seemed reasonable since his lifetime of training had been concerned solely with how to most efficiently kill them.

His gait stretched out into the conservative pace to which he'd grown accustomed, and his mind wandered into meandering thoughts concerning his destiny. As yet, he had no inkling that the very people in whose hands his destiny lay were presently hunting him.

The gelding's hooves dug twin furrows in the road's hard-packed surface, a grunt of displeasure escaping the horse's nostrils with a cloud of steamy breath. Mya jerked the rein smartly, bringing the willful horse into line. She'd been riding hard all night, but had kept her pace well within both her and her mount's limits. The last thing she needed was a dead horse a day out from Twailin. But now she rubbed her eyes and wondered if she were pushing herself too hard. Maybe the elixir that Targus had given her was making her see things. She blinked hard and refocused, squinting through the bright sunshine.

"Well, I'll be damned," she muttered to herself, sure now that she was actually seeing what had caused her to rein in her mount so sharply. A boy, skinny and dressed in peasant garb, stood in the middle of the road less than a furlong ahead, looking back at her. She could see no detail from this distance, but thought immediately of their quarry. Her mind raced with options as she sat astride her fidgeting horse, watching him watch her. There was no way from this distance that she could tell for sure that this was the one they sought, so she would have to get closer, perhaps within killing range, to find out. She had no idea how violent the boy was, or if he only killed when threatened or told to do so. She couldn't hope to subdue him, but perhaps there was another way, a less dangerous way, to get him to Twailin and to the Grandfather.

She kicked her mount into a trot, making a show of taking a long drink from her waterskin and nibbling on some trail rations from her bag. While doing so, she carefully loosened the lacings of her tunic. Perhaps her best weapon against such a boy was the one he would never know hit him. The boy turned away and continued walking at a brisk pace as she came upon him and prudently guided her horse to keep a respectful distance between them.

"Hello there," she said, trying for her most amiable tone, friendly without being too familiar. "You headed for Twailin?"

"Hello." His voice was a pleasing tenor, totally without fear, or any other emotion that she could detect. "What is 'Twailin'?"

"Twailin's a city." She tried not to sound incredulous. "It's the city where this road leads. You'll be there before midday tomorrow if you keep that pace." She nodded, indicating his brisk walk, a fast walk even for her horse.

"What's a city?"

"What's a city?" She couldn't help her tone at this, then admonished herself for her outburst. The Grandfather had said that the weapon might act strangely, and this boy's manner was puzzling, to say the least. "Like a town or a village, only larger. A lot larger. Twailin's home to more than twenty thousand souls."

"Then, yes, I'm headed for Twailin."

She took another drink and levied her best smile at him. "Thirsty?" She bent down from the saddle, holding out her waterskin, her loose tunic flapping in the light morning breeze. "It's gonna get hot today."

He looked at her, and she could see his scrutiny; he was sizing her up. She watched, smiling as his eyes roamed over her. They stopped several times, but not where she thought they would.

"Yes, I'm thirsty." He sidestepped and took the skin from her hand, his movements absolutely fluid, as graceful as any dancer she'd ever seen. He tilted the skin back and drank as he walked, and she watched his feet move like ghosts over the road's surface, not a scuff or track left to read in his wake, even to her trained eye. There was absolutely no doubt that this was the weapon they sought. He handed the skin back, once again watching her warily as their hands neared. He didn't say thank you for the water.

"Say, I'm carrying a message to Twailin, and I'll be there by late this evening. If you want, you can ride with me." She patted the horse's rump behind the saddle. "Both of us together don't weigh much more than most men. It won't slow me much, and it'll give me someone to talk to."

"Why would you want someone to talk to?"

"I just like company, you know." She smiled again, trying a more direct approach. "You might like a friend who knows the city if you've never been there before. I might even know a place where you could stay."

She watched his eyes inspect her again. They lingered on her belt, her boot, and her face. She couldn't imagine that he feared her and saw no emotion at all on his face, just a blank, open scrutiny. She knew then that her attempt had failed.

"I don't wish to offend you, but I must refuse your offer."

"You *must*?" She grinned openly at his manner. "Well, I don't think I've ever been turned down in a nicer way. Suit yourself, and look me up if you find yourself in need of a friend in Twailin. It's a big place, you know. Just find the *Golden Cockerel* and ask for Mya. I live there."

"The golden cockerel? What is that?"

"It's a pub, but the innkeeper rents rooms upstairs." She kicked her mount into a prancing trot and shouted over her shoulder. "Anyway, just ask for Mya!" She waved and kicked her mount again, surprised when the boy hesitantly raised his hand in a poor attempt at a wave. He really *was* strange. She rode at a conservative pace until she was out of sight, then dug her heels in hard. If she got to the Grandfather soon enough, they could lay a trap on the road for the boy, but if he reached the city, finding him would be virtually impossible.

Lad let his hand drop to his side, continuing his loose-limbed gait and wondering why he had refused the young woman's offer. If he had joined her, he may well have shortened his traveling time by half a day. But there were some things about her that didn't fit. With a short sword and dagger at her belt, and another dagger in her boot, she wore more weapons than seemed needful of a messenger, and although she rode well enough, her clothes looked worn more from walking than from sitting a horse. That she had been riding hard all night was the truth, at least, for he could see the mount's lather and smell her sweat as well. He also wondered why she wore such a poorly fitting tunic. He'd worn less for most of his life, but if she found the garment so constricting that she felt the need to loosen the lacings until it was almost falling off, why not just go without?

Well, the meeting hadn't been a complete waste; he now knew exactly how far he had to travel before reaching his destiny. Lad reached into his bag and took out the slab of jerky. He bit off a mouthful and chewed the tough, smoked meat into submission before swallowing. Another bite, followed by two bites of hardtack, and his belly was less empty. After the impromptu meal, he quickened his pace slightly, easing into a mile-eating jog. His food would last the trip easily, and he'd reach the city of Twailin well before the following morning.

Lad had no illusions that his destiny would be easy to find in a city of twenty thousand people, but he knew that he could earn his way without creating trouble now. He'd find somewhere he could work for food and a place to sleep and search the city from there. Perhaps he'd also find Mya and learn what she knew of the city.

CHAPTER VIII

"Clear the road!" Mya yelled at the top of her lungs, lashing her exhausted mount with the reins and kicking him with her weary legs. "Out of my way!" She ignored the yelps and shouts of protest from the late-evening throngs walking the narrow streets near the Grandfather's estate. She'd run them all down if she had to.

She clattered around a corner too fast, and her horse skittered on the cobbles, losing its footing. She jerked the reins and kicked hard, trying to straighten the gelding out, but the shod hooves just threw sparks from the smooth stones, finding no purchase. With a squeal of terror, the horse went down, and she barely got her foot out of the stirrup in time to avoid being crushed. She flung out a hand and tried to roll, but the unyielding street slapped her hard; her left wrist bent at a bad angle and pain lanced up her arm. Then her head struck a cobble, dimming her vision for a moment.

Shouts from the crowd lashed at her wavering consciousness, the groping hands of strangers jerking her to wakefulness.

"Get away from me!" she shouted, lashing out with her uninjured hand. Her fist hit something yielding, and she heard more shouts.

"She's crazy!"

"Gotta be drunk!"

"Look at that poor horse! Why it's rode out!"

"Get away, damn you all!" Mya lurched unsteadily to her feet, cradling her injured arm. One glance told her that something was broken, but it didn't matter. She stumbled to her mount, shoving the crowd aside. The gelding heaved ragged breaths, convulsing in shudders that told her it was dying. She'd ridden it to death, but that didn't matter either. She was but a few blocks from the Grandfather's estate. She only needed it for a few more minutes.

"Get up!" she shouted, grabbing the reins and lashing at the curdled froth of the beast's withers. "UP, damn you!" The spent horse tried to comply, its legs churning, the broad neck bowing as it tried to right itself, but it couldn't.

"Leave be, girl!" a man's voice shouted from behind her. A broad hand landed on her shoulder, and she swept her sword out and around in a slow broad arc. He jumped back quickly enough to save himself from being gutted, but just barely.

"Back off!" she yelled, glaring the crowd into submission. "This is no affair of yours! I'm a messenger for *The Guild*!" The tone she used implied exactly which guild she meant, and that, if nothing else, brought fear into the eyes of the ugly throng.

She turned back to her horse, but its eyes had already glazed over, and its breaths were the shuddering convulsions of its last death throes. Cursing, she cut loose her saddlebags and started to turn away. The horse's dying eyes drew hers as if by some magical impulse, and a sliver of pity surfaced in her mind. She looked at the blade in her hand, and with one stroke ended the animal's suffering. The crowd let out a collective gasp at the death stroke, but she just glared at them, turned, and ran up the street toward the looming spire of the Grandfather's estate.

"Hold up there!" a voice called through the dimness of the foggy evening darkness. The glow of a torch poorly lit only the man who had spoken, but Targus knew there were more; he could hear the hooves of at least four more horses and the creaking of a wagon or cart through the fog that was playing tricks with the sounds. He pulled back on his mount's rein, hissing a warning to Jax to do the same.

"Ware, travelers!" the half-elven Hunter called out, limbering his short horn bow from its scabbard as a precaution. "We're searching for a friend of ours, long overdue in the city. He was to have come this way and may have met trouble."

"Well, if one of these be your friend," the speaker said wearily, moving his short column of horsemen into clearer view, "methinks he found trouble." Two men were leading a two-wheeled cart by the reins, the bed piled high with canvas-wrapped bodies.

"Good gods, man! What in the names of the Nine Hells happened here?" Targas really didn't expect a coherent account, but he thought this response would be more believable than a more calculated one.

"I'm Constable Burk from Thistledown and I'll have your name before I answer any of your questions, sir," the man said as three more horsemen pulled up to flank him closely.

"My name is Targus, if that means anything to you, and if that's the cart I think I recognize, there are two among those piled upon it that I may know. One was a man who was to have delivered something to my guildmaster; the other would be his nephew, a boy of sixteen summers." Truth mixed with falsehood was always more believable than falsehood alone, Targus knew. He couldn't have described Corillian, so withheld any attempt to depict him. He also knew that the weapon wouldn't be found among the dead, so any description of the boy that he might think up would mean nothing.

"Come into the light, then, Mister Targus. Have a look, and tell me if there are any here you know," the man said, raising his torch high. "We had a disturbance there that I'm sure you heard about if you stopped for the night at the *Inn of the Copper Pot*. We traveled this way to find the cause of that disturbance, but only found seven people slain and lying in the road, and an old man slumped in his cart with an arrow wound through his neck. Looks to me like bandits attacked him, but we couldn't tell the outlaws from their victims. If your friends are among them, I'd appreciate any explanation you could provide."

Targus kicked his mount forward, placing his bow back in the scabbard. "I would wager that the old man you describe is the one we seek. His name was Corillian, and he was an artisan of no small skill." As he approached, the smell of the seven aging corpses hit Targus like a slap in the face, even though the bodies were wrapped in canvas. He raised his hand to his face to ward off the stench. "That's his cart surely enough, but I'd rather not try to identify them at this point, if you don't mind." He noted the two additional horsemen riding behind the wagon, and the three horses they trailed.

"Well, if it's any consolation, we found no half-grown boy among the dead. Mayhaps your friend decided not to bring his nephew along on this trip." Burk moved his horse back to shed light on the laden wagon. "And the old man gave a good accounting of himself if he was alone, though how he felled seven brigands before falling himself is a mystery to me."

"Master Corillian was more than an artisan, good constable." Targas kept his mount at such a distance that he didn't have to endure so much of the stench. He couldn't blame the men for trailing the team along by their traces instead of driving them properly. "He knew more than a little magic, and could use it well when it came to protecting himself."

"Magic didn't kill these men. The old man and two of the others died from arrows, one from a dagger in his heart, and four from, well, something I can't quite explain." The man looked uncomfortable, as if he'd found something that scared him a lot more than a simple bandit attack.

"Such was his skill, to send arrows flying where he wanted," Targus lied. "But you say you found no boy among the dead? That is good news among the ruin, at least." He peered into the cart, stifling the smell with a kerchief. "If the bandits didn't take everything..."

"Didn't look like they took *anything*, to my eye," the constable said, motioning the entire entourage forward again. "Good weapons lying around, money still in the old man's belt pouch... Some strange stuff in that cart, mind you. Scrolls and pots of dust that don't smell like anything I know of, but if you say he was a magician, that explains a lot. Don't know how he managed to kill all the bandits and then end up dead himself, though."

"A tale we'd all like to hear, but never will." Targus kicked his horse away from the stinking cart, motioning Jax to follow. "If you would, good constable, please keep the cart and its contents secure in Thistledown. The guild will send a representative to see what may be salvaged."

"What guild do you mean? And why shouldn't we search through the magician's things? We found it deserted, and by law, anything in it belongs to Thistledown."

"By law, you may be correct, sir. Take what weapons and money you found as your compensation; we have no need of those. But unless you have a competent wizard in residence in Thistledown, I would suggest that you not go poking into things best left untouched by those without mage-skill." He kicked his mount into a canter and shouted back. "And what guild would you think has dealings with wizards?"

Targus and Jax rode back the way they had come, ignoring the muttered curses of the motley group behind. They had at least confirmed that Corillian was dead and that the weapon was roaming loose somewhere. They settled into an energy-conserving pace; Twailin was three days away, and Targus felt that he would need that long to think up an adequate explanation for his failure to the Grandfather of Assassins.

"Hold there, lassie!" a burly guard snapped, stepping up to the wrought-iron gate that was the entrance to the guildmaster's estate. The gate was closed and barred, as it always was after dark, which made the guard's warning a little ridiculous in Mya's mind.

"You expected me to crash right through, maybe?" she said with a scoff, cradling her throbbing arm, her breath coming in long, ragged gasps. The days without sleep or rest were taking their toll; she felt giddy with exhaustion and the lingering effects of Targus' potion. "I'm on the Grandfather's business, guard, and as you can see," she held up her deformed wrist, "it's left me a little worse for wear. I need to speak with him immediately! My name is Mya; I work with Master Hunter Targus."

"Aye, we've been told to expect someone from Targus, so

that'll get you through the gate." They worked the squeaky bolt and opened the heavy portal just enough for her to slip through. She started for the main house, but the guard snapped, "Not so fast there! I told you that'd get you through the gate. You'll not go traipsing around the estate without an escort." He snapped his fingers at one of the others standing the gate post. "Hollas, you go with her. And from the looks of that arm, you might have one of the boys call for a healer as well."

"Aye, sir!" Hollas said, falling in beside Mya. "Let's go, girlie, but at my pace, not yours."

"Fine." Mya was just about through arguing. All she needed to do was stay on her feet long enough to tell the Grandfather what she'd found, then she could rest. "Lead on!"

The two entered the main house and were immediately met by two more guards. A short explanation that the Grandfather need be summoned sent one of them in search of the guildmaster's valet. The man cared for more than the Grandfather's clothes, Mya knew, and was a veteran of many contracts. Nobody saw the Grandfather without going through his valet. Mya took a moment to look around, having never been allowed to enter the estate proper. The ceiling of the entrance hall arched two floors high, the center of the dome dominated by a single, magnificent, wrought-iron chandelier. The lamps held in its twisting embrace were turned down, and she could see how the whole apparatus could be lowered by a huge chain set in a pulley system. The entry hall was dominated by an immense, white marble stair that swept gracefully upward to bifurcate at its peak, extending into the two wings of the second floor.

Her mind wandered as she waited, her breath returning quickly from her short run. Her arm throbbed at a slower rate as her heart calmed. One of the guards offered her a drink from his waterskin and she took it, the sweet, clean liquid washing away the dust cloying her throat. By the time the portly man who she knew was the Grandfather's valet descended the broad stair from the upper floor, the combination of pain and exhaustion had her nodding sleepily on her feet.

"What's this about then?" the man asked, eying her up and down as the guard who'd delivered him trotted off to find a healer.

"My name is Mya," she said, trying for calm respect through the clenched teeth that kept her from crying out in pain at every throb of her badly swollen arm. "I work for Master Hunter Targus. I have information that the Grandfather needs to know right away. I *must* see him."

"And how did you hurt your arm?"

Mya stared for a half second, wondering if she'd heard correctly. "What the hell difference does that make?"

"The difference between seeing the Grandfather and spending the next few days decorating the wall of a dungeon." His tone was mild, but his eyes were as sharp as twin daggers. "Answer me."

"Fine." Mya bit her lip against her temper. "I broke my arm when the horse that I'd just ridden to death to get here as quickly as possible fell on me. I was rounding the corner of Serpent Way and Ironmonger Street, riding too fast for cobblestones. I ran the rest of the way on foot." She glared at him, matching stares. She had little doubt that this man could kill her before she could clear her sword from its scabbard, but felt confident that he would find himself tacked to a wall without his skin if the Grandfather found out he'd been deprived of her message. "Now, do I get to see him?"

"In the morning." He started to turn away, but her hand shot out, grabbing his sleeve at the shoulder.

"Wait just a minute!" The rasp of steel loosened her grip even before the valet turned his evil stare upon her. The two guards had their swords out, one pointed directly at her throat from the side, and the other behind her, ready, she felt sure, to split her skull. She let her hand drift away from the valet's arm, open and unthreatening.

"Just let me explain." She took a deep breath and glanced at the guard to her right, but he did not lower his blade. "I've got a message regarding something of great value to the Grandfather. If you won't let me see him, just tell him that I've found his weapon. He will see me. If he doesn't learn of it before morning, *neither* of our lives will be worth *spit*!"

The valet turned back to her, waving the guards away and squaring his round shoulders. "I decide what is important to the Grandfather, little girl." He took a half step closer. "He is entertaining this evening, and will probably keep his guest until morning." Another half step and his lips drew back in a feral sneer. "I was told not to allow him to be disturbed." One more half step brought his nose only inches from her own, his breath hot in her face with every word. "In comes a slip of a girl telling *me* she's got something more important than my direct order from the Grandfather not to allow him to be disturbed!" The sneer dissolved into a sweet, placating smile that turned her stomach with its insincerity. "After briefly considering the consequences of disobeying a direct order from the Grandfather of Assassins, I have decided that you will see him *in...the...morning*!"

She stood there fuming as the fool turned and strode back up the sweeping stairs, his smug confidence more painful than her throbbing arm.

"Swaggering idiot!" she spat as she eased herself down to sit on the lowest step of the grand marble staircase, cradling her arm in her lap.

"You can't stay here, missie," one of the guards said, his tone incredulous.

"Have me removed, then!" She winced as she leaned back, crossing her tired legs. "They can bury you right next to that pompous twerp who's keeping me from delivering my message to the Grandfather. The message that he's *specifically* been waiting for."

The guards looked at one another, and the one who'd escorted her across the courtyard said, "She's your problem, Jeffer. I gotta get back to my post."

As the gate guard left, a tired-looking man in a long crimson robe entered the foyer from a side passage, escorted by the guard who had summoned the valet. He walked up to the pair, eying the girl lying back with her arm cradled in her lap and the guard standing over her, the latter obviously trying to decide what to do with the former.

"I presume this woman is the one who requires my attention." The healer raised an eyebrow at the guard and knelt beside Mya. "Your arm, I venture to guess?"

"Yeah." Mya raised the deformed member for him to see. "Either broken or sprained, I think."

"Are you kidding? Broken at the least, I should think!" The man produced a pair of gleaming silver scissors from under his robe and started to cut the embroidered cuff of her shirt.

"Hey, wait a second! This is a new tunic!"

"Well, I've got to get at your arm!" He sat back on his heels and folded his arms. "You'll never roll up the sleeve past that swelling. Either you let me cut it or take it off."

"Fine, but you'll have to help me." She began pulling the hem up with her free hand.

"Hey!" The guard's voice was shrill, his face red. "You can't do that here!"

"Let's get this straight, Jeffer," Mya said flatly, pulling the hem up and, with the healer's help, over her head. "I'm staying here until I see the Grandfather. Unless you've received specific orders to not let me stay here, you're not in any trouble and you won't end up dead in the morning, unlike the valet and, quite probably, me."

To the guard's relief, she wore a shirt of light linen under the tunic. Unfortunately, for him at least, her recent run had soaked the material through with sweat. Her breath caught in a hiss as the healer eased her arm out of the garment.

"Hold still," the healer said, rotating her arm slowly and eliciting another hiss of pain. "I'm going to have to straighten it before I heal it."

"Jeffer!" she snapped to the guard, who was looking on in shock at the half-naked woman sitting on *his* steps, or at least the steps that he was supposed to be guarding. "You got a kerchief?"

"Er, yeah." He produced one from a pocket. "Why?"

She snatched it from his fingers. "Because I don't particularly feel like rattling the windows when he straightens this thing!" She stuffed the kerchief into her mouth and nodded to the healer. She was satisfied that she hadn't underestimated how painful the procedure would be, nor the need for the kerchief to keep her screams from escaping.

# Chapter IX

A sea of yellow stars flickered before Lad, as if the night sky had fallen in liquid form to fill the broad valley in a glittering pool of brilliance. It was a wonder he could never have imagined. Two swaths of blackness converged in the midst of that valley of lights, two rivers merging into one, dividing the twinkling sea into thirds. A great black wall encircled the vast sea of lighted streets and buildings; the lanterns of men walking upon the wall bobbed along in the darkness. More light bloomed outside the wall, as if the bubbling pot of humanity had overflowed and spilled out in sparkling patches of yellow. At the center of the brightest portion of the city, tall spires adorned a hillock where the two rivers joined. Mighty walls surrounded the high, palatial estate on all sides and torches flickered from the battlements. Other tall buildings could be seen in the lower portions of the city, and huge square towers stood at each point where the rivers entered and exited, their grim countenances glaring jealously down on the dark water. Lad stood there for a time absorbing the sight, and his mind slowly expanded to encompass what those many lights really meant.

"So many people..."

The thought escaped his lips without his knowing. His destiny lay before him like an oyster open on the half-shell, but it lay among twenty thousand of its kin, and he knew not how to tell one from another. A needle in a haystack would have been child's play by comparison, for when one finally finds the needle, it's at least recognizable from a bit of straw. Here lay twenty thousand people, any one of whom could hold his destiny in the palm of their hand, and he wouldn't know them if he saw them.

The task that he had thought so straightforward had just become immensely more difficult, and, for the first time in his young life, Lad felt daunted by something. It would take *years* to find his destiny in this mass of humanity.

"Years..."

But Lad had mastered many tasks that had required years of study and practice; his whole *life* had been a single task to perfect his art, adding the skills of many masters to create one perfect weapon: the perfect killer. Years, indeed, a lifetime he had spent at this, and if it took another lifetime to find the source—the impetus for all his work, all his mastery—he would spend that lifetime searching.

And he would succeed. Lad would find his destiny among the people of Twailin, or he would die in the attempt. It was all he could do. It was what he was *made* to do.

A soft night breeze ruffled his hair, stirring him from his quiet musing. He stood immobile in the center of the road for a time, his gaze slowly rising up to the glittering canopy of the stars overhead, then falling back down to the carpet of lights that beckoned him into their midst. His thoughts finally coalesced into one clear idea.

"How?"

This was, of course, the next logical question, his next decision. Unlike any other decision he had made, this wasn't a simple yes or no, right or left, hide or stand question. This task was complex, and he had no master or instructor to guide him. He was alone. He would have to rely on himself and what he knew of what he was and what he was looking for.

The former was simple; he was a weapon, trained to kill in any environment without being detected, caught, or killed. Who might want such a weapon? He had no idea. Warriors used weapons, he knew, but rarely did warriors use others to do their fighting for them, at least that he knew of. So, if he were a weapon, who would wield him? Someone who could not wield a weapon for

73

themselves?

Lad knew nothing of the wants or needs of men; power was a concept of which he was totally ignorant. Would a man use his skills to protect himself from others, or simply to slay his enemies? Neither struck Lad as a questionable pursuit, for he had certainly never been taught concepts of right and wrong, good and bad. He was made to kill—efficiently, economically, and silently if need be—without being killed himself. With that in mind, Lad stretched out his foot and took the first step down the hill into the valley of Twailin where his destiny lay, his curiosity burning within him like the fires that lit the city below.

When the sun's first rays touched the highest spire of the estate of the master of the Assassins Guild, the door to the Grandfather's private chambers burst open with a resounding crash.

"Valet!" His voice cracked through the corridors with the echoes of his mistreated door.

"Yes, Grandfather." The man materialized from the shadow of an alcove, bowing low, alert and attentive as always.

"Send a messenger to the House of Seven Sins." He strode past his prostrate servant, continuing his instructions. "Inform them that their trainee did not withstand my attentions. She expired sometime in the hours of the early morning. The agreed-upon sum will be sent via courier."

"At once, Grandfather." The man recovered from his bow and trotted to catch up to his master. "Your bath has been drawn, and breakfast awaits in the morning room, Grandfather. Also, a girl claiming to be in the employ of Master Hunter Targus arrived late last night with a message for you. She is waiting in the foyer."

"From Targus?" He stopped so quickly that the valet had to sidestep to avoid bumping into him.

"Yes, Grandfather. She spouted something about finding a weapon that belonged to you. She wouldn't leave. She was injured, but the healer has seen to her."

"My weapon..." The valet kept his gaze lowered respectfully and so didn't see the narrowing of his master's eyes, the thinning of his lips, or the flush of color that flooded those wizened features. "Follow me."

"Of course, Grandfather."

The valet's steps whisked quietly behind the utterly silent ones of his master as the two descended to the second floor, trod the carpeted halls to the front of the estate, then finally started down the broad sweeping stair that emptied into the foyer. So quiet was their approach that the slumped figure seated upon the lowest step didn't stir until the glowering guard tapped her with his boot. The girl scrambled up. Her sleepy eyes darted around the room and centered on the guard, who nodded up the stair to the descending pair. She whirled and dropped to one knee at the last step, her hands out and open, palms up, her face down.

"Grandfather!" Her voice was thick with fatigue, her hair and clothing disheveled. "I bear news of your weapon, sir. I saw him on the eastern road yesterday. I rode as fast as I could to bring you the news. He's headed this way, but may have already reached the city."

At a twitch of his wrist, a broad-bladed dagger dropped into the Grandfather's left hand. He brought the blade down in front of the girl's face and angled the tip upward until it touched her chin. She didn't flinch, but tilted her head back as that deadly pressure indicated she should. Her face was slightly pale, and a light sheen of sweat had broken out on her brow, but her eyes were clear and sharp, and they met his without wavering.

"What is your name, girl?"

"Mya, Grandfather." Her voice betrayed some of her fear, but not as much as he had expected.

His lip twitched with a combination of disappointment and intrigue, the tip of the blade turning her head slightly. Her face bore a wide bruise and several scrapes from jaw to temple.

"And when did you arrive here with this message, Mya?"

"Last night, sir. Just before midnight."

"And why, dear Mya, didn't you deliver your message upon your arrival?" The tip of the dagger pricked her skin just enough to allow a drop of blood to ooze down the blade. She remained perfectly still, eyes fixed on his, her lips working without her jaw moving in an attempt to keep the blade from piercing deeper.

"Such was my intent, Grandfather, but I was told that you were not to be disturbed. I had little hope to win past your guards and your valet to bring you the news."

His eyes left hers and fixed the guard standing behind her with a narrow stare.

"Is this true?"

"Yes, Grandfather."

His eyes returned to hers, and his lip twitched once again. The dagger left Mya's chin for the span of one fluttering heartbeat, and when it returned it was drenched to the hilt. A fine spray of blood spattered Mya's upturned face, but again, she didn't flinch. A gasp from the Grandfather's left evolved into a gurgle, and the valet fell past them, his throat slit neatly from earlobe to earlobe. He was dead before he hit the floor.

"Stand up, Mya."

His dagger stayed at her chin as she stood upon legs shaky from fear or a long sleepless night on a hard marble floor. She was not tall—the top of her head was still below his shoulders as he stood upon the lowest step of the stair. Young and fit, but slight of frame, he remembered her from the courtyard when he sent Targus on the hunt. There was less fear in her eyes than he would have liked, but that also could have been blunted by her obvious exhaustion.

"When last did you see my weapon?" He lowered the dagger slowly, but kept it in his hand.

"Yesterday just before midday, Grandfather." Still, she didn't move, even to wipe the blood from her face.

"And where?"

"A quarter-day's hard ride west of the crossroads to Melfey, Grandfather." She swallowed and blinked once. "At his pace, he would have arrived just at dawn."

"Guard, find Sereth and send him on horseback to the east road gate. Tell him to watch for a boy entering alone. If he sees this boy, he's to follow without being seen or heard. Go."

"Yes, Grandfather!" The guard started off, but Mya's shout brought him up short.

"He's dressed like a slave: brown tunic, rope belt, short trousers, and no shoes. He's got sandy hair, and he's thin. About my height." The guard looked at her, then at the Grandfather, confusion evident on his face; the guildmaster's guards were trained to take orders from one person only, not some upstart second apprentice.

"Anything else?" the Grandfather asked, one eyebrow cocking in amusement.

"Yes; he walks like you, sir. More grace than a dancer, and he leaves no tracks. He's strange to talk to, like he knows nothing of the world. He asked me what a city was."

"Tell Sereth all of that. Now go, and tell him to hurry. We may still be lucky." His eyes lost focus for a moment, his thoughts racing ahead to all the possible permutations of effect this new information could set into motion. He snapped to focus again, his eyes fixing onto Mya's like a hawk acquiring prey.

"You will come with me, Mya. I've been informed that there is a bath waiting and breakfast after. You look like you could do with both. And while you bathe and eat, you'll tell me every detail since you left this estate with Targus."

"Yes, Grandfather."

"Good." Two more guards entered the foyer as the Grandfather turned, his right hand extending to guide Mya up the stairs. "Guards, have my valet removed. We no longer require his services. And send my scribe and artist to the morning room."

Lad's steps were those of a man in a trance. As the glow of predawn lightened the dark streets, then turned into morning, his awe of his surroundings doubled and redoubled. People began appearing on the streets, in doorways, on balconies, all of them busy talking, working, laughing, some even singing, a sound he'd never dreamt to hear from a human throat. A girl dashed up the street with a basket of brightly colored flowers, her skirts a swirl of color rivaling the riot of hues cradled in her arms. A man pulled along a cantankerous beast that was tall with a back humped high; it bawled a warning at anyone they passed. Another pushed a two-wheeled cart mounded with dead sea creatures, his voice calling out in sing-song fashion, listing his wares. A woman from a balcony shouted down, and he tossed a flat fish up to her waiting basket, then caught the coin she threw down.

It was all too much for Lad to take in at once.

He came to the lower river, wide and slow-flowing and lined with stone quays. Long, wide boats were tied with ropes thicker than his arm. He watched as men loaded and unloaded goods, produce, fish, boxes, barrels, and even livestock. As he stood there, another barge worked its way up the river against the lazy current, men with long poles walking from bow to stern, then pulling up their poles and walking back to the bow in a never-ending succession. Other craft, narrow and quick, darted up and down in zig-zagging patterns, propelled by the wind and a single large triangular sail.

And the people...

Men, women, boys, and girls of all shapes, shades, sizes, races, and classes crowded the streets in a never-ending throng of humanity. A tall figure in white on an even taller horse the color of slate rode up the center of the street at a canter; as they passed Lad noticed the rider's gracefully pointed ears and narrow, sweep-browed features. He had heard of elves and knew this was one by the description in his mind's eye, but he had never hoped to see one. A boy half Lad's height hawked pots and pans from a cart pulled by a huge shaggy dog, but as he turned to Lad with a huge nose and a grin that was far too wide to be human, Lad realized that it was a gnome.

Lad continued on, working his way aimlessly from the busier portions of Twailin that bordered the rivers through twisting residential streets that followed the contours of the land and finally into areas where business and trade pursued a more leisurely pace. The buildings here were lighter, older. Where cut stone girded the outer wall and the docks, plaster and slate lined these streets. He walked in a daze, aware, but overwhelmed by his surroundings.

Finally, as the sun climbed halfway to its zenith, his stomach made his first decision for him. As he was walking past a wide drive that opened into the turning yard of an inn, the scents of well-cooked food struck him, and his stomach growled loudly.

The inn was three floors, the bottom one of cut stone, the top two of white-washed plaster, with a roof of slate. To the left of the huge turning yard stood a barn of wooden planks painted red, and to the right were a well with a long watering trough, a row of hitching posts, and a low coop. A flock of tuft-footed chickens pecked around the yard; the rooster looked at Lad sidelong, then scurried off after a hen. A man of immense girth stood on the inn's lowest step, talking with another who stood before a box-wagon with the stylized heads of a pig and a cow on the side. The two were talking in a language that Lad could barely understand; it concerned cuts and marbling and corn-fed versus grain-fed. As he walked carefully forward, the smaller man finally threw up his hands and disappeared into his wagon. He came out with a huge side of meat balanced on one shoulder and two legs of mutton tied together at the shank over the other.

"That's four and two, Forbish, and I'll not have any of that southern coin!"

"Still robbery!" The big man fished six coins, four gold and two silver, from a pouch under his stained apron and handed them over to the smaller man. "Just bring it into the kitchen, and I'll—"

"I'm a butcher, not a porter," replied the merchant as he handed the legs of mutton over and started to unload the beef.

The other man held up a hand. "Hold on just a moment! I can't heft that or my back would surely pain me for a fortnight. Let me call one of the maids out, and I'll—"

"Sir?"

The two men looked at Lad as if he had sprouted up out of the ground. The innkeeper's eyes inspected him at a glance, from head to foot and back.

"Yes? What do you want?"

"I want to work, sir." The big man opened his mouth to speak, but Lad continued before he could. "I'm stronger than I look and a good worker. I only want food and a place to sleep that's warm." He looked at the two men, and at the strain on the butcher's face from the heavy load on his shoulder. "I can take all of that for you."

"Oh, now, you can't heft that!"

Before the man could protest, Lad lifted the side of beef from the butcher's shoulder and relieved the innkeeper of his mutton as well. He bounded up the ten steps to the inn's porch in three strides, and turned around to say, "If you would tell me where the kitchen is, I'll take this meat there."

"Uh, through the common room and to the right. Tell Josie to show you where the locker is. You can hang them in there."

"Looks like you just got yourself a new stable hand, Forbish!" the butcher said with a laugh as Lad nodded and entered the inn.

"I ain't hired that skinny kid yet, you bloody-handed land-pirate. You just get back up on your meat wagon and..."

Their voices faded into the murmur of the common room as Lad entered, balancing his heavy load easily. There were four men at two tables, and a woman pouring mugs of black, steaming liquid into cups on their tables. The room could have easily seated forty. All of their eyes were on him as he walked through the room and pushed open the swinging door to the right.

The kitchen was a sweltering maze of counters, washbasins, chopping blocks, pothooks, stoves, ovens, grills, and huge iron and copper pots and pans. A quick turn around confirmed that there was nobody there. There were two doors besides the one he'd come in through, and he had no idea where or what the "locker" was. Not knowing what to do, he stood and waited for "Josie" to appear.

"Who are you?"

Lad turned toward the voice and saw a girl standing at one of the doors; she held two metal pails brimming with milk. Her stance was slightly askew, looking at him somewhat sideways as if she were frozen in mid-step, unsure of whether she should enter or back up. Her knuckles were white on the handles of the pails, and Lad could see the concentric ripples on the milk within that betrayed her shaking.

"I'm Lad." This got nothing but a raised eyebrow. "Are you Josie?"

"Wiggen." She took a step into the kitchen and put her pails aside, dusting her hands on her apron. "You work for the butcher?"

"No." She stopped again and gave him that same, wide-eyed, sidelong stare. "Do you know where the locker is? I was told to put these there."

"Who told you?"

"Forbish."

"My *father* told you to bring that in here?"

"What's a father?" She looked at him blankly, eyebrows arched in astonishment. "Forbish is your father?"

"Yes," she said carefully.

"No."

"What?"

"Forbish didn't ask me to take this meat in here."

"What? You *just* said that he—"

"Forbish told me to ask Josie where the locker was and to hang these in *there*, not here. You're not Josie, but you work here, so I asked you where the locker is. If you don't know where the locker is, I can wait for Josie."

The girl shook her head and took a half step back, then turned away and opened one of the other doors. "The locker's this way."

Lad followed her through the door and down a passage lined with large barrels and smaller casks. The passage had a yeasty smell that was heady, but not unpleasant. At the end of the passage was another door. Wiggen opened this door and entered. Lad followed. The room was cool, thick stone on all sides, and the walls were crowded with shelves full of crates. Barrels stood on the floor, some full of apples, some potatoes, and one full of pickles swimming in brine. Wiggen took a small lamp from beside the door and lit it with a match she struck with her thumbnail. She took the lamp to the center of the room and pulled up a heavy oak-planked hatch. A steep stair vanished into the darkness below.

"That's the locker, but you'll need help to get that beef down there. I can take one end and—"

"If you take this," he handed the bound legs of mutton to her, "I can take the large piece down.

"Don't be silly! If you— Wait!"

Lad repositioned the heavy side of beef and merely stepped into the empty space of the hole. His eyes had penetrated the gloom of the locker easily, and he knew the floor was only twice his height from the hatch. He just flexed his knees upon landing and looked around for something to hang the meat on. It was very cool and dry in the stone-lined locker, and there were many hams, sides of smoked meat, and a much-diminished side of beef hanging from hooks.

"Are you—"

"Wiggen! Did you see a—"

Lad ignored the chatter for a moment as he found one of the heavy meat hooks. He placed it firmly into the side of beef and looped the eye over one of the pegs on the ceiling, then wiped the grease from his hands onto his trousers and ascended the steps through the hatch.

"—don't like the idea of you hiring a street urchin to—"

Lad lifted the two legs of mutton from Wiggen's hand, and she jumped like she'd been slapped, whirling on him and glaring straight at him for the first time. Forbish stood behind her, his eyes wide in surprise.

"I didn't intend to startle you, Wiggen." He looked at her face and noted the deep scar that ran from her ear almost to the point of her chin. But Lad had seen many scars and thought nothing of it. He lifted the mutton to show her. "I'll take these down into the locker now." He stepped off into the hole.

"See what I mean? Did you see what he did? He did that with a whole side of beef, Father! It's probably ruined, smashed on the floor like that!"

"Now, Wiggen, he's just a poor beggar boy. Don't you take that tone. He asked me for work and wants nothing but food and a warm place to sleep in return. With Tam gone, we could use the help, and he seems capable enough. I'll check on the meat."

But Lad was already back up the steps, silent as a mouse on a rug. "I hung the beef next to the other one, and the mutton next to that." He looked at Wiggen and cocked his head in question. "Did I do something wrong? The meat didn't touch the floor."

"Now he's lying," the girl said flatly, backing away until she was half behind her father. "He couldn't have kept it from hitting the floor, jumping down like that. I don't think you should hire him, Father." She lowered her voice to a whisper. "And he told me his name was 'Lad.' That can't be true. Nobody names someone that."

"My name *is* Lad." He tried to understand why she was afraid of him. All he'd done was try to be helpful.

"Well...Lad," Forbish said, looking to his daughter, then back to Lad. "Show me where you hung that meat, and I'll decide whether or not you can work for me. Is that all right?"

"Yes." He turned and stepped through the hatch again, landing lightly on the floor. Forbish followed more slowly, working his bulk backward down the steps. Wiggen handed down the lamp and the big man looked around carefully. He touched the meat and checked the floor, and then looked at Lad.

"Looks fine to me," he said with a shrug. The big man worked his way back up the steps. By the time he handed the lamp back to his daughter and dusted off his hands, Lad was standing beside him, waiting patiently. "Whoa! You do move quick, don't you, Lad?"

"Yes." Lad stepped back, since his appearance at the man's elbow had startled him so, and asked, "Will you let me work for food and a place to sleep?"

"Father, I don't like the idea of having a stranger staying in the inn."

"Now, Wiggen. We have strangers stayin' here every night, so you'll have to come up with a better excuse than that. Lad didn't lie about the meat; it didn't touch the floor. And I've heard stranger names than 'Lad' in my time. He can sleep in the tack room out in the barn, if that'll suit you, Lad. We serve three meals a day. You can have leftovers after you've finished the work. Will that be all right?"

"Yes." He waited patiently for a few breaths, then asked, "What work do you want me to do?"

"Wiggen can show you," the big man said. "And don't you give me that look, girl! He's workin' for us as of right now. Just show him where to wash up. He can take his meals in the kitchen." Forbish turned and led the way back through the taproom to the kitchen.

"After lunch you get Josie to pull down some extra blankets. We can wash his things tonight after supper." He looked at Lad with a raised eyebrow. "Do you have any other things? Clothes and such?"

"No."

"Well, there's Tam's old things that he'd grown out of. Some of that might fit. Can't have you runnin' around in naught but rags, you know. Gives the *Tap and Kettle* a bad name!"

"The tap and kettle?"

"Aye, that's the inn, Lad! The *Tap*," he waved to the taproom, "and *Kettle*!" he waved to the huge copper kettle on one of the stoves. "Best beer and blackbrew in all of Twailin!"

"I understand," Lad said, though he didn't know what blackbrew was.

"Good!" The big man sighed gustily and fixed his daughter with a meaningful stare. "You show him around now, Wiggen, and don't be mean. He's gonna be here a while."

"Yes, Father," she said, her voice and manner less than enthusiastic. She still stood sideways to Lad, and he noticed that she wore her hair down over the off-side of her face. "Come on, Lad."

Chapter X

Soft, warm water scented with exotic oils cascaded over Mya's tired shoulders, leeching the exhaustion from her fatigued muscles and easing her aches and pains. Her eyes closed in bliss as one of the servants massaged her scalp with fragrant soap for the second time and once again rinsed the soap away with more luscious water.

"How is this, Lady?"

Mya opened her eyes and found herself staring into the face of the Grandfather's weapon rendered in charcoal pencil on fine parchment. The likeness was amazing, but there was something not quite right.

"The eyes are too dark," she said, easing up out of the water and accepting a thick, warm towel from a servant. "He has eyes the color of mica, a very light tan, almost like they were made of colored glass."

The artist went back to work, rubbing out the darker irises and sketching in lighter ones. Mya stepped out of the huge copper tub. Two servants dried her hair and legs and the towel she had been wrapped in was replaced by a warm robe of emerald silk. When the servants were finished, she slid her feet into slippers of black satin and looked again at the artist's rendering.

"Yes. That's him." She turned to the Grandfather and nodded to the sketch. "That's your weapon, Grandfather."

"Ah, yes." The Guildmaster of Assassins eased himself up

from the thickly upholstered chair next to the window. The morning sun bathed the chair, and the old man's wizened features were flushed with color from the warm rays. He bid his artist come near with a flick of one hand and the man complied, presenting his work for his master's scrutiny.

"We meet at last." He stood there utterly still for so long that Mya would have thought he had slipped into a trance, except for his eyes. Those slitted orbs danced within their wrinkle-rimmed sockets, flickering over the artist's rendering like a mosquito hovering over warm skin. Then his eyes snapped up and met hers.

"See that copies are made of this and distributed to all the district supervisors," he said, handing the sketch back to the artist while never taking his eyes off Mya's. "Come sit with me for a while, my dear. We must discuss your role in the coming hunt."

"Yes, Grandfather," she said, bowing slightly, more in an attempt to break his discomforting scrutiny than as a sign of any reverence she felt.

They moved to a small table set by the windows, and servants immediately brought an array of food and drink. Mya suddenly realized that she was famished; the luscious aroma of sausage, egg, bread and steaming blackbrew started her stomach to growling. At that moment another servant entered the morning room and bowed before making his announcement.

"Milord Grandfather, one of your operatives, a young apprentice named Sereth, has returned. He wishes to speak with you."

"Send him in," the Grandfather said, his eyes leaving his guest for a moment while the apprentice entered and bowed low. Mya kept her gaze lowered, trying to silence her tumultuous stomach by clenching the muscles of her midriff.

"Grandfather, I've found some evidence that your weapon entered the city through the east gate sometime in the early morning hours." The apprentice's voice was steady, but there was a faint timbre of fear beneath the placid surface. Years under the tutelage of Targus had taught Mya to recognize such signs, so she knew the underlying dread for what it was.

"What evidence?" the Grandfather asked, his own tone heavy with foreboding.

"I spoke with the morning watchman at length, Grandfather." As he spoke, the Grandfather filled his plate from the platters on the table. He didn't give Mya leave to touch the food, however, and her plate remained empty. "He's not one of ours, but enough silver loosened his tongue. I asked if a lost boy had entered the city though his gate and he finally remembered a scrawny youngster who'd come through in the early morning hours, a couple of glasses before first light. He remembered because it was well before the normal morning traffic started. Just a peasant lad, or so he thought, with no baggage and no shoes."

"Thank you Sereth. You may go, but stay in the compound." The Grandfather's voice sweetened like honeyed wine as he said, "You have shown resourcefulness in this, Sereth. I may have need of your services soon."

"Thank you, Grandfather," the youth stated flatly, turning on his heel and quick-stepping out of the room. Mya watched him leave with professional scrutiny, then returned her gaze to her host and found him watching her again.

"You find him interesting, Mya?" he asked, watching her watch him as he picked up knife and fork, cut off a piece of sausage, and dredged it through an egg yolk. He brought the bite slowly to his mouth, chewed carefully, and swallowed.

"No, Grandfather," Mya said, swallowing. She hadn't eaten a real meal since the inn at Thistledown; her mouth watered at the smell of food and the sight of him eating. "I've never seen him before this day." He knew she was hungry, she realized, and was using it as a distraction to reveal any hidden motives she might have. It made her slightly angry, but she refused to let it show.

"But your eyes followed him with more than a passing glance." He tore the corner off a slice of steaming bread and methodically dabbed it into the egg.

"You told him that you might need his services soon, and he had been searching for information about your weapon." She licked her lips, trying to ignore the food. "I was memorizing him, as I've been taught to do."

"Ahh, yes. Targus has taught you well." He poured a dollop of cream into his blackbrew and swirled it with a tiny spoon, then brought the cup to his lips. When the cup touched the table again he smiled at her thinly. "I wonder why Targus hasn't brought you to my attention before. You're most capable for your age, steadier of nerve than many trained guild members; and show remarkable fortitude and self-control."

"Thank you, Grandfather," she said, again forcing herself not to react as he thought she would. "I often thought that Master Targus deemed me too brash."

"Are you hungry, Mya?" he asked.

"Yes, Grandfather."

"But you haven't asked me for food. That's not the manner of a brash young woman."

"It's not my place to ask, Grandfather. You've already shown me much kindness." She nodded to the still-steaming tub and fingered the lapel of her luxurious robe.

"Yet you're hungry. If I offered those things, shouldn't I also offer a simple meal?"

"I'm your servant, Grandfather. It's not for me to say what you should or shouldn't offer." She clenched her jaw and swallowed again, hiding her annoyance at this ridiculous sparring. "I don't take you for a fool, Grandfather. You know I haven't eaten. You know Targus' opinion of my temperament. You're testing that assessment, offering me one indulgence, then not offering the next." She let the corner of her mouth quirk upward slightly. "I am not so brash that I'd be rude to my master's master simply because I'm hungry."

"You may eat," he said evenly, his wizened features unreadable.

"Thank you, Grandfather." She promptly filled her plate and began eating in relaxed, controlled movements, relishing each bite, but refusing to show her bliss.

"Yes, I think Targus may have underestimated you, dear Mya. And since you're the only person in my employ who has actually *seen* my weapon, I'll require your services in directing the search for him." He continued eating, still watching her, still trying to read her reactions. "You *will*, of course, require some kind of rank within the guild other than apprentice in order to supervise such an endeavor."

"Of course, Grandfather." She sipped blackbrew, black and strong, watching him watch her over the rim of the cup. "And if I may be so brash as to ask, what might that rank be?"

"Junior Journeyman, I think will be sufficient."

"Thank you, Grandfather," she said, bowing her head in gratitude. "Will I still be under Master Targus' supervision?"

"I don't think that would be prudent, Mya." He paused, reached, and refilled her cup from the silver pot. "You'll report directly to me. Sereth will be at your disposal. Any disposition of manpower will require my approval, but you'll have much autonomy as well."

"Thank you, Grandfather," she said, bringing the cup once again to her lips, thinking that both Targus and Jax were going to be positively furious with her promotion to journeyman. She *should* have been an apprentice for at least two more years, and Jax was in his *fifth* year of apprenticeship. When her eyes met the Grandfather's once again, however, her stomach clenched upon the few bites of food she'd eaten. His gaze had turned hard, cruel, and infinitely malicious.

"Don't fail me in this, Mya."

"I shall not, Grandfather." She forced her eyes away from his, hearing her own fear in her voice and hating herself for that weakness. She picked up her fork and took another bite, but the delicious food seemed to turn to ashes in her mouth.

Wiggen hefted the heavy bucket with a sigh and headed off toward the barn. It had been a long day, and they had more guests than usual: six merchants, one with his young son, and a man who was traveling alone. She'd spent half the morning showing their strange new stable hand how to do his job, which had put her behind in her other chores. Granted, if he'd done all she told him to, he had cut her work in half, but she had her doubts about him. His manner was odd, as if he knew nothing at all. She remembered his question when they'd first met, "What's a father?" and shook her head. *He must be an escaped slave or something*, she thought, her fear and suspicion easing into cautious pity for his obviously inadequate upbringing. Granted, her own childhood hadn't been exactly easy, but at least she had a father.

She stepped into the barn and stopped, her eyes widening slightly at the state of the place. Everything was spotless, or as spotless as a barn could be. The floor was swept clean, the tools were all put away, there was no clutter at all, and every stall was strewn with a fresh layer of straw. The four saddle horses and the team of two matched bays were all stabled, groomed, fed, and watered, the merchant's heavily laden wagon was moved to the back and looked to have been scrubbed. She certainly hadn't expected such a thorough job, not on the first day with the small amount of instruction that she'd given him. But now he was nowhere to be seen.

"Probably off sleeping somewhere," she mused, her frown tugging at her scar, which always made her frown the more. "Lad?" she called toward the tack room.

"Yes, Wiggen."

She turned in time to see him plummeting from the hayloft and almost let out a cry of alarm, but he landed as light as a feather. She tried to hide her startlement as he looked at her with that curious askance tilt of his head and placed the broom he'd been using carefully aside.

"Why do you do that?" she asked, putting the bucket down to rest her aching shoulder.

"Do what?"

"Leap down like that. You could hurt yourself, and there's a ladder right over there."

"Jumping is quicker and easier. I couldn't hurt my*self*."

"Well, be careful anyway." She turned her head partially away to hide the scar and inspected him sidelong. He certainly looked like he'd been working all day; he was grimy to the elbows, sweat streaked his tunic, and bits of straw riddled his hair and clothing. His bare feet were nothing short of filthy. She nodded to the bucket. "I thought you might want to wash up before supper, so I brought you water, some soap, and a towel, and there's some of Tam's old clothes in here, too." He took the bundle from her without a word and placed it on the nearby workbench.

"The guests have eaten, so you can come in whenever you like." She watched curiously as he sorted the pile of clothes and picked out the towel and soap. "We usually all eat in the kitchen after the guests have finished, so just come in the back way when—" She stopped suddenly as he stripped off his filthy tunic and began working on the knotted rope belt of his trousers. "What are you *doing*?"

"I'm washing." He stopped instantly, his face a blank question. "You were correct that I wanted to wash. Shouldn't I?"

"Not *here*!" Didn't this boy have any decency at all? Why, he was standing in plain view of the courtyard and she was only three feet away. Her eyes lingered on the layers of corded muscle that his tunic had covered; he wasn't as skinny as she'd thought, and all of his weight was muscle. His skin was tan beneath the sweat and grime of a day's work, and so thin that she could see the individual fibers playing in waves along his abdomen and chest.

"Why not here?"

"Uh...because!" She snapped her eyes away, hating the rush of heat that washed over her face. "It's not decent! People can see!"

"Where should I wash then, Wiggen?"

She looked back to him, taken aback at the utter lack of scorn, sarcasm, or spite in his voice. On his face were nothing but complete trust, curiosity, and concern that he had done something wrong. She nodded toward one of the stalls, thinking again what a bleak childhood Lad must have had.

"You can wash in one of the stalls for now. We have bathing rooms in the inn, but you're a little too dirty to be walking through the common room." She turned her back as he took the soap and towel and stepped into the first stall. "We like to keep the inn as clean as we can, Lad. The customers like it that way, which means more customers and more money coming in." She heard him splashing and scrubbing and kept her attention on the courtyard. "If one of our own walks through all dirty and tracking filth from the stables, word might get out that the whole place was dirty, even the kitchen, and then we wouldn't have any customers at all, see?"

"I understand," he said, and she heard one more great splash as he dumped the rest of the bucket over his head in a final rinse.

"Do you need more water?" she asked. "I can get another bucket from the well if you do."

"I don't think I need more water, Wiggen." She heard the flutter of the towel as he dried himself. "But I forgot the clothes that you brought. I don't want to stand where people can see."

"Oh, well, here." She stepped to the workbench and picked out a pair of trousers and a nice blue tunic that she had always liked when Tam wore them. "These should fit closely enough." She stepped to the stall door, fully expecting him to be wrapped in the towel. She stopped with a gasp, her eyes popping wide at the sight of him standing there amid the damp straw, the towel flung casually over his shoulder.

"Aren't I clean enough?" he asked, looking down at himself and turning a circle before her. "I couldn't see my back, but I tried to wash well."

"No." Wiggen gaped, forcing herself to turn away and hold out the clothes. "You're clean."

He lifted the clothes from her hand and she stepped out of the stall, her eyes still wide but focusing on nothing, her hands clenching her apron. Well, he was *definitely* older than he looked. Earlier she'd thought he might be a tall, lanky thirteen or so; now she knew she'd underestimated by at least three years, which made him only a year or so younger than her. She shook her head sharply and clenched her eyes closed, but she felt as if the sight of him standing like that would be burned into her eyes forever.

"Did I do something else wrong, Wiggen?"

"No, er...yes. I mean... Oh, never mind! Just get dressed!"

"I'm dressed," he said in that same expressionless tone. No malice, no trick, no sly seduction that she would have expected from anyone else. She turned back and knew instantly that she'd made a mistake in giving him those clothes.

"Is something wrong, Wiggen?" Evidently, he could see the discomfort on her face.

"Oh, nothing. You just remind me of Tam in those clothes."

"Who's Tam?" he asked, retrieving his soiled things and the towel from the stall and taking them to the workbench.

"He was my brother." She reached for the clothes. "I'll take those back to the inn."

"He's not your brother any longer?" As he handed over the dirty things, his hand brushed hers slightly in passing. She drew back a step, snapping her eyes at him. Her ire melted at his blank stare, so honest and empty.

"No, he... He died about a year ago."

"Oh. I understand." He took the rest of the clothes and blankets and opened the door to the tack room. Through the door she could see that the entire room had been cleaned and reorganized. The saddles gleamed with oil, the harnesses glittered in the evening sunlight streaming through the one tiny window, and the narrow cot that had formerly been piled with old saddle blankets was clean, the pallet packed with fresh straw.

"You've done a lot of work today."

"Yes." He stood before her and patted down his new tunic. "Am I clean enough to go into the inn?"

She looked at him and smiled at the way his damp hair was sticking up in odd directions. "You're clean, but... Here." She reached up to pat it down, and he moved, snapping backward a half step, one hand rising as if to fend her off. "Hold still, Lad. I'm not going to hurt you. Your hair's just a little ruffled." She took another step forward and he held still while she finger-combed his tumultuous hair into a semblance of order. "There. You're presentable now." She took a step back and smiled again. "Hungry?"

"Yes." His voice was slightly different, as if he were strained or scared. She shook her head and smiled. He certainly was a strange young man, but she knew now that she'd been wrong about him at first, and she was glad for it. It would be nice to have someone her own age around for a change.

"Well, follow me, then, and we'll get something to eat." She turned, and he followed her to the back door of the inn, so silent that she twice turned back to make sure he was there. He was there both times, half a step behind and to her left, like a shadow.

Or a ghost, she thought, her smile fading once again with thoughts of Tam. She frowned and felt it tug at the year-old scar on her face.

After dinner, Lad left the inn and strolled back toward the barn. Evening's light was still fading, but stars had come out, and the moon was already halfway across the sky. He stopped and looked up for a moment, remembering Flindle's love for sitting beside his forge in the evening and looking up at the stars. His mind wandered over his recent experiences and he wondered once again about his destiny and where he might find it. His eyes were drawn to the courtyard gate and the city beyond, so large and daunting.

"So many decisions to make," he said to himself.

He looked back at the inn, recalling the warm feeling of sitting down and eating with Forbish, Wiggen, and the surly serving woman, Josie, who bustled in and out with tankards of ale and wine. There was another decision, he realized suddenly; he could choose to stay here and not pursue his destiny at all. These people were kind, the food was good, and they enjoyed his help and his company. They cared for him, and he worked for them; the relationship was perfect, seamless, like a sword slipping into its scabbard.

But the curiosity nagged at him, his master's words ringing in his mind over and over. He longed to know what he was made for, what purpose he was meant to serve. It called to him like a siren song and before he realized he was moving, Lad found that his steps had taken him across the inn courtyard and out the gate.

The city of Twailin engulfed him and Lad began meticulously

memorizing every detail, every street, building, signpost and storefront as he carefully began a systematic search through the twilight city streets for his destiny.

CHAPTER XI

As the faintest glow of predawn lightened Lad's room, his eyes opened as if on cue. It was cool in the tack room and the blankets were warm, but Lad had never known luxury or had the option of sleeping late. He sat up slowly, weary from his long night of prowling the city. His skin rose in gooseflesh, but he didn't don his clothes yet. He rose and began a series of slow exercises that he had learned from one of his teachers; gentle stretches evolved into a liquid sequence of moves that prepared his body for the stresses of the day. The exercises became a fluid dance of slow strikes, sweeps, and turns. He moved and flowed, becoming more limber with each successive position, his concentration guiding him flawlessly through the complex series. When he was finished, his skin was warm, though he hadn't broken a sweat. He donned his tunic and sat lotus upon the floor, his mind slipping into the calming meditation that ordered his thoughts.

First the body, then the mind, and the two become one.

This had become his routine over the last week: rise with dawn's first light, stretch, exercise, meditate, see to his duties around the inn and stables throughout the day; then, after dinner, when darkness and silence took over the inn, he would slip out into the streets and prowl. He had memorized about a third of the city in his first seven nights' excursions, ordering the jumble of streets and buildings into a pattern in his mind. He knew not what he was looking for, but he felt that becoming familiar with his environment was a reasonable first step. The need for sleep always brought him back to the inn sometime after midnight, but habit and training opened his eyes at first light. There was a structure to this routine, a rhythm that he either craved innately or was compelled to require by the magic that was ingrained into his soul. Of course, Lad knew nothing of craving or compulsion; the routine just felt *right*.

He stood and donned his trousers, awake and alert and ready for the day.

The first wisps of smoke fluttered from the kitchen chimney as he left the barn. Forbish was stoking the fires in the kitchen stoves to life when he entered, and greeted Lad with his usual morning exuberance.

"Morning, Lad! Sleep well? There's a bite of bread for ya on the sideboard. Go ahead and lay a fire in the common room for me."

"Good morning, Forbish." He took a slice of the dark bread and ate it as he entered the main room and quickly laid a fire. The door to the kitchen squeaked, and he knew it was Wiggen even before he turned his head.

"Good morning, Wiggen." She brought a bit of burning tallow from the kitchen fire to kindle the larger one, and smiled as he stepped aside for her.

"G'morning, Lad." Her voice was thick with sleep. He knew she wasn't at her best in the morning by her own admission that she rarely slept well, though he knew not why. He waited while she lit the tinder and coaxed the little blaze to life. He added two larger pieces of wood to the fire and watched them catch, but Wiggen just sat there staring at the flames. Usually she was up and back in the kitchen by now, helping Forbish with the morning bread and sipping at the dark brew that was half of the inn's claim to fame. This departure from routine brought him up short. Had he done something wrong? Her eyes were locked onto the growing blaze as if some secret could be delved from its depths.

"Wiggen?"

"Oh! Sorry, Lad. I was just lost there for a moment, you

know."

"Lost?" He placed two more pieces of wood on the fire and stood with her. She still stared at the flames, but wasn't transfixed by them now.

"Yeah. I was remembering a dream I had last night, and my mind wandered."

"A dream?" This was one more term that he didn't know.

"A bad dream, about the day Tam died. Sometimes in my dreams I see him alive again, and sometimes I watch him die again, just like before." She looked at him and he could see water pooling in the crescents of her eyes. "I have them a lot. It's why I don't sleep very well, I guess." She wiped at her eyes, a frown of annoyance tugging at the corners of her mouth. She moved her hair to cover the side of her face that was scarred. "I know it's silly. It's been over a year, but I still..."

Lad still wasn't quite sure what she was talking about, but he could see that she was troubled somehow. These dreams she spoke of sounded more like memories to him. He didn't understand how memories could be good or bad, they just *were*. He had acute memories of his upbringing, his training, every fight he'd ever been in, and every moment he lay under his old master's hands, feeling the press of the needles and the rush of power from the magic. His memories lay like books upon a shelf in his mind, there if he needed them, but only *when* he needed them. Perhaps others' memories invaded their thoughts like unwelcome guests.

"Your memories trouble you."

"Yeah." She sniffed, and turned to go back to the kitchen. "I wish I could forget it all."

"You cannot forget, Wiggen, but your memories need not cause you trouble."

"What?" She turned back, her eyes narrow and skeptical.

"You can order your thoughts." He found it hard to explain the concept of meditation. "Your memories, those which cause you trouble, can be placed where they belong in your mind so that you recall them only when you need to. I was trained to do this. I will teach you, if you wish."

"How?"

"The mind is like the body; just as you can teach someone to do something, like you taught me to milk the cows, you can teach the mind to perform certain tasks." He shrugged, stumbling over the concept. His memories of the training were perfectly clear and most of his words were those of the one who had trained him. "It isn't hard to learn, but very difficult to master. It may help you."

"I don't—"

"Wiggen!" The call from the kitchen was obviously Forbish, and he didn't sound pleased.

"After breakfast, Lad," she said, whirling toward the kitchen.

Lad squatted back down in front of the fire, adding two more lengths of pine and watching the flames lick at the pale wood. He looked into the flames, watched their patterns swirling in the constant upward spiral that was faintly hypnotic. No memories lurked in the flames to torment Lad's mind; all of his memories were securely locked away and wouldn't come to the surface unless he needed them.

"This is unprecedented, Grandfather." Targus' boots whisked along the flagstones of his master's courtyard, half a pace behind the Grandfather's silent steps. Jax followed them both, and Targus could feel the young man's temper smoldering like a bed of coals. "She is naught but a girl, and a headstrong one at that! You'll rue putting her in such a critical position."

"*I* will rue?" The Grandfather stopped in the span of a single stride, his eyes flashing dangerously. "Speak not of actions to be regretted when you commit them yourself, *Master* Targus! You overreach yourself when you deign to tell *me* what I'll do!"

"I spoke out of turn, Grandfather," Targus said, the muscles of his jaw bunching and relaxing rhythmically. "I'm simply concerned that you've put a witless girl in a position that may cause you difficulty in the future. She'll serve herself in this, not you."

A dagger stood before Targus' left eye before he could blink it, the needle point a finger-breadth from ending his life. He stood perfectly still, knowing better than to try anything as foolish as drawing a weapon. Even if he could have cleared the weapon from its sheath before being pithed, he was bound by more than words when it came to raising a hand against the Grandfather. He clenched his left hand on the obsidian ring that encircled his finger and bound his soul to his master.

"The only reason you still live, Targus, is that you are a very valuable Hunter. I need your skills and I need your obedience. The former without the latter is useless to me." The dagger vanished into the Grandfather's sleeve in a flick of motion. "Do you understand me, Targus?"

"Perfectly, Grandfather." Targus held his tongue. He had said all that he thought he must say to make his opinion known. Anything further would unnecessarily endanger his life. "I live to serve you."

"Good! Start by assigning your apprentice to assist Mya."

"What?" Jax sputtered. "Grandfather, I'm—"

Targus felt Jax start to move and whirled. The backhand blow met with his apprentice's jaw with all the force he could deliver, knocking the stupid young man to the ground and probably saving his life. Targus placed his boot carefully on Jax's chest and glared down at him.

"Who gave you leave to speak, apprentice?"

"No one, Master," Jax said, his words slurred through his clenched and bloody teeth.

"Then don't. Your life is mine to spend, Jax! If I tell you to fall on your sword, you will fall on your sword. If I tell you to assist Mya to the best of your abilities, you will assist Mya. Do you understand me?"

"Yes, Master."

"Good! Now get up and see to our things. Stow your gear in the barracks." He removed his boot from his apprentice's chest.

"Yes, Master." Jax rolled easily to his feet, bowed and whirled toward the stables. The two men watched Jax until he disappeared into the low building.

"My apologies for the behavior of my apprentice,

Grandfather," Targus said with a bow. "He's skilled, but short of sight."

"He will learn to tread carefully, or he will perish," the Grandfather said with a wave of one hand, as if the matter was of no consequence. "I have something else for you, a task that will require your absence from the city for some days."

"The wizard?"

"You're astute, Targus." The Grandfather's smile was thin and bore perhaps enough warmth to melt a single snowflake, a small snowflake. "Take one of my mages to deal with any spells. You were wise to tell the authorities in Thistledown to hold Corillian's body; he may have trinkets stashed about his person that will help us in our search for my weapon. If you find anything interesting, return. But if your search of his person is fruitless, proceed to Krakengul Keep and see what you can find out."

"I'll leave at once, Grandfather," Targus said, hiding his disappointment. This would be his third visit to the dismal little village of Thistledown in less than a fortnight, and he felt that this one would be no more productive than the others.

It was late afternoon before Lad and Wiggen got a break from the relentless list of chores that piled up every day around the *Tap and Kettle*. Finally, when the milking, haying, baking, mucking, feeding, egging, cleaning, washing, grooming, stoking, hauling, washing, pressing, and cooking were done, the two slipped off to the barn.

"So, what's this mind trick you mentioned this morning?" Wiggen asked, her tone blatantly skeptical. "Is it some kind of magic?"

"Magic? No." Lad led her up to the hayloft and they sat in the open haying door, the sun streaming in on them. "It's a discipline of the mind. It's like learning how to read or speak a language."

"I don't believe you can change the way you think just by wanting to hard enough." Wiggen's voice was almost angry now, and the scar that marred her face grew livid. "It's like saying I could fly if I flap my arms hard enough. It'll never happen!"

"Let me show you what your mind can do." Lad's voice had taken on a quality that she'd not heard before, and her temper seeped away, leaving behind a faint ghost of fear. How well did she really know this strange young man? Would he spell her and steal her thoughts or was it just a trick?

Lad reached into his tunic and withdrew a stale heel of bread. He brushed a bit of the loft floor clear of hay and crumbled the bread. Then he looked up into the rafters and twittered a whistle, high and shrill. Immediately, a small flock of sparrows fluttered down and began to peck at the crumbs. They scuffed and pecked and pushed one another about, and Wiggen thought them the most adorable things she'd ever seen.

"Which one do you like best?" Lad asked, his voice calm but not a whisper. The birds paid no attention, as if he didn't exist.

"What?" *What does he mean?* she thought.

"You like the birds. I've seen you watching them when you feed the chickens. Of these here," he crumbled more bread and let the bits sift through his fingers, bringing the little birds closer, "which would you like to hold in your hand?"

"I don't know." *This is ridiculous!* What did birds have to do with her bad dreams? "That one in the back, I guess. He's smaller than the others and only gets the littlest bits."

"Okay, now watch him closely and concentrate on him."

"Fine."

Wiggen stared at the little bird, widening her eyes and studying his every detail. Suddenly, Lad moved and all the birds fluttered away, their wings beating the air in a rush.

"What? Why did you—?"

"And here he is," Lad said, holding out his gently cupped hands. The tiny sparrow sat there, its head cocking around to look at them from between his thumb and forefinger. Its tiny wings were pressed snugly down to its sides in Lad's hands, but it wasn't hurt. It knew it couldn't fly away, and surely it was scared, but it didn't struggle, as if it were resigned to its fate.

"How did you *do* that?" she whispered, awed that anyone could catch a bird in their hand, but at the same time, drawn to the little scared creature. "Don't hurt it."

"I won't hurt it, Wiggen. Now, place your hands over mine in the same position."

"What?" She stared at him as if he'd told her to put her hands in a fire. "I can't!" But her hands moved, as if of their own volition. Her palms settled over the backs of his hands, and she was startled to find his skin so much warmer than hers. She let her hands rest there, and slowly, he pulled his back. The tiny bird fluttered a bit, but found her hands as unyielding as his had been. In a moment it settled down, watching her with first one eye and then the other.

"Now what?" Her voice quavered and she could hear her heart pounding in her ears.

"Now hold him," he said simply, his voice different again. She looked to him, expecting a smile to match her own, but there was nothing on his face. Only his voice held any emotion. "Let him trust you, Wiggen."

"Huh?"

"Let him trust you."

She looked down at the tiny frightened bird and instantly felt sorry for it, so scared and alone. She wanted to hold it, but at the same time, she didn't want it to be scared any longer. Slowly, she started to understand what Lad meant. She brought her cupped hands close to herself and whispered to the tiny bird. She could feel its wings pressing against her hand, its gentle struggles against her overwhelming strength. She could feel its fluttering breaths, its hammering heart. She cooed to it gently, trying to put peace and calm in her voice. Slowly, after long minutes, the bird began to still. Its breathing slowed and its heart beat at a less frantic pace. It looked at her now with less fear than it had.

"Now," Lad whispered, "slowly open your hands."

Without questioning him, she slowly lifted the pressure from the tiny bird's wings, gently pulling away her constricting hand until the creature sat there peacefully upon her other. Its wings fluttered once, but it still sat there, staring at her. She watched the bird for what seemed like forever, but was only a few breaths, before Lad's gentle whisper drew her attention.

"Now, what are you thinking about, Wiggen?"

"Huh?" The question meant nothing to her, it had no bearing upon the beauty she held in her hand.

"Where are the memories that troubled your sleep last night?"

"I, uh, don't know."

"Have you forgotten them?"

She thought for a moment of the horrors she'd witnessed, the violations she'd endured, and the pain that had been dealt her. The memories lay there in a lump, but they didn't compare to the glory of the tiny sparrow in her hand.

"No. They're still there. I just wasn't thinking about them."

Finally, the little bird fluttered off, twittering a shrill cry as it soared up to the rafters to join its flock. She stared up after it, then lowered her eyes to Lad's, and she began to understand.

"For the time you held the bird, your mind was free from those memories, yes?"

"Yes," she said, knowing it was true. For that moment, nothing had mattered but the here and now, and the beauty in her hands.

"So, you see? You can free your mind of those thoughts that cloud your peace."

"But I can't catch birds," she said, smiling despite her claim.

"You don't need to." He passed his hand over hers and she again felt the warmth of it. "Close your eyes."

She did so, unquestioning now.

"Now, see the bird in your hand." She felt something tickle her palm and, without conscious thought, resurrected that moment in her mind. She held the bird again, and her mind was at peace.

"Good," he whispered, his voice smooth and calming, "now stay there."

His hand slipped from hers and her thoughts wavered, but she grasped at the feeling, holding it like she'd held the fluttering life in her hands, gently but firmly. She refused to let go. She felt herself sink into it, the soft warmth of calm. Peace...

"Wiggen."

"Huh?" Her eyes fluttered open and she was staring at Lad's face, expressionless, but exuding calm.

"Time to go." He nodded out the haying door toward the inn.

"Already?" She sighed and pushed herself to her feet. "Well, I guess a moment's peace is better than none."

"Longer than a moment, Wiggen." He gestured to the sun, and she noticed that it was approaching evening. "It's been half a glass and more."

"What?" She looked back at where they'd sat. "But we just..."

"Half a glass ago." He gestured her to the ladder and she descended. When she reached the bottom, he was standing there waiting for her. For once, his sudden appearance didn't startle her. "How do you feel?"

"Good." It was the only word she could think of, unless, "Rested."

"You've done very well for your first try at meditation, Wiggen." He walked toward the inn with her, talking as they strolled. "Tonight, before you begin to sleep, think of the bird in your hands. Still your mind. Find the place where you were today and stay there. Your sleep won't be troubled."

"I—" She stumbled over the words, trying again as they walked around the corner of the inn to the kitchen door. "I don't know how to thank you, Lad."

"Then don't." He opened the door and she stared at him in passing. She would have expected some kind of joke from anyone else, but she knew he was serious. "I'll show you more tomorrow."

She entered the kitchen and he closed the door, heading off to the cow byre to continue his endless chores.

Chapter XII

The owner of the *Golden Cockerel* backed through the door into the pub's only private room, balancing the heavy tray as his lips moved in a constant muttering curse. He stopped when one of the hulking thugs that guarded the door waved a foot-long dirk under his nose.

"You best learn to knock, barkeep."

"And you best learn manners, boy." The barman moved into the room, ignoring the thug's grim mien. "I was servin' yer master's master in this pub when you wasn't even a bulge in yer pappy's drawers."

"You got a mouth, old man," the thug growled, taking a step. He stopped in his tracks, however, with one look from Mya.

"Leave off, Donik." Mya managed a thin smile for the barman, motioning toward the least-cluttered portion of the broad table she was using as a desk. "You can put it there, Paxal. Thanks."

"Aye, Miss Mya." He put the heavy tray down.

There was enough food and blackbrew for her and her two bodyguards here, and the *Golden Cockerel* didn't even serve food. He must have gone to the cafe on the corner and bought all this. For the first time in a week, she thought of the cost to her landlord of this impromptu invasion she'd spearheaded into his domain. She'd been just a tenant to the man, taking an occasional drink in the bar before climbing the stairs to her one-room flat, and she'd only ever been called "Mya" or "Girl" by him in those years. Now, all of a sudden, he called her "Miss" and was fetching her food day and night. This was costing him dearly.

"You're keeping track of the reckoning, I trust," she said before he turned away, taking up the blackbrew kettle and pouring a cup.

"There's no reckoning, Miss. It's been seen to."

She wondered for a moment just how much Paxal knew, then dismissed the entire matter. If Paxal said it had been taken care of, she could rest assured that it had been. She'd already gone back to her maps and lists of names, sipping the life-giving blackbrew and rubbing her tired eyes, when there was a knock at the door. She looked up with a silent curse at the interruption, but immediately changed her outlook at the sight of Jax and the gaily-clad man with him.

"Master Hensen of the Moneylender's Guild," Jax announced, his tone flat. He'd been utterly stone-faced with her for the two days he'd been here. That he was angry with her was obvious, but Jax was a professional and kept his feelings to himself. That was good, because Mya had more than enough on her hands trying to locate the Grandfather's weapon.

"Master Hensen," she said in greeting, standing and waving at a chair and the tray that Paxal had just brought. The man may well have been a master in the Moneylender's Guild, but he was also a high-ranking boss in the Thieves Guild, and Mya needed his help desperately. "Please sit and have something to eat and a cup of blackbrew."

"Delighted, Miss Mya," he said with a glittering smile. He swept his crimson cloak aside, straightened his green velvet doublet, and sat, accepting a cup from her hand.

"Cream?"

"Please."

"There's sugar or honey as well, here. Please feel free."

"Thank you." He put two heaping teaspoons of sugar into his cup and swirled the syrupy brew.

"Master Hensen," she began, watching him sip daintily, "we're all friends here, so I'll speak bluntly."

"Please do, Miss Mya." He put the cup down and smiled again, his eyes narrowing with hidden knowledge. "Our two...organizations have always worked closely together."

"Quite closely," she agreed. It was true that the Thieves and Assassins Guilds worked together, but they were often bitter rivals as well, and turf wars between the two had spilled blood in the streets and alleys of Twailin more than once. She had no doubt that any help she got from Hensen would cost her dearly. And she also knew that she could, under no circumstances, allow him to know the value or origin of the Grandfather's weapon. But people like Hensen had ways of knowing when they were being lied to. She must be careful in her deceptions.

"The plain fact is that I require your aid in a rather delicate situation." That much was true, at least.

"From the look of it," he said, pointedly eying the maps and lists littering the table, "you're searching for something or someone."

"Your powers of observation are uncontested. As a matter of fact, we seek a young man." She produced the sketch of Lad; it had been enhanced with colored chalk and fine graphite pencils by a master artist, and the likeness was flawless. "This is the closest rendering of his face that we have."

"Hmmm, a lovely young man," Hensen said with a raised eyebrow. "Did he...steal something of yours, perhaps?"

"Nothing of the kind, Master Hensen. He was to have served my Grandfather in some way, the details of which I'm not privy to. He's disappeared, but resides somewhere in the city, we feel sure." She made a shooing motion as he handed back the sketch. "Please, keep it. I have many copies."

"And just how long have you been looking for this young man?" Hensen rolled the parchment and placed it carefully into a pocket in the lining of his cloak.

"Nine days."

"And he's eluded you for that long?" One immaculate eyebrow arched delicately. "He must be skilled in the art of evasion."

"Which is even more curious, Master Hensen, for we doubt that the young man even knows that he's being sought. As you know, we're not unskilled in the art of finding people, even when they don't wish to be found." She sipped her blackbrew, ordering her thoughts carefully. She couldn't give too much away, but the more Hensen knew, the more he could help her.

"Indeed," he agreed, waiting patiently.

"Our entire network has been alerted to watch for him. We feel sure that he must be working somewhere, a stable or warehouse, somewhere out of open view, else we would have found him in short order."

"And you want us to apprehend this young man for you?"

"Not at all, Master Hensen. We simply wish help in locating him, without his knowledge would be best. *We'll* bring him in."

"Is he so dangerous?"

She paused long enough in thinking of a proper answer that she knew she may as well have said yes, but instead, for the sake of propriety if nothing else, she said, "The depth of his skill isn't known to me, Master Hensen, but it would be best if he wasn't confronted directly, for his own safety, if nothing else."

"This young man must be very valuable to your Grandfather, Miss Mya." Avarice, pure and clear, glinted in Hensen's eyes.

"His precise value is also unknown to me, Master Hensen. But if the lengths to which we seek him are any indication, I surmise that your estimate is correct."

"Well, we must help you find him, then, and with all alacrity!" Hensen stood, and Mya followed suit.

"Thank you, Master Hensen," she said, taking his proffered hand in a perfunctory clasp. "Your usual fee for locating missing persons, I assume?"

"Quite." He swirled his cloak around himself and made for the door. "I shall send a messenger when the young man is located, Miss Mya. You need only await my word."

"I will, Master Hensen." When the door closed behind him, she muttered, "Cocky bastard," barely loud enough for her own ears to hear.

She stood silently for several breaths, weighing every word that had been said. Finally she took her seat and sipped her blackbrew, perusing the maps once again.

"Permission to speak, Junior Journeyman?"

Mya looked up to find Jax standing stiffly in front of the table, his hands clenched behind him. She could see the strain in him and wondered just how much he hated her for passing him by so suddenly.

"Of course, Jax. What is it?"

"Hensen is no fool. He knows that the boy is valuable. He'll capture him and hold him ransom. He'll name his price, and we'll risk war if we don't pay it."

"Give me *some* credit, Jax. Hensen may very well be a genius, but he's an ignorant one." Mya took a scone from the tray and bit off a corner, chewing thoughtfully while Jax squirmed in discomfort. "He doesn't know how dangerous the weapon is. If he doesn't take the hint I gave him and tries to apprehend the boy, all we'll have to do is follow the trail of dead thieves straight to him."

"You play a dangerous game, Mya," he said, inclining his head in a mock bow.

"We all play the same game, Jax. We've been playing it since the day we joined the guild. Some of us just *know* how dangerous it is." She briefly searched her sheaf of papers and recovered a tightly bound scroll. "Take this to Brin in The Sprawls and tell her I want an answer by highsun."

"At once, Junior Journeyman." Jax took the scroll and went away. Mya wished she could make all her problems go away so easily.

* * *

"Hey! What do you—"

"Stop that, you!"

"What now?" Forbish muttered, dusting flour from his hands and rounding the kitchen table for the common room. Josie sounded angry. All they needed was another problem with one of the guests. He shouldered the door aside, drawing breath to settle the squabble, but a fist roughly the size of a tankard of ale came out

110

of nowhere and met with the side of his head. The blow sent him to the floor, but the same huge hand grasped his tunic and lifted him bodily.

"Well, here's Fat Man Forbish himself!" a voice thundered in his face. A smaller hand slapped him twice and the stars that were swimming in his vision cleared. Forbish knew immediately that he was in trouble.

"Urik!" he said, still dazed, but able to take in the mayhem that had overrun the common room.

Josie struggled in the grasp of another ruffian, and one of the two guests who had been taking a late breakfast was picking himself up from the floor. There were four of the thugs in all: the huge brute who held Forbish, one who held Josie, another who was threatening his guests, and Urik, their boss. Forbish knew this one, and that alone was enough to confirm that this was no ordinary trouble.

"That's right, Fat Man. Urik the Knife." The man drew his namesake and brandished it before Forbish's face. "And this is your wake-up call."

"What's this about?" one of the guests asked, his voice shaking with impotent rage. All four of the thugs were armed and they would take what they wanted, that much was obvious.

"Unpaid taxes!" Urik bawled over his shoulder at the two men. "This place is under new management! Now show these two the door, Davish. They look like they need to take a walk."

"You heard him," the ruffian said, waving a short sword under the guests' noses for emphasis. "Take a walk. Come back fer supper, and you can settle up accounts."

The two men needed little encouragement. That these were not the duke's representatives was obvious, but being merchants themselves, they knew there were other kinds of payments that the business owners of Twailin had to pay. The two merchants left, their departure accompanied by the raucous laughter of the four thugs.

At that point, Forbish heard the thump of the kitchen door swinging into the back of the hulking brute holding him, and a startled, "What the—" that could only be one person.

"Run, Wiggen!" he shouted, thinking only to save his daughter from the horrors that he knew were to come, horrors of which she had already seen too many.

The crash of crockery hitting the floor and a scream as the back door banged open told him that she had fled. Two more screams and a man's coarsely shouted curse told him that he'd failed. Forbish struggled to break the grip on him. He finally got a look at the brute and knew why he felt so weak against the hold. The man towered over him. His skin was the color of a rotten egg yolk, and two short tusks protruded from between black lips. The man had ogre blood in his veins, and the grip that felt like a vise was being tightened upon his arms.

The kitchen door slammed open and the thrashing, screaming, cursing bundle of skirts that was Wiggen was carried bodily into the room by the thug who had been waiting by the back door.

"Lookie what I caught!" the man crowed, grabbing a handful of hair and silencing Wiggen's struggles with a jerk. He had four parallel welts running from his ear to the tip of his jaw that were beginning to leak blood. Her struggles hadn't been totally ineffectual. "You remember this one, don't ya, Urik?"

"Oh, indeed I do!" Urik stepped around Forbish and up to the terrified girl. "But I see she hasn't completely gotten over our last visit, has she?" He traced the scar on the side of her face, then jerked his hand back from her gnashing teeth.

"Let her go, Urik!" Forbish was pleased that his voice didn't show how terrified he was. "I've got your damned money. Let her go and you can have it."

"You don't understand, Fat Man," the thug said, turning from Wiggen to Forbish. "Money's not the point anymore; you broke the rules. Rules that we had to teach you once before, and you still broke 'em." He waved his dagger in front of Forbish's face for emphasis. "The last time we had to teach you cost you a son and left your girl here marked for life, though she don't look too much the worse for wear." He eyed Wiggen over his shoulder and grinned maliciously.

"I'll double it!" Forbish cried, trying to think of anything to save his daughter.

"Double, triple, it don't matter, Fat Man. You broke the rules." He nodded to his men, and then at the kitchen door. "Let's go someplace where we can discuss this private-like."

Forbish, Wiggen, and the terrified serving woman, Josie, were pushed and prodded through the kitchen, tap room and finally into the storeroom. There, the hulking creature who held Forbish bound his hands and tied them to a hook that supported sacks of onions from the ceiling in the corner. The women were held, and Urik brandished his dagger, pacing the floor and chuckling dangerously.

"Nice thick stone walls in here. Good. We're not likely to disturb the neighbors. Now Forbish, I'll let you choose which of these lovely young ladies we're going to entertain first." He flipped the knife—a foot-long, double-edged fighting dagger—and spun it expertly in his palm. "Your daughter or your employee?"

"Damn you, Urik!" Forbish struggled, but every move threatened to dislocate his shoulders.

"Oh, you want *me* to choose. How kind." He strolled to Josie and leaned close with a predatory smile. "I think the serving wench first, then. That way the girl can see what's in store for—"

Josie spat in his face.

"Filthy cow!" Urik's dagger swung in the dim light, but it was the hilt, not the blade, that impacted upon Josie's temple. The woman collapsed, sagging in the grasp of her captor. Urik wiped his face and waved the woman away as if she could respond. "Let her rest for a while, Baral. I'm sure she'll wake up before we're finished with the good innkeeper's young daughter."

Baral dropped Josie in the corner. She landed like a sack of grain, utterly senseless, blood oozing from the shallow cut on her temple. Urik turned to Wiggen, and the girl's struggles redoubled, even to the point where she broke one arm free and flailed at her captor.

"That just won't do, Tomi. Let Quegul hold the girl." He brandished the knife as Wiggen was handed off to the hulking half-ogre. Hands closed on her arms like iron manacles, and all her struggles didn't affect the brute's grip in the slightest.

"Now..." He stepped forward and put the tip of his dagger under Wiggen's nose. "Hold still while your daddy learns why he mustn't break the rules anymore, lassie." Without pause, he gripped the neck of her dress firmly in his free hand and jerked, tearing the material open to the waist.

Wiggen's scream rose on the air like a dying bird, piercing and horrible, and it broke her father's heart as surely as if a knife had been thrust through it.

"NOO!" Forbish wailed, wrenching forward against his bonds, heedless of the pain.

"Oh, so much over so little?" Urik laughed, grabbing a handful of the girl's hair and wrenching her head back. "I haven't even touched her yet and you're both crying like spitted pigs!"

Wiggen's tears streaked her face, her eyes clenched tightly, her chest heaving with each sobbing gasp. Forbish couldn't take the sight of it, his daughter, his only child, naked and weeping. "Anything..." he cried, falling against his bonds. "Anything you want..."

"Oh, we'll take what we want, Fat Man. You can be sure of that." He brought his blade to the unscarred side of the girl's face and said, "And what I want first is to give this young lass a little symmetry."

"What are you doing?"

At the strange voice, everyone's attention suddenly snapped to the door. Lad stood there, eyes wide, hands at his sides. Wiggen's eyes snapped open, her sobs coming up short. The thugs stared in wonder at being surprised. The two at the door brandished their weapons, and Forbish saw Lad's eyes shift left, then right, then back to Urik and Wiggen behind him.

"We're just teachin' this young lass some manners, boyo," Urik growled, jerking the girl's hair again and waving the knife. "Unless you wanna be next, I suggest you take a hike."

"Stop. I won't let you do this." Lad's voice was the same calm timbre as ever, but there was a tremor in his jaw that Forbish had never seen.

Wiggen screamed, "No, Lad! Run!"

"Yes, run, laddy," Urik laughed, turning back to Wiggen and raising the knife. "Show him the door, boys."

Forbish's eyes were on his daughter, so he didn't see what happened while his heart hammered twice in his chest. He heard a crack, a gasp, then a sickening crunch and the sound of a body hitting the floor. He looked back, fully expecting Lad to be lying in a pool of blood. His jaw dropped at what he saw.

"Unholy mother of—"

"What?" Urik looked back and his eyes widened until Forbish thought they'd pop out. One corpse lay at Lad's feet, its head twisted backward on its body, a look of utter astonishment painted on its features. The other man still stood, but the thug's own sword, still gripped in his hand, was thrust up his nose and through the back of his skull. Lad released his bloodied grip on the man's wrist, and the twitching corpse dropped.

"Let her go." Lad took a step forward, poised, blood dripping from his fingers, his eyes welded to Urik's.

Urik grabbed Wiggen's arm and stepped behind her, nudging his huge companion and nodding toward Lad as his blade tucked under the girl's chin. The third thug limbered up two broad-bladed hand axes and stood ready, the weapons held on guard.

"Kill him," Urik said simply, and the huge brute lunged like a cat at an unsuspecting mouse while his companion spun in a sweeping two-bladed attack.

Forbish was watching this time, and still Lad's movement was almost too fast to follow.

Lad spun low. The heel of one lashing foot intersected the axe-wielding thug's knee. Bone splintered and the thug went down screaming, but one of his sweeping axes was right on target. An inch before the blade would have cleaved Lad's neck, it was clapped between the boy's two flat palms and twisted from the man's nerveless fingers. Lad's deadly pirouette continued. The stolen weapon flipped in his grasp and swept around to meet the charging half-ogre's skull just above the jutting brow. The creature landed with a resounding thump, its skull halved like a melon on display. The other thug lay crumpled and weeping, clutching the shards of bone that jutted from his leg.

Lad stood among the carnage, his eyes once again on Urik's. He took a step and, to everyone's astonishment, dropped the hand axe. He stood two strides from the embraced pair, but Urik's dagger was firmly nestled at Wiggen's throat.

"Now, let her go."

"I'll cut her pretty throat, boy. Quick as you are, you can't keep me from killing her!"

"You won't kill her." Lad's voice quivered like a tuning fork, the muscles of his jaw and neck bunching and relaxing rhythmically.

"Won't I, boy?" Urik grinned maniacally, jerking the girl's hair back again.

"No, you—"

But Urik had seen something neither Lad nor Forbish had detected, and the innkeeper's yell of warning couldn't prevent the dagger from plunging into the boy's back.

"Lad!" he yelled as the man on the floor lunged, but it was too late.

He watched the dagger go in just below the ribs. It slammed to the hilt, and Lad stood there, perfectly still. Forbish could see the blade tenting the skin of the boy's stomach and thought he must be in shock. But Lad wasn't in shock. Reaching back in a flash to grip the man's wrist, he tightened his grip until Forbish heard the bones of the man's forearm crack and splinter. Screams shook the air as the man released the dagger, but none were Lad's.

Then, as everyone stood in horror, Lad reached back with his free hand and pulled eight inches of bloodied steel from his back without so much as a twitch of pain. Crimson cascaded down his trousers as he brought the dagger around and economically drew it across the man's throat. The screams died in a gurgling torrent.

Lad dropped the dagger, turned to Urik, and took another step. He stood within striking distance now, and there was naught but terror in the thug's eyes. Lad held out a bloodied hand.

"Give me the knife."

"I'll cut her gods-damned throat!" Urik threatened, his voice trembling in stark fear.

Forbish stood stunned as Lad's jaw clenched. He saw the muscles of his forearm and neck writhe under the skin. Then, as he watched, a faint spider web of light shone through the skin, green-white, like runes or symbols. Forbish was three feet away and could feel the heat emanating from Lad in waves, as if he were on fire.

"Wiggen." Lad's voice was a whisper, calm and soothing.

"Wha—" Her attention snapped to his eyes, to the peace there, so contrasting the strain of his muscles.

"The dagger," he whispered, his eyes narrowing as one foot moved minutely, "is a sparrow."

She stood for a moment, then Forbish saw the most curious thing: Wiggen smiled and closed her eyes.

In the next instant, Lad's hand was wrapped around the blade of the dagger, his fingers between its edge and her throat. He pulled the blade away slowly, and Urik's hand came with it, his eyes wide with shock and surprise. Urik jerked and pulled at the blade, and blood poured over it, the edge grating against bone, but Lad's features remained calm, his grip like iron.

Then Lad moved.

His foot whisked over Wiggen's head, brushing her hair in passing. The leading edge impacted upon Urik's nose, smashing bone and driving his head back into the unyielding stone. Lad's kick drove on, crushing bone, pulping flesh and sinew until his foot struck stone. The small room shook, dust falling like snow from the rafters as Urik's body slumped to the floor.

"Lad!" Wiggen lunged forward, her arms flung around him in a crushing embrace. "Oh, Lad!"

Forbish watched in shock as the boy stumbled backward with her weight. The strain and the odd green light were gone, or maybe never were, just a figment of an old man's pain-ridden imagination. But his daughter's sobs of relief were real, and watching her smother the stunned boy in teary kisses took much of the pain from his shoulders away. Then Lad's hand opened slowly, and he saw the deep cuts as the dagger fell away.

"Wiggen! Stop it, girl! He's hurt!" *More like dying*, he thought, remembering the deep stab in his back.

"Oh, gods!" Wiggen flung herself back, grasping at his hand. She snatched at her riven dress, tearing off strips of cloth to wrap his hand. "You're bleeding!"

"It's amazing he's even standing, lass!" Forbish shouted. "Cut me loose and see if you can wake Josie. Someone's got to run for a healer, and you're in no condition."

"I'm not hurt," Lad said, wiping his hand on his trousers. While Wiggen fumbled for the dagger that would have ended her life, Lad took a step and parted Forbish's bonds.

"Not hurt?" Forbish's arms fell, pain lancing through his shoulders. "You should be *dead*, Lad! That was a killing stroke you took! Hold still while I have a look. You're witless with blood loss, is what you are."

"It's not so bad, Forbish," Lad said as the man turned him and tore open the tunic at the hole the dagger had made.

"It was in to the bloody hilt, Lad!" He wiped the congealing blood away, but there was just a thin pink line in Lad's skin where there should have been a gaping hole. "What in the name of the gods…"

"It's healed. See?" Lad held up his hand for Forbish and Wiggen to see. As they watched, the torn skin closed. "I heal fast."

"Fast?" Forbish gasped, taking a step back. He made a warding sign with his fingers.

"It's magic!" Wiggen stood in awe, her eyes as big as saucers.

"Yes," Lad said calmly. "It's the magic that heals me."

"Magic? What magic?" Forbish stared at him suspiciously now, wondering just what kind of being he'd let into his household. *Whatever he is*, he thought suddenly, *he saved Wiggen, sure enough. That ought to be good enough!*

"The magic my master gave me."

Forbish opened his mouth to ask something more about this magic, but a moan from the corner told them that Josie was waking. Forbish's mind clicked into the orderly mode that had served him throughout his life, and he was giving orders even before he knew what he was saying.

"Get something on, Wiggen, and fetch some cool water and a cloth for Josie." His daughter clutched the tatters of her dress to her blood-smeared torso and tiptoed through the gore toward the kitchen. "I'll see if Josie's okay, but we may still need the healer. Lad, you, uh... Well, you just stand there for a bit. Maybe clean up some of this. Gods, the storeroom's going to stink like a slaughterhouse if we don't scrub it down quick."

"Yes, Forbish," Lad said, bending to lift Urik's decapitated corpse. "Where do I put this?"

Chapter XIII

The last of the five bundles thumped into the bed of the ramshackle cart. The axle creaked alarmingly, but Forbish didn't seem to notice. The man was still nervous, his orders to Lad and Wiggen curt and as sharp as his kitchen knives. Lad didn't understand why Forbish was so keyed up; the thugs were dead, the storeroom was clean after hours of scrubbing, and the bodies were now securely wrapped in old saddle blankets and stowed in the borrowed cart. They would take them down to the river late at night and slip them into the dark water when nobody was watching. The stones they'd wrapped in with the corpses would ensure that the bodies remained undiscovered. They were out of danger.

"Well, that's that!" Forbish dusted his hands on his apron, although they weren't really dirty. Lad had done most of the lifting, though the portly innkeeper had helped him carry the heavy half-ogre.

"Yes," Lad agreed. He didn't understand how 'that' could be anything else, but it seemed logical.

"Well, since all of the guests have left, thanks to these noisy bastards, we've got a nice quiet night ahead of us." Forbish dusted his hands again and waved Lad toward the inn. "Let's get in and cleaned up, and have a nice early dinner. It's going to be a long night."

"How can this night be any longer than last night, Forbish?"

Lad asked as they left the barn. Sometimes people said things that really made no sense.

"Oh, well, it's just a figure of speech, Lad." The older man looked at him and shook his head. "Tonight will *seem* longer, because we'll be workin' half way 'til morning."

"I understand." It seemed to Lad that people often said things that meant other things. These 'figures of speech' that Forbish was talking about were nothing but confusing; if you wanted people to understand what you wanted to say, why not just say it?

"Here we are," the innkeeper said unnecessarily as he opened the inn's front door. As usual, the smell of well-cooked food was overwhelming. Wiggen backed out of the kitchen door with a platter of bread and cheese in one hand, and two foaming tankards of ale in the other.

"There you are!" She smiled at the two and put her burdens down on one of the tables already set with three plates, eating utensils and cups of water. "Dinner's ready, so wash up."

"What's all this?" Forbish picked up one of the tankards and sipped. "Hmm, Highland Summerbrew, my favorite, but—"

"Just you go and wash up, Father. We've no guests. The roast was already on for tonight, so we're having a little celebration, just the three of us." Josie had gone home with a splitting headache and a bandage, with orders from the healer not to get out of bed for a day.

"Sounds like a good idea," Forbish said, taking a healthy gulp of ale.

"That's *supposed* to be for dinner, Father," Wiggen scolded good-naturedly, swatting at him with the dishtowel. She took the tankard from him and scooted back toward the kitchen. "I'll refill it, but just this once! Now go and wash."

"Women!" Forbish said with a laugh. "Come on, Lad. We'd better get washed up, or she'll feed our dinner to the chickens."

"Would the chickens eat—" Lad stopped as Forbish led the way to the bathing rooms. "A figure of speech. You didn't *mean* that the chickens would really eat our dinner. You meant something else."

"Ha! Now you're gettin' it, Lad! Come on."

"What did you mean?"

"I meant that my daughter is becoming a fussbudget! Now, hurry up and wash. I'm hungry!"

Lad had no idea what a 'fussbudget' was, but decided not to ask. He hoped fussbudgets weren't dangerous. He couldn't imagine Wiggen becoming something dangerous.

The two men washed quickly, scrubbing hands, arms, and faces with the hot water and fragrant soap that Wiggen had put out for them. They were back in the common room in a matter of minutes and the table was fully laden when they arrived.

A steaming platter of roast beef, yams, and onions lay among lesser dishes of stewed greens, spicy peppers, sliced tomatoes, cheese, and a huge loaf of freshly baked bread. A cup of wine sat before one of the place settings. Forbish indicated one of the chairs with a wave, and the two men sat, but the innkeeper didn't touch the food. Lad wondered why. Was there something wrong with it? Was there some custom he was missing? Forbish had never paused before eating when they took their dinner in the kitchen. Perhaps things were different when dinner was in the common room.

Wiggen entered, taking off her apron and smoothing her dress. Forbish was watching her, his face strange. Lad began to wonder if something was wrong.

"Dessert's cooling on the sideboard." She sat down and looked at her father, her head cocking in question. "What?"

"You just reminded me of your mum there for a bit, Wig." He smiled and reached out to take her hand. "You're very like her, you know."

"Oh, stop it, Father." She gripped her father's hand firmly then let go.

"I'm very lucky to have you, Wiggen. I won't put you at risk like that any more. Even though Urik and his mob are dead, someone'll come for their payment, and I'll have it ready."

"Oh, Father..."

"Which leads me to something else." He raised his tankard and looked at Lad. "Here's to our young savior, Lad. I don't know how you did it, but I'm thankful to you."

Lad watched as Wiggen raised her cup of wine and touched it to Forbish's tankard. This was a custom he'd seen some of the patrons perform while they ate their dinners. It was called a toast. He didn't know if he should join them, so he just watched.

"To Lad," Wiggen said, sipping her wine. Her eyes glittered strangely in the lamplight. "Now, eat, before this all gets cold."

They feasted.

Lad ate more than he ever had before, encouraged to have second and even third helpings if he wished. Everything delicious, as always, but there was a different feeling about this dinner than any of the others he'd had with Forbish and Wiggen. The conversation was sparse, mostly concerning the food or the delicious ale, which was new to Lad. When they'd all eaten their fill, Wiggen excused herself to the kitchen, and returned with a tray of small bowls and cups of steaming blackbrew. The bowls were filled with a sweetened mixture of baked apple and spices, drenched in fresh cream. They ate slowly, savoring the flavors between sips of the stimulating black beverage.

"Everything was delicious, Wiggen," Forbish said, pushing his chair back a few inches and loosening his belt a notch. "You've really outdone yourself."

"Thank you, Father," she said with a blush. She fiddled with her hair that draped over the left side of her face.

"And thank you again, Lad, for saving my daughter's life. Though where you learned to fight like that, and that magic that healed your wounds... I've never seen anything like that."

"I learned to fight from my master and the teachers he brought to train me. The master gave me the magic, too." He traced a finger up his forearm, over the invisible lines of power that resided under his skin. "Every day."

"Was he a wizard, then, this master of yours?"

"A wizard?" Lad didn't know what a wizard was, but he'd heard the word before from people that stayed at the inn. "He was skilled. He made me and gave me magic and taught me the skills I have."

"He *made* you?" Wiggen's voice trembled slightly. "What about your family? Your mother and father?"

"I do not remember a mother or father. Only the master." Lad's voice was as calm as ever, but he saw the fear that his words elicited from the two. He wanted to calm their fears, but he didn't know how.

"So this master of yours; did he have a name?" Forbish took a sip of blackbrew, but his eyes never left Lad's.

"I do not know. If he did, I never heard it."

"Did you run away?" Wiggen asked.

"No." This was the same question that the others had asked. He didn't want to make them laugh, and maybe instigate a fight as a result, so he skipped the next part, and said, "He was dead, killed by men that came out of the forest while we were traveling. I didn't know where we were going, but he had said that my destiny was somewhere down the road."

"Your destiny?" Forbish's eyes widened.

"Yes. I walked down the road, and eventually came here. I think that my destiny is somewhere here, in Twailin."

"And what exactly is your destiny, Lad?" He could hear the strain in Wiggen's voice.

"I do not know." Lad thought for a moment, wondering if they could, perhaps, help him find his destiny. Maybe, if they knew more about him, they could. "I am a weapon. I think that—"

"What? You're a what, Lad?" Forbish's cup clattered into its saucer.

"My master said that I am a weapon. I was taught to fight, run, climb, use and defend against weapons, move quietly without leaving a trace, order my thoughts through meditation, discipline my body, and channel and focus the power of mind and body. The master gave me magic to make me strong, fast and heal my wounds."

"But why?" Wiggen's voice was a trembling whisper.

"Why is any weapon made?" He paused, but they didn't answer. "A weapon is to be wielded, used for combat. I feel sure that my destiny is to be used by someone, as a weapon is used. To kill." He watched their faces slacken and wondered if fear had overcome them. He didn't understand their fear. Surely they knew that he was no danger to them.

"Don't fear me. I won't hurt either of you. You've given me much here. Food, a place to stay, and..." He stumbled over his thoughts. He didn't know how to say what he felt for these people, how to describe what they had given him.

But Wiggen did.

"Friendship." She reached out, but Lad withdrew his hand. The withdrawal was automatic, the aversion to be touched that had been drilled into him for years. Wiggen stopped, her hand frozen, and he could see the pain in her eyes.

"I did not mean to—"

"It's all right." She smiled, looked to her father, then back to Lad, and carefully put her hand on top of his. "You've never had friends, have you?"

"I...don't know." He didn't know precisely what a friend was. He'd heard the term used many times, sometimes even between those in heated debate. He was finding it hard to concentrate with her hand resting on his. It felt cool, comfortable against his skin, but there was the underlying desire to withdraw, to defend himself. "Friends are people who you don't want to hurt? Like you and Forbish?"

"Well, kind of." Forbish grinned. "We're family, Lad, and that's more than friends. Though I've heard of families that weren't very friendly to one another. I guess we're both, family and friends. Friends are just people you like."

"I understand." Lad looked at Wiggen's hand atop his own. The compulsion to withdraw swelled within him, but he didn't want to cause her pain again. Fighting the urge was playing on his nerves like a bow on overly taut fiddle strings. His temples began to pound with his pulse, though there was no pain. "Friends aid one another, like allies in combat combine their skills against a common foe. I helped you against Urik and his men. That makes us friends, right?"

"Close enough." Forbish pushed himself up from the table and started clearing the dishes. "You go and get some sleep, Lad. You've done enough work already today. I'll wake you later for our little trip to the river. I'll wash these up, Wig."

"Oh, I'll help, Father." Wiggen took her hand from Lad's and pushed herself away from the table.

The tension in Lad eased immediately.

"I know you don't like to—" She got up and reached for a dish, but Forbish pulled it away.

"Tut, tut! You just go have a rest. You've been through enough today." He loaded the dishes onto the platter and backed through the door to the kitchen. Lad could hear the man whistling tunelessly while pots and dishes clattered and splashed.

"I'll go." Lad got up.

"Do you mind if I walk out to the barn with you?" Her voice was pitched low and she glanced at the kitchen door, her lower lip clenched between her teeth. "I want to talk to you, Lad."

"Yes. I'd...like you to talk to me, Wiggen." She smiled and followed him out the front door of the inn.

Jingles wasn't happy. And as a general rule, when Jingles wasn't happy, people got hurt.

"Hit him again, Burke."

Burke hit him; a sharp jab straight to the nose with a satisfying wet crack.

The shopkeeper's head snapped back, flecks of blood and sweat spattering the floor. The man moaned through split and bleeding lips. He was learning a difficult lesson, one that needn't have been so painful.

"Are we learning yet, Mister Joanis?" Jingles rattled the golden chain that wrapped his wrist, enjoying the sound that had earned him his nickname. The chain was linked with tiny silver rods, each as long as his thumbnail; they made a very pleasing sound when he jingled them. There was a significance to these silver rods that only his associates within the Assassins Guild knew. He might add another today, but he hoped this lesson wouldn't have to go that far; it was hard to get money from a dead man. Joanis moaned incoherently, and Jingles grabbed the man's hair.

"Look at me, Mister Joanis." He shook the man by the hair, the jingling jewelry louder than the man's weak moans of pain. "Open your eyes and look at me. Tell me you've learned your lesson for today, and I'll let you go back to your shop."

One swollen eye cracked open; the white, shot with the red of a burst blood vessel, was barely visible between the puffy purple of the lids. "I've learned..." the man croaked miserably.

"Good." Joanis' head lolled forward as Jingles let go of his hair. "Get him out of here, Burke. And don't forget to get my money from him. He owes me for two months, and another twenty gold for the inconvenience of having to have this little talk."

"Straight away, Jingles." Burke lifted the bloody rag of a man from the chair and dragged him out of the room.

"And send someone in to clean this mess up!" Jingles shouted, stepping back behind his desk and sitting down carefully. "One damn problem after another," he muttered, rifling through the pages of his ledger.

He wet the tip of his quill and checked off the note he'd made beside Joanis' name, then ran a finger down the long list of his sources of income. Jingles was only a sub-boss, and his area of influence was relatively small, about a dozen blocks in a rough radius around his headquarters. The list included the names of every shopkeeper, innkeeper, pimp, and wholesaler in his district, and now, after dealing with Joanis, there was only one name without a check mark beside it to indicate that their payment had been made.

"Forbish," he mumbled. There was a note that he'd dispatched one of his Enforcers to take care of that stubborn old man, but there was no check. Urik wasn't back yet. "Damn cocky bastard better not be crossin' me."

There was a tap at his door, and his assistant Dragel came in with a bucket and mop.

"After you've finished there, Dragel, send a runner to Urik. I want to find out why he hasn't brought me the payment he was supposed to collect."

"Sure, Jingles."

Dragel wiped down the chair with a rag and moved it out of the way, then mopped up the spattered blood. He was done in less than a minute and out the door. Jingles watched the wet patch of floor for a while, enjoying the patterns of moisture glistening in the lamplight as it dried. His wrist twitched absently, the musical chime of his jewelry bringing a smile to his cruel lips.

"I wanted to thank you again, Lad," Wiggen said as they walked across the courtyard. Evening's twilight was fading to night, the crimson and orange of a blazing sunset deepening to purple. In the east, over the crest of the inn, the first stars were peeking out from the shroud of darkness that enveloped the land.

"You saved my life today." Her voice shook with the memory of the assault, the horror of helplessness that had paralyzed her. "They were the same ones, Urik and his gang. They were the ones who killed Tam, and..." Her hand moved unconsciously to the scar, her fingertips brushing it, kindling the memory. "I don't think I could have taken that again."

"I don't understand why these men came here. Why did they try to hurt you, Wiggen? Forbish said they were here for money."

"Blood money. They're outlaws, thieves, I guess." Lad didn't answer so she tried a simpler approach. "They threaten all the shopkeepers. They say they're providing protection for the money, but that's a lie. If the shopkeepers don't pay, they're hurt or their businesses are broken into and looted or burned. Sometimes people are taken, killed or beaten, held for ransom. It's illegal, but the constables say that they can't prove it. It happens everywhere. Most people pay, but Father's stubborn. He hates them for what they did when I was little, and more now, for what happened to Tam...and me." They stopped just inside the barn door; Wiggen leaned against the foot-thick wooden beam of the old building's frame and sighed.

"I don't understand." Lad's voice was that same calm tone. She wondered if *anything* ever changed the tone of his voice. Sometimes it was infuriating, but most of the time she found his voice comforting. "They threaten you, and hurt or kill if you don't pay. It makes no sense."

"You're not *supposed* to understand, Lad. You weren't *made* to understand, and that's what I really wanted to talk to you about." She looked up to him, realizing for the first time that he was actually slightly taller than her. His sandy hair was askew, as always, and she fought the desire to straighten it. His eyes were so strange, so deep, but showing no emotion. She wondered if he was *made* to feel emotion, and realized that he probably wasn't. Killing would be easier if he didn't feel. "I'm worried about you, Lad."

"Why?" His head cocked to the side, the curiosity written on his face. "I'm in no danger."

"I think you are, Lad." His eyes flashed left and right, and she knew he had misunderstood. "No. Not right now. Let me explain."

"Yes. Explain what danger I'm in." He was tense now, wound tight; he looked calm, but she knew better.

"I think I know why your master made you the way you are, and I don't just mean the way you fight, and how you're so fast and strong. I mean the way you don't know how you should feel about people; the way you were never taught what family or friends are, all the things that most of us learn when we're little children and take for granted." She paused, biting her lip, wondering if she should continue.

"Go on, Wiggen. I want to know what you think."

"Okay, but try to understand...you *scare* me, Lad. I like you, but...you scare me."

"Don't fear me, Wiggen." He raised a hand, and for a moment, she thought he would touch her, but he pulled away again. She could see the strain in him now; the quickening pulse in his neck, the flush of heat that she could actually feel from a foot away.

"Okay." She steeled her nerve and continued, heedless. She owed it to him. "You were made to kill, Lad."

"Yes. I know this, Wiggen."

"No, you *don't* know. Listen." She reached out slowly and took his hand. "Your purpose, this destiny you're looking for... You were made to be someone's assassin, Lad. You were made to kill for someone who doesn't want to do it for themselves…or can't. You were made to follow orders and kill whoever they want, without feeling anything, without knowing you were doing anything wrong."

"Wrong?" She felt a quiver of tension in his grip. "Killing is wrong?"

"Yes, Lad. Killing is wrong. It's the worst crime you can commit. Unless you're protecting someone, like today, killing makes you bad, evil. Like Urik and his men. They would have killed me today. You were made to be like them, but worse, without feeling."

"I—" Lad's eyes were wide with his tumultuous thoughts; she could see the confusion, the denial. "I don't want to be like they were, Wiggen. They were going to hurt you. I wouldn't hurt you. I *couldn't*."

"Not me, Lad. I know you wouldn't hurt me, at least not intentionally. I'm talking about other people. Someone went to a lot of trouble to…well, to have you made the way you are. They could use you to kill anyone, anywhere, and you'd do it without remorse or fear or hate even. They took those feelings away from you, Lad; I don't know how, probably magic, but…you don't…." She didn't know how to put it into words. She knew there was something holding him back, something suppressing his humanity, but she couldn't say what was missing. She squeezed his hand harder, part frustration, part willing him to understand.

"I don't want to be evil." The words were an affirmation to everything she was trying to tell him.

"Then *don't* be!" She gripped his hand with hysterical strength, trying to make him feel something. Anything. "You don't have to follow this path your master put you on, Lad! You could run away, find another way to live."

"But today," he said, his voice calm, his body strained, "I killed those men. You said that wasn't evil."

"Yes, Lad. That was good. You helped us."

"So, my destiny *could* be to protect, to prevent harm." She could see that his mind had latched onto this explanation like a drowning man reaching for any floating object. She couldn't make herself tell him that she thought he was wrong and dash his hopes.

"Yes, Lad. That could be your destiny."

"Then I'll stay in Twailin. I'll find my destiny. If it's evil, I'll leave. If it's not, I'll stay and fulfill what my master intended for me."

"You *must* be careful, Lad. I'm afraid..."

"I won't let anyone make me evil, Wiggen. Don't be afraid for me."

"I know you don't *want* to be evil, but you might not be given a choice. You *must* be careful!" She brought her other hand up slowly to his face. He tensed, but didn't withdraw. Her palm brushed his cheek, and his whole body quivered at an incredibly high pitch, almost a vibration. His skin was very warm as she let her hand caress up to his ear, and into his hair to twine the sandy strands between her fingers. "Just be careful, Lad. For me."

"I'll be careful, Wiggen." His face was still a blank slate, devoid of emotion, but his body sang with suppressed power.

"Thank you," she said as she brought her face up to his.

She pressed her lips to his, feeling his warmth now even more, his skin tingling with heat. His lips were soft, but unmoving, passive. When she opened her eyes, she found him staring into her soul with that bottomless gaze of his. She withdrew, dropped his hand and took a step back.

"This," Lad said, his fingers drifting up to his lips, his head cocked in a question, "is something that friends do?"

"Yes." She didn't know how to explain what a kiss was, let alone what she was beginning to feel toward him. "It's called a kiss. It's a way for our friendship to grow."

"This kiss felt strange to me, Wiggen. I felt like I should defend myself or flee, but I wanted to stay, too." His fingers touched his lips and his brow furrowed in thought. "I'm glad you're my friend, Wiggen. I've learned many things from you."

"Don't tell Father about the kiss, okay?" She bit her lip, wondering if she'd made a horrible mistake. "He wouldn't understand."

"Forbish doesn't know what a kiss is?"

"He knows, Lad. Just don't tell him I kissed you. Please."

"If you don't want me to, then I won't."

"Thank you." She found that her fingers were wound into her hair, pulling it down over her scar. She felt ashamed, like she'd taken advantage of him, ruined their friendship. "I better get back to the inn. Goodnight, Lad." She turned to go.

"Goodnight, Wiggen," she heard him say from behind her, but she wasn't sure if he said anything else. Her heart was pounding too loudly in her ears.

Chapter XIV

Targus' nostrils twitched at the heavy odor of death that pervaded the enclosed space of the stable. He sniffed carefully, thinking, *A fortnight at the least*. Death in all its forms and stages was something with which he was intimately familiar; it was his business. But that didn't mean he liked the smell. He wetted a long kerchief from his belt and tied it around his face.

"Here," he said, handing another kerchief to Jorrel, the mage who had accompanied him from Twailin, "it dampens the stench."

"Thank you." The mage followed suit, stifling a cough at the thick odor.

"That mage's cart's there in the back," Constable Burk told them from the door to the stable. "I made sure nobody touched it, but that wasn't hard with such a stink. Even the stable boy's sleepin' in the inn these last few days. If you don't mind, I'll just stay here."

"That's fine, constable. You've been most helpful in this matter. The guild will see that you're compensated for the inconvenience."

Targus kept his tone civil, though his mood was much darker. He loathed being sent back to Thistledown for no other reason than to babysit this weakling mage. It had taken them four days to travel from Twailin, with a full camp set up every night, and Targus cooking for the both of them. Jorrel wasn't as insufferable as many mages he'd dealt with, simply soft, with his satin robes, pointed shoes, and superior air. He tolerated Jorrel by necessity, but much like the smell, he didn't have to like it.

The two approached the large two-wheeled cart carefully; it was well lit with the afternoon sun streaming through the stable windows, but wizards secreted many dangerous items among their things when they traveled. Jorrel had assured him of that. Why, even the cart might not be *just* a simple cart, though with the bumbling constable and his men handling it for so long, anything dangerous should have made itself known by now.

"Hold here for a moment, if you please, Master Targus."

Targus stopped and watched the dainty little man wave his fingers in an intricate pattern and press them to his forehead, eyes closed. He knew Jorrel was performing a "seeing," a simple scan for magical energy. He also knew that all the finger waving was window dressing, a show to make his art seem more mysterious. Seeings didn't require a spell, per se, just proper concentration on the part of the wizard. He thought for a moment about unveiling Jorrel's sham, but restrained himself; there was no point in stirring up animosity.

"The wagon is mundane, but there's much magic here."

"Just tell me what not to touch." Targus moved to the back of the cart and peered in at its contents. There were several bags, boxes, and even a small coffer piled under the broad seat. And there was, of course, the tightly wrapped shape of Corillian's corpse. The bodies of the others had been disposed of.

"There are many individual items here that may hold some danger for us, Targus." Jorrel waved his thin hand in a vague manner. "The body, of course, but we'll have to unwrap it. That coffer, and the smallest box, also. The rest is mundane, and can be searched at leisure."

"Let's get the body down first, then you can go over it while I look through the other stuff."

"I'd really rather not—"

"Helping me lift one corpse down from a wagon won't tarnish your mystique, Jorrel. Just grab his feet and pull."

Jorrel complied with a grumble that Targus found amusing, though he stifled his smile. Once the body was on the ground, the Hunter produced a blade from his belt and applied it to the canvas wrappings. The knife was short and curved, designed for separating hide from sinew, and parted the thick material with little resistance. What lay beneath crawled with pestilence.

"Hooaaa!" Targas exclaimed as the full stench of the decomposing corpse hit them like a ram. His head swam for a moment, dizzy with nausea.

"Here," Jorrel said, producing a small vial from a pocket, "spirit of peppermint. Dab some on your finger and wipe it under your nose." He demonstrated and handed the vial to Targus.

"Thank you." He applied some of the extract to his upper lip and immediately decided to revise his opinion of the mage. When his nausea had vanished in a heady swirl of peppermint, the two carefully unwrapped the late Master Corillian.

The search was long, painstaking and, for the most part, fruitless. Jorrel cooed like a child at midwinter gift-giving and pocketed many items, but Targus couldn't have cared less. He was interested only in anything pertaining to the master's weapon; the mage could stuff his pockets with magical trinkets to his heart's desire for all he cared. Only when the wizard finally cracked the magical locking mechanism on the small coffer was Targus finally intrigued.

"A scroll?" Jorrel said, crestfallen. "All that over a simple scroll?"

Targus peered at the red velvet interior of the coffer; one simple roll of parchment wrapped in black ribbon lay there, the container's sole occupant.

"And it's not even magical!" Jorrel scoffed, after a brief seeing. "What could possibly be so important as to warrant a magically warded coffer?"

The mage reached for the scroll, but Targus' hand moved like a striking snake, snatching Jorrel's wrist before his fingers could brush the rolled parchment.

"Have a care, mage! Not all traps are magical!"

"What?" Jorrel's eyes widened until Targus released his wrist. "What do you sense?"

"Sense? Ha!" He removed a thin probe from his belt pouch and held it up to the light. "I sense nothing. I've just got a healthy amount of paranoia running through my veins, and it's kept me alive for a very long time. Watch and learn, mage."

He ran the probe along the rolled parchment, barely brushing the velvet bed on which it lay. When the probe met the black ribbon, it caught there instead of simply bumping over the thin material.

"That's what I thought. The ribbon is the trigger. It passes through the velvet and around something beneath, but I can't tell whether releasing it or pulling it will set off the trap."

He stared at it for a moment as if willing its secrets to the surface.

"It was my first inclination to grasp the scroll and lift it from its bed," the mage offered. "I think most would do so."

"A reasonable assumption, but let me check something before we test that theory." Targus freed another probe, this one hooked, from his pouch. "If I can get a peek under the covers..."

He teased up one corner of the velvet bedding and peered underneath.

"Very nasty indeed." He peeled back the coverlet for the mage to see, revealing a glass container filled with silvery metallic filings. Under that lay a shifting layer of liquid. The two containers were separated by a thin layer of glass, which was connected to the black ribbon by a golden wire.

"Elemental potassium, unless I miss my guess," Jorrel said with a sigh of mixed fear and relief. "That's probably water beneath. Break the glass and the two mix. The explosion would not only destroy the scroll, but very likely reduce the unlucky burglar to cinders."

"Nice." Targus very carefully untied the bow restraining the parchment and lifted it free. "Now, let's see what's so important." He unrolled the stiff scroll carefully. His eyes widened, and he immediately rolled it back up and stuffed it into a pocket in his cloak.

"Wait! What was it?" Jorrel stood as Targus lurched to his feet and started out of the stable. "Where are you going?"

"Back to Twailin. This must be taken to the Grandfather."

"Now? But we haven't even had a meal!" Jorrel trotted after him, past the dumbfounded constable to where their horses were hitched. "You can't be serious!"

"Stay here, Jorrel." Targus leapt into his saddle, his feet touching the stirrups only after his backside was in place. "Go through the rest of Corillian's things. Keep it all, for all I care. If you don't want to travel alone, I'll send someone back for you. I'm going to be moving too fast to have you tagging along."

"But what about the—" Jorrel leapt out of the way as Targus kicked his mount into a gallop. "Targus! Wait!"

But Targus was already gone, and the damned constable was already standing at Jorrel's elbow, waiting expectantly for the compensation that Targus had promised.

"Welcome to the *Tap and Kettle*, good sir."

Forbish wiped his hands on his apron and waved at the all-but-vacant common room. There were just two other customers, a young couple from out of town who were spending the night before traveling downriver. After the recent trouble, rumors were flying around the city like leaves on the wind; their business would suffer for a fortnight at the least. But this man looked wealthy enough to make up for some of the slack.

"Would you be wanting a room for this evening, or is it just a meal and a draught from one of our fine kegs that you're here for? We've quite a selection of fine ales and stouts, if you're interested."

"Actually, I was recommended to this place by some business associates." The man dabbed his brow with a kerchief. The gaudy gold-and-silver jewelry at his wrist jingled with every movement. "They said you ran a fine inn and kept a well-stocked cellar. You must be Master Forbish."

"Why, yes!" Forbish offered his hand and gripped the other's firmly, noting the shrewd narrowing of the man's eyes. "You're a local businessman, Master...?"

"Jarred," he answered, retrieving his hand and nodding to the common room. "And yes. I do my business in many inns throughout the city. I often entertain clients visiting from out of town, and I'm always looking for a new bit of local color to show off to them. Twailin is so diverse, you see."

"Yes, of course! Of course!" Forbish showed the man to a table, knowing immediately that this was a very important customer. The innkeeper was no novice at gauging people, and he knew that both he and his establishment were being sized up very carefully. There was scrutiny and a peculiar wariness in the man that he found discomforting. "And your business?"

"I'm an importer." He waved a hand inconsequentially, the bracelet chiming. "Just a middleman, so to speak. I handle merchandise between those who supply it and those who sell it to the public. For a small percentage, of course. I was told your ale selection was second to none, which is why I'm here. When I entertain I like variety and local flavors."

"Perhaps you'd like a sample of what we have to offer?" The door to the kitchen creaked as Wiggen brought the couple their dinners. Forbish cast a glance at her and smiled. "I'll have my daughter bring you a sampler of our best ales."

"That would be delightful, Master Forbish. Thank you."

Forbish scurried off, following his daughter into the kitchen.

"That's a very important customer at that table, Wiggen. Get him a sample of each of our best. None of the dregs, now, mind you. In fact, tap a new barrel of the Keeshire Red. The one on tap's been open too long."

"Why's he so important?" Wiggen asked, placing the tray on the preparation table and selecting half a dozen small glasses from the rack.

"He's an importer! Entertains all types of rich merchants and the like! He wants to bring people here to impress them with what Twailin has to offer!"

"Or he's just trying to get a free drink out of a gullible innkeeper," Wiggen scoffed as she went to fill the glasses.

"Now, Wiggen, don't you start with me! Here's a chance to bring in some business, and you're laughing at me! What do you want me to do, tell him he's got to show me his money before he's gettin' a sip from any of my kegs?"

"No. I'm sorry, Father." She moved into the taproom and began filling the glasses with foamy amber liquid. "Why don't you put out a plate of cheese and bread for him to nibble. There's that nice dark-red Liechester we got the other day. It'll go nicely with these."

"An excellent idea!" Forbish snatched up one of his many knives and sawed off a corner of a warm dark loaf, and then reached for the cheese. By the time he had several thin wedges cut and placed on the plate with the bread, Wiggen was back with her tray of ales. "Let's go present this to him together, shall we?"

"No, Father. You—"

"Now, I won't hear of it!" he snapped, nudging her toward the door before she could duck her head and refuse. "I want to show *all* of the *Tap and Kettle's* best points, Wiggen, and you're one of them, so you just straighten up and be nice to the man."

"All right, Father, all right." She backed through the swinging door and turned to the room, balancing the tray on one hand and brushing her hair down over her scar with the other.

Forbish sighed and followed her to the man's table, smiling as they approached while wishing that his daughter could see past the scar on her cheek. She was a beautiful young woman, but she felt that she had nothing to offer because she'd been abused, damaged beyond wanting. Forbish knew differently; he saw how men watched her, even those who had seen her scar and knew its origin. Some men were shallow enough not to see beyond it, but most weren't. Why couldn't she see that?

"Here you are, Master Jarred. Six of our best ales, and a bite to smooth your palate between tastes." He put the platter of bread and cheese next to the ales, and said, "Thank you, Wiggen," as she curtsied, keeping her face averted.

Forbish turned back to his guest. "I think that you'll find the Highland Summerbrew to be... Master Jarred?"

But Jarred was paying him no attention. In fact, the man was staring straight past both Forbish and Wiggen as if caught in a trance.

Forbish glanced over his shoulder to see what the man might be staring at, and was utterly surprised to see Lad standing there with two large burlap bags balanced on one shoulder. The weight would have staggered Forbish, but Lad stood easily, waiting patiently. He realized immediately what a shock this must seem to his guests.

"Oh, Lad! Just put those in the kitchen for me, please."

"Yes, Forbish." The boy moved easily to the kitchen door, but his eyes strayed to the visitor before he left the room, undoubtedly uncomfortable under the stranger's stare.

"Don't mind the boy, sir." Forbish assured his guest. "That's just Lad, a beggar boy I hired some time ago. He does the heavy work since my back's gone out on me these past months, and a right strong boy he is."

"Of course," Jarred said, waving his hand in dismissal and filling the air with the chiming of his bracelet. He sipped one of the ales haphazardly, and nodded. "Yes, this is very good!"

"That one's from the lowlands. Velrigh spring ale. It's a bit thick for summer, but..." Forbish watched in surprise as the man took three more gulps of three other ales in quick succession. "Master Jarred, you should really take your time and savor—"

"Time is the problem, good innkeeper. These are all very good indeed, but I've just remembered an appointment that I'm quite late to attend." He stood suddenly, bowing stiffly and rounding the table. "My apologies, but I must be off. I'll return, you have my promise! And I'll bring my associates to sample your wonderful array of ales!" He tossed a silver to Forbish even as he backed away and whirled for the door.

"Thank you, Master Jarred." Forbish waved, dumbfounded at the other's abrupt departure. "Hmph." He pocketed the silver and turned back to the kitchen, only to find Lad standing in the doorway, staring after the retreating visitor.

"Something wrong, Lad?" Forbish asked, picking up the two trays and moving to the kitchen.

"Who was that man, Forbish?" The boy relieved him of the platters and placed them on the table as Forbish entered the room. The innkeeper retrieved one of the untouched glasses of ale and a wedge of cheese before they were out of reach.

"Just a customer. He's an importer. Wants to entertain some people here, so he wanted to sample our wares." He tossed the small glass of ale back and sighed in contentment, nibbling at the sharp cheese.

"Why do importers carry so many weapons?"

"Weapons?" Forbish nearly choked on his cheese. "What weapons? He wasn't wearing so much as a dagger!"

"He wore four daggers and a short sword, Forbish."

"What?" That was Wiggen, looking worriedly at her father and Lad in turn. "What weapons?"

"Now, Lad. Where would he put that many blades?"

"Two of the daggers were under his sleeves, and probably made for throwing. He wore a dagger in each boot top hidden under his pants, and there was a long knife or short sword hidden under his cloak in an inverted sheath strapped to his back."

"*What?*"

"How could you see all that?" Forbish asked skeptically.

"One of my... I was trained to see such things, Forbish. If he was an importer, it must be a very dangerous business."

"Or he wasn't an importer." Wiggen stared first at Lad, then at her father.

"But if he wasn't an importer, what was he?" Forbish liberated the last untouched glass of ale from the tray and downed it at a gulp to steady his suddenly frazzled nerves. "And why did he leave so suddenly?"

The innkeeper looked to his daughter and Lad, but neither could answer his rhetorical question.

"I don't understand the necessity for me to accompany you to see the Grandfather." Jingles glared at Mya and twitched his hands nervously, filling the small carriage with discordant music as they passed through the gate into the courtyard of the guildmaster's estate. "I found the boy-weapon. My duty's been performed, and my job's finished!"

"The *necessity* is that the Grandfather won't be satisfied with hearsay." Mya stepped out of the carriage as it stopped and told the driver to wait. "I know him better than I care to, Jingles. He's subtle in ways you'd never understand, and he doesn't tolerate mistakes."

"Tell me something I *don't* know!" He exited the carriage like a man being dragged to the gallows. "I've never met him, and I don't particularly care to."

"And I don't particularly care what you do or don't care to do, Jingles." Mya narrowed her eyes at the man, someone she wouldn't have even considered crossing words with a month ago. But her position had changed, and with it her nerve. Jingles was a senior journeyman and, technically, outranked her within the hierarchy of the guild, although his position wasn't directly over her. There were five divisions within the guild; she answered to Master Hunter Targus, who answered only to the Grandfather. But Mya was under direct assignment from the guildmaster, which gave her the authority to give orders that were backed by him.

"Now, come on! Keeping him waiting won't increase your chances of walking out of here with your skin intact." She turned her back on him, knowing he wouldn't dare put a knife between her ribs, at least not here and now. Later, she would have to be more careful.

Jingles followed, muttering curses and wringing his hands to the accompaniment of the sound that had earned him his nickname.

The lofty doors to the estate opened before they reached the top of the courtyard steps. Two armed guards bowed and ushered them into the entry hall. One of the guards she recognized, though this was a far cry from the circumstances of her first arrival into the Grandfather's sanctuary. A rather short and skeletally thin man in a dark-red waistcoat and breeches greeted them with a nod.

"The Grandfather is expecting you. Please follow me."

"My messenger arrived, then?" Mya asked, her steps falling in behind those of the new valet. She briefly wondered if this one knew how the last one had met his end.

"Of course." He looked back at her, his sneer a mask of derision. "How else could he be expecting you?"

"Through some means other than my messenger, obviously. Which would mean he had someone watching me. Which would have been of concern to me. Which was why I asked if my messenger had arrived." The valet's neck stiffened, and she wondered if all such menials took on a mantle of inflated self-importance. "Any other questions?"

The valet walked on without looking back, and they followed. The stream of muttered curses from Jingles increased in both volume and tone enough for her to hear the words "lunatic" and "suicidal" clearly. She just turned to him and smiled thinly, knowing that his opinion of her brazenness would better her reputation within the guild. Nobody got *anywhere* within the guild without earning a reputation.

They followed the valet down a flight of stairs and along a well-lit hall. At the end was a large double door, which he opened with a key that hung on a chain under his doublet. Even before the door opened, Mya heard the sound of metal striking metal at a feverish cadence. As the portal was pushed aside and they were ushered through, her eyes widened at the spectacle.

Upon a broad gray mat, the Grandfather sparred with three opponents. A long fighting dagger flashed in each hand as he faced three curved swords wielded expertly and in perfect coordination. His opponents were young men bearing the ringed tattoos of one of the martial guilds, their blades flashing almost too fast for Mya to see. But the Grandfather moved like a whirlwind, his dark robes fluttering and fanning out with his spinning attacks and evasions.

Mya watched in awe; she had known that the Grandfather was skilled at arms despite his advanced years, but she had never known, nor sought to know, just how skilled. The four moved ceaselessly, attacking and defending in such a blur that she often lost track of which blade was where or even whose. As she and Jingles stood transfixed by the deadly ballet, the valet moved to a small chime set into a wooden frame beside the door. He struck a single note on the tubular rod, sending a clear tone ringing throughout the chamber.

The sparring stopped, weapons frozen in mid-strike and parry.

"Cease."

At the single word from the Grandfather, his three opponents lowered their weapons and bowed, backing away several steps. The older man glanced at the door where Mya and Jingles stood waiting.

"Ah! Very good!" He turned back to his sparring partners. "Return to your master, gentlemen. Come back here at the same time day after tomorrow."

"Yes, Guildmaster!"

As the three bowed and left through another door, Mya noticed that their tunics were drenched with sweat, their chests heaving with labored breathing. The Grandfather, on the other hand, stood relaxed and cool, his wizened features not even flushed.

The daggers he bore vanished into his dark robes as he approached, and Mya began to wonder exactly *what* he was. No man could fight like that against three opponents and not break a sweat. She bowed as he came before them, fighting to keep her face neutral.

"Dear Mya, well done!" He smiled openly at her. "And this must be Senior Journeyman 'Jingles' Jarred. Master Youtrin has told me good things of you. It was your sharp eye that spotted my weapon, was it not?"

"It was, Grandfather." Jingles bowed, the jewelry at his wrist chiming with the movement.

"Ah, and I see how you got your nickname." One gray eyebrow arched at the clattering silver rods. "They hold some significance, I suppose?"

"One piece for each life that I have taken in your service, Grandfather." He held up his hand and twitched his wrist proudly.

"Twenty six in all."

"Impressive." The eyebrow dropped. "Now quiet that incessant noise. I find it irritating."

"Yes, Grandfather."

"Follow me, both of you." He turned to go as Jingles fumbled the noisy bracelet into a pocket while trying to keep it still. "First, tell me how you are sure that this was my weapon."

"He bore a perfect likeness to the image Mya distributed to the bosses, Grandfather. Aside from that, other than his movements, I wouldn't have marked him as anything other than a skinny kid."

"Movements?" The Grandfather whirled in mid-stride, catching both of his subordinates off guard. Mya side-stepped out of the way, but Jingles stumbled to a halt only inches from bowling into the guildmaster. "What about his movement?"

"He, uh, moved like a dancer, Grandfather." The two stood face to face a hand-breadth apart. Mya watched carefully, knowing the power of the Grandfather's scrutiny. Jingles' hand twitched behind his back, either from the long habit of rattling his bracelet, or from the need to be filled with the hilt of a weapon. "He bore two large sacks of meal on his shoulder, maybe ten-stone weight, and he stood there like he was waiting for a carriage on a street corner."

"Enhanced strength. Yes." The Grandfather's eyes narrowed. "What else?"

"Uh, he walked like, well, like *you*, Grandfather. Fluid. Graceful. Even with that weight."

"Hmm, yes. Excellent." He turned and walked briskly to another door, opened it without pause, and ushered them through. "So the weapon was hiding in open view. Either he knew we sought him and was using the tactic, or he's still ignorant of our intentions."

They followed him down a short hallway that ended in three doors, one on each wall and one straight ahead. "What was your impression of the boy when you saw him, Jarred?" the Grandfather asked, working a key into the middle door. The lock clicked, and Mya heard the telltale clatter of machinery that said a trap of some kind had just been disarmed. "Was he wary? Were his mannerisms guarded?"

"I think he saw me for more than the simple businessman I was posing as, Grandfather. The innkeeper called him Lad, like it was a proper name, and the boy answered him like any boy might his master. His eyes were on me the whole time, but he didn't look afraid, just curious."

"The weapon cannot fear."

They followed him into a long, low room lit with overhead glow crystals that brightened as they entered. Shelves crowded with bottles, jars, pots, and jugs lined the walls. As they followed the Grandfather, Mya gaped at the array of neatly labeled potions, elixirs, poisons, and salves. The collection must have taken a lifetime to amass, several lifetimes perhaps.

"Did the weapon recognize you for what you are?"

"No, Grandfather. I left as quickly as I could without causing a stir after I spotted him. There's no way he could have known I was an assassin."

"Let us hope so."

The Grandfather chose a small jar from a shelf without pausing to read its label and handed it to Mya. She took it without hesitation, reading the neatly scribed lettering that described the jar's contents. She hid her reaction, but held the jar very carefully after that. The Grandfather stepped past them both and they followed him out of the room.

"You'll use a two-phase technique to acquire the weapon, Mya." She hid her surprise that she was being put in charge of the hunt. Jarred was her senior by two ranks, though they answered to different masters. Her being put in direct command over him was a breach in the chain of rank, but the Grandfather's word was law. The door closed and was relocked with the clatter of protective machinery. "Reconnaissance followed by stealthy assault."

"Yes, Grandfather." They both followed as he walked briskly back toward the sparring room.

"Choose your best man for the reconnaissance, Jarred. His goal is to discern where the weapon sleeps, if he sleeps."

"Yes, Grandfather."

"If, and only if, that information is gleaned, you will choose four of my best Blades to accompany you and Mya to claim the prize." They followed him into the sparring room, and Mya noticed that the valet stood exactly where they had left him. "Choose your people for stealth and skill with envenomed weaponry, Jarred. Mya, you'll use a single drop of that mixture on each of the weapons, no more."

"Yes, Grandfather," they both said.

"Have a care that only one dose is administered. The effects are immediate and overwhelming, but too much can kill." He leveled a glare at the two that would have soured milk. "If the weapon is killed, using the rest of that mixture on yourselves would probably be the best course of action. It would be much less painful than my wrath. Do I make myself perfectly clear?"

"Yes, Grandfather."

"Good. Now, go, and don't fail me."

They were ushered silently out by the valet, but Mya noticed the smug smile on the man's lips as he held open the door. She suppressed the urge to wipe that smile off with the edge of her dagger.

CHAPTER XV

L ad stepped from the front porch of the *Tap and Kettle* and breathed deeply of the night air. The scents of the city filled his mind in a heady swirl. Each flavor—the bitter tang of the tanner's vats three blocks to the east on Highwall Street, the pungent mingling of blood and offal from the slaughterhouse farther south in The Sprawls, and the lighter aroma of the herbalist's shop a block to the southeast—lent its own hint to city's distinctive bouquet.

Lad smiled, a thing he had learned from Wiggen to do when something pleased his senses. The city of Twailin had come to please him as he, in turn, grew to know it. He had explored much of it in his nocturnal jaunts: all of Eastmarket, where the inn resided, and across the bridge to Westmarket. He had also ventured south to The Sprawls with its rows of cheap tenements, and the South Dock District with its wide stone quays that lined the river, and the river sailors who drank and wenched in the bars lining the wharves. He'd even ventured into Barleycorn Heights and West Crescent, with their palatial estates, high-walled manors, and expensive shops. He had not yet gone across the river to the north into the quarters of Hightown and The Bluff. The duke's palace dominated the promontory of The Bluff and overlooked the entire city. It was the highest point of land within the city walls, a fitting position for the governing ruler.

Perhaps I'll venture across Narrow Bridge and into that

quarter tonight, he thought, starting across the courtyard toward the barn. *Perhaps my destiny lies among the royalty that rule this wonderful place.* For Lad had truly grown to believe that he was made to live in such a place, to use his skills among the variety of humanity that now surrounded him.

Yes, he thought, lengthening his strides in eagerness. Today had been a full and interesting day, though Wiggen had not, as he had hoped, accompanied him to the barn for another kiss. That was another thing that brought a smile to his lips, though he knew not why. There was a danger and a yearning to that simple pressing of lips, something that challenged the magic that infused him, something that caused his blood to race and the heat to rise in him. He pushed the memory aside, refocusing his thoughts. *Tonight will be the night I venture into the quarter of the royals.* But when he stepped foot into the barn, his plans for the evening suddenly changed.

Something wasn't right.

Had this been the first time Lad had entered the barn, he might not have noticed, but he was familiar with the place now. He knew its sounds and scents. He knew the patter of the mice that nested in the hayloft as they scampered across the rafters. He knew the odors of dung and horse sweat, cloying but not unpleasant. He knew the cooing of the mourning doves at daybreak and the chirping of the crickets in the evening.

But now those familiar sounds and scents had changed: the mice were not moving, hunkered in their den of rotting hay and leaves; the crickets were silent, unheard of for this time of night; and the scents of horse and hay were mingled with those of men.

Not just men, he thought, letting his eyes scan the darkness as he breathed in the air of the barn. *Many men, and at least one woman*, he decided, taking a cautious step toward the first stall.

All of the horses were in their stalls, fed, watered and reasonably complacent, though one of the mares stomped a foot at him, startled that he appeared without her hearing his approach. He soothed her with a pat and a few soft words, then stepped back into the wide aisle that ran the length of the barn. He stood and listened, closed his eyes and strained to hear that which makes no sound, to sense the darkness, to feel the air.

A near-silent creak of leather. A hint of a breath being taken in too quickly. A heartbeat too loud to be muffled by the sinew, bone and flesh surrounding it. The scuff of a finger on wood. The click of metal against bone. At least five people were hidden in the dark, out of sight, waiting.

The memory of a thousand ambushes flashed through his mind, all orchestrated by his maker to prepare him for this moment. He stood in the darkness, ready, his senses taut, his muscles relaxing into the state of preparedness that had been drilled into him by masters of flesh and mind.

Lad smiled, and spoke.

"I'm ready for you." He heard two quickly indrawn breaths that told him his taunt had scored. The tactic was simple and time tested: when an ambush is discovered, impart that knowledge to the ambushers and reap the benefit of their shattered morale. "To those who seek me harm, I tell you this: If you leave this place now, I'll let you go unharmed. If you stay, you'll die by my hand." And he meant it, for he had learned from Wiggen that killing was wrong. He didn't want to kill if he didn't have to.

His answer came as he expected it would, with an attack.

The sound of air being puffed out of a long tube reached his ears a bare instant before the dart would have struck home, but Lad hadn't lied when he said he was ready.

He moved.

The technique was called displacement, taught to him by one of his trainers as a defensive measure against an attack from concealment. It involved moving every portion of one's body from its previous position in the assumption that whoever is shooting at you is aiming for where you are, not where you will be. The twisting leap took him ten feet to his left, and the dart that would have pierced his flesh stood quivering in one of the stall doors. The mare in the stall huffed and stomped her foot.

Lad took a half second to analyze the weapon, a slim feathered dart from a blowgun, and calculate the angle from which it had come. His next move took him in a bounding leap to the man's perch above the tack room. The utter surprise on the assassin's features lasted only a second. His hand was reaching for another dart, but shifted to the dagger at his belt. His fingers never touched the hilt. The heel of Lad's hand impacted upon the bridge of the man's nose, sending shards of shattered bone into his brain. He fell dead to the floor of the barn, surprise and shock still etched upon his face.

Lad didn't pause to gloat, but moved again. Three more shots, one dart and two tiny arrows, followed his tumbling progress across the barn. Two missed, and one he caught and flung back at his attacker. He heard the arrow strike flesh, even as he vanished into the shadows. It surprised him when he heard another body strike the floor of the barn. He had surmised that the missiles were envenomed, but few poisons acted so quickly that a man struck would drop senseless in the span of a few heartbeats. He'd have to take care, lest he fall prey to that venom.

"Two of you lie dead," he said, taking care to cast his voice to one side. The jittery mare reared in her stall, neighing loudly at the scent of blood. "How many more must die? Leave now, and live." He was answered only with silence.

He moved through the shadows like blackened quicksilver flowing among the cracks and crevices of darkness, silent and deadly. The other horses were nervous now, the scent of blood and strange sounds arousing their instincts, but he heard the scuff of a boot through their shuffling hooves. His quarry was moving.

The edge of the loft was above him now, and he knew that at least two of them hid among the bales and sacks stacked there. There was one sure way to draw them out, but there was risk in it. There was no fear in him, but there was concern, for if he fell he would see his new friends no longer, and they would be in danger with these assassins about. Weighing the risks carefully, he made a decision.

Lad leapt from the darkness like a cat, catching the ledge of the loft in a grip like iron as he flung his legs up and thrust himself into a whirling, somersaulting loop. The danger was that once he was airborne, his trajectory was predictable. He had little doubt that his stalkers would send more envenomed darts his way, but he was ready for them.

Two missed by wide margins.

Two did not.

He landed in a crouch, holding a dart by its fletching and a short arrow between the toes of his right foot. The latter he cast aside, for it interfered with his movement. The former he kept.

He heard the two in the loft fumbling to reload their weapons, and moved. The first crouched behind a hay bale which, when Lad kicked it, sent him sprawling. The dart in Lad's hand found a sheath in the assassin's neck before he was forced to move again by more flying missiles. A woman moved from hiding amid several sacks, her blowgun cast aside in favor of two long fighting daggers.

Lad deflected another missile from an assassin hidden in the rafters as the woman lunged to the attack. One blade he evaded easily, the other was immobilized by his grip on her wrist, which he twisted as his foot lashed out at her midriff. The woman actually surprised him when she flipped with the twisting arm, neatly evaded the kick, and aimed the other dagger at his wrist. He released his grip, snatched the other wrist as it passed, and planted a firm kick into her armpit. Ribs splintered under his foot, and the shoulder popped out of joint. He evaded another tiny arrow as she fell gasping to the floor.

He vanished into the shadows, pausing to reacquire his targets.

The one he'd pierced with the dart lay still, barely breathing. The woman was curled in a protective ball gasping for breath, her consciousness waning. From the sounds of scuffing leather and the number of attacks he'd evaded, there were still two assassins out there, though they remained hidden, even to his senses. He gauged their positions by sound and moved through the shadows, calculating the best angle of attack.

"Two of you remain," he said, casting his voice afar. "I offer you another chance to save yourselves. Leave now, and you'll remain alive."

Chris A. Jackson

He really didn't expect an answer, let alone one of assent.

"I yield!" a woman said from the darkness. She was among the rafters and well hidden. "I'll have your word that no harm will come to me if I move into the open."

"You have it," he answered immediately.

He heard her move, careful steps of soft leather on wood. She dropped down from the rafters to the top of the tack room, then to the floor of the barn. He risked a glance, and saw that she stood in the open, her hands away from her sides. She still bore weapons, but he hadn't asked her to disarm.

"Jingles! Come out." Her voice was flat and hard, that of one in command.

"I will *not* betray my guildmaster!" a male voice said from the darkness of the tack room.

"Then you'll die here!" she spat, taking another step away from the door where her reluctant accomplice hid. "He's more than we bargained for, and that's what I'll tell the Grandfather. He won't kill us for failing to acquire his weapon."

His weapon? Lad thought, his mind snapping to the allusion to his destiny. Perhaps this was a hint to the reason for it all, the foundation for his creation.

"On your word, Mya," the male voice said amid the scuffing of his boots. The revelation of the woman's name caught him off guard as Lad watched the man move into the open. This was the woman he'd met on the road. She'd been searching for him.

"Mya!" he called, moving into the open. "Before you leave, I wish to speak with you." He wasn't much concerned with the two; he could vanish into the shadows long before either could bring a weapon to bear.

"Why?" She sounded suspicious and a little scared. That was good.

"I wish to know more of your master. You said you were here to acquire his weapon." He took another step and stood at the edge of the loft. "I am his weapon?"

"Yes, you are."

"No, I'm not." Lad stepped off the platform and dropped easily to the floor of the barn. The two stood ten paces in front of him, obviously uncomfortable with his approach. This suited Lad fine, for their fear was his ally. He took three careful steps, moving into the diffuse moonlight. "I won't serve the man who sent you here, if his tactics include attacking innocent people from hiding. Go to him and tell him that I refuse to be his weapon. If more are sent to take me, they'll meet the same greeting as you have."

"You've learned much since our meeting on the road, Lad."

He blinked in surprise at her use of his name, then took the time to recognize the man who stood next to her. It was the man who had visited the inn yesterday, the one with the jingling bracelet and the hidden weapons.

"I've learned much, Mya." He took another three steps, stopping barely within striking distance. He could kill them both in an instant if he had to. "I've learned that I don't want to be a slave made only to kill. I've learned what friends are, and I've learned that I can say no."

"My master won't be happy with that."

"Then your master won't be happy. Tell him this: if he doesn't let me go, I'll kill him."

"I'll tell him." She took a cautious step forward. "You're a worthy adversary, Lad, and I would have your hand on this agreement: I won't seek to harm you from this day on, even if my master tells me to do so." She held out her hand for him to take.

He stared at her for a moment, suspicious, but her hands were open and empty, and she knew he could kill her in the blink of an eye if she tried something foolish.

"Very well."

He stepped forward and took her hand into his.

This was the only time the magic that protected Lad from pain and injury betrayed him, for he didn't feel the tiny prick of the needle hidden inside the ring Mya wore. He only felt the invisible grip of the narcotic as it enveloped his mind and sent him sagging to the ground.

Exhaustion gnawed at the muscles of Mya's back and shoulders; it had been a long night, and it was only going to get longer.

"Careful with that, damn you!" she snapped at the two ham-handed guards who were unloading the boy's bound form from the carriage. If they split his skull on a flagstone, all of this would be for nothing.

It had taken her and Jingles an hour to remove the two dead and two unconscious members of the team from the barn and scour the place clean of any trace of their presence. The hardest part had been finding the spent arrows and darts that had missed their mark, but she felt sure that all had been accounted for. The two wounded members of the team would recover, one by morning, since the wound was a simple prick and the drug would wear off in about six hours. The other, Keewa, the woman with three broken ribs and a dislocated shoulder, would take longer to mend. Once everything was cleaned up, and the boy bound and hoisted into the guild's carriage like a sack of grain, they had gotten some help from Jingles' people and acquired an escort to ensure that nothing happened to their precious cargo before it was delivered to the Grandfather.

That task, at least, was done, and it was no small glow of satisfaction that warmed her as she stepped out of the saddle and handed her reins to one of the grooms. But she knew there would be questions to be answered and accounts to be given of the incident. All she really wanted was to go to bed.

"Grandfather!"

She turned and bowed at the guard's exclamation, knowing what was to come and dreading it more than a beating.

"Excellent! Excellent! Hold there a moment while I have a look." The Grandfather of Assassins strode down the steps of his estate, drawn to the bound form of the boy like a great black moth to a flame. "Most excellent indeed!" His wrinkled old hands caressed the boy's unconscious features like a blind man memorizing a face by touch. He pinched the flesh, tested the eyes and felt for pulse at neck and wrist, all in the span of a few breaths.

"Yes, this will do nicely. Take him to the interrogation room and place him in the restraints I've prepared. He should remain senseless for several more hours."

The guards, led by the Grandfather's valet, carried the wisp of bound flesh up the steps and into the manor house. *Swallowed like a dragon gobbling down a choice morsel*, Mya thought.

"Mya!" The Grandfather's voice was like the crack of a whip, wrenching her from her exhausted musings and snapping her shoulders out of their slump.

"Yes, Grandfather," she said, bowing shortly and meeting his gaze evenly. His wizened features were stretched into a mask of glee, and from the lines and wrinkles that were being crisscrossed by those of mirth, she could tell this was not his usual mien.

"You've performed beyond all my expectations." He laughed a short bark of amusement that set the hairs at the nape of her neck on end. "Truth be told, I expected the weapon to slaughter you all like lambs in a pen!"

"Then I'm happy that, in that expectation only, I've disappointed you, Grandfather." Though she chose her words carefully, she saw that the affront had not gone unnoticed. Mya was far too tired to let such a comment go unchallenged, be it from the Grandfather of Assassins or Duke Mir himself. She smiled and bowed again, wondering if he'd kill her on the spot for her insolence.

She didn't hear him move, but she hadn't expected to. She managed not to jump as his cold fingers settled upon the nape of her neck, chilling her like the touch of a ghoul. *Well, it could have been a dagger*, she thought, willing herself not to shiver.

"You *do* know that I've killed for less, Mya." There was no mirth in his voice now, but nor was there malice, only warning. The pressure of his fingertips intensified for a moment and her head swam with dizziness.

"Yes, Grandfather," she managed, as the pressure abated.

"See that you remember it. And you, Jarred." He turned from her and shook Jingles' hand. "Well done! You'll be compensated for the people you lost this night, of course, and for the healing of the one who was wounded."

"Thank you, Grandfather," he said with a bow. "But it was Mya who took the prize this night, sir. We'd all be dead if not for her, and your weapon would be that much the warier."

"Oh?" The old man's gaze slid sideways to Mya once again, his eyes narrowing ever-so-slightly, either in scrutiny or warning, she couldn't tell. "How so?"

"He knew we were there the moment he walked into the barn, sir." Jingles bit his lower lip, but continued with his account, ignorant of Mya's glare. "We lost two Blades before we got as many decent shots off, one of which the boy plucked out of the air like a bat pickin' off a juicy moth. He would'a cleaned us up slicker than spilt grease if Mya hadn't tricked him."

"Tricked him?" His eyes snapped to focus again on Jingles, and the man shrunk under the scrutiny. "Tricked him how?"

"Well, when two more of our people were down, and the boy said that we'd be safe and let go free if we just gave up, she made like she would take him up on it." His eyes flickered back and forth from Mya to the Grandfather, but there was no contest as to where the greater threat lay. "She even had me fooled with the way she played right into his offer. Stood right out in the open and ordered me to come out. Well, I refused flat out, but she said you wouldn't kill us for lettin' the boy go since we were so much overmatched, so I came out."

"You believed her?" There was the slightest edge of sarcasm in that ancient voice, Mya thought.

"Well, not really, sir. But she was in command of the operation, like you said. And then when he came out, she tricked him into shakin' her hand, and he dropped like a pole-axed steer!"

"You had an envenomed ring?" the oldster asked, flicking her a stare that would have stopped a charging bull in its tracks.

"I did, Grandfather." She left it at that, refusing to embellish.

"That was most deceitful of you, Mya," he said, one gray eyebrow twitching upward.

"Thank you, Grandfather," she said with a short bow. She did *not* smile at his irony.

"And very quick thinking, to change tactics so drastically in the middle of an operation. I must say that I'm impressed." He turned to Jingles and said, "You may go. You can expect a package from me tomorrow."

"Yes, Grandfather." Jingles turned on his heel and mounted, calling the rest of his people together with the snap of his fingers. Mya didn't particularly like the man, but felt his departure keenly. She was now the only target for the Grandfather's wrath or gratitude, whichever he chose to wield, and at this point she wasn't particularly sure which she'd prefer.

"Come with me, Mya." He turned and entered the estate, and she was forced to follow.

She followed him down the same stairs that she knew led to the sparring chamber and the repository for his potions and poisons. She still had the pot of narcotic extract in her belt pouch, and thought that might be where he was taking her. Surely he'd want the mixture back; such potent extracts were exceedingly rare and ruinously expensive. And indeed, they did pass through the sparring room and down the short hall that ended in three doors, but as her hand drifted to her belt pouch, the Grandfather worked a key into the door on the right instead of that on the left. Beyond was a descending stair cut out of the living rock; he started down without a word, and she followed. At the bottom was another simple oak door. The Grandfather's keys rattled as he opened it. She swallowed and followed him through.

The interrogation room turned her stomach.

The room was a wide half-sphere crowded with a maze of machinery and shelving. The implements on the shelves and most of the larger devices were designed for a common purpose. She'd seen many such devices before, and was even trained in the use of some, but she'd never had a taste for torture. She was a Hunter, not a butcher.

The guards were clapping padded manacles around the boy's wrists, arms, legs, and ankles upon a bed of stone padded with supple leather. The restraints and the slab itself were made neither for comfort, nor to cause pain, the only device in the room so designed. All the devices looked well maintained and well used.

Mya focused upon her master, refusing to let the surroundings unnerve her.

The guards finished their work and left without a word, but the valet lingered, hovering like a skinny little vulture waiting for something to die. The Grandfather stood at the side of the boy's pallet, staring down at his prize, silent as a grave, his mien every bit as warm. He stood there until Mya thought he might have forgotten she was there. Her eyelids were beginning to sag as his voice brought her back like the prick of a needle.

"I must admit that I'm at a bit of a loss about what to do with you, Mya." His tone was even, and his eyes never left his newly acquired weapon. "Over the last few weeks, you've been privy to much that is dear to me, much that could be put to use against me."

He paused, and Mya began to wonder if she would ever again see the outside of this room.

"Usually, when someone possesses such information, someone whom I don't yet fully find worthy of my trust, I neutralize the threat. You, however, have shown remarkable fortitude, considerable intelligence, and an uncanny ability to make decisions under pressure; yet you are young and somewhat untempered."

She didn't reply, not knowing if she should agree, disagree, or thank him.

"What would you choose if given the opportunity to guide your own destiny, Mya?"

"I'd choose to be a Hunter," she said without pause, meeting his eyes as he turned to assess her response, "if Master Targus would take me back."

"I don't think Master Targus would be willing to take you back as apprentice, considering your recent promotion. I'll send his other apprentice back to him when he returns from Thistledown." He paused again, and his attention slipped back to his weapon. "But I do see the potential for your skills in the use of my new weapon, if you're interested."

"If I may be so bold as to ask, exactly how would my skills be put to use?"

"Very prudent, Mya." The Grandfather turned to a nearby table and picked up a glistening pair of shears. He examined them closely, working them open and closed as if he relished the sound of sharpened steel against sharpened steel. He then deftly applied them to the boy's tunic. "There'll be much to do once my weapon is put to work. The first phase of my plan involves a number of specific assassinations of very powerful and influential people. Until now, they've been untouchable. But such a weapon isn't to be used carelessly. I'll need meticulous reconnaissance of each target."

The tunic was removed, slit up the arms and down the chest, then teased out from under the restraints. He began on the trousers, the shears flashing in the bright lamplight, slicing through the sturdy cloth easily.

"The skills of a Hunter, specifically one with the ability to think on her feet, would be of much use in that reconnaissance." He snipped through the last of the cloth and removed it. The boy lay naked before them, his skin flawless, unmarked and unscarred. "Exquisite, is he not, Mya?" he asked, catching her off guard.

"Yes, Grandfather." Her answer was automatic, but accurate. The boy was perfect. Lithe and muscular, he was without as much as a birthmark marring his flesh. She averted her eyes when she noticed that the Grandfather was watching her.

"So, would you like to hunt for me, Mya?" he asked, setting the shears aside and turning to her. "I'll pick the targets, you'll delve into their protections and vulnerabilities, then we'll plan the appropriate action, which will be executed by my weapon here." He patted the boy's leg, and Mya shivered.

"How would I be compensated for my services?"

"I think the standard junior journeyman's rate will do, with a sizable bonus for every target that we eliminate or manipulate through your efforts." He smiled thinly and motioned for her to follow him as he moved toward the room's single exit. "You would also get rooms here at the estate, the services of the staff, and whatever equipment you need to perform your duties." He stopped at the door and turned to her with that same thin smile of warning.

"If this is not acceptable..."

"Your offer's most generous, Grandfather." She'd known from the start of this conversation that she'd have no choice in the matter. "I accept. I'll retrieve my things from the *Golden Cockerel* this morning."

"Excellent. Just report to my valet. He'll have everything ready for you."

"Yes, Grandfather." She stepped past the grinning valet, who bowed to her mockingly, and followed the Grandfather up the stairs, wondering with every step what exactly she was getting herself into.

Chapter XVI

"L_{ad?"} Wiggen entered the barn warily. It was late morning, past milking already, and Lad hadn't come to the inn.

"Lad, are you here?" She peeked into the tack room carefully, remembering the time she had interrupted his morning exercises. She'd watched enthralled for more than a minute before she realized that she was intruding and backed away. He had later told her not to worry, that he had known she was there but was too busy to answer. But today there was no one in the tack room, and Lad's bed didn't even look slept in.

"What the—" She entered the room and placed her hand on the cold pillow, felt between the cool sheets. No one had slept in the bed.

Now she was worried.

A quick search of the tack room yielded no sign of him, but Lad had no possessions, so there was nothing to go missing if he'd left. Out in the barn proper, there was no sign that anything had happened. All of the horses were in their stalls, albeit hungrily expecting something from her, having missed their morning oats. None of the tools were missing, no blankets or gear were gone. It was as if he'd simply walked away and not come back.

"I don't believe it," she said to herself, adamantly refusing the notion that Lad would simply leave without saying anything, regardless of the circumstances. She quickly fed and watered the horses and returned to the inn, worry growing in her with every step.

She burst into the kitchen, red faced and panting. "Father, Lad's gone!"

"What?" Forbish set down the immense kettle from which he was pouring blackbrew. "Gone where?"

"I don't *know* where!" She clenched her fists and pounded the air. "He's just *gone!*"

"Oh, come now, Wiggen. Maybe he's just gone for a walk down the market. I said we needed some more barley flour. He's probably just gone to fetch it."

"His chores haven't been done and his bed hasn't been slept in. Something's wrong! He's left, and it's *my* fault!"

"Your fault? Now, how could it be your fault?" He rounded the table and took her by the shoulders, but even his embrace couldn't keep the tears from coursing down her cheeks. "Come, now. What could you have done to make Lad want to leave? You two were getting on famously!"

"It's not what I did, Father, it's what I said." She wiped her nose on the handkerchief he supplied and looked up at him, guilt painting her features with misery. "The other night, after we had dinner together, after those men tried to hurt us, I told him—" She broke down, unable to continue, her shoulders heaving with her sobs.

"Oh, Wiggen." Forbish buried the girl in his embrace, squeezing her tightly, his solidity steadying her like an anchor. He held her until her sobs subsided, whispering the comforting things that fathers whisper to crying daughters. Then, when she was still, he asked the question that was the underlying cause of her distress. "When did you fall in love with him?"

"Huh?" Wiggen stepped back, dabbing her eyes and sniffling, but taken aback by her father's question. "When did I *what?*"

"Well, you wouldn't be cryin' your eyes out if he didn't mean that much to you, now would you, girl?" Forbish crossed his beefy arms and smiled down at her. "Was it before he saved your life or after?"

"Uh..." Wiggen wrung her handkerchief, her eyes darting

down to her feet then back up. Her father obviously knew more about what she felt toward Lad than she did, and he didn't look or sound particularly angry about it. "I, uh, don't really know. Before, I think. He helped me. I'd been having those nightmares again, not sleeping much, and he taught me how to clear my thoughts before I went to sleep." She smiled weakly.

"And did it work? Did he cure your nightmares?"

"After a couple of nights, yes. I had to practice some before I could do it without him to help me, but it worked." She blinked and sniffed again, and with a wrenching pang of remorse, the tears began again. "But now he's gone, and I'm the one to blame! I told him that killing was *bad*, Father. I told him that whoever made him the way he was made him to do evil! I told him to run away!"

"And so you think he did? You think he just up and walked out without a word?"

"Well, it doesn't sound much like him, but I thought that he might, if he thought he was becoming evil."

"Well, I don't think it sounds much like the Lad I know." Forbish's brow knitted together into a nest of thick wrinkles. "I don't think he would have just walked out of here. Leastways, not without sayin' goodbye!"

"Then what happened to him?" Her voice trembled with more than anguish now, for there was fear in her for what may have happened to Lad.

"I think his destiny finally found him, Wiggen."

Her heart sank in her chest, her breath coming in short gasps. "His destiny?"

"Yep, and I think you were spot-on about the men who made Lad the way he was. There's some powerful people out there who've put a lot of money and time into making Lad the perfect killer."

"And you think they came and took him?"

"Well, I don't think Lad would have gone without a fight, and we've both seen him fight; so, since the barn's not chockablock with dead bodies, I'm thinkin' they may have just talked him out of here." At her skeptical look, he elaborated. "Think how much he wanted to know about his destiny, Wig. If they promised him what he wanted, a purpose to his life, maybe he just went with 'em."

"No," she said adamantly, shaking her head. "No, he wouldn't have gone with them without saying goodbye. They must have tricked him somehow."

"That's possible." Forbish rubbed his multiple chins in thought. "He wasn't the sharpest pitchfork in the barn, you know."

"So they took him," she finished, her voice wavering with suppressed tears. "But where?"

"I don't know, girl, but one thing's for sure: Twailin's a fair big city to find one person in, and we don't have much of a chance, just you and me walkin' the streets yellin' out 'Lad! Oh Lad!' dawn to dusk every day." He gestured toward the tray that was ready to be taken out to their waiting customers. "Even if we weren't busy with the inn, we couldn't find him on our own."

"So we just forget him?" she asked, a splinter of accusation edging her tone.

"No, we don't just forget him, but we gotta go about this smart like." Forbish picked up the tray and forcefully handed it to his daughter, pushing her toward the door to the main room. "I got some friends who know a little about how things work around Twailin, Wiggen. I'll call in a few favors and see what we can find out."

"Thank you, Father," she said, sniffing back the last of her tears. At least they weren't just going to forget about him, not that she thought that she ever could.

Lad's mind surfaced through the fading fingers of narcotic, and his senses gradually cleared. He didn't awaken, since he hadn't been asleep, but rather unconscious, so as his senses returned, he carefully took stock of his surroundings.

The air on his skin elicited the same faint whispers of sensation from his head to his toes, which meant that his clothing had been removed. This didn't really matter, but it was interesting. He felt a slight pressure on his arms, wrists, legs, and ankles, which told him he was restrained. He didn't strain against his bonds, but rather felt them; the leather against his skin was soft, but there was no give against the gentle pressure he exerted.

Iron or steel, he thought, *but padded with leather.* This was also interesting.

He listened. There were two low voices, both male and neither familiar. They were discussing something, many of their words strange to his ears, another language perhaps.

"Corillian's use of elvish for the phrase of bonding is ingenious," one voice said, the tone careful and measured. "There are few enough true elves left in the lowlands, and any who happen by aren't likely to use this particular phonetic of the phrase."

"Why is that?" The second voice was quiet, but there was power beneath it. It was the voice of a man who was used to being obeyed.

"The pronunciation makes the phrase nonsense. This character is feminine, while the other is masculine, and neither should be used in the context of the third. It's like saying 'The woman's beard is having a baby;' it makes no sense."

"So it would never be uttered by mistake, even from one who spoke elvish."

"Exactly, and what's more..."

Lad listened for a little longer, but their words meant little to him, concerning hidden script, elvish characters, and intonation in the various elvish tongues. He focused on the rest of his surroundings, deciding to keep his eyes closed for now. He didn't know if anyone was watching him, but if someone were, opening his eyes would let them know he was awake. There probably wasn't much of an advantage to feigning sleep, but there might be, and he had the definite feeling that he needed every advantage he could get.

The air itself was warm, smelling of wood, oil, leather, sweat, and the smoke of lamps and torches, which told him that he was probably underground or in a windowless chamber. He also detected a faint metallic tang that was either rusted metal or blood. He heard the flutter of a guttering flame, probably a lamp, and the rustle of cloth, parchment, and leather, all to his left. There were also other people about; he could hear the faint breathing of someone farther to his left, and occasionally caught the sound of a heartbeat to his right. He breathed in the air again and thought he caught a familiar scent: something from last night, something warm and spicy.

"He's awake, Grandfather."

Lad snapped his eyes open and turned his head to the right to look at Mya, who stood barely within arm's reach if his arms had been free. She'd been watching him and had detected the change in his breathing.

"You're observant, Mya."

"Yes, I am." She looked down at him for a moment, her face carefully expressionless. Then she bowed to the men who approached from his left.

"Excellent!"

Lad turned and watched the two men walk over, his eyes taking them in professionally. One was a tall half-elf in soft leathers and high boots. He walked smoothly and wore a sword like he could use it. His eyes were sharp and snapped about as if memorizing every detail of everything before him, even as his motions were relaxed and fluid. He brought with him the smell of sweat, leather, and horse, and there was a slight tremor to his hands that spoke of fatigue.

The other man was cloaked in black, though Lad could see the outlines of several weapons beneath the garment. The hood of the cloak was thrown back to reveal a wizened face with bushy white eyebrows. The lips were curled back from teeth that were slightly yellowed with age, and the man's head was capped with a wispy mop of snow-white hair. His eyes, however, were sharp and cunning, and never left Lad for an instant. But the most telling feature of the old man was the way he moved; every step was perfectly balanced, every motion fluid and controlled, and not a whisper could Lad hear from either the black cloak or the man's feet. His gait screamed of training, years of it, decades of control and precision.

This man was a master.

But a master of what, and of whom?

"And how is my weapon feeling after his nice long rest?"

Lad watched him carefully; he knew the question was directed at him, and he remembered the term that Mya had used the previous night. He also remembered what she'd said. The answer was still the same.

"You're the one Mya calls Grandfather." It wasn't a question, but the old man smiled and nodded, nonetheless. "I'm not your weapon. I'm not anyone's weapon."

"Oh, but you are, boy," the man cooed, soft laughter bubbling up his ancient throat like air escaping a pit of quicksand. "I contracted you to be made, and made you were. Had Corillian not met with an untimely end on the trip here, you would have been delivered and paid for." He laughed again, this time with what appeared to be genuine mirth. "I must find the robber who put an arrow in that old wizard's throat and thank him. He saved me an embarrassing amount of money and accomplished what I would have never thought to attempt!"

His mirth continued, and the tall half-elf beside him smiled. Mya's face, Lad noticed, remained expressionless. He focused his attention on the old man and tried again.

"My name is Lad. I'm not your weapon. I won't serve you. If you don't release me, I'll kill you."

"Brave words from one bound on a pallet, boy!" the old man said, his voice transforming in one sentence from mirthful to malicious. "You'd be wise to address your new master with more respect."

"My master is dead," Lad said, immune to the old man's threat. "You're not my master."

"Oh, but I am, you see." The Grandfather held up a scroll, waving it as if it bore some mystical power. "Corillian made you for me, and this is the key that will make you my weapon. This will make me your master. This is why you were made."

"No." Lad's voice was flat and dangerous. He couldn't hate, for that too had been denied him by the magic, but he could still refuse. "I won't kill for you. Killing is evil."

"Oh, *is* it now?" The old man's eyes widened with amazement, his mouth stretching into a rictus grin of malevolence. "Are soldiers evil, then, for the killing they do at the behest of their lords? Are constables evil for the thieves and murderers they kill in the streets? Surely the duke's headsman is more evil than any, for how many have died beneath his axe? Even Duke Mir himself, I daresay, must be evil for all the hundreds he's had put to death by his judgments."

The old man's face turned cold after the last, and he leaned over to stare down, his breath warm on Lad's cheek.

"Strange, isn't it, how a man who kills one is a murderer, while another who kills hundreds or thousands is a patriot or a vanquisher?" The ancient eyes narrowed slightly, and Lad could feel their contempt, though they sent no fear through him. "You'll find out very shortly, boy, that evil and good are as meaningless as any two words that men use to describe the souls of other men. What do men know of evil who have never stared death in the face and embraced it?"

"I don't want to kill," Lad said, knowing his words fell on deaf ears. He began to slowly test his bonds, pulling against the thick iron restraining his wrists. "I won't be your slave."

"And what gives you the slightest impression that I give a bent copper for what *you* want?" the Grandfather asked, straightening and holding the scroll up once again. "You *will* be my slave, boy, and this is what will make you so."

As the knobby old hands began to unroll the scroll, Lad suddenly realized what all the talk had been about. The scroll was magic, and whatever was written on it would make him this man's slave. He could not, *would* not allow it!

As the old man drew breath to read the words that would make him a slave forever, Lad brought all the strength he bore into one forceful movement to free his left arm. He couldn't break the iron bands that bound him, that he knew, but the flesh of his wrist was weaker, and pain meant nothing to him. Sinew and bone popped and crackled like dice on a stone bench as he wrenched his hand through the manacle. Skin and muscle tore away, blood wetting his wrist and hand as he ripped free.

The tall half-elf shouted a warning, lunging forward to restrain him, but Lad wasn't quite loose yet. His wrist was free, but the iron band that encircled his upper arm still restrained him. He shifted his torso away, popped his shoulder out of joint, and wrenched the torn limb through, leaving more flesh behind.

Then the half-elf was on him, trying to hold him down, his voice harsh as he yelled, "Read the bonding phrase, Grandfather! Read it!"

But the old man didn't read. He simply stepped back out of Lad's bloody flailing reach and grinned in amusement.

The half-elf's full weight bore down on Lad's mangled arm as the bones of his shoulder popped back into the socket, but he twisted the blood-slicked limb free. His thumb hung from a tatter of torn flesh, so he had no grip, but his fingers were intact. He evaded the half-elf's grasp and jabbed him in the throat hard enough to crush the larynx, then brought his hand around to slam his assailant's head down onto one of the iron manacles. Bone shattered with the impact, and the man went limp, falling away, leaving Lad free to struggle against his bonds.

"Oh, impressive!" the ancient man cooed, laughing at his loyal servant's demise. "Very impressive indeed! But I'm afraid not enough." He brought the scroll up and began to read aloud.

Lad wrenched at his other arm even as he felt the magic course through his body. It infused him, filled him, and wound around every fiber of his being. The runes that lay beneath his skin flared green-white, and all the muscles of his body twitched with their power. Then the magic was gone, and Lad renewed his struggles.

"Stop trying to free yourself!" the old man snapped.

To his own amazement, Lad obeyed. He lay there straining to make himself wrench free, his eyes wide with wonder at his inaction. He had just *obeyed*, as if his muscles acted of their own volition. He looked around, trying to find something, someone who could help him escape.

The only other person near was Mya, and the horror on her face was plain to see. He reached his mangled hand toward her, but she backed away, aghast either at him or at what he'd done to the half-elf.

"Look at me." The command was undeniable. Lad turned his head and looked at his new master.

"You won't try to escape from now on," the old man commanded, and Lad felt the force of it. All the drive to flee, to escape, suddenly left him. "Do you understand me?"

Lad looked at him, tried not to answer, but said, "Yes," despite his effort.

"You'll address me as 'Master.' Do you understand me?"

"Yes, Master," Lad found himself saying, though he clenched his teeth against it. A battle raged within him, his mind versus the magic that bound his body. He knew he wanted to free himself, to flee this prison, but he couldn't make himself do it.

"Good!" His new master stepped forward, but stopped just beyond Lad's reach. His next command was predictable. "You will never harm me, either by action or inaction. Do you understand me?"

"Yes, Master." Lad felt lost, alone and helpless. He couldn't flee and he couldn't fight. He didn't want to obey, but was compelled to do so. He knew from the impotence of his internal struggle against the binding magic that its control was complete; the Grandfather could command him to do anything, and he'd do it. He couldn't disobey.

But his mind was still his own. He might be a slave, but he was an unwilling one, and his voice was still intact.

"I must follow your commands, Master," he said, leveling a dangerous glare at the old man, "but the magic can't change who I am. My name is Lad. I'm only your slave because the magic makes me so. You can't make me evil."

"Evil? Bahh!" The Grandfather waved one gnarled hand in dismissal. "I'll not bandy words with a witless slave! From this point forth, you'll only speak to me when I request it or ask you a question. Do you understand?"

"Yes, Master," Lad said without thinking. He focused his thoughts inward, trying to slip into meditation as an escape, but the next of the old man's commands snapped his concentration like a twig.

"Good, now hold out your arm."

Lad did so, allowing the man to inspect his already healing injuries. The bone and sinew were knitting, the gaping flesh slipping back into place. Blood still smeared the limb from the elbow down, as well as much of his left side and the pallet beneath him, but the damage was very nearly gone.

"Very good." He tested the strength of Lad's thumb and nodded in satisfaction. "Mya, bring a towel from that bin and wipe all this blood away. Valet! Send word for someone to come down here and pick up this fool's corpse. Oh, and come here and get Targus' ring." He toed the body at his feet to indicate the half-elf that Lad had killed.

The skinny man by the door obeyed immediately, shouting a few words to the guards stationed outside, then moved quickly toward them. Lad watched, waiting for him to come within reach.

"Grandfather," Mya said, standing just farther than Lad could lunge and holding a damp towel in her hands. "If you don't order the weapon not to harm us"—she nodded toward the advancing valet—"he'll kill us both as soon as we're within reach."

Lad looked at her; she was observant indeed, and very careful, not just of him, but of her master. She hadn't disobeyed his command, just informed him of what would happen if she complied. This woman was very interesting. The valet stopped in his tracks, well out of Lad's reach, glancing nervously at his master, then Mya.

"Oh, well, I don't suppose we can have that." The Grandfather reached out and took Lad's chin in his hand, pulling him roughly back to look into those sharp ancient eyes. "You'll harm none of my people," he said, glancing at Mya and smiling thinly, "without my orders. Do you understand me?"

"Yes, Master."

"Good." He nodded to Mya, and she moved forward and began wiping the drying blood from Lad's arm. "Be thorough, Mya," he said, pulling the iron pins from the other restraints. He

172

worked his way around the table, opening the restraints until Lad was free. "A good weapon must be kept clean and sharp."

The valet knelt and pulled a black ring from one of the dead half-elf's fingers, wiped it clean on his tunic, and handed it to his master. The Grandfather looked at the ring briefly, then slipped it into a pocket without another word.

When the last restraint clicked open, Lad sat up. Mya took a half-step back, eying him warily, but the Grandfather just smiled. Lad took the towel from her hand and began cleaning himself, stepping off the pallet and scrubbing at the blood that had dried.

"Good," the Grandfather said with another smile. He gathered his valet with a glance and strode slowly toward the door. "Stay here and see that he is cleaned, clothed, and fed, Mya. Then you may come up to my chambers and we'll discuss our first task for my new weapon."

"Yes, Grandfather," she said, retrieving another towel from the bin and attending to the few flecks of blood that Lad couldn't reach.

"Oh, and as for you, boy. This is your new home. Don't damage anything, and stay here until I bid you leave. Do you understand?"

"Yes, Master."

"Good." The Grandfather and his valet left the room without another word.

Two burly guards came in and lifted the lifeless form of the half-elf. Lad watched them go as he finished with the towel and dropped it on the floor. While Mya picked it up and deposited it in an empty barrel, he took a moment to inspect his prison.

The room was a dome of mortared stone, perhaps a hundred fifty feet across and a third that high at the center. From wall to wall, and suspended from a large portion of the ceiling, the place was crowded with devices, most of which Lad had never seen before. Having just been strapped down to one of them, however, he quickly realized that the purpose of all of this equipment was to restrain and cause pain to people. What reason someone would have to do that was still beyond his ken, but he had a deep knot in the pit of his stomach when he looked at these machines and imagined them in use. He was beginning to understand what Wiggen had meant by evil, and he didn't like it at all.

"Here."

He turned to see that Mya had retrieved some clothing from a shelf next to the bin. He inspected her, his mind sorting through a hundred ways that he could kill her in an instant, none of which the magic would allow. Her eyes flicked over him quickly whenever she could not avoid looking at him, as if he made her nervous.

"Put these on." She put a dark pair of trousers and a similarly hued tunic on the pallet.

"Why?" Lad stood staring at her, commanding her attention. If making her uncomfortable was his only weapon, he would wield it. "What difference if a slave wears clothing or not? Or if another slave sees one without clothes."

"I'm not a slave," she said dangerously. Lad watched carefully as her face flushed with color and her nostrils dilated with every breath. His taunt had scored.

"You may not think you're a slave, Mya, but you're as much bound by the Grandfather's commands as I." He smiled, letting her see that her discomfort amused him. "At least I *know* what I am."

"I'm a Hunter!" she spat, taking a half-step and glaring into his eyes, her discomfort transforming to rage. "I *work* for the Grandfather. You're a weapon, one of flesh, but a weapon and nothing more. You were *made* to be a slave, and that's what you are."

"What we're made to be is not always what we become." He let his voice soften with that, wondering what other emotions he could provoke from her.

"You were told to put these on." She snatched up the clothes and thrust them at him, her eyes hard as flint.

"No, you were told to see that I was dressed." Lad made no move to take the clothing. "I must obey my master, but not *you*."

"Refusing to obey me will get you nowhere, Lad. If you don't put the clothing on, I'll simply tell the Grandfather that you refused, and he'll order you to do so." She held out the clothing once again. "It wouldn't be wise to antagonize him. He could make you do things that you wouldn't enjoy."

Lad's thoughts immediately centered upon Wiggen and Forbish, and he saw in Mya's eyes that she knew what he was thinking. She could easily tell the Grandfather that he cared for the innkeeper and his daughter. The result would be predictable and, as she had said, something he wouldn't enjoy.

"If you're not his slave, Mya," Lad asked, taking the clothes and slipping into the dark trousers, "why do you stay here?" He drew the drawstring tight and reached for the tunic. The material of both garments was smooth and slick to the touch; he'd never felt its like. "Clearly, you don't enjoy following his orders."

"I do my job." She turned and walked to another cabinet and began putting things onto a tray. "Whether I enjoy it or not doesn't matter."

"Why not?" He slipped into the tunic as she turned back with a tray full of food.

"Because I'm bound by my contract." She placed the tray upon the pallet. It bore two large pieces of dried meat, a bowl of porridge, and an apple. "Eat."

"Then you're a slave." He picked up one piece of meat and bit off a mouthful.

"No, I'm indentured. There's a difference."

"What's indentured?"

"It means that I have an agreement with the Grandfather to serve him until I'm fully trained." She watched him eat for a few bites.

"Who decides when you're fully trained?"

"The Grandfather."

He watched her face and smiled.

"But that doesn't mean I'm a slave!"

"You and I are more the same than we're different, Mya."

"No, we aren't." Her eyes grew hard again and her hand drifted to her dagger's hilt. He ignored her threatening posture.

"Both of us will escape the Grandfather the same way." He sampled the porridge. It was sweetened with fruit and sugar, but was nowhere near as good as Forbish's porridge.

"You'll never escape the Grandfather, Lad. Not unless you're—" Her eyes flared with anger and she whirled away, storming toward the door without looking back.

"Not unless I'm killed," he said before the door slammed. Lad stopped eating and let the false smile fade from his mouth, wondering if his taunt would prove all-too-accurate in the end.

CHAPTER XVII

High upon The Bluff, amid the opulent estates and townhouses of the neighborhood known as Duke's Court, a shadow moved across a sliver of moonlight. It moved without sound, without a scuff of boot or creak of leather, flickering from darkness to darkness like a wraith. It moved with such stealth that one of the many patrolling Royal Guard walked within two feet of it without knowing. Never had ignorance saved a life with such certainty.

Lad watched the guard until the noisy fellow disappeared around a corner, then he listened. When the sound of the man's footsteps faded away, he moved to the spot Mya had told him to seek. Here, just like she'd said, the stone was rough and the two walls were set against one another at a sufficiently acute angle to allow easier climbing. He listened for a moment to make sure the next guard was not near, and then scaled the two adjoining walls like a spider climbing a cellar door.

At the top there was nowhere to go; the edge of the roof was adorned with a decorative crenellation that wouldn't support his weight, though how Mya had learned this, he had no idea. He was forced by the magic to follow her instructions, so he didn't even consider testing her information. The nearest window was fifteen feet away. Lad remained perfectly still, hands and toes gripping the stone easily, his breathing steady and silent.

The second guard passed without looking up.

When the man was gone, Lad leapt without the slightest hesitation, aiming for the stone sill below the window. It didn't occur to him that if Mya's information was slightly off and the sill didn't support his weight, he'd fall fifty feet to the cobbled street. He'd been told to accept her instructions, and though his mind was still free, the magic wouldn't allow him to disobey.

His outstretched fingers snatched the window's narrow ledge and gripped it like a vise, his legs dangling freely. The stone showed no sign of giving way. He easily chinned himself up and contorted into a braced position in the window's frame, leaving his hands free to work. The window was just as Mya had described: two bronze-framed panels made up from small panes of thick leaded glass. It was made to be opened inward and secured with a simple turn-latch. The hooked pick that had been secreted in the collar of Lad's dark shirt slipped through the crack and lifted the latch without a sound. He pushed gently, listening with every ounce of concentration he could muster for the faintest squeak.

The near-silent grating of the old bronze hinges might have gone unnoticed even to an astute observer, but to Lad the sound was deafening. He'd been ordered to be silent, and obey he must, so with the window only a hand's width open, he stopped. He could hear rhythmic breathing from those within the darkened chamber and easily discern the two sleeping shapes, but he couldn't reach them through the partially opened window.

Well, he thought, *I can't just sit here forever. The magic compels me, but it restrains me, so...* An idea came to him finally, though whether from some magical compulsion or his own agile mind, he knew not. He had a single weapon that he had been instructed to use for a single purpose, but that didn't preclude his using it for other purposes.

He slipped the slim stiletto from its sheath and placed the tip through the minute crack onto one of the offending hinges. Then he slipped his finger slowly down the razor edge, letting his blood slide down the blade in thick droplets onto the squeaky bronze. *Blood is a poor lubricant, but when none other is available it makes metal slide against metal more easily*, the memory said in his mind, as if his old instructor were perched invisibly over his shoulder. After treating each hinge similarly, he sheathed the blade and carefully pushed the window. His ears still caught the faintest of noises, but he knew that no other human could have heard it.

He slipped through the open portal like black water poured from a pitcher and lay upon the floor of the chamber, a shadow amid darkness.

He remained still for some time, ensuring that both of the people in the bed were indeed sleeping peacefully. When he was sure, he stood and looked upon his unwary victim. Regret, sorrow, and remorse weren't part of him, but Wiggen's words rang in his mind as he retrieved the stiletto from its sheath and moved to the side of the bed. He knew she had told him the truth: what he was about to do was evil. He didn't want to be evil, but the magic made him comply. He stood for a moment and looked down at the face of the one he was going to kill, and he felt a tension in his stomach that he knew was his friendship for Wiggen telling him what he was doing was wrong. There was something akin to pain in that feeling, for he knew he was betraying that friendship, even though it wasn't of his own volition.

With a single lightning stroke, he thrust the blade into its intended sheath. Lad left it there as he'd been instructed. He also took the ribbon-bound parchment from inside his shirt and placed it where he'd been told. He turned to go, his grim task complete.

But then Lad stopped.

His appointed task was finished; his only remaining orders were to return directly to the Grandfather's keep without being detected. There was no compulsion to hurry, so the magic that bound him left only a vague desire to return to the Grandfather's estate *sometime* that evening. He was free to act within the bounds of those orders, and decided to exercise that small spark of freedom.

He returned to the bedside, remembering something Wiggen had once said to him. He then did something that he knew might put his life at risk in the future, but he hadn't been instructed *not* to do this specific thing, so the magic had no compulsion over him.

When he was finished, he turned to go, closing the window behind him with the same care he had used while breaking in. He perched on the window's sill for several long breaths, listening and timing the passage of the guard patrols. When everything was quiet, he simply stepped off the sill into fifty feet of empty air. There were three more windows between the one he'd left and the street, and he used each to slow his descent. With no more noise than a leaf falling from a tree, he landed in a crouch. He stepped into the shadows and listened carefully again, before becoming one with the darkness that enveloped him.

"Good to see you, Toby!" Forbish said with a genuine smile. He gripped the hand of his old friend and perched his bulk on one of the tiny bar stools.

"Likewise, Forbish." The man was thin, his dark hair somewhat gray around the ears, with an open smile and eyes brimming with mirth. He placed a tankard of ale in front of the larger man without having been asked. "How's business?"

"Can't say good, but I'm still makin' a go of it." Forbish sipped the ale and restrained a grimace of distaste. It was nowhere near up to the standards of the *Tap and Kettle*, but people didn't come to Toby's to drink fine ale. "There's just me and Wiggen now, you know."

"Yeah, I heard about Tam." Toby pulled a pipe from his pocket and began stuffing the bowl with sweet-smelling tobacco. "Sorry." He lit it and exhaled a plume of smoke into the already smoky air.

"Nobody's fault but my own," Forbish said solemnly, sipping his ale. "You'd think I'd have learned my lesson by now."

"Well, never you mind about that now, my friend. I got your note, and I've called him in." He nodded past the tables where patrons were playing various games of chance to a corner booth usually reserved for private card games. "He's over there."

But as Forbish rose from his stool, Toby reached across the bar and gripped his forearm, holding him back.

"Just be careful what you get yourself into, Forbish." His tone screamed a warning, which Forbish knew was sincere. "He owns the note on this place, and always will. They get their hooks into you, they never let go."

"Don't worry, Toby. I just need his help to find something. Nothing complicated."

"Nothing ever starts out complicated. Always seems to end up that way, though."

Forbish could tell that his friend was bitter about his interminable relationship with these people, but he was also sure that Toby was speaking from long experience. These were the same type of people who had taken Forbish's son away from him. He clenched his jaw and nodded. "I'll be careful, Toby."

"You do that."

Forbish turned from his friend and worked his way through the busy gambling hall's main floor. There were tables with cards, tables with dice, tables with blocks of ivory with dots in strange patterns on one side, and even a table with a great flat wheel and several colored balls that rattled around the slotted surface as it spun. Forbish was never one to gamble, unless you considered running an inn a gamble of sorts. He was far too tight-fisted to put money on a table and watch as it was whisked away at the whim of chance or luck.

Forbish didn't believe in luck. He believed in hard work. He also believed in his family, or more precisely, his daughter, who was the only family he had left.

He reached the corner table where he was immediately faced with two dangerous-looking men wearing weapons, their arms crossed in defiance. Forbish would have laughed at their stern demeanors if his mood had been lighter; that they considered him a potential threat in a room full of half-drunk dock workers and bargemen was almost funny.

"I've come to speak with your master about some business." He tucked his thumbs in his belt and hitched up his trousers, setting his formidable belly jiggling in a most non-threatening manner. "I'm not armed."

"Let him through, gentlemen," the fellow at the table said, his voice calm and as slick as a greased cobblestone. "We didn't come down here for the wine, after all."

"Thank you," Forbish said as the two goons parted and his host waved one immaculate, bejeweled hand across the table. He took the proffered seat, struggling slightly with his girth in the narrow booth.

"May I buy you a drink, Mister Forbish?" the man asked, now waving his hand in the direction of the bar. The gesture summoned one of the busy barmaids in a flash.

"Yes, milord?" she said with a curtsey and a patently false smile. "You want something else?"

Her dress was cut low, as were those of all the serving staff and the "ladies" who were paid to keep the gamblers company. The displayed cleavage drew stares from neither of the two men, however. They were too busy watching one another to have time to show interest in her. Her smile faded like a watercolor in rain.

"I'll have another glass of wine, something better than this swill if you can manage, and my associate will have..."

"Just a mug of water, if you please, Master Hensen." Forbish had gauged his order carefully, not wanting to appear either rude or beholden to his host.

"Water then." The man smiled thinly, twitching his cuffs into perfection as the woman bowed again and left.

"So," Hensen said, sipping his wine, "my friend Toby tells me that you require my help in finding something. Something you've lost."

"Not exactly require, if you please, sir. I'd welcome your help and I'll pay you for the service, but it's not a requirement. Also, it's not some*thing* so much as some*one* who's gone missing."

"You choose your words carefully, Mister Forbish," the elegantly dressed man said, nodding to the barmaid as his new glass of wine and Forbish's water were delivered. "I find that both refreshing and somewhat worrisome. You speak as though you're afraid I'm trying to trick you with words."

"I'm just a careful sort, sir. No insult was intended."

"That's good." Hensen sipped, then raised his eyebrows either in warning or in appreciation of the wine. "My associates don't like it when people insult me."

"Then your associates and I should get along just fine." Forbish sipped his water, more for something to do with his hands than from thirst.

"So, this person who has gone missing. Are you sure they didn't simply wander away, get lost in the city perhaps? Or maybe they fell victim to the common thugs that prey on the unaware."

"No, sir. He didn't just get lost, and he was quite capable of defending himself." Forbish sipped again, choosing his next words with extreme care. "I'm sure he was taken. Abducted, that is."

"Abducted?" Hensen's eyebrows shot up as if they were attached to strings. "Was this friend of yours so valuable that he's being ransomed?"

"No, sir. There won't be a ransom. Lad had only been working for me for just over a fortnight. He's just a boy."

"Have you no idea why the boy might have been taken? Slavers, perhaps?"

"I don't think so, sir. As I said, Lad was more than able to defend himself from common thugs. In fact," Forbish paused, unsure how much he should tell this man of Lad's abilities, "it may have been those very skills for which he was taken."

"What skills exactly do you mean?" Hensen was showing far too much interest for Forbish's comfort, but there was no way to avoid the question.

"He's quite an amazing young man, Lad is, sir. He can move fast and do things with his hands and feet that I've never seen nor thought could be done."

"He's trained in fighting then? As a swordsman?"

"No, sir, not with a sword, though I did see him use a hand axe once. Lad didn't need a sword."

"Didn't *need* a sword? What do you mean?"

Forbish took a deep breath and another sip of water, wishing it was ale after all. "What I mean, sir, is that I watched the boy kill four armed men without a weapon in his hand. He saved my daughter's life, he did. Them men would've killed us all, and Lad saved us. Now he's gone missin', and I think it was because he could do those things."

He didn't want to tell this man Lad's entire story, not unless it was necessary, but Hensen's eyes were narrowing now, as if the thoughts behind them were making connections he didn't particularly care for. He stared at Forbish hard, as if willing more information out of him, but the innkeeper feared that he had already said too much. He sipped his water and let his eyes explore the patterns of wood grain in the table's surface.

"I'll tell you something, Mister Forbish," Hensen said finally, sipping his wine and returning to his carefully neutral mien. "This is the second time in as many weeks that I've been approached to aid in finding a young man."

"Really?"

"Yes, *really*." His tone blatantly implied that he did not care for interruptions. "The previous search was much more vague in some respects and much more direct in others. I wasn't given any information about this boy, but a very accurate description. That search was called off yesterday morning, and here I have you asking me to look for a young man who has gone missing the very next day."

Forbish kept his mouth carefully shut.

"I'm not one to believe in coincidence, Mister Forbish, but the occurrence could have happened by chance, so I'll ask you to give me a description of this young man, and we'll see if it matches the one of my previous employer."

"Yes, sir. He was not so tall as me, maybe a hand shorter. Thin, though not what you'd call skinny. More like wiry, I guess you'd say. He had sandy hair, fair skin, though he'd been out in the sun and was a bit tan, and his eyes were a very light color, almost like fresh-cut oak." He shrugged, wondering what else to add. "He wore a simple homespun tunic of blue, the last I saw him, and trousers of brown. He never wore shoes."

"I see." Hensen appeared to lapse into silence for a long, uncomfortable time during which Forbish kept his eyes down. He knew it wouldn't be healthy to attempt to pressure the man, but after a while his gaze drifted up. Hensen was staring right at him, but his eyes were glazed over as if he were staring at a distant scene. Forbish looked back down at the table, sipped his water and concentrated on the endless spirals of grain in its surface, trying to ignore the man's relentless stare. Finally, after minutes of discomfort, Hensen reached inside his cloak and retrieved a roll of parchment. He handed it to Forbish and smiled thinly.

"Please have a look at that and tell me if this is the young man you seek."

Forbish's fingers trembled as they untied the thin ribbon that bound the parchment. His thoughts whirled in chaotic circles. Why would this man have a portrait of Lad? Who had been searching for him? Why was Hensen being so cagey? He unrolled the parchment and found himself staring into features that were all too familiar.

"That's his very image, sir."

"I thought so." Hensen took the parchment back and made it vanish into his cloak. He then took another, deeper drink from his glass and stood up from the table.

"I'm sorry, Mister Forbish, but I can't help you recover your friend."

"Why not?" Forbish started to rise, but sat back down at the man's gesture. "I'm willing to pay you!"

"Money's not the issue. I know precisely who took your friend from you, and let me assure you, no amount of money could induce me to attempt to recover him." He fished two gold coins from his pocket and placed them on the table. "Have a drink on me, Mister Forbish. Have several. But forget your young friend. He's either dead or so far beyond your reach that he may as well be."

With that, the man and his two bodyguards turned and left Forbish to sit and stare at the gold on the table. A day's profits lay there for the taking, but he would rather have touched a viper. He sat and stared a long time, thinking of the words that Hensen had used, thinking of Lad, and thinking of his daughter.

"Would you like anything else, sir?"

The barmaid's return jolted him out of his reverie. Forbish looked up at her and shook his head, then worked his way out from the narrow booth.

"No, that'll be all, thank you." He looked once more at the money on the table. "You can keep that."

He left the gambling house and walked slowly back to the *Tap and Kettle*, wondering all the while what he was going to tell Wiggen.

Chapter XVIII

Captain Norwood had seen a lot of murders. He'd seen everything from professional assassinations to crimes of passion, insanity-driven mutilations to careful poisonings that had taken weeks to kill. After thirty years in the duke's Royal Guard, he'd thought he'd seen it all.

"Guess I thought wrong," he said to himself as he stepped past the hysterical Count Dovek into the man's bedchamber. He closed the door carefully, stifling the wailing gibberish that was coming from the count. The man might be able to give an accurate account later, but not now. He surveyed the room at a glance and his lip curled back involuntarily.

"Good morning Captain," one of his sergeants said, turning from his work to salute. Two other guardsmen who were helping the sergeant examine the crime scene saluted and returned to their work.

"What's good about it, Sergeant Tamir?" Norwood growled, letting his gaze smolder into the man for a moment before moving on.

"My da always used to say that any morning you could get out of bed was a good morning, so..." He nodded to the bed. "Ain't exactly her best morning now, is it, sir?"

"No, it's not, Sergeant." He cringed as the wailing from beyond the door rose in pitch then subsided again. "The count's a complete wreck. We won't get anything out of him today."

"Aye, sir. I can't say as I blame him, though. Said he woke up before first light wondering why his wife was so cold. Did what any husband might, I guess, trying to warm her. He didn't know until he opened his eyes."

"Damn," Norwood muttered. They'd be lucky if the man *ever* recovered.

He stepped up to the bed and looked down at the young countess. She was a beautiful woman, her beauty now marred by the stiletto thrust through her eye. Her head was wreathed in crimson; her blond hair and the silken pillow to which she was pinned were both saturated with blood. There was only a slight look of surprise on her features, and the tip of the blade had actually passed through the lid of her eye. She'd been killed in her sleep. Death had been instantaneous.

"Like a butterfly pinned in a case," the captain murmured, clenching his jaw against his tumultuous thoughts.

Back to work! he thought venomously, forcing himself to examine the knife. The early-morning sun shone through the window at a sharp angle, illuminating the scene all too clearly. The blade was well-made—double-edged and narrow, meant for stabbing, its crosspiece short and dark. He couldn't see the hilt because a ribbon-bound roll of parchment had been slipped over it. The parchment wasn't wrinkled, so it had been put there after the woman was dead. What really had the captain scratching his chin, however, was not the fact that the count's wife had been stabbed through the brain while the count slept next to her, nor the note left behind. He positioned himself so that his face was aligned with that of the dead woman and read the single word that had been written upon her forehead in her own blood.

"What the—? 'Sorry'? That's odd."

"What's that, Captain?" The sergeant paused in his inspection of the window and moved up beside his commander. "Oh, that. Yeah, that's a real brain tease, ain't it?"

"The dagger, the note, or the apology?"

"I was thinkin' you meant the blood on her forehead, sir. I've seen the like before, usually from some crazy sap who don't know what he's doin'. But this job's all pro. This was a pressure hit or I'm a doxy, but I never seen a professional apologize."

"I couldn't agree more, Sergeant." Captain Norwood stood straight, his blunt nails raking at his gray stubble again, reminding him that he'd been in too much of a hurry to shave this morning. "Well, I guess we should see what else this apologetic assassin has to say besides 'Sorry,' hadn't we?"

"Aye, sir," Tamir agreed as his commander carefully slipped the rolled parchment off of the dagger's hilt, untied the ribbon and read it.

"Damn." It was a list of names and dates. Every single one of them was a relative or loved one of Count Dovek. They all lived in Twailin, and all the dates save one were in the future. The top name was that of the count's late wife, and there was a single line through it, and yesterday's date. "You hit that one on the head, Sergeant. Pressure. But from whom, and to do what?"

"Well, my guess would be to use his influence with the duke, but to what end, beats me all to hell." He looked at the distinguished list of names. "Pretty cocky to put dates there. They can't be stupid enough to follow through with that schedule. We'll be watchin'."

"Damn right we'll be watching them. The next is his son the viscount, and the date is only two days away."

"Do you think we should show it to the count?"

"He'd go catatonic, Sergeant." He pocketed the scroll and glanced around the room. "Okay, let's have the rest of the details. What have you got?"

"Well, sir, you're not going to believe this, but the assassin came in through that window there. There's no evidence that he used a rope or hook, or came down from the roof. The stonework's sound and tightly fit, so I don't see how anyone could climb up. Magic maybe. He opened the window with a wire hook; you can see where the metal's scratched, but there's one thing I don't get."

"What's that, Sergeant?"

"There's blood on the hinges. Just the ones on the left side there, see?"

"Yeah." The captain looked closely at the hinges. "Take a sample of that and give it to his lordship's mage. I want to know if it's hers," he indicated the deceased countess with a nod, "or someone else's."

"Yes, sir."

"I want two guards on Count Dovek every minute of every day until I say to stop. Is that clear, Sergeant?"

"Crystal, sir."

"I'm also putting you in charge of the duty roster for this. I'll have to have some men pulling double shifts, but we've got to make sure this stops here. Understood?"

"Yes, sir."

"Make sure this room is examined carefully. I don't want to miss anything on this one." He continued speaking as he moved toward the door. "I'll be in my office, working out a watch schedule for the duke's court and wondering where I'm going to get enough men to watch all these people." He patted the rolled parchment in his belt and left the sergeant to his work.

In the outer chamber, the scene had devolved into one of mildly suppressed chaos; the count was red-faced and hysterical, and a woman Norwood recognized as the count's younger sister was holding his arm, trying to calm him. *There's number three on the list*, he thought. Two additional guards were at the door to the hall holding several more royals at bay. Concerned neighbors, friends, and relatives were already descending to offer support and condolences, as well as to make sure there wasn't some inheritance or title transfer they were missing out on, no doubt.

I wonder how many of them are on the list? he wondered before pushing his way through the crowd.

"Wiggen?"

Forbish tapped on his daughter's door timidly. The usual hour of her rising had passed, but he had let her sleep late on purpose. There were only two guests staying at the inn, and Josie was now back at work and could handle the morning chores easily enough. Besides, what he had to tell Wiggen would be hard, and he was putting it off as long as he could. He knew he had to tell her what he'd found out the night before, but *how*? How does a father tell his only daughter, a daughter who had been through so much already, that the young man she loved was dead?

"Wiggen?" he called softly, cracking the door and peering into her room. She rustled beneath the blankets of her bed, hair tousled, eyes blinking away sleep as they peeked over the thick down comforter.

"What? Oh!" She noticed the angle of the sun coming through her window and instantly sat up. "I'm sorry, Father. I just didn't wake up, I guess. Why didn't you wake me?

"Because I wanted to let you sleep, Wiggen." He entered the room and shut the door quietly behind him. "I've got something to tell you, honey, and I don't know where to start." He stood there wringing his hands, not knowing whether he should just blurt it out, or if there was some way he could break the news more gently.

"It's about Lad, isn't it?" Her voice was cold, her hands clenched white on the blankets.

"Yes. It's about Lad." He stepped over to the bed and sat at the foot, his broad hand covering hers on the blanket. "The man I talked to last night said he knew who had taken him."

"*Who*?" Wiggen asked, eyes wide.

"He wouldn't tell me. Not for any amount of money."

"What? Why not? Why wouldn't he?"

"He was afraid, Wiggen." Forbish hadn't really realized that fact until he said it. Hensen was terrified of whoever had taken Lad, and that was enough to terrify Forbish. "He's a very powerful man, powerful in ways that have nothing to do with law or royalty. The people he works for have their fingers in every gambling hall, tavern, brothel and shipping business in the city, and they don't scare easy."

"So why was he scared, if he is so powerful?"

"Because there are people who are even more powerful, more ruthless..." Forbish sighed and gripped his daughter's hand. "He had a portrait of Lad, Wiggen. This other bunch of...of people were looking for him, and they were paying a lot of people to help them look."

"And they found him, didn't they?" Her voice quivered, shaking with the horror of what he was telling her, but he couldn't lie to her. She had to know the truth.

"Yes, Wiggen. They found him, and they took him."

"But he knows! This man knows who it was!" she snapped accusatively. "We can tell the constables, and they can *make* him tell who took Lad. They can get him back!"

"No, Wiggen. We can't tell anyone what we think happened to Lad, and I'll tell you exactly why."

"But Father, I—"

"I know, Wiggen, but listen. Just listen." He took another deep breath. "The people who took Lad are killers. Maybe they're the same ones who threaten us, maybe not. I don't know, but I *do* know that they won't hesitate for a moment to kill anyone and everyone who tries to interfere with them. They killed Tam because he went to the authorities, and they hurt you because I was going to go to the duke's Guard. If we tell anyone about Lad, neither of us will live another day."

"But what about Lad?" Tears hovered in the crescents of her eyes, held back by sheer will. She wouldn't cry for him; he could see her holding it back. Crying would be admitting he was gone.

"I don't know, Wiggen." Forbish shook his head in sorrow. He knew Lad was as good as dead, but maybe there was a chance he could get away from these murderers. "Lad's an amazing young man, honey. We know he was made to be a killer, and it's my bet that they plan to use him for that. But they never intended him to get away from his master. He's not as blind as they wanted him to be. He won't do their killing for them. If he has a chance, he'll get away from them."

"Or they'll kill him." Her lip trembled with the words, her voice cracking with pain.

"They might if they can't control him, which is one more reason we have to stay quiet about all this. If they find out Lad cares about you, they'll use you to get to him."

"But what do we do?" One tear escaped, but she wiped it away before it could make its track halfway down her scarred cheek. "We *can't* just leave him!"

"We can't do anything, Wiggen. I'm sorry." She tore her hand out of his grasp and rolled over, shutting him out. Her breath was deep and ragged, but still she would not cry. Still, she wouldn't let him go. "I'm sorry."

Mya descended the stairs from the Grandfather's private rooms in a rush, her stomach knotting on her breakfast and her jaw clenched so tightly that her head pounded with her racing pulse. This was *not* what she had hoped it would be, that much was certain. The boy had performed flawlessly, eliminating both targets he'd been told to kill the night before just as easily as the one the first night, but so far her job had been nothing more than giving instructions that the Grandfather had worked out to the most minute detail months ago. She had done no reconnaissance, no investigation, no tracking...no *hunting* at all. She should have known that the intended targets had been well researched ahead of time; he'd been planning this for *years*. Now she was nothing but a babysitter.

See that the boy eats! she thought venomously. *See that his clothes are cleaned! See that he continues his exercises! See that he understands the instructions!* She turned a corner to the cellar stair and almost bowled over the guard who was posted there. He moved out of her way without a word, and she wrenched the door open and started down.

"Next it'll be, 'See that the boy wipes his *ass* properly!'" she growled under her breath as the door slammed.

She strode through the sparring room, studiously ignoring the two swordmasters from the Mercenaries Guild waiting patiently for their morning bout with the Grandfather. He sparred every morning, she'd come to learn, usually with the best-trained professionals the martial guilds could offer. He paid handsomely for the service, and even more handsomely for services from other guilds.

Mya shuddered with that thought, slamming the next door

behind her and descending the stairs into the Grandfather's interrogation chamber.

"More like torture chamber," she said to herself, slowing her pace and unlocking the door. She pushed it open carefully, though she didn't know why she was showing such trepidation. Lad sat upon the same stone slab where she'd seen him bound and unconscious less than two days before. The restraints had been removed; it was now his bed. He sat placidly, legs folded, hands on his knees, his palms up and open. His eyes were closed.

Meditation, she thought, descending the few steps to the floor and wondering why anyone would teach a weapon to meditate. *Might as well teach a sword to play three-card mango!*

"I've got your instructions for tonight, Lad," she stated flatly, stopping a stride in front of him. She noticed that the silk pants and shirt she'd sent down were sitting folded next to him, clean and ready to be put on. He wore only a short breechcloth, and his skin shone with the sheen of sweat.

He didn't respond to her at all, even to the extent of opening his eyes. She tried a more direct approach. "You've been exercising?"

He didn't even twitch.

Mya's temper, left over from her less-than-satisfying breakfast with her master, suddenly burst into a rage. How *dare* this slave boy ignore her. She was a professional, a journeyman in the guild.

"Wake up!" she shouted, but there was no more response than before. This was intolerable. "Wake UP!" Her open palm lashed across his face with a report like the crack of a coachman's whip.

Lad sat perfectly still as her handprint flushed red on his cheek and slowly faded.

Mya's anger smoldered like a bed of coals. He'd been ordered to follow her commands, and now he was ignoring her. He was supposedly controlled by magic—she had seen the effect the Grandfather's words had on him—but if he'd been ordered to obey her, why wouldn't he?

"You've been ordered to obey me, Lad," she said dangerously, her hand on her dagger. "Now, open your eyes and get off that table."

She jumped back as his eyes suddenly snapped open and he vaulted off the table to stand perfectly still before her. His face still bore that same placid expression, as if he were half-asleep.

"You were awake the whole time," she snapped accusatively. "You heard every word I said!"

He remained perfectly still, his eyes not even tracking her. She was beginning to wonder if his mind had fled, or if she were being goaded. *Yes, that must be it!* she realized, letting her anger ebb. *He's trying to goad me into killing him! He doesn't want to be a slave, and he knows the only way he'll ever be free is to die.* She stood there, amazed by his stoicism.

"Why didn't you respond to me earlier? Answer me."

"You didn't say or do anything that required my response," he stated flatly, his eyes remaining fixed to a point just over her left shoulder.

"You didn't wake up when I ordered you to. How do you figure that didn't 'require your response?'"

"I didn't respond because your order couldn't be followed."

"What? What do you mean?"

"I wasn't asleep, so I couldn't wake up."

"Hmph!" She glared at him, disgusted with his childish taunt. "But you knew I wanted you to answer me. You were just being insolent." He remained silent, a statue hewn from flesh. "You were baiting me, admit it."

"I don't know what you mean by 'baiting'." His eyes shifted slightly toward her, and then back. "I can't answer your question."

"You're still doing it. You're trying to make me angry. I know you have enough free will to do as you wish within the bounds of your orders, Lad." She smiled, knowing she was right in her surmise. "You hope to make me angry enough to kill you. Isn't that right?"

"Yes."

"Well, it's not going to work. Now sit down. We've got a lot to cover before tonight, so pay attention. You have two targets to eliminate before morning."

"You mean two people to kill, don't you?" He sat on the slab, legs folded, staring at her with those strange eyes of his.

"Yes, that's exactly what I mean. Now pay attention." She unrolled the scroll from her belt. "The first is the nephew of Duke Mir himself. He is of middle age and is not in line for the duke's title, which is probably why he and the duke are so close. His estate is well guarded, and he's a capable fighter. He has a wife and two children, and a mistress he keeps in a flat in Westmarket. That's where he'll be tonight."

"What's his name?

"What? Why would you want to know that?"

"I want to know the people I kill."

"Why?"

"Because not knowing them, not caring about them, would be evil. I'm not evil."

He said the last with such calm assurance that it took Mya off guard. She'd never really thought of herself as evil, but she supposed that her profession couldn't really be called good or honorable. But she'd also grown up fighting everything and everyone around her just to survive; she had seen real evil, and snuffing out the lives of a few fat nobles in their sleep didn't hold a candle in comparison.

"His name is Treyland Vossek Mir. Happy?"

"No, Mya. I'm not happy." He offered nothing else: no explanation, no thanks, and no feeling.

"Fine, then." She laid the map of Westmarket flat on the slab beside him and indicated a building with her fingertip. "This is where the mistress lives. He usually takes her to one of the eating establishments nearby. They eat, share a bottle of wine, and go back to her place for sex."

"What's that?"

"What's what?"

"Secks," he said, mispronouncing the word slightly.

"You're joking."

He looked at her with eyes that seemed to her incapable of joking.

"I'm not. I don't know the word."

"Well, I'm not going to explain it to you." She changed maps in a rush, pointing out the woman's flat in the corner of the building. "She lives above a clothier. They sleep after, and that's the best time to strike. Just wait for the sound of their breathing to change, then kill him." She handed over the dagger he was to use. It was identical to the ones he'd used the night before.

"Same technique," she said, handing over a rolled parchment, "different message."

He placed the dagger and the scroll on his clothing, his face impassive.

"As for the rest of it, your orders are the same as the two last night. Don't be seen, don't kill anyone you don't have to, and don't leave any clues that might implicate the Assassins Guild."

"What about the woman?"

"Don't kill her unless she sees you well enough to recognize you." She thought his face might have twitched slightly at that, and wondered why.

"Choose the way in that's the quietest and least likely to get you spotted."

"What about guards?" he asked, drawing a suspicious glance from her.

"This is a woman's flat in a working quarter of the city, Lad. There aren't any guards."

"Okay."

"Any other questions? We've got one more to go over."

"Yes." His eyes left the map and drew hers like a magnet. "Will you help me kill the Grandfather?"

She felt the blood leave her face as she stumbled back a step. Would she *what?* She set her jaw and glared at him. He was trying to make her angry again.

"I told you to stop trying to goad me!"

"I'm not."

"Then you're stupid, Lad," she scoffed, retrieving another parchment from her belt. "You can't *seriously* expect me to help you assassinate the Grandfather. Now pay attention. This is your second target." She pinned the parchment flat for him to see.

"I don't expect you to help me, Mya," he said, his attention on the map, "but you've done many other things that I haven't expected. I couldn't know if you'd help me or not, unless I asked."

"Well, now you know. Don't ever ask me that again!"

He didn't respond, his attention on the map as she had ordered. The subject had been dropped—forgotten, she hoped. If the Grandfather even caught a hint that Lad was trying to persuade her to kill her master, her life wouldn't be worth spit.

CHAPTER XIX

You there!" Captain Norwood advanced on the hapless corporal, pinning him to the side of the carriage with a fist pressed to the man's chest. "What's your explanation for this? Viscount Dovek dead and not so much as a decent description of the assassin? Were all four of you sleeping?"

"No, sir!" The man was sweating despite the cool night air, and with good reason. The captain would have him busted to private and cleaning sewer pipes in The Sprawls by morning if he found out any of the squad had been negligent in their duty.

"Then explain to me how the one man the four of you were told to protect is dead, while none of you have so much as a scratch!"

"It happened too fast, sir!" the poor man said, obviously shaken. "We were all on watch, three of us on the outside of the carriage and Mori inside, sittin' right across from the viscount. One second we were rumblin' along Wyvern Street, then we rounded the corner onto East Run, and out of nowhere this thin shape comes leapin' out of the shadows and right through the carriage window without even touching the casement. By the time Mori even got his dagger out, the deed was done and the culprit out the other side window! Mori says he never seen nobody move that fast! All he saw was a blur of black."

"The assassin came through *that* window?" the captain asked skeptically, inspecting the small square portal in the carriage's door. It was no more than twice the width of his outstretched hand. "And the carriage was moving?"

"Yes, sir! Not fast, but we were movin' along at a jog, I'd say."

"Have you been chewing lotus, Corporal? Nobody could get through that window at a run!"

"I wouldn't have thought so either, sir, but that's what happened. Truth be told, Clem was the only one to see the culprit comin'. Didn't see nothin' but a black shape, thin, maybe an elf. The feller just took three runnin' steps from where he was hidin' and dove right through. The carriage lurched when he hit the far wall inside, but by the time anyone could even so much as yell, he was out the other side and the viscount was—well, like you see him, sir."

"Blast!" The captain released the man and wrenched open the door of the carriage. The young viscount sat there, his head pinned to the back of the carriage seat by a long stiletto, a tightly rolled note secured to the hilt with a black ribbon. "I can't believe this! And the bastard *told* us!"

"Sir?" The corporal's confused shock begged for an explanation. Norwood wasn't usually inclined to offer information to his guardsmen, but the man had been through a lot and deserved something.

"Three days ago the count's wife was murdered in their bed while he slept next to her. Same method. Same note. The assassin is telling us who's next and when. There have been four more killings between then and now, two each night, and different notes and dates with each telling when the next person in that particular noble family will be killed. Two barons, another count, and the duke himself have lost family members. Now the assassin's making good his promises, and it looks like there's nothing we can do to stop him."

"Holy gods! Er... sir, I mean..." The corporal's stammering devolved into silence as the captain looked around the carriage, searching for clues. There was nothing—nothing but a dead viscount, the dagger, and the note.

"Well, I guess he didn't have *time* to apologize for this one,"

Norwood muttered to himself, raking his stubble of beard with his blunt nails.

"Apologize, sir?" The corporal looked even more baffled.

"Yes, Corporal, apologize is what I said!" He reached into the carriage and jerked the dagger free. The young man's corpse slumped forward. "The other five victims had the word 'Sorry' written on their foreheads in their own blood. He was evidently in too big a hurry this time."

The corporal remained wisely silent as Norwood removed the note from the dagger's hilt. The parchment was crumpled, meaning it had been bound to the hilt before the knife was thrust through the viscount's eye. He handed the dagger to the corporal, who took it like a man might handle a live scorpion. The note was predictable, if not informative.

"Cocky bastard!" The note was identical to the one they'd found with Count Dovek's wife, except for the single line through the viscount's name. The count's sister was next on the list, and the date was two days away. "Well, we are *not* going to take any chances on this one! Corporal, I want you and your men to take charge of Count Dovek's younger sister, Patrice. She is to be protected. Do you understand?"

"Yes, sir!" The man's face told the captain that he wasn't looking forward to the assignment.

"I'm putting you on this job, Corporal, because you understand what we're dealing with here. If an assassin can kill his target inside a moving carriage with four armed guards watching, and still get away without a scratch or even a decent description, we need to step up our security."

"Yes, sir!" The man sounded a little more steady, determination taking the place of stark fear.

"Good. I want you to draw three more guards from the roster, and give two of them crossbows. Explain to the count's sister that she'll be under house arrest for her own protection until three days hence."

"She's not going to like it, sir."

"I think she might like a dagger through the eye a little less."

"Should I tell her that?"

"If she makes trouble, yes. Just keep her alive, Corporal. We'll handle the political consequences later."

"Yes, sir."

"Oh, and send word to Sergeant Tamir to step up security on the other targets. He's coordinating the duty roster, so he'll have to make some changes."

"Yes, sir."

The corporal turned and left the captain to inspect the crime scene. There wasn't much to inspect. He took another look at the carriage window and shook his head in amazement; it was nowhere near as wide as his shoulders. Whoever this assassin was, his skills were truly astounding.

"This reeks of magic like a wizard's old underwear," he growled, wondering how many more would die before they got lucky and put an end to this murdering scum.

"What is it?" Duke Mir looked up from his desk at the guard who had just knocked on his office door. The man looked decidedly ill.

"It's Count Dovek, milord. He requests an audience."

Duke Mir cringed. He'd been expecting this. The man had lost his wife and now his son, in a span of three days. The duke's own nephew had fallen to the same assassin, and now all the nobles were running scared. Pressure was being applied—some subtle, some not so subtle.

"Show him in." The duke closed his ledger and steeled his nerves.

"Very well, milord." The guard closed the door, and it reopened a moment later. Duke Mir barely recognized the man who shambled in behind the guard.

"Dovek, my good count!" He was out of his chair and around the desk before he knew what he was doing. He offered first his hand, then a warm embrace to the wreck of a man. Dovek had never been very strong; his title was inherited for the fourth generation. He wasn't military, and wasn't used to violence or death. Mir had lost loved ones to violence before. He knew how to handle the pain, knew that there would be an end to it eventually. "Hold fast, man. We'll make them pay for this, I promise you!"

"Can you, milord?" the man asked, stifling a sob and breaking the embrace to stare imploringly into his lord's eyes. "That devil isn't mortal. He's a black wraith. The guardsmen who came to look after Patrice told her. They *saw* it!"

"Calm yourself, Dovek. Here." The Duke drew him away from the door to a small nook in the corner of the office. From a cupboard he produced a bottle and two glasses. "This will calm your nerves." He poured two fingers of good brandy into each glass and pressed one into the count's trembling hands. They both took a steadying drink.

"Now, what's this the guards said?"

"The ones who were watching over my son. They said the one who killed him couldn't have been human. He was all black, and he came right through the carriage's window! They say he was a wraith!"

"Now, Dovek, they would say that just to make their own failure seem less. Wraiths don't use daggers, and they certainly don't leave threatening notes."

"But the guards said—"

"The guards don't *know*, Dovek! Come here." He virtually dragged the other man over to his desk, opened a drawer and pulled out several sheets of parchment. "These are not from some *wraith*, my friend. They're from someone who is trying to manipulate me, both directly—by killing my nephew and threatening to kill the rest of my family, one by one, unless I do as they say—and indirectly, through threatening those in my court. I'll wager you've gotten several of these the last few days."

"Well, yes, I did get some notes that were unusual, but I didn't think they had anything to do with this."

The count's voice had changed, Mir realized. He'd made a career out of reading people's intentions and knew that Dovek was not wholly ignorant in this.

"I mean, people send me notes all the time asking for favors, or asking me to ask you for some favor. How do you know these are from the assassin?"

"I do have *some* resources, Dovek," he said with a smile, keeping his own tone even. "Master Woefler is very adept at discerning things. The ink on the notes found on my nephew and your wife is the same as the ink on these notes, *exactly* the same, as is the parchment they're written on. Just looking at them side by side, I could tell you that the hand is the same. And there's this." He retrieved a small clear vial half full of a dark granular material. "This is blood, my friend, the culprit's blood. He's human, male, and no more than twenty years old, by Woefler's reckoning. Someone is pressuring me, and they're using the threat of killing everyone we care about to exert that pressure. It's all about money, Dovek. They want me to relax the trade restrictions with Morrgrey, the tariffs on barge traffic. It's that simple."

"My Lord! I never thought..." The count's face was even paler than when he'd come in.

"I've got my very best man on this, Dovek. Captain Norwood has more experience hunting down scum like this than any man I know. He'll put an end to it, I promise you."

"But the rest of the court, milord. They're starting to talk." He glanced at the ever-present guards and lowered his voice. "They say if the murders don't stop, they'll force a vote of no-confidence on you. They'll ask the emperor to replace you."

"Oh, they *will*?" Duke Mir squared his shoulders and clenched his jaw to curb his temper. "Tell them this, then; if we accede to these threats, we will forever be under the thumb of these murderers. I will *not* be dictated to by those who use murder and fear to dominate others! If my *court* demands that I do, they will *also* find that I am rather noncompliant when threatened."

"Yes, milord," the count said with a stiff bow.

"They killed my nephew, Dovek," he growled, his eyes narrowing to slits that would have shot arrows if they could have. "I bounced that boy on my knee thirty-five years ago. I'll *not* give in. Not now, and not if every noble at court comes crying to my door."

"Milord! I didn't come to—"

"I know, Dovek. I know," he said, knowing that that was *exactly* why Dovek had come calling. He patted the man on the shoulder and raised his glass. "To finding the murdering scum who did this, and seeing their heads roll for what they've done."

The two men drank.

"Now, please, leave me. I've got so much work stacked up here that I'll never get out of this damned office."

The count bowed and left, and Duke Mir sat at his desk and sighed. He then drafted a note to his captain of the Royal Guard. The first part of the message was quite heated, and concerned the flapping mouths of his guardsmen. The second related the disturbing trend among the nobility. Count Dovek was cracking under the pressure, or had already cracked. He and others like him would have to be watched closely, before they did something stupid.

✳ ❄ ✳

Forbish nudged the kitchen door aside with his ample stomach and pushed through, placing a heavy bag of flour on the counter and settling another bag of rice beside it. His face was red from the exertion, and his back was in flames.

"You all right, Father?"

"Oh, fine, dear. Just my back, is all." He straightened himself with several audible pops and forced a smile. "Nothing a night's sleep won't cure."

"Do you want me to help?" Wiggen moved from behind the counter where she'd been chopping vegetables for the evening stew. "I can lift one end."

"Thank you, Wiggen. I asked that worthless boy the miller has delivering his goods, but he said some nonsense about having to finish his rounds." He lifted one end of the bag of rice while Wiggen lifted the other, and together they moved it into the storeroom. "He said the whole city's stirred up like a nest of chatter vipers. Seems some rich noble got killed in his sleep, and everybody's frettin' like they're next."

"I've heard more than that, Father," she said as they went back through the taproom to fetch the bag of flour. "I've heard that six have been killed in the last four days." She stopped when they got back to the counter, pinning Forbish with her eyes. "It's Lad, isn't it?"

"I think so," he said, trying to keep his voice steady. Wiggen had been close to the edge for days; any little thing sent her into tears. "I think they've found out a way to make him do what they want."

"You mean they're making him kill for them." She took the bag of flour from him and flung it over her shoulder. "It makes me *sick* to think about it!"

"Here, Wiggen! Let me help. You're going to hurt yourself!"

"I'm fine, father," she said, "and I'm stronger than you think I am!" She strode through the taproom and heaved the bag onto the shelf with an ease that surprised him, and when she turned back to him he could see the anger in her. He'd *never* seen her like this.

"Now, Wiggen. Just calm down."

"No, father, I *won't* calm down! They're making him into a *murderer*, and it's not right!"

"No, it's not right, but there's nothing we can do about it." He saw the blind determination in her eyes, determination driven by love, which was equally blind. "If we get involved, they'll come after us."

"I'd be *dead* if it weren't for Lad, Father. Worse than dead! You *know* what Urik and his goons were planning to do to me. Right here! In this room! They would have raped me and then killed me right in front of you. If they come for me now, after having threatened that, how much worse could they hurt me?"

"Wiggen, I—"

"I know. You don't want to lose me. Well, we didn't want to lose Tam either, and you didn't want to lose Mama, but they're gone. But we didn't lose them, Father. They were *taken* from us! Taken by the same murdering filth who are making Lad into one of them."

The tears were flowing now, but they weren't tears of fear, sorrow, or loss; they were tears of righteous anger. Forbish, to his surprise, was quickly learning that his daughter was no longer a little girl who needed his protection; she was a strong-willed young woman, and maybe...maybe she was right.

"What do you want to do, Wiggen?"

"I don't know." She bit her lip and wiped the tears away with her sleeve. "I don't think we can just walk into the constable's office and say 'By the way, we know who's killing all those people,' but I feel like we should do something."

"Telling them we know Lad won't do anyone any good," he agreed. "It'd just put us in danger and make the constables think we had something to do with it. What we need to find out is who's controlling him. Who took him."

"Your friend, the one you spoke with the other night. You said he knew, but wouldn't tell you."

"Well, he's not really a friend, Wiggen. I've only met him that one time. He's a powerful man, and didn't want any part of it. Too much to lose, probably."

"What about that other man, the one who owns the gambling hall?"

"Toby? I don't know if he could help us, but I can ask."

"And if he can't help us?"

"Well, if he can't help us, maybe he knows someone who can."

"Come in, Mya." The Grandfather finished penning the note and set it aside as she entered his private rooms. She'd been here before, but was still in awe of the expensive appointments—the rug she was standing on had probably cost more gold than she would make in a lifetime. "I've got some questions for you, and some more instructions."

"Yes, Grandfather." She stood in front of the desk with her hands folded behind her back.

"My first question is regarding some of the rumors I've been hearing about the killings that have been taking place up on the hill." He looked at her and cocked an eyebrow.

"I have heard many rumors about the killings, Grandfather."

She didn't know what game he was playing, but it was a safe bet that this was something serious. "All of them are as inaccurate as they are outrageous."

"All of them?" His sharp gaze told her that at least one of the rumors had some validity to it.

"All of the rumors I've heard, yes, Grandfather. There may be some that I haven't heard, but I haven't been actively listening." She paused for a breath, and when he didn't interrupt, she said, "I could look into the matter if you wish."

"I will tell you the rumor, and you will tell me if there's any truth to it."

"Yes, Grandfather."

"There's been a rumor that the perpetrator of these killings has left a certain message upon his victims."

"If you mean the notes, I don't think that's what I would call a rumor." She let a smile crease her lips. "But that's not what you mean, is it?"

"No. I mean that our young apprentice has been leaving his own calling card."

"He has?" Mya was honestly surprised. "He's been specifically told to leave nothing that can implicate you, Grandfather."

"Yes, I know." He smiled thinly at her. "But he's not been told to leave no trace whatsoever, and couldn't be told such, because he *has* been told to kill someone and leave a dagger and a note. What he *has* left behind, seemingly of his own volition, is an apology."

"An *apology?*" Mya's jaw dropped in astonishment. "I find that very hard to believe, Grandfather. He hasn't the wit to know what an apology is, let alone that he's doing something that might *require* an apology."

"Nevertheless," he continued, with a casual wave of his hand that told her to be quiet as effectively as a finger over pursed lips, "upon the foreheads of five of the six targets, he has left the word 'Sorry' written in their own blood."

"Sorry?" She endured his glare and clenched her jaw against her next thought. Apologizing now might be seen as being flippant, which could be lethal.

Chris A. Jackson

"My question is, where do you suppose he learned this?"

"My guess is that he learned it somewhere when he was on his own." She shrugged, knowing what his next command would be. "Maybe the inn where we found him."

"Well, it matters little. We must break him of this behavior. Please see to it."

"Yes, Grandfather." She turned on her heel, but he brought her back with a word.

"Mya?"

"Yes, Grandfather."

"I may also need your specific skills to look into one of our future targets."

"Which target, Grandfather?" She suppressed the heat of excitement that surged to her face; this was the first time he was actually asking her to do something she was trained to do. Until now, her title should have been 'Boy Keeper' instead of 'Hunter.'

"Count Dovek's sister Patrice is under heavy guard." He reached into a drawer of his desk and retrieved a thick roll of parchment. "She's being kept in the Dovek Estate under house arrest. There are at least five guards watching her throughout the day and night, even in her sleep." He handed the roll over to her. "I need to know where and when we should instruct the boy to kill her. You know the date, but any time during the day or night will do. Please bring your information to me so that we can make an intelligent decision together."

"Yes, Grandfather!"

"Also, there's one last item."

"Yes?"

"We must make sure that the boy understands that no one who sees him commit any of the killings may be allowed to survive."

"He's received this instruction, Grandfather, but I'll make sure he understands. Has there been some instance when you think he might have broken that order?"

"There were four guards watching Viscount Dovek when the boy killed him. By all accounts it happened so fast that no one got a good look at him, but they *did* see him. I don't understand how he could have *known* that none of them could identify him. He should have killed them as a precaution, but he didn't."

"I'll word my instructions carefully, Grandfather," she said, bowing shortly.

"See that you do. Our young apprentice may be actively seeking to thwart our instructions. Avoiding killing the guards, for instance."

"He'll understand and obey, Grandfather."

"Good. You may go."

She turned on her heel and left the chamber, wondering how such a creation as Lad could come up with the notion that he should apologize to the dead.

Chapter XX

Lad moved through the dance of death, his mind focused only partially on the intricate series of motions that he had performed and perfected every morning for more than four years. His first martial trainer, Master Xhang, had instructed him in the exercises; they could be modified to accompany many weapons and had been adapted to incorporate many styles of combat. Years of the exercises had honed him into the perfect killing weapon.

...step...sweep...strike...twist...kick...step...block...

He performed the series flawlessly, as always, but his heart wasn't in his work. The exercises no longer served to calm his mind and unify his thoughts with his body's actions. They only served to remind him of what he was. The dance of death was just that, a means to make him a better killer, a more efficient weapon to be wielded by an evil hand.

...step...turn...kick...block...thrust...twist...turn...

He had grown uncomfortable with this morning ritual, despite its familiarity. Only in meditation could he now find peace, but he had been ordered to perform his exercises. He couldn't disobey.

...lunge...strike...step...sweep...strike...block...turn...

He heard her coming.

She was his only hope, his only glimmer of light in the sea of evil that had swept him into its ebb and flow. She didn't enjoy this life, that was clear; he could hear the strain in her voice and in the lies that she had repeated so many times that she believed them. He could see under that shell, that armor of bravado and caustic wit; beneath it, she was scared, and her fear was the only real weapon he had.

...step...turn...kick...kick...turn...sweep...

She was descending the steps, but not muttering to herself as she had many other times. Also, there was a swiftness, a power to her gait that was different. She opened the door and stood on the landing, frozen in place.

...turn...sweep...strike...block...kick...turn...

He could feel her watching him, but he continued his exercises. He wouldn't respond to her until she commanded him. This was just one of the ways he provoked her, one of the ways he peeled away the layers of armor to get a glimpse at the small, frightened woman beneath.

...sweep...step...kick...turn...

She descended the steps slowly, trying to be quiet, but he heard her heartbeat quicken. He had noticed that before: when he was exercising or when one of his taunts scored, her face would remain impassive, but her heart would betray her.

...kick...kick...turn...strike...block...

"These exercises. Where did you learn them?"

Her tone told him she knew he had detected her approach. Why was she still moving like she was trying to be quiet? There were still many things about Mya that Lad didn't understand.

...lunge...strike...twist...kick...

"Answer me."

"My first martial trainer." ...step...strike...turn... "His name was Xhang."

"What style is it? I don't recognize the form."

This conversational manner was unusual. Lad wondered what was going through the woman's mind as he continued the series. ...turn...sweep...strike... "It is many forms."

"How many?" she demanded in her usual tone; her armor was in place now.

"Six formal styles." ...kick...turn...sweep...strike... "And some of my own."

"*You* modified one of the formal styles of combat?" Her tone was accusative now. Lad wondered why.

"No." ...sweep...strike...step...stand... and ...bow. He turned and regarded her, the series finished. "I modified all six. Master Xhang's use of the styles together was flawed. I changed them to flow better."

"And who told you to do *that*?"

"No one. I did it myself."

"Why?"

"Because it was wrong, Mya." He cocked his head, wondering what she was getting at. "When you find something wrong, something you can change, you change it."

"Oh? You do?"

"Yes." He examined her more closely and noted a hint of sweat on her upper lip and a slight flush to her face. She was definitely worked up about something, but what? Perhaps some careful sparring would bring it out. "You know, for example, that what the Grandfather is doing is wrong. You could change it, but you don't, so *you* are wrong."

"I told you never to bring that up again, Lad."

"No, you told me never to ask you to help me kill the Grandfather again. I haven't."

"No, you haven't, but you brought up the subject, which is the same thing without *exactly* voicing the question."

"Yes."

"So, you do what you're told to do, and beyond that you can do what you *want*. Is that right?"

"Yes."

"No, it is *not* right, Lad." She took a step and glared right into his eyes. He could see the pulse pounding at her temples, hear her heart racing, and smell the sweet tang of her nervous sweat. "You do what you're *told* to do and nothing else. Is that clear?"

"It's clear, Mya, but it's not possible."

"Why not?" She was even more livid now.

"Because there are many things that you've never told me to do that I'm required to do to live." He shrugged. "Breathing, for example."

"Oh, that's ridiculous! You know what I mean, so just follow my orders."

"I do follow your orders, Mya."

"Yes, but you do other things that you know perfectly well are against my wishes."

"I do?" He knew what she was talking about now, where this conversation was going. He didn't know how she had discovered it, but she knew. And now she would order him to stop.

"Yes, you do! The little apologies you write in blood on your victims. It has to stop, Lad. It's foolish and it could get you caught."

"If you order me to stop, I must stop, but I don't see how it could cause me to be caught."

"There are things you don't know about, Lad. Things like sorcery. There are spells of divination that might lead a wizard to you using the messages you wrote."

He didn't respond; there was nothing to say. She may well be telling him the truth, but that didn't change anything. He'd continue leaving the messages unless he was specifically ordered not to. He could see the anger smoldering behind her eyes.

"Will you stop with these foolish apologies?"

"If you order me to stop, I must stop."

"Then I order you to stop. You'll leave no messages, apologies, or other written communication on or near your victims. Is that clear?"

"Yes."

"Good. Now tell me what possessed you to do such a thing?"

"Nothing possessed me, Mya. I wished to do it, and I did."

"But why? What purpose could apologizing to the dead serve?"

"I wasn't apologizing to the people I killed. I was apologizing to the ones who are their friends. They'll be hurt by the deaths we've caused, and I'm sorry for it."

"Who told you to be sorry for anything? I know your old master would never have put such a stupid idea in your head."

"No, it wasn't my master." He didn't like the direction this was taking.

"Then who *was* it?"

"It was someone I met later."

"Yes, I *know* that. Stop being evasive, Lad. Who told you that you should be sorry for hurting people? Answer me!"

"Wiggen."

"And who is Wiggen? Tell me, and be specific!"

"She's a young woman who is the daughter of the innkeeper, Forbish, who owns the *Tap and Kettle*. She's my friend." The words left his mouth despite his desire to hold them in; he couldn't even clench his teeth against the facts that could mean Wiggen's death.

"Your *friend*?"

"Yes, Mya, my friend. My best friend." He knew what would come next: the order to kill them, the order he had worried would come since the day he'd been taken by the Grandfather. He didn't feel true dread or fear, but there was a twisting discomfort within him not unlike the desperate hunger of starvation. Once again, Mya surprised him.

"Well, she must be pretty pathetic if she chose a witless boy like *you* for a friend." She took two scrolls from the case at her belt.

The discomfort within him fell away, leaving him swimming in a sea of relief, but curiosity soon replaced that. Why would Mya suddenly drop the subject when she knew he was at her mercy? This wasn't the tactic of a Hunter.

"These are your targets for tonight. The first is Baron Volkes' niece, the second is Count Tirian's son. Both are well guarded. And this brings up another of your transgressions, Lad. You were told to kill anyone who saw you and might be able to identify you. The guards in the viscount's coach saw you. You should have killed them."

"What's a transgression?"

"It's when you do what *you* want instead of what *I* want. From now on I want you to kill anyone who witnesses the murder, whether you *think* they could identify you or not." She rolled out the first scroll. "Now look at this closely."

"So it is *you* who wants these people dead, Mya?" His eyes were welded to the scroll by her order, but the rest of his mind was free to bait her. "I thought it was the Grandfather."

"Shut up and listen to me," she growled, her features darkening with rage. "You know I could order you to kill your friends, yet you taunt me. Do you think that's wise?"

He looked at her, unable to speak because of her first order, but compelled to speak by her question. The discomfort within him swelled, prickling his skin into gooseflesh as emotions he couldn't feel battered against the magical restraints like a butterfly in a glass jar; friendship, anger, resentment, fear, and desire all struggled impotently for supremacy over the magic.

"Answer me. Do you want me to order you to kill Wiggen?"

"No." He could feel the heat of the magic restraining his desire to lash out in one lightning blow and end the threat to Wiggen's life. Mya was less than half a step away; a simple snap kick to the throat would end it. He willed himself to attack, planned it in his mind, and told his muscles to do it, but the magic wouldn't let him. He stood there, quivering, unable to move.

"Then don't bring up the Grandfather again. His orders come through me. That's enough for you to understand." She reached out and took his chin in her hand, pulling his face close to hers. "Do you understand me?"

"I understand you, Mya." The desire to kill her was overwhelming. A simple thrust-twist and it would be over. The heat washed over him in a torrent, and he saw something in Mya's eyes that he knew was stark fear.

She stumbled back a step, her eyes wide, and her hand on her weapon.

"What the hell was that?"

He didn't respond. He wasn't ordered to respond.

"Answer me!" she raged, drawing her weapon and taking another step back. "What was that?"

"What was what?" he asked, the heat subsiding. "I don't know what you're asking, Mya."

"That light! Some kind of light though your skin! It was like writing. Like layers and layers of runes etched in green light."

"That was the magic."

"What magic?"

"The magic that makes me do as you say. The magic that makes me strong and fast. The magic that makes me not feel anger, or pain, or pity." He stared at her for a moment, and thought the rest of it was warranted. "The magic that keeps me from killing you."

"You must *really* hate me," she said, her words a quivering whisper.

"No, I don't hate you."

"But you would kill me. If you don't hate me, why then?"

"You're a threat to my friend. Killing you would end that threat."

"I have no interest in having you kill anyone, Lad. The people I order you to kill are those the Grandfather wishes dead. They mean nothing to me. Your friend is safe as long as you follow my orders and don't try any stupid little tricks like leaving messages. Okay?"

"Yes." Her statement in no way lessened the threat to Wiggen, but there was no other way to respond. Perhaps provoking Mya's anger wasn't the way to get her to help him. Maybe there was something else he could provoke.

"Good. Now examine those," she indicated the scrolls with a nod, "and plan the best way to kill the targets. That means the plan that's most likely to succeed without you being identified or killed. Is that clear?"

"Yes, Mya."

"Good." She turned to leave, but Lad stopped her with a word. "Mya?"

"If you ask me about the Grandfather again, Lad, you know what my next order will be." She spoke without turning, her warning smoldering like a coal.

"I wasn't going to ask you about the Grandfather."

"What then?"

"Do you have a friend?"

"Do I *what*?" She whirled and glared, clearly suspicious of another taunt.

"I want you to understand about Wiggen, why threatening her made me want to kill you. But I don't know if you have a friend like that."

"I have friends," she said, but he could hear the lie.

"Good. Then you understand." He was quite sure she didn't understand, but this strategy was safer for Wiggen. "I don't want to see her hurt."

"Then follow my orders." She turned and walked out, but Lad could hear her breathing change as she ascended the stairs beyond the door. Before she passed totally beyond his hearing, he thought that perhaps there was another sound. The other door squeaked open and slammed, and he could no longer hear her. He could have been mistaken about that sound. After all, Mya didn't have any reason to cry.

"Come in, Captain." Duke Mir waved his personal guards forward. "Guards, please wait outside. I'm sure I'm quite safe with the commander of the Royal Guard."

The two bodyguards bowed, turned, and left. Captain Norwood stood like a statue, hands clasped behind his back, eyes fixed on an invisible point somewhere across the room. He didn't doubt that the Duke was safe, but his own safety might be less secure.

"At your ease, Captain." Mir rounded the desk and headed for the cabinet to his left. "I didn't call you in to chastise you for not finding this assassin. I just want to get a few points across." He poured himself a drink without offering one to Norwood. "Points that I think you'll find interesting."

"Yes, milord?" Norwood relaxed his stance, but still stared at the same invisible point.

"First of all, these are notes from Master Woefler regarding the samples of blood, the notes, and the ribbon binding the notes to the daggers. You may read it at your leisure, but I'll tell you the gist of the report." He scooped up the scrolls and handed them to the captain. "The blood on the victims was from the victims. The blood on the hinges of Count Dovek's bedchamber window was from a young man whose name Master Woefler couldn't discern. The same hand penned all of the notes, and the same parchment and ink was used for each note. The person who wrote the apologies on five of the six victims was *not* the same person who wrote the notes."

"Master Woefler can divine a name from a spot of dried blood, milord?"

"In most instances, yes, if that person's name is reasonably well known. In this instance he could say only that the blood came from a lad of about seventeen years of age."

"Seventeen?" Norwood's eyes snapped from his invisible point to his lord's in a blink. "Just a boy?"

"So it would seem."

"And you trust the wizard's accuracy in this, milord?" The captain's tone stated blatantly that he did not.

"I do, Captain Norwood, and so should you." He took the drink he had poured himself in one shaky hand and downed it at a gulp. "Master Woefler is many things, but incompetent is not one of them."

"Yes, milord!" Norwood fixed his gaze once more upon infinity.

"The other point of which I wish you to be aware is this." Duke Mir scooped a scroll off his desk and flung it at the captain of his Royal Guard as if the piece of parchment offended him. "This is a copy of the letter that is, as we speak, on its way to the hand of the emperor."

The duke strode over to his cupboard and poured himself another brandy while Norwood read the letter. That it was drafted by a politically minded noble was obvious; it was full of half-truths, rhetoric, and gushing praise concerning Duke Mir's handling of the current crisis. What wasn't stated in plain language, but was evident to anyone with any experience at court, was that the duke's court was dissatisfied with the performance of their lord and wanted imperial aid or a replacement.

"With all due respect to the duke's court, milord," Norwood said, rolling the scroll and placing it deftly upon his lord's desk, "they're full of horseshit."

His tone was flatly neutral, his eyes once again fixed upon infinity.

"Really." Duke Mir sipped his brandy and regarded the man whose foremost job was to protect his life. He knew Norwood, had known him for years, and he trusted his judgment in most things political and *all* things military more than any member of his court. Which was exactly why he had called him in. "How do you come to this conclusion?"

"First, milord, His Majesty the emperor won't even see this note for a week. Then, if he makes a decision on how to handle it in less than three days, I'll eat my socks with mustard and call them smoked oysters." That, at least, earned a smirk from the duke, which was a good sign. "Third, if he decides to send aid, who will he send? It'll take another week to find someone competent, then another week or more to get them here."

"Almost a month."

"Yes, milord."

"And when that aid arrives?"

"Well, at the current rate, we ought to be nearly out of nobility by then, milord, so—"

"Including ME!"

The Duke slammed his glass down on the desk, spilling brandy over the papers. His eyes burned holes in the captain while Norwood silently cursed himself for his glib tongue.

"I do *NOT* take this situation lightly, Captain! One of the dead is my own nephew, a man I watched grow from a lad to a fine man with a family! Now he's dead, his wife a widow, and you're unable to catch the murdering filth that buried a dagger in his eye!"

A fine man with a family, killed right after he finished busily boffing his mistress, Norwood thought silently, eyes fixed, face impassive.

"I want a suspect, Captain," the duke growled through clenched teeth.

"Yes, milord."

"And I want some arrests! Even if they're trumped up!" He sat down stiffly, scowling at the mess the alcohol had made of his neatly stacked notes. "You must have informants who know someone who might be involved in this mess. Maybe some action, productive or not, will get these jackals off my back."

"Yes, milord." Norwood remained standing, staring into nothing. He hadn't been dismissed, and he'd stretched his insubordination just about as far as it would go today.

The duke glared at him for a while longer, then finally said, "That's all. Now get out."

"Milord." Norwood bowed and left, running through a mental list of people he could put pressure on to produce some likely suspects, real or not.

✳ ✸ ✳

The tiny barstool was as uncomfortable as Forbish remembered, but he sat down anyway. He even ordered an ale, knowing it wouldn't be to his taste. The ale arrived just ahead of the proprietor, who he'd come to see in the first place.

"Forbish! What are you doing here?" Toby finished polishing a mug and stacked it on the shelf behind the bar. "Master Hensen told you he couldn't help you, as plain as day. He won't change his mind on it."

"Don't expect him to," he said with a mighty shrug, sipping at the bitter ale. He didn't make a face, though it took some restraint. "Came to talk to you, my friend."

"When you say 'my friend' like that, I know you want something." The barkeep picked up another mug and began polishing with the same dirty rag. Forbish stopped wondering why the ale tasted funny.

"No, really. I just want to talk." He forced himself to sip again, just to help put Toby at ease. "I want to get some ideas about how to find my friend. Hensen won't do it for me, so maybe I'll hire someone else who will, but I can't just ask someone without having any ideas at all, can I?"

"No, I don't suppose you can." The barkeep finished and picked up another mug, eying its tarnish dubiously. "So what do you want to know?"

"Well, it struck me strange that a man like Hensen would refuse to help me in the first place. I offered to pay him, I mean." Forbish pushed two gold coins across the bar. The price of the ale was two coppers. "Why would a man like that turn down good coin?"

"He needs coin like I need another mortgage," Toby said with a smirk, eying the gold. "But he's got good reason for not wanting to cross these people, reasons that you're a lot safer not knowing, my friend."

Forbish nodded, knowing that Toby was trying to save him trouble. But trouble had already found them. Now he was trying to get out of trouble.

"Oh, he can keep his reasons to himself, for all I care. I just need a name, a starting point, you might say. If I was going to hire someone to start looking, where would I have them look?"

"You're asking *me*?" Toby stopped polishing and leaned on the bar, lowering his voice. "I don't know these people, Forbish, and I don't really *want* to know them. I've got nothing against earning a little extra coin, but," he pushed the money back across the bar, "I can't give you what I don't have."

"Just think of that as a tip, Toby." Forbish pushed the money back. "I don't expect you to go digging into something that's going to put you in trouble. I just need some direction. A name will do."

"Well, I don't know any off the top of my head, but I can ask around. There are plenty of people who will think it worth taking a risk for a little money." He scooped up the two coins and pocketed them. "It may take a day or two."

"That's all I can ask." Forbish pushed his tankard across the bar and stood, wincing at the punishment the stool had done to his backside. "Just send word, or drop by the inn. I'll treat you to a nice lunch." Toby opened his mouth to protest, but Forbish cut him off with a raised hand. "No, I won't hear it. Even if you find nothing, I'll have you over for lunch. We can talk about old times, if nothing else."

"Sure. I'll come by either tomorrow or the day after."

"See you then." Forbish waved and left, working the stiffness out of his backside as he climbed the stairs to the street.

"It's a wonder the stool didn't give way," Hensen said at Toby's elbow even before the door closed behind Forbish's considerable bulk. "I knew he'd be back. Good that I had him followed, otherwise I wouldn't have been here to hear that little chat. He's persistent, isn't he?"

"Yep," Toby said, returning to his polishing.

"Well, I can't have him poking around." Hensen tugged at his waistcoat and sniffed noisily. "Sorry, Toby, but your friend has earned some gentle discouragement."

"Do you have to hurt him?" The barkeep's voice was guarded; he knew Hensen could put the same kind of pressure on him as he could on Forbish.

"Oh, I'm not going to hurt him, Toby. Don't worry. We're not a bunch of muscle-bound thugs, unlike some other organizations in Twailin." He sniffed again and produced a tiny silver snuffbox from his waistcoat pocket. He took a pinch and inhaled it with a snort. "In fact, I think I'll defer this to the authorities."

"The authorities? But what are you going to—"

Hensen forestalled his question with a raised finger and an explosive sneeze. He produced an expensive handkerchief from his sleeve and dabbed his nose, smiling with satisfaction.

"Oh, don't worry so much, Toby. I'll just spread a little rumor and let Duke Mir's own capable guardsmen handle the rest." He tucked the handkerchief away and turned to leave. "After all, there's a killer on the loose. They're bound to be interested in someone who is inquiring as to the whereabouts of said assassin, don't you think?"

Toby kept his mouth shut and went back to his polishing as the owner of his club swaggered out of the bar. After the man was gone, he fished the two coins from his pocket and dropped them in the tip jar. The gold had grown far too heavy to keep.

Chapter XXI

The hallway was straight and narrow, sixty feet from the corner where Lad stood to the two men guarding the door. Each guard held a cocked crossbow at the ready. Flames flickered in the six oil lamps set along the length of the hall, banishing all shadows; there would be no sneaking past these guards as he had the others. He knew there would be more guards in the room. Mya's reconnaissance was flawless, as always.

This was the approach most likely to succeed without his being identified or killed. It wasn't the approach he would have chosen, for it wasn't the one most likely to achieve the goal without killing people unnecessarily. The only difference between the tactic Mya had instructed him to take and the one he would have taken on his own was risk. Lad was willing to risk his own safety to save even one unnecessary killing; Mya was not. The guards were just men doing their jobs, men like Forbish, trying to earn a living and feed their families. They probably had daughters and sons, wives and friends who would be hurt by what Lad was about to do.

But the magic wouldn't allow him to disobey.

Lad stepped out into the corridor and walked toward the guards at an easy, relaxed pace. He made it much farther than he thought he would before one of them raised a weapon. He watched as the man's fingers tightened on the trigger.

"Stop right there!"

The man's shout sent Lad into action. The guard fired without hesitation, and his aim was excellent, but his target was no longer where he had aimed. Lad careened off of first one wall, then the other, as the second guard fired. This one's aim was even better, and Lad felt the bolt's fletching brush his cheek in passing.

They both cleared short swords from their sheaths before he fell upon them, but the blades were useless against him. He dodged one stroke and caught the other between his palms as his foot smashed through ribs, killing one guard instantly. The other man released his trapped weapon and reached for a dagger, but the stolen sword slipped between his ribs before the dagger was in his grasp.

Lad stopped and listened.

Three men were moving within the room; he heard the clicks of crossbows being cocked. No one spoke a word, which meant they were ready for him. Their reactions would be swift and well-rehearsed.

He stood to the side of the door and jiggled the handle. Two heavy crossbow bolts smashed through the door and clattered down the hall, and he was moving even before they came to rest. He took one step back and kicked the door into splinters.

The room was well lit, which was no surprise, and the three guards were ready for him. The one who hadn't fired at his ruse did so now, but Lad was already moving, and the bolt missed by a safe margin. He was on the guard before the man could reach another weapon, and his kick sent the man flying; either the kick or the wall that interrupted his trajectory killed him, which one was unimportant. The young woman in the bed screamed, but Lad ignored the noise, for the other two guards were attacking with short swords and daggers. They fought well, and one even managed to score a gash in Lad's arm before they both fell.

Lad turned to the girl.

"P...please," the girl stammered, backed up to the ornate headboard, clutching the covers up to her neck. "Don't..."

Lad had to do as he was ordered, and what was more, he couldn't hesitate. He could hear more guards coming, the ones he'd evaded earlier. The longer he waited, the more would die. He moved to the bedside and drew the stiletto. If he struck quickly, she'd feel no pain. That was the best he could offer. But as he neared her, the blankets jerked and Lad stumbled back.

He looked down.

The fletching of a crossbow bolt barely protruded from his stomach.

He felt a wave of weakness, and knew the damage was dire. The shaft had hit something vital, and he was bleeding inside. He'd heal, but not until the shaft was removed. He reached behind and snapped off the four inches of bolt that protruded from his back, then drew the shaft from his stomach and dropped it.

The weakness lessened, but he had lost a good amount of blood. The wound in the great vessel that supplied blood to his legs had closed, and his stance steadied. He looked to the horror-struck woman in the bed. She sat trembling, eyes flung wide open, her gaze locked on his bloody hands. Her hands shook on the small crossbow, making its outline through the blanket evident.

"I'm sorry," he said, and his words did seem to calm her a bit. He moved so quickly that she didn't even flinch before she died.

He placed the note and left, streaking silently through the halls of Baron Volkes' estate. He had one more target to eliminate this night, and the magic that controlled him wouldn't let him rest until the job was done.

A skinny girl in drab skirts and a stained leather corset stepped into a small pub on the edge of The Sprawls. She stood blinking into the lamplight that seemed bright compared to the darkness outside. It only took her a moment to spy her quarry. She approached the table at a quick walk and plopped down in the chair across from the man who wore the duke's seal on his shoulder.

"I got somethin' you want, Master Sergeant." She put her hands flat on the table, just in case the big guardsman was fool enough to take her for a threat.

"I don't doubt it," he said, eying her up and down, "but I don't consort with whores, so be off."

"Found a steady girl, then, did ya?" He sneered and started to reply, but she waved a hand and cut him off. "That ain't what I mean, and you know it, Master Sergeant." She reached across the table and snatched his tankard, earning a scowl. "I'm talkin' about information." She sipped the ale and raised her eyebrows. "You can afford good ale, Master Sergeant."

"What makes you think I'm looking for information?"

"Oh, come on. It's all over the streets about them poor royals of the duke's court droppin' like flies to some assassin's dagger." She sipped again. "If your coin's as good as your ale, I'll tell you where to find someone who knows this killer."

"You know this murderer?"

"No, but I can point you in the right direction, Master Sergeant, and that's more than you've got now by a long shot." She drank deeply, draining the tankard, then pushed the empty vessel back across the table to him. "Fill that with gold instead of ale and I'll tell you where you can find someone who knows him."

"Three gold crowns," he offered, producing the coins and placing them on the table for her to see.

"Ten."

"Five."

"Seven."

"Six, and that's more than you earn on your back in a fortnight, so let's have it!" He pushed the coins across the table.

"And just how do you know my prices haven't gone up, Master Sergeant?" She looked at the money, then at his glowering features. "You ain't *paid* for my services in a long time."

"Take it or leave it. I couldn't care less which."

"Okay then." She scooped the coins up and stuffed them into her corset. "The *Tap and Kettle*. It's an inn up in Eastmarket. The innkeeper's the one you want to talk to. His name's Forbish or somethin'."

She got up and left, letting herself smile at the irony of being paid twice by two different people for the same task. "And I didn't even have to hitch up me skirts," she mumbled to herself with a quiet chuckle.

Lad squirmed over the wall of the Grandfather's estate and dropped to the ground in a graceless heap. He lay there for a moment, struggling to breathe, concentrating on remaining conscious. He coughed and tasted blood. The magic prevented pain, but the weakness was overwhelming. All he wanted to do was lie down and sleep.

But the magic wouldn't let him rest.

He struggled to his feet; it was difficult with his left arm not working and his consciousness waning with every ragged breath. The lucky shot from a guard atop a buttressed wall would have killed any man, and had nearly killed Lad despite the healing magic that prevented him from bleeding to death. But if he couldn't breathe he would eventually die, which was his only desire. Unfortunately, the magic drove him on.

He entered the secret door at the base of the north tower and descended the stairs to the sparring room. After passing through there at a shambling half-run and down the short hall, he opened the door to the stair that led down to his chamber. He'd never counted the stairs, but there seemed too many, and at the bottom he bumped into the door before he saw it in the gloom. His hand fumbled with the latch, and he felt the door swing away from him as it opened. He couldn't catch himself, and fell heavily onto the landing. He had fulfilled Mya's instructions; he had returned to the interrogation chamber. Now he could rest. Now he could die.

"Lad!"

He felt cool hands on his face, a strong grasp checking the pulse at his wrist.

"Gods, Lad. What the hell happened?"

Mya's voice sounded strange, but the weakness was taking him down a spiral of darkness where everything seemed strange. She turned him over and gasped when she found the arrow and her fingers came away bloody.

"I...almost...escaped you." His voice was a croaked whisper. He fumbled for her with one hand, trying to stop her from tending to his wound. If he put her off long enough...maybe.... The image of a scared young boy cowering in a corner amid the bodies of the guards who had just given their lives trying to save him visited his mind. The memory hit him like a wave of nausea. He couldn't stand to remember what had followed.

"You what? Hold still!"

"Please..." he said, forced to hold still by the unrelenting magic. "Let me go."

"Shut up and don't fight me. I've got to get you to the table. Can you walk?"

He carefully gauged his strength, or the lack of it, before answering.

"No." It wouldn't be long now.

"Then just don't fight me."

He felt one hand under his knees and another under his back, and heard her strain with his weight. She was stronger than most women her size, and lifted him with some minor cursing. There were a few bumps as she descended the steps, then a solid thump as she virtually dropped him onto the stone slab that was his bed.

"Now, let's see about that arrow." A knife parted his shirt from neck to cuff, and he heard a sharply indrawn breath. He opened his eyes and looked curiously up at the expression on her face. It was as if the arrow had found her flesh instead of his, so twisted with pain was her visage. "Gods, Lad. This is in to the fletching!"

Her fingers probed where the wood met flesh just in the hollow of his collarbone. The shot had been from directly overhead, and he'd moved just enough to keep it from piercing his skull. The shaft had entered him in the soft tissue between the collarbone and his shoulder blade, and had passed straight down through lung and diaphragm and into his viscera, severing the nerves that controlled his arm. He had tried to pull the arrow out, but the barbed head dragged at his insides, causing the weakness to spread.

"Yes," he said, though she hadn't told him to answer. It wouldn't be long now; he could feel the weakness slowly enveloping him. There was no point to sparring with her.

"What do I do?"

He looked up at her, remembering the boy's sobbing pleas, and said, "Let me die."

"No." There was something in her face that Lad couldn't read. It was familiar, but the weakness was playing with his consciousness and he couldn't remember. "No, I won't let you die. Tell me, was the arrow's head barbed or straight?"

"Barbed."

"Damn." She bit her lip and cast a glance around the room. "Hold still."

She left him for a moment, and he heard the clatter of metal instruments. There were many tools in the room—tools of torture. He could discern the sounds of knives, pliers, and pincers, and knew what she was going to do. He could only hope that she wasn't as adept at surgery as with her quick wit.

"Now hold still, Lad. This will hurt, but—"

"No, it won't hurt. I feel no pain."

"Oh, yeah. Handy, that."

"No pain," he said, his voice fading to a whisper. "No remorse. The child…was someone's son, someone's best friend. More sons…best friends…wives…husbands…will die if you don't let me go. I don't want to kill anymore. Please..."

"Shut up, Lad. You're delirious."

He could see in her face that she knew he was not delirious, but the magic made him remain quiet.

"Now, show me where the tip of this arrow is."

He indicated a spot just below the lowest rib on his left side.

"Great. Now hold very still."

He felt the knife part his flesh and heard her astonished gasp.

"Gods! It closed right back up!" She muttered and grabbed another instrument from the tray. "You're going to have to help me here, Lad. I'll part the flesh and put this in," she held up a flat-bladed hook made for pulling bones from living flesh. "You'll have to hold the wound open. Nod if you understand me."

He nodded.

"Fine. Now."

The blade parted his flesh again and he felt the cold metal of the hook as it went in.

"Hold this."

He grasped the handle and pulled, feeling his ribs lift with the tension. Dimness crept into the edges of his vision.

"Good! I can see it. There's a lot of blood."

Lad heard a spattering sound, like rain overflowing a clogged gutter. Something touched the arrow, sending a tremor through his flesh. He heard the snip of heavy shears severing the head from the shaft, then felt Mya grasp the arrow by the fletching and pull the entire length out in one smooth motion. His grip slackened on the hook.

"No! Don't let go! I've got to get the arrowhead out. Stay still."

His breath was coming in rattles, and he felt the need to cough, but she had ordered him to stay still. Dimness advanced across his vision as she probed with the pliers. His eyes sagged shut.

"I'm sorry," he said in a gurgling whisper, not knowing who he was apologizing to this time. There were so many—so many faces of wives and sons and friends he'd murdered. He saw them all in the darkness of his mind. "I'm sorry for everything."

"Got it."

He felt a wrenching pull, and the handle of the hook slipped from his limp grasp.

"There, now. You can let it go." Her voice was faint in his ears. "Lad?"

He tried to answer, but couldn't.

"Lad, concentrate! Breathe!"

He forced himself to take a breath, but he was too weak. It was barely a rattle.

"Breathe! Now!"

He felt something press against his lips and fingers pinching his nose, and then air flooded into his collapsed lung. He coughed spasmodically and heard cursing, but breathing was easier. His eyes fluttered and he saw Mya wiping blood from her face. His left arm tingled as his nerves knit together. He reached for her. He didn't know why, but she was there, and she was solid.

"No, Lad. You rest. Sleep." She took his hand and folded it across his chest.

Whether from the compulsion of the magic or the overwhelming exhaustion of the trauma, he found her suggestion irresistible.

"We got something, Captain!"

Norwood was out of his chair before the man was even through his office door. Truth be told, he'd been half-asleep, exhausted from hours of writing letters to wives and husbands of guardsmen who would never see their spouses again. But he was up now, and the bright-eyed sergeant's enthusiasm was better than a cup of fresh blackbrew.

"Where, Sergeant?"

"An inn in Eastmarket by the name of *Tap and Kettle*. My source said the innkeeper, a man named Forbish, knows who the assassin is."

"Good!" He started to grab his uniform jacket, then stopped as he noticed that it was still pitch black outside his window. "What's the hour, Sergeant?"

"Oh, about two glasses before first light."

"So early? Hmph." He put his coat down. He'd started drafting the letters just after midnight, and had finished most of them before exhaustion and sorrow had taken him. "Well, put on a pot of blackbrew and get a squad together. I'm going to finish these tonight even if it's the death of me."

"Yessir." The sergeant noticed the letters on the captain's desk and his broad shoulders slumped. "How many, if you don't mind me askin', sir?"

"Besides the two targets? Ten." He sat down and straightened the papers. "Ten good men and women, Sergeant. And we're going to find the murdering bastard who killed them and string him up by his innards!"

"Yessir!"

The sergeant turned and left his office, and Captain Norwood returned to his letters. He had his doubts about this informant. What would an innkeeper know of the murders, let alone who was committing them? But the maneuver might serve to flush the quarry into the open. Even more important, it might bring whoever was ordering these murders out of the slimy hole he lived in long enough for Captain Norwood to put a sword through his liver.

He sharpened his quill and tried to think of a kind way to tell a wife that her husband was never coming home.

 CHAPTER XXII

Black cloaks and steel whirled in blurring entropy.

Dagger met sword, turning the stroke that would have taken his life, then darted in like a striking snake. His target twisted away, sword arcing through an intricate series of feints before it struck again. Steel met steel once more in three sharp blows before both adversaries broke off, circling, watching for weakness.

The Grandfather let his foot land on a patch of blood-dampened stone and slipped minutely.

The sword slashed without pause, but the slip had been a feint, and he flipped over the sweeping stroke, both daggers stabbing. One was deflected. The other was not, and the tip pierced flesh before the target twisted away.

"Three to one!" said the thin figure standing well to the side, ignored by both combatants.

They squared off, his opponent breathing heavily and protecting his left side where the dagger had struck for the third and most telling stroke. Blood, dark and sweet, dripped steadily from the man's elbow.

The scuff of a boot from the open hallway behind him snapped the Grandfather's attention away from the sword he faced.

"Hold!"

The sword's tip dropped, and the blademaster quickly clamped a hand upon his bleeding arm.

"Forgive me, Grandfather." Mya bowed as he turned and

advanced upon her. "I didn't mean to interrupt your bout."

"Of course you did, Mya." He put his daggers away and took one cleansing breath that returned his heart to its steady slow beat. "I know that you're quite capable of moving silently. The discreet noise you made with your foot was intentional, well timed, and politely executed. Next time just clear your throat and stop putting on pretenses."

"Yes, Grandfather."

"What's that you've got?" he asked, nodding to the bundle of black silk she cradled in her arms. "The boy's clothing?"

"I, uh..." She peered past him at the tall blademaster who was lashing a quick bandage around his left arm. She ignored the Grandfather's valet, since the man knew more of the guild's private affairs than Mya ever would.

"You may speak freely, Mya. He's a Kossnhir apprentice." She swallowed visibly, a common response to meeting a blademaster of Koss Godslayer; they had their tongues cut out at the age of eight to prevent them from divulging the training secrets of their cult.

"It was the boy's clothing." She held out the sodden shirt in one bloody hand, and he noticed that there was also blood on her neck and shoulder. "It's little more than a rag now. That's why I need to talk to you. Your weapon was injured last night."

"How badly?" He felt a chill of worry. *Injured, she said, not killed. Not so soon. Not yet!*

"Would have killed him if he wasn't held together with more magic than muscle."

There was something in her tone that the Grandfather didn't like. He wasn't sure exactly what it was, but there were feelings beneath that sharp wit and hard exterior. *How troublesome.*

"He took two arrows. I didn't know about the first until he told me this morning. He'd taken it out himself. The second he couldn't remove without killing himself, so he just came back here. How he made it over the wall is beyond me."

"You removed it?"

"I cut it out of him." She fetched the broad head of a crossbow bolt from her pocket and held it out for him. "I had to dig this out of his spleen before he'd stop bleeding."

"Interesting." He took the arrowhead, turning it over in his hand. There was still blood and tissue stuck to the barbed wedge of iron. "And he is recovered?"

"Aside from some weakness due to losing about half of his blood, yes." She smiled crookedly, something he found oddly irritating. "He's doing his exercises and eating like a starved cloud cat. He'll probably be fine by tonight."

"Good." He started to turn back to his own morning exercises, then noticed the impatient shuffle in her stance. "Was there something else, Mya?"

"There is, Master, but I'm not sure how to say it." She bit her lip and shrugged. "I don't know if it's important or if it will anger you."

"Telling me something is amiss, then not telling me what it is, will surely anger me." His hand itched for his dagger, but killing Mya wasn't a good idea right now. Her reconnaissance of the added security measures of the Royal Guard had been flawless and invaluable. If not for her efforts, it was very likely that his weapon *would* have died. "I won't hold you responsible for the bad news you bear, Mya. Your skills are far too valuable for me to waste in a fit of temper."

"Yes, Grandfather." She steadied herself visibly and continued. "Your weapon is very near the breaking point, Master."

"Near the breaking point? What do you mean? You said he was healed."

"Physically he is healed, Master. His mind, however, is damaged, and I don't know if that will heal."

"His mind? That's impossible, Mya. The magic prevents him from feeling anything. I made sure of that."

"I don't doubt it, Grandfather, but there's something moving within him. I think it's because he was exposed to others. He's learned what others feel, and his curiosity has caused him to expect it in himself. He's been told that killing is bad, so he doesn't want to kill, but he's forced to follow our orders. He doesn't *feel*, but he knows he should, and that's causing a conflict that's inflicting a kind of pain that the magic doesn't prevent."

"Do you think this pain is affecting his efficiency?" If the weapon was showing weakness, the longevity of the Grandfather's project could be severely curtailed. Many plans had been put into motion that hinged upon the pressure being put to bear with his new weapon. If the pressure eased, the plans would crumble like a house of cards.

"It's not his efficiency that worries me, Grandfather, but his sanity. He doesn't want to live, but he's compelled to continue. He begged me last night to let him die." She looked at the bloody shreds of silk in her hand and shrugged. "He can't even hate me for saving his life. The magic won't let him."

"I worry more for you than my weapon, Mya." Her eyes snapped up to his, wary of some taunt or mocking jab. "The weapon is just that. Remember, he's a made thing, like this dagger." He produced the blade from the folds of his cloak and raised it for her to see. "Would this blade feel differently if it were used to kill a man or a dog? I think not." The blade vanished in the blink of an eye, and he smiled at the effect the sudden motion had on her. She still feared him, which was as it should be. The moment she no longer feared him, she would have to die.

"The boy isn't a dagger, Master," she said evenly, bowing and backing away a step. "Perhaps only in that he has a mind and the dagger does not, but that's the crux of the problem." She paused, obviously choosing her next words with the utmost care. "Is there no way the schedule could be postponed a day, simply to allow him to recover?"

"Wheels have been put into motion that cannot be stopped, Mya. The schedule must remain inviolate."

"Very well, Master." She turned to go, then stopped and looked back at him, her eyes admirably emotionless in their scrutiny. "He's going to crack. I don't know when, but he will eventually. Then, magic or no, both of us will have to start watching our backs for daggers."

He watched her go, resisting the compulsion to put a dagger

between her shoulder blades. Her questioning of his prudence was more than enough reason to kill her, but her utter conviction told him that she was being honest with him, something he valued almost as much as her loyalty. There was still enough fear in her to keep her in line, but that appeared to be waning. She didn't leave in the direction of her quarters, as he suspected she would, but back down into the interrogation chamber. Back down to his weapon. He clenched his jaw rhythmically for more than a minute before he turned back to his exercises. He drew his daggers and wondered which of his weapons would have to be disposed of first.

Exclamations of surprise and alarm rang through the kitchen door from the common room. Before Forbish even had a chance to think, his largest cleaver was in his hand. *If those damned cutthroats are back, I'll show them what for!* he raged inwardly as he pounded through the swinging door.

"Here now, you—"

He came up short at the sight of six royal guardsmen standing at the ready in the common room. Their hands were on the hilts of their swords, their faces grim as death. And all of their eyes were on him.

"Forgive me, milord Captain!" he spouted, recognizing the insignia on the leader's collar. He bowed low, putting the cleaver aside. His mind raced for a reason why royal guardsmen would be in the *Tap and Kettle*; it had been hard enough to get a constable to pay a visit when they'd been harassed by Urik and his goons. But his heart knew the answer even if his mind did not, and it leapt into his throat at the prospect of whom they sought. "I heard shouts, and we've had trouble of late with ruffians."

"Rest easy, good innkeeper," the broad-shouldered captain said, his smile strained with fatigue or pain. Something dire lurked behind the eyes of the gray-haired man, something that Forbish was quite positive he wanted no part of. "We've just come to ask some questions. There's no trouble here."

"Questions?" He gathered Wiggen to him with a wave of his hand, and he felt her tremors of fear as he drew her close. Josie glared at them all, her caustic tongue muttering curses. "What questions, Captain?"

"As I'm sure you've heard, there have been a number of murders of late." One of the few customers seated in the common room rose to leave, but he sank back down into his seat at one glance from the guard captain. "We have been told by a reliable source that you have information as to the identity of the assassin."

"*Me?*" Forbish squeaked in poorly feigned astonishment. "What do I know of assassins and royalty, milord Captain? I'm but a simple innkeeper!" He knew in an instant that the guard captain hadn't been fooled.

"Even simple men may hear things or know people, Mister Forbish." The man moved forward casually, his men following as a unit, never letting him lead them by more than two strides. Then the captain's flint gray eyes flashed dangerously, pinning Forbish with their intensity. "Eight members of the duke's court have fallen to this assassin's dagger, and ten of my best guardsmen!"

He took one more step and stood directly before Forbish and his trembling daughter, his stern visage glowering down on the both of them and inspiring as much fear as any thug ever had. The innkeeper's fingers itched for the handle of his cleaver.

"The only description we have of this assassin is that he's a slim young man with sandy hair." He took a deep breath, letting it out slowly as he regarded his quarry. "If you know anything of this young man—a name, who he is, who commands him—it would be well done if you told me all."

"Please, sir. We don't know anything about such a man." He felt Wiggen's fingernails digging into his arm and feared that she'd blurt out the story. "We don't have anything to do with these murders."

"Oh, I don't doubt that, Mister Forbish, but I don't think you're telling me the whole truth, either." He turned away and surveyed the inn's common room as if he were looking to buy the place. He sighed gustily, his broad, warrior's hands rubbing at the cabled muscles of his neck.

"I'm tired, Mister Forbish," he said, walking casually to the fireplace, and Forbish could hear the truth in his words. "I'm tired of these murders, I'm tired of not being able to protect those under my charge, and I'm tired of writing letters to the wives and husbands of my guardsmen who were killed by this assassin you know nothing about."

"Captain, please! We've never even been north of the river! How could we know anything of these killings?"

"But most of all, Mister Forbish," the captain continued, turning back to the fearful pair and rubbing his weary eyes, "I'm tired of being lied to."

"Sir!" Forbish spouted, trying to sound indignant. "I'll not be called a liar in my own inn, even by the Captain of the Royal Guard! We know nothing of this assassin." Unfortunately, Forbish was at heart an honest man, and he could see in the captain's face that his performance wasn't having the desired effect.

"Very well, Mister Forbish." The captain motioned two of his men forward. "I know from several of your neighbors and business associates that you had a boy working for you for several weeks who fit this description quite well. They haven't seen him for several days, but they remember him. If you're having a lapse in memory, perhaps we might remedy it."

Without another word from the captain, the two guardsmen peeled Wiggen from Forbish's arm and held her.

"No! Please don't hurt her, Captain! She's got nothing to do with it!" He surged forward, but the captain placed one broad fist against his chest, forcing him back. Forbish's breath came in short gasps, his head spinning with dizziness. "Please, sir. She's the only family I've got left!"

"We're not going to hurt her, Mister Forbish," he said, disgust souring his tone. "We're not thugs! When you remember more about this young man who worked for you, your daughter will be released."

"We did have a lad working for us, Captain, but..." He stopped short at the look in his daughter's eyes. She hadn't spoken a word or uttered a peep of protest, and now he understood why. There was fear in her, but not for her own safety. She was afraid for Lad, afraid of what the Royal Guard would do to him if they caught him. Her eyes were wide with horror, and her head shook once, denying him the words that meant her freedom.

"But what?" The captain advanced upon him again, hands on his hips, eyes like arrow slits ready to shoot the portly innkeeper dead. "What aren't you telling me?"

"He stole from us." He put all he could into the lie, and hoped. "He wouldn't admit it, but he stole, sure enough. I didn't want him to go to prison for it, so I just sent him away. I don't know where he went after he left." The last part was true enough.

The captain's eyes roved over Forbish, then shifted sideways to scrutinize Wiggen. "It's plain to me that either one or both of you knows a good bit more than you're telling. My apologies for this, Mister Forbish, but there are lives at stake." He nodded to the men who held Wiggen. "Take her out."

Forbish stood trembling helplessly as they took from him the only thing in the world he truly cared about.

Sweat trickled down Mya's torso as she moved through the intricate dance, her body straining to accommodate the elaborate mixture of forms.

"Left turn, block with right palm..."

Lad took her through the dance, watching as he accompanied her, his movements mirroring hers. His voice was a mantra in her ears, her mind enveloping it, her body moving as he directed without her conscious thought.

"...twist, kick left, turn and strike. Sweep and block right..."

Time and thought flowed through her like water over a miller's wheel, turning her, bringing her forward, but not really moving her. The moves of the dance were so fluid, so *right,* that she was lost in it, barely needing his prompts even after only a few hours of instruction.

"...sweep, turn..."

The exercise had started out simply as something to take his mind away from the tasks that were appointed him, the tasks that were slowly driving him over the brink of darkness from which there would be no return. She sought only to distract him, to lure him away from his troubles by teaching her the exercises he performed every morning.

"...strike...yes...yes..."

He'd asked many questions at first: Why did she wish to learn? What did she already know? How many years had she practiced? What weapons was she proficient with? Had she ever been trained to fight without them? At first, she'd been awkward and slow, trying to memorize the dance as if it were something she could learn by rote. It was not. It was more than a series of movements, she knew now; it was art, music, poetry and dance all combined in a martial genre. Now it flowed through her body like water through a funnel, directed but still moving, unchanged.

Lad's voice faded away, and still they moved together through the forms of the dance. She'd felt nothing like it, such synergy with another. It was the closest to intimacy she'd ever been.

"Mya."

She reacted without thinking, whirling toward the unfamiliar voice, her posture slipping into the defensive crouch of the dance.

"What are you doing?" the Grandfather asked, descending the stairs into the chamber with his usual fluid grace. His countenance was stern and unreadable. Her mind raced for a moment with all the possible reasons he was here. He hadn't come down to the interrogation chamber since Lad's arrival. Three reasons for his presence occurred to her, and two meant her death.

"I'm learning the exercises that your weapon has been taught, Grandfather." She bowed, thankful that she had retained a breechcloth and halter despite Lad's suggestion that her clothing was too restrictive to perform the dance properly.

"Why?" He stopped before them, less than striking distance away, his hands invisible within his cloaks. She wondered briefly if they were clutching the hilts of his daggers.

"Two reasons, Grandfather," she said, finding herself strangely calm at the prospect of facing his wrath. Lad stood beside her, but she knew he couldn't help her if the Grandfather decided to strike her down. She could rely only on herself, as she always had. "First, for reasons we discussed earlier, I thought to distract him. Second, I find the forms of his exercises interesting and wished to learn them for my own purposes."

"And have you?"

She shrugged noncommittally. "You ask the pupil if she's learned the lesson properly. I don't know." She glanced sidelong at Lad. "Ask the teacher."

"Well," the Grandfather said, his eyes flickering to his weapon, "has she?"

"No, Master."

Mya's eyes were on the Grandfather, so she saw the corner of his mouth twitch minutely in amusement. She had expected Lad's admission, so there was no surprise for her. No one could assimilate such a complex repertoire in such a short time. She'd learned the moves, but to learn the forms and how they interacted to create the dance would take many months. Even then, to become proficient would take years.

"Well, then," he said, turning back to her, his tone shifting from amusement to ire, "have you at least accomplished *something* this day?"

"Yes, Master. He's been instructed regarding this evening's targets, and he's recovered fully from his previous injuries."

"All of them?"

"All of the physical injuries are healed, and he's regained his strength and agility. As to the other, I have no idea." She looked at Lad again and could see the curiosity whirling behind his eyes. "Time will tell."

"Good enough." The Grandfather took a small scroll from within his robes and handed it to Mya. "There's an additional task that must be performed tonight. My spy within the Royal Guard has informed me that they have procured a witness, someone who has evidently seen or known our reluctant weapon."

Mya unrolled the scroll, recognizing the sketched layout of the barracks of the Royal Guard.

"This threat must be eliminated. Instruct him to see to this first. The holding cells beneath the barracks should be no more difficult

Chris A. Jackson

to access than any of the other fortified buildings in which we've eliminated targets." He turned in a swirl of cloaks and ascended the stairs, a silent cloud, malignant and terrible in his indifference. "After she's dead, he is to eliminate the scheduled targets."

"Yes, Master," Mya said, her eyes still absorbing the details of the scroll. The door closed, snapping her attention from the task detailed before her to the one to whom it would befall. Her stomach clenched at the thought of giving Lad his instructions.

"She's being held beneath the barracks complex, one level down. There'll be at least a dozen guards. One will have keys to the cell."

"Who is it?" he asked, innocent and unknowing.

"You know who." She handed him the scroll, shivering as the sweat of her previous exertions cooled on her skin. "Read it."

"It's Wiggen." His voice was as calm and matter of fact as always, but she could see the strain in him. "They found out where I stayed before you took me. They took her to get to me."

"Yes." She watched the realization dawn behind his eyes, and hated herself for what she knew she had to tell him.

"You're going to order me to kill her." His tone was flat, emotionless, but his eyes were alight with pain.

"Yes."

"She's my friend, Mya. You cannot— I *will* not kill her." The parchment fluttered from his quivering grasp. She watched him, saw the telltale signs of the conflict building within him.

"I'm sorry." The words came from her mouth before she could stop them, and their effect on Lad was astounding.

"You're *sorry*?" Tracings of light flared along his sweat-streaked torso, and she knew that the magic that restrained him was the only thing keeping her alive. "How can you be sorry? This is something you can change, Mya. You don't have to order me to kill Wiggen. You can run away. Flee. Go from here and you won't have to order me to kill my friend."

"It wouldn't matter, Lad." She glanced over her shoulder at the room's one door. "If I didn't, he would."

"Then help me k—" The plea ended with a flare of light from

245

the runes that imprisoned his soul. He couldn't ask it; she had ordered him not to. The light and heat dimmed, and Mya hadn't shied away from it. "Help me do as I have asked."

"He would kill me." She was surprised that there was so little fear in that admission.

Lad stood there, the magical light of the runes fading completely as they stared at one another. How much time passed, she couldn't tell. It was like during the exercise, the dance he had taught her; time moved past without touching her.

"Read the scroll," she said finally, breaking that implacable gaze. She turned away and recovered her tunic from the table. "One glass after the sun has set, go to the barracks of the Royal Guard and kill the girl they're holding in the cells below. Kill anyone who sees you. Kill anyone who tries to stop you. Don't allow yourself to be captured, injured, or killed." She struggled into the garment, her damp skin hindering her actions. "When you've done this, proceed to the other two targets, unless you're badly injured. If you're too injured to perform the other tasks safely, return here."

Mya recovered her trousers, stepping into them mechanically. She cinched the belt tight and looked at him still standing there immobile, a statue of flesh and bone. "Do you understand?"

"Yes, Mya. I understand." The words were totally without feeling, without anger or remorse, pain or anguish. Then Lad turned to her and regarded her with eyes she felt were looking straight into her soul. "But do *you* understand?"

She felt the words like a blow to the stomach.

There was only one answer.

"Yes, Lad. I understand."

She walked past him and climbed the stairs, wondering if she would ever truly feel human again.

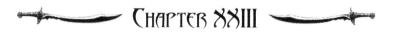 Chapter XXIII

Blood and shadow flowed through the barracks of the Royal Guard.

A second-floor window with squeaky bronze hinges yielded, and two guards died before they were fully awake.

One... Two..., he thought. *Wives, sons, daughters, friends...*

Outside the door a guard walked by, his boots thumping on the stone floor. The door opened. The guard turned and died before his hand could touch his sword. He was lowered gently to the floor, his last breath escaping from between his killer's fingers.

Three...

Lad put the body with the others. Ten minutes would pass until the guard was missed.

The stairs took him down to the main mess. Four guards sat at a table chatting and drinking blackbrew. Their conversation was predictable; they were talking about him. He couldn't take four silently, he knew. Others would come. Lad could hear the shuffling feet of two more as they stood outside the doors to the mess. His goal lay beyond this room, and there was no way around. He might be able to skirt the shadows of the room and remain unseen, but that would mean taking a risk that his orders forbade: *Kill anyone who sees you.*

Wives, children, friends...

He lunged from hiding, and two men died before the others could even react. One managed a truncated shout before he was deprived of the ability to breathe. The other drew steel and spent his last moments fighting for his life. The result was the same.

Sorry...so sorry...

The noise brought more guards. One died with a short sword thrown through his chest. The other raised a crossbow and fired, but before she even lowered the bow, the bolt came back upon the path it had flown. Her puzzled expression lay frozen, transfixed by the shaft. Lad closed her eyes with two blood-slicked fingers and moved on.

Husbands, children, mothers, fathers.... Eight... Nine.

The door to the lower level and the holding cells was locked, but the guards had lost their keys along with their lives. He descended the stairs, listening to the breathing of the two guards standing at the bottom.

Ten... The edge of Lad's hand met with one guard's throat, and the gasp of alarm turned into a strangled cry. The other swung a loaded crossbow, a poor weapon. Lad jerked it out of his grasp, flipped it, and fired point blank into the man's heart.

Eleven...

They both fell with a clatter of weapons and keys.

Daughters... Sons... Wives... Husbands...

Lad saw all their faces as he lifted the ring of brass keys from the lifeless fingers of someone's loved one.

I'm sorry...

Wiggen snapped awake, wondering what had suddenly broken her sleep. Her cell was quiet, the bunk warm and, if not cozy, at least comfortable. Orange torchlight flickered outside, casting fluttering shadows of the bars against the opposite wall. She knew there were two guards just down the long hall; she'd fallen asleep to the sound of their whispered conversations and the occasional jingle of keys.

Now they were quiet.

She fluffed her lumpy pillow and let her eyes sag closed.

Keys clinked faintly. One of the guards must have sneezed or something and woken her up. Her eyes fluttered open for a moment, then closed, and into her mind settled the image of the flickering shadows on the wall of her cell, the bars, and the silhouette of a man...

"Who—"

She jerked awake, bolting upright, but it wasn't one of the guards who stood outside the bars of her cell.

"Lad!" She lunged out of bed, flinging the blankets aside. Her hands gripped the bars with hysterical strength, her voice lowered to a husky whisper. "Lad! What are you doing here? You shouldn't have come! There are guards all over the—"

Something was wrong.

His face was pale, eyes staring at her blankly. He was dressed not in the homespun clothes she'd seen him in, but in fine black silks, his feet bare. Flecks of blood stood out on his hands and neck, more on the dark material; she could smell the sweet tang of it on him. The guard's keys jingled faintly as he lifted them. Blood dripped from his fingers as he put one into the lock of her cell. Her gaze slid off of him and took in the two crumpled bodies lying at the end of the hall.

"I'm sorry," he mumbled through slack lips.

"Oh, no, Lad. You shouldn't have. They weren't hurting me; they were just keeping me here until Father told them about you." The key turned with a click, and the iron padlock fell open.

"That's not why I'm here, Wiggen," he said, lifting the lock from the ring and pulling the cell door open slowly.

"What? I don't understand." She took a step back without knowing why. He was acting strangely, his eyes fixed on her as if something drew them like a magnet.

"I have a new master, Wiggen." He took a step, leaving the cell door open. "He sent me here."

"But..." Realization hit her like a blow—there was only one reason Lad would be sent here. "Then you've come to..."

"I've come to kill you, Wiggen."

The room spun in her vision for a heartbeat, then steadied. It was as if the world had just disappeared out from under her feet, and she was falling. There was nothing she could do; if he was here to kill her, he would kill her. It was that simple. Her hammering heart steadied, and she felt a strange peace settle over her. Perhaps it was resolve, or perhaps it was the hand of some beneficent deity readying to take her soul when it was over.

She didn't know where her strength came from, but it came to her then, and as Lad took another shuffling step toward her, she didn't back away.

"Do you *want* to kill me, Lad?"

"No."

"Then why? Why do as your master tells you?" Wiggen had little hope that he'd listen to reason; she knew something was wrong with him. This wasn't the innocent boy she'd fallen in love with. This was someone else.

"The magic." He took another step, and she stayed unmoving. His chest was now only inches from hers, and she could feel the warmth of him. "The magic has made me his slave, Wiggen. I can't disobey him."

One of his hands rose slowly. She didn't shy from it as his palm brushed her cheek and ear. He cupped the back of her head, his fingers spread out in her hair, and she felt her breath come up short with it. So like the caress of a lover, yet so deadly. His other hand rose, and she knew the end was coming.

"Before you kill me, Lad," she said, surprised that her words stopped him, "tell me that you feel nothing for me. Tell me that you hate me. Tell me that you *want* to kill me." She looked deeply into his eyes, and through the blank stare, the unfeeling stoicism, she could see the pain in him.

"I...I do feel...something. You're my friend. I don't hate you, Wiggen," he said, his voice cracking. His mouth twitched at the corners, and his eyes fairly sang with strain. She could feel the heat of the magic in him now like a furnace through the thin silk of his shirt. "I feel...something..."

"It's your heart, Lad!" she said, bringing one hand to his chest. Wiggen could feel the trip-hammer blows against her palm, like a beast trying to escape a cage beating itself against the bars. She smiled at him then and saw the surprise in his face. "It's love."

250

"Love?" His head tilted and she almost laughed out loud at that quizzical gesture that had melted her heart the first time she'd seen it. "What's love?"

"Love is when you feel more for someone else than you do for yourself. When you'd rather hurt yourself than see that one hurt." She pressed both hands against him, clawing at the warmth of him, feeling the tremor of his struggle against the magic. "It's what I feel for you, Lad. I love you."

"You...love...me?" Tiny droplets of sweat broke out on his lip and brow, and the hand cupping her head begin to quiver. "But I must..." He now laid his other hand upon her face. The touch was gentle, but she could feel both hands quaking with the strain of unreleased violence.

"No, Lad!" She raised her own hands to his face, grasping him desperately. "No, you don't have to do it!"

"I must obey...."

Spider webs of green light began to glow beneath his skin. Waves of incandescence showed through, layers of glowing letters that she couldn't read. Runes of power exerted their force against him, and Lad strained to combat their will. But the pressure of his grasp was increasing.

"No!" Wiggen grasped his wrists and pulled frantically, her strength impotent against his. Heat seared her palms, as if his skin were on fire. "Fight it, Lad!"

"I can't... I...must..." Tendons stood out upon the glowing flesh of his neck, his face contorting with the strain. Tears streamed from his eyes in rivulets.

"Love me, Lad!" she screamed, not knowing where the thought came from. She released his wrists and grabbed him, pulling him closer. "Love me!"

"I...love..."

His lips curled back in a grimace of strain as his grip on her tightened inexorably. But as she felt the pain begin to throb between her ears, as the smell of burning flesh reached her nostrils, he also began to draw her closer. The runes flared so brightly that Wiggen thought the light would blind her as she watched his skin blister and heal and blister again. Hysteria strengthened her as she raked her fingernails into the glowing flesh of his neck and pulled him to her.

Their lips met in a painful, desperate kiss, her hands clenching him closer. She screamed into their parted lips, eyes closed tightly against the pain, kissing him more strongly, grasping him desperately. Her fingernails gouged his glowing flesh, blood slicking her grip, but the pain in her skull was too much. Her struggles weakened.

Suddenly, light erupted through her closed lids, and a wave of heat lashed against her.

Lad's arms flew apart, and with the sudden release of pain and pressure Wiggen fell back onto the cold stone floor. When she opened her eyes, she beheld something that made all the pain, all the fear, vanish in a rush of warmth.

Lad stood like a statue, his eyes flung open in shock and his face alight, not from the magic, but from something within him. He looked through her as if blind, eyes wide and staring, pupils dilated as if something were broken within his mind.

"Lad?" she said, pushing herself up. He still stood unmoving, arms out straight, eyes fixed upon her, but unseeing. "Lad, you did it! You're free!"

"Free?" His voice was faint, distant. The runes glowed no more, but she could see where they had been, for in their wake blisters had risen on his skin.

"Yes, free. Your love freed you. My love." She reached out to him, brushing the blistered skin with her fingertips. "You broke the magic."

"Ahh!" He drew back from her touch, his eyes wide with surprise. He touched the blistered skin gingerly, flinching. "Love *hurts*!"

"You were able to love me." She cupped his face in her hands, the only flesh she could see that was free of burns, and drew him close again. "Do you feel it?"

"I feel many things." He looked at her with eyes she barely recognized. "Pain. And the burns aren't healing." He touched a blister and winced. "The magic is gone!"

"All of it?" she asked, hearing the fear in his voice. He'd never felt pain before, and it scared him.

"I don't know. I feel…different. Strange. I feel like killing my master. I feel…all the people I have killed. I feel their deaths inside me; it makes me want to cry out, and...." Tears resumed their tracks down his cheeks. "All those people… But at the same time I want to hold you and touch you. I feel warm and weak at the same time. Is that love?"

"Oh, yes." She drew him closer. "But that's just part of it." She kissed him again, this time with tenderness instead of desperation, and when she felt him kiss her back, it was as if the heavens had taken her heart.

Suddenly he broke away, his eyes wide with panic.

"The guards!" he hissed, grabbing her hand and pulling her from the cell, fear plain on his face. "We've got to go!"

"No, Lad. Just you!" She stopped him, not by force, for he seemed as strong as ever, but her words brought him up short. "You go. They're not after me. I'll just slow you down. I'll tell them something, and you can find me later."

"There may be no later, Wiggen!" He waved a hand at the dead guards. "How can you explain this? They'll kill you if you don't tell them who did this."

"But I can't—"

"You can, and you *will*, Wiggen!" He dragged her out of the cell, snatching the keys from the lock in passing. She saw the stark desperation in him. Not only was he scared, he was scared of feeling scared. All the emotions that the magic had blocked—the emotions that had been denied him his whole life—were rushing down on him, and he didn't know what to feel. "We must go!"

"All right!" It was impossible for her to fight him, she realized, although she had no idea how the two of them would get out of this place.

"This way." He snatched a torch from the wall and handed it to her, then pulled her along at a run, keeping the keys quiet in his free hand. They stepped over the bodies of the guards and lunged up the stairs. At the top there were two doors. Wiggen could hear faint cries of alarm; more guards were coming.

Lad slipped a key into the lock of the door to the left and broke it off, then unlocked the right-hand door and pulled her through. On the other side he locked the door and again broke the key off in the lock. They stood in a store room a dozen strides long and half as wide. There were shelves holding everything from manacles to rope to blankets, but there was no way out.

At the back were barrels full of torches, one of long iron bars, and a rack of short, wooden batons. He took two of the batons and handed her one.

"What's this for?"

"Can you see in the dark?"

"What? No, of course I can't."

"I didn't think so." He moved to the corner and tipped the barrel of iron bar stock, wheeling it out of his way. "It will be dark, and I don't think the torch will stay lit. You can use the baton to feel your way. Just run it along the wall in front of you."

"Where are we going?"

"The river." He retrieved one bar from the barrel and came back to look at the floor.

"The river?" Now it was her turn to be frightened. "But Lad! I can't swim!"

"Swim?" He jammed the iron bar into a small hole in the floor and pried. To Wiggen's astonishment, a large flagstone tilted up. He was certainly as strong as ever. Under it was an iron-bound wooden door with a thick padlock. One of the keys clicked in the lock, and he heaved the portal open. "We won't need to swim, Wiggen. We're going *under* the river."

"Under it?" She stared in astonishment as he took the torch from her and dropped it through the hole. It landed many feet below with a hiss and a splash. The room was plunged into darkness, the only light a faint yellow wedge from beneath the door.

"Uh, I'm not so sure about this, Lad." Wiggen peered down into the dark hole dubiously.

A sharp crash sounded behind them. The guards were breaking through the first door.

"No time," Lad whispered in her ear. "Hang on to me."

He gripped her tightly and stepped into the dark hole. It was all Wiggen could do to refrain from screaming as they plunged into the darkness.

Mya woke to the stunning shock of a backhand slap across the face. She rolled off the bench, her mind reeling from the blow. For an instant she thought she was home again, a young girl fending off the blows of an abusive mother. Her arms came up defensively and she curled into a ball on the floor, expecting the first kick.

Then she remembered. And the present was almost as frightening as the past.

"Where is my weapon, dear Mya?" the Grandfather asked, his tone deadly sweet as he stepped around the stone bench.

"What?" She rolled to her feet, her mind still waking up, disoriented from the shock of the slap and the surprise that she was still in the interrogation chamber. She'd been waiting for Lad's return and must have fallen asleep. She fingered her stinging cheek. She tasted blood, but the blow hadn't been as hard as she'd thought, not as hard as she'd felt as a child. None of her teeth were loose anyway. She fought the urge to fill her hand with the hilt of a weapon and answered, "Probably still out killing royalty. Why? What's wrong?"

"It's nearly morning, dear Mya." He stepped closer, and she suppressed the urge to back away. That was when she noticed the gleam of rage in the Grandfather's face. His lips were drawn back from his teeth in a rictus smile, like a dog ready to bite, and his eyes... She shuddered.

"He hasn't returned, and my spies inform me that his latter two targets are still breathing. What do you suppose happened to him?"

Sarcasm dripped from his question, and Mya realized the source of his anger—he thought she had something to do with this.

"I don't know, Grandfather." She kept her voice level, vowing not to show fear. She knew what happened when you showed a dog or an abusive parent that you were scared. "Did he kill the girl?"

"I've not yet received a report from my spy with the Royal Guard. Perhaps you'd like to discover that little tidbit of information for me." His stance shifted slightly under his robes, settling, returning to a resting posture from one ready to strike. "Perhaps you were correct, and my weapon has been over-taxed."

"I'll find out, Grandfather." Mya turned to go, but was brought up short by his voice.

"Please do so, my dear. And do remember to come back, especially if you *don't* find my weapon." He followed her slowly up the steps, silently, as if he was stalking her. "I'd hate to lose *both* of my best young weapons in one night."

"Thank you for your concern, Grandfather," she said tightly, bristling at the implied threat. "I'll be careful."

At the top of the stairs she opened the door and stepped through, but as she held it open for her master, she realized with a start that he was no longer behind her. He had vanished without a word or sound, as invisible and intangible as death itself. She hurried to her chambers and changed quickly into the clothes she used for reconnaissance. She left by the main gate, hitching up her skirts and breaking into an easy jog, heedless of the shadows that deepened in her wake.

Lad wormed his way up through the thick iron storm grating and reached his slime-slicked hand back down for Wiggen. She gripped it dubiously, knowing hers was as wet and slick as his. But his grip was like iron, and he lifted her out easily. She squeezed her shapely frame through the bars, smearing even more filth down the front of her dress.

"This will *never* come clean!" she hissed in frustration, wiping her grimy hand on the equally grimy material.

"Quiet," Lad whispered, nodding toward the dim lights in the ramshackle buildings that littered this quarter of the city. "Some people are awake already. We don't want anyone to see us."

"But where are we going?"

"There are places where no one lives here in The Sprawls, Wiggen," he explained, tugging her along the edge of the litter-strewn street.

Her shoe slipped on something slick and she cringed, not wanting to think of what it might be. She supposed there was a bad smell—she knew The Sprawls smelled from the times when the wind blew from the south—but hours of slogging through the sewers of Twailin had inured her to bad smells. She wondered if she'd ever be clean again.

"Here," he whispered, pulling her into the deeper shadows of an alley. "This is the one."

"The one what?" Wiggen looked up at the abandoned building skeptically. The windows were all boarded, and the place looked like it was ready to fall down.

"The one I was looking for." He led her to a low window well set half below the level of the alley. The glass was miraculously intact, and the latch yielded to whatever tinkering he did. She couldn't see, but she thought she heard the click of metal on metal before the window creaked open. "Quickly!"

He held out a hand to her, and as she wiggled through she noticed that the panes were not dark glass as she had thought, but black iron. The window was actually a vent damper, and she found herself in a pitch-black shaft that led down at a shallow angle.

"Lad?" she said, trying to keep the tremor of fear out of her voice. She waved her baton ahead of her as she shimmied down.

"Yes, Wiggen. I'm coming."

Then she heard the creak of the damper and she realized that it really wasn't completely dark, at least not until the door clicked closed and her vision failed her completely. She waved her hand in front of her face, but saw nothing. *Now that's dark!*

"I can't see anything! I'm afraid to move!"

"Don't worry, Wiggen. I can see." She looked toward his voice and saw the two faint motes that she knew were his eyes. She didn't know how some of the magic in him had remained while some had been broken, but he seemed as strong, quick, and agile as ever. The burns that outlined the shattered runes, however, had failed to heal, and she'd seen him grimace every time he brushed one of the rows of tender blisters. Pain was a new experience for Lad, as were all the whirling emotions that she knew were now rattling around within him like beans in a cup. She'd caught him smiling on more than one occasion for no apparent reason, and he kept watching her as if the mere sight of her was entertaining.

He squeezed past her in the narrow shaft—it was big enough to crouch in, but not a lot more—and she felt his hand on her wrist.

"Come on. It's not far."

"What's not far? How do you know this place?"

"I did a lot of exploring in the weeks I worked for Forbish. I found this place one night. I think it used to be a laundry. This shaft opens up under an old furnace they used to heat big pots of water."

"Like the one on Copper Street?" For years she had taken their sheets and blankets to the big laundry house run by a family of Westerners a few blocks from the inn. "Do you think we could wash?"

"I hope so; we won't get far smelling like this."

She felt him step down into a depression, then thought she caught the glimmer of light from around him.

"Hold still for a moment, Wiggen. I've got to get this old door open."

She held as still as she could while she listened to him tinkering with some kind of metal mechanism. Then rusty iron squealed, and a dim light flooded the low area ahead of them.

"Come on."

She wasted no time in crawling through the underside of the furnace and out the old ash door that Lad had opened. She stood up and stretched in the early morning light that streamed through the cracks in the boarded windows. The furnace room was cavernous, ceilings of brick arched high over her head. The place was strewn with strange equipment and tools. It seemed as if the owners had barely taken anything when they left.

"Come on upstairs," Lad said, smiling at her and taking her hand again. "This place is big, and the room where they washed the clothing is right above us."

She followed him up the steps, daydreaming of soap and water and piles of crisp clean sheets to fall asleep upon. They'd been slogging, crawling, wading, and scrabbling through dark dank tunnels all night. She was exhausted and more than a little hungry. At the top of the stairs Lad pushed open a heavy, oaken door and they entered the laundry proper.

"Uh..."

The place wasn't exactly what she'd been hoping for.

"It's kind of dusty," he said, running his hand over a heavy iron press and leaving a streak of black metal behind. Before, it had been gray. "But the cisterns are full."

"This is nothing like Mister Feng's laundry," she said, gaping at the wrist-thick bronze pipes and big copper pots, each chest high and shaped like an oversized teacup on great, wheeled trolleys. "This place is huge!"

"I think they moved these big pots around to carry water. The pipes over there," he pointed to a row of bronze pipes along one wall, "come from the cisterns on the roof. They filled the pots, wheeled them over there," he pointed to slotted grates in the floor where heated air would come up from the furnaces below, "and when the water was hot, took them over there to do the scrubbing."

"I can't believe they left all this here. Why didn't they take it with them?"

"I don't know." He pushed down on the edge of one of the deep pots, and it tipped in its trolley. There was a geared mechanism and a crank to tilt the pot even if it were full. "These tip to pour out the dirty water. See?"

"Hmmm." She peered down inside the pot; it was dusty and there were even some desiccated insect parts amid the filth. "Needs a good scrubbing."

"Let's see if the water will flow," he said with another smile, pulling her over to the wall with the pipes. There was already a pot under one of the pipes. He reached up to the rusty iron lever that controlled the flow of water and pulled. It opened with a horrendous screech, and out poured...

"Dirt!" Wiggen gasped, waving her hand at the wave of dust

and dander that rose from the pot. "Nice."

"Well, maybe one of the others will work. I know there's water in some of the cisterns. I've seen it."

"Maybe we should just go up to the roof to wash."

"This will be better," he assured her, tipping the dusty contents of the pot out on the floor, then pushing it under the next spigot. He pulled the handle, and a torrent of dirty water plunged into the dirty pot, swirling in a turbid mess.

"Ew!" Wiggen said with a cringe, backing away. The stagnant water smelled horrible.

"It should clear," he said, and as they watched, the water went from brown to tan, and finally clear. "There! See?"

She cupped her hands under the flow and scrubbed at her face and arms, still wrinkling her nose at the smell of the water in the pot.

"Here," he said, turning off the flow and pushing the pot out of the way. He wheeled it over to a wide, bowl-like depression in the floor and tipped it. The filthy water swirled down the drain. He pushed it back and ran some more water into the pot. "There are some old rags in that bin," he said, pointing. "We can scrub this out and use it like a tub."

"Uh..." She retrieved a rag and helped clean the pot, her mind wavering over the idea of Lad's suggestion. Not that the thought of a bath didn't sound wonderful; she was just unsure of where it might lead. Lad no longer had a magical inhibition suppressing his emotions, and she knew that he had strong feelings for her. She had strong feelings for him, too, but she didn't want things to go too far either. "You first. I'll wash your clothes out while you scrub, then you can do the same for me."

"All right."

Wiggen breathed a little easier. There was no hint of disappointment in his tone. She didn't know what she was scared of, really. She knew he wouldn't hurt her. She loved him, but he still frightened her a little.

When the pot was clean and rinsed one more time, he stripped from the black silk shirt and trousers without hesitation. She had intended to avert her eyes, but was caught unaware by the rows and rows of raised blisters from his neck to his ankles.

"Oh, gods, Lad! I just thought these were on your chest and arms!" He looked down and turned around. There were areas where the blistering was less severe, and even a few patches that were relatively free of damage, but, for the most part, his skin was a patchwork of red, raised flesh. "These must be killing you!"

"I don't think they'll kill me," he said, brushing some of the blisters on his flank and wincing, "but they hurt. I've never felt this before. It's distracting."

"Well, the cool water should help." She opened the valve and let the clean water fill the pot. "Can you climb in without tipping it over?"

"Yes."

He did so easily while she tried not to watch the muscle rippling in corded waves under his blistered skin. Wiggen gathered up his filthy clothes and looked around for something to wash them in. There were some smaller pots stashed in a corner. She retrieved one of these, along with a washboard and soft bristle brush. This place was obviously geared to handle vast amounts of dirty clothing and linen. When Lad's tub was full enough, he closed the valve.

"Does that feel better?" she asked, dipping her smaller pot into his.

"Yes. The cool water takes the pain away." He ducked his head under water and scrubbed his hair vigorously.

"I don't suppose there's any soap?" she asked when he surfaced.

"I don't know. There are many things in that bin with the rags." He astonished her by splashing her and smiling with mischief. "Ha! You look like the cat in the barn after it's caught in the rain!"

"Thanks!" She laughed despite the remark. He'd actually made a joke. And laughed. "You've never laughed before, have you?"

"No. Why?" He splashed at her again, missing intentionally. "Am I doing it wrong?"

"Only if you want me to wash these," she said, smiling and holding his clothes over the drain hole. "It'd be a shame if you had to walk around the city naked!"

"It would draw attention to us, Wiggen," he said, serious once again.

"I was joking," she said with a sour look. He might be regaining his emotions, but he had far to go before he developed a sense of humor. She opened the bin and began rooting through the piles of rags, blankets, brushes, and stirring rods. There were several large blocks of harsh lye soap, but she knew that would be no good for regular clothing, let alone Lad's silks. In the bottom of the bin, she found a small box that held four colored balls of scented soap, each a different fragrance.

"Here," she called to Lad, tossing him one that smelled of spices. "Use that, but be careful of the blisters. Try not to break them open."

"It smells like Forbish's pumpkin bread."

"I like his pumpkin bread." She smiled at him as he sniffed the soap and applied it gingerly to his skin.

She applied a second ball of soap to his clothes, scrubbing off the grime. She rinsed them three times before the water stayed clear. By that time Lad was standing beside his tub shivering. He reached for the clothes, but she pulled them out of his grasp.

"No, Lad. Find a sheet or something from the bin to wrap yourself in. These will have to dry before you put them on or you'll just get a chill."

"Oh. Yes, I *am* cold." He turned to the bin as she pushed the heavy tub to the drain. Tipping it out wasn't as hard as she thought it would be. The crank on the side was geared, and the tub was balanced to make it easier. There was a locking catch to keep it from tipping by accident. By the time she'd pushed it back under the spigot, Lad was wrapped in two reasonably clean blankets and was watching her, his shivering gone and his smile intact.

"Feeling better?"

"Yes!" He shook his head and droplets of water scattered from his hair. He winced as the blanket tugged at his tender skin. "The burns still hurt, but less."

"I don't know what caused the burns—the magic, I guess. I'm sorry you hurt, Lad."

"Don't be sorry, Wiggen. You freed me. I'd still be a slave and you'd be dead if you hadn't loved me." He reached out a hand and brushed her cheek, and she leaned into the caress. "Thank you, Wiggen."

"You're welcome." She smiled back at him, lost in his strange, wonderful eyes.

"Do you want me to take your clothes off now?"

"What?" She gaped at the question.

"Your clothes. You'll need to take them off to wash, and I can wash them like you did mine. Do you want help?"

"Oh! Uh, no, Lad. I can take them off."

"Okay." He stood there watching her, waiting.

"Um, you stay here and fill the tub. I'll go over there and take my dress off, okay?"

"All right," he said with a shrug. He reached up and pulled open the valve, watching the water rise in the tub as she walked quickly over to the bin and snatched up the biggest blanket she could find.

She managed to wrap the blanket around herself, hold it in her teeth and squirm out of her dress, all without exposing herself, a feat of which she was secretly proud, especially since Lad kept glancing over his shoulder at her, cocking his head quizzically. When she finally stepped out of the filthy dress, slip, and underclothes and tiptoed across the dusty floor to the tub, he was looking at her as if she was painted blue.

"What?" she asked defensively, tucking the blanket around herself more tightly.

"I don't understand why you did that with the blanket. It looked uncomfortable."

"It was uncomfortable, but I couldn't just peel out of my clothes right in front of you."

"Why not?"

"It wouldn't be *decent*, Lad." He reached up and shut off the valve. "It's different for you. You were never taught to feel modesty."

"Modesty?" His forehead crinkled in question.

"It's feeling uncomfortable without clothes in front of people," she explained, trying to keep it simple, "especially in front of someone you don't know well."

"But you know me, Wiggen."

"Yes, but... Well, I'm just uncomfortable, all right?"

"Okay."

"So, will you not *watch* while I get into the tub?"

"Oh. All right."

He turned away and busied himself sorting through her grimy clothes, putting some into the smaller pot to be washed. While he was busy, she tried to figure out a way to get into the tub without losing her blanket. Lad had simply climbed in like a squirrel up a tree. She couldn't match his agility, let alone while holding a blanket around herself. With a glance at Lad, she let the blanket drop and scrambled up and into the huge copper pot, splashing loudly and cracking her knee sharply on the edge. She bit back a cry of pain and massaged the injured joint. The water was cool, but not cold, and it felt absolutely wonderful. Slowly, she began to scrub away the caked-on filth.

"Do you feel better?"

"Wha—?" She whirled in the tub. Lad stood right beside the tub, looking down at her with that same quizzical smile. "Lad! What are you doing?"

"Getting water for your clothes." He lifted the smaller pot in emphasis, obviously surprised at her manner. "Don't you want me to wash them?"

"Uh, sure." She crouched in the tub. "Could you push me away from the spigot and fill it there?"

"Yes." He pushed her several feet away, and filled the smaller pot. Just as she started to relax again, he said, "Oh, and here's some soap for you." He handed it to her and smiled. It smelled of lavender.

"Thank you, Lad. Now, please, let me wash without you

264

watching. Okay?"

"Oh." He took a step back, understanding dawning on his face. "I'm sorry. Yes. I'll wash your clothes over here. I won't watch."

"Thank you."

"You're welcome." He turned his back and began scrubbing her clothes.

Wiggen slowly relaxed and washed away the grime, sweat, and fear of the last half day. Her hair took three washes before it felt clean, and when she was finished, the water was turbid.

"Wiggen?"

"Yes?" She looked, and smiled. He was standing ten feet away, turned sideways, his eyes carefully averted. He wore his damp trousers, but his shirt still hung over the corner of the bin.

"I should go out while it's still early. I need different clothes, and we should have some food. Do you need anything before I go?"

"Oh, uh, actually, yes." She hadn't thought about this before, but the inside of the pot was very slippery, and it was all she could do to kneel on the bottom. "I can't get out of here by myself. Could you just tip it over a little near the drain so I can climb out?"

"Yes."

Still averting his eyes, he pushed her over to the wide funnel set in the floor and worked the mechanism that tipped the big pot over. She managed not to let herself slip out of the pot with the water, and to her surprise, when she stepped gingerly out onto the floor, Lad was waiting with her blanket, his head turned to the side.

"Thank you." She enveloped herself in the material and smiled up at him. "You can look at me now."

"Good." He looked at her and smiled. "I like looking at you." He settled his palm onto the side of her face again, a strange gesture that she was learning to love. She stood there for a moment, relishing the feel of it. "I should go now. I'll be back as soon as I can."

"Okay," she said, brushing her cheek where he'd touched her. "Be careful."

He nodded and waved as he disappeared down the stairs. She

settled onto the blankets near the bin, listening to the rattle of the furnace door and then the outside flue vent. She laid her head down, her fingertips brushing where he had touched her face. Briefly, she wondered if her life would ever be the same, and if she wanted it to be. And not once while she lay there thinking did she remember the scar that marred her cheek.

Chapter XXIV

Bloody damn waste!" Norwood cursed, clenching his jaw against his temper as he watched a cloak being drawn over the last dead guard's face. He looked around the barracks lockup with a glare that could have melted the locks off the cell doors. "Eleven! Right here in the gods-damned barracks! This can't happen, Sergeant! Not in *my* city!"

"No, sir!" The guardsman stared past his captain at nothing, his face like stone, neck as stiff as an oak tree.

The man was scared, Norwood realized, and not just of his commander. All the guardsmen were. They were terrified and trying desperately not to show it. Well, he was getting a little scared, too, but not of this ghost of an assassin who seemed able to cut through his men like a scythe through so much wheat. He was scared for his city, for his duke, and for what would happen to both if these killings continued and he remained impotent to stop them.

"Sir!" A bright-eyed private descended the steps in a rush. "Sir, we've found how they got out!"

"About bloody damn time! Show me!"

He followed the man back up the stairs, but instead of turning left into the main hall, the guard led him into the storeroom. It was obvious enough where they'd gone. The flagstone over the bolt-hole had been pried up, and the trap door was still open.

"Blast! How in the Nine Unholy Hells did they know about this?" No one thought to answer the rhetorical question as he knelt and glared down the dark hole. "It hasn't been used since the old walls were torn down! I've never even seen it opened!"

"Yes, sir. Most of us didn't even know it was here." The private peered down the hole dubiously. "What's it for, if you don't mind my askin', sir?"

"It's a bolt-hole, Private." Norwood scratched his chin and stood. "Every keep has one, just in case the walls are breached and the royal family has to scoot. This used to be part of the original fortress, before the new palace was built up on the bluff. It won't do any good, but we better have a look down there."

He looked around at his guardsmen; they all shrank back like beaten curs.

"Sergeant Fursk, take two men and have a look. Don't you go too far, but if there are signs someone's gone through there, I want them followed. We might have to hire a tracker, but I want to know where this bolt-hole ends up. Got it?"

"Yes, sir!" The sergeant's voice was steady, at least. He picked two men and started laying out supplies of torches and rope.

Norwood turned and stalked out of the room, clenching his fists at his sides as the shrouded litter bearing one of his guardsmen was maneuvered up the stairs from the holding cells. Instead of following it, he turned down the steps. His feet took him to the open cell that had held their one and only lead in this whole messed-up investigation.

"Why take her?" he asked himself, smacking his fist into his palm as he examined the empty cell. There were no signs of struggle: no blood, no torn clothing. Nothing. He sighed deeply, and a faint scent in the air provoked an image of meat roasting on a spit. He shook the ridiculous thought out of his mind. There was no sign of fire in the cell, and nothing to burn. It was just his over-tired mind playing tricks on him. "Private!"

"Yes, sir!" The man was standing at his elbow in an instant.

"Tell Sergeant Tamir that we're going to have another talk with that innkeeper, Forbish."

"Yes, sir."

"And tell him to bring enough men to tear that inn apart.

There's got to be something we're missing, but I'll be damned to all Nine Hells if I can think what it is."

"I'll tell him, sir."

The guard left, leaving him alone to ponder the empty cell. He rubbed his chin thoughtfully and took a deep breath, trying to calm his murderous thoughts. That smell…cooking meat, or…ridiculous! Whoever this girl was, she was important enough to be the only person this assassin had taken the trouble to abduct instead of simply kill. There had to be a connection, and the only person who might know something was an innkeeper who had already made it very plain that he wasn't going to talk.

"Captain?" He turned to see Sergeant Tamir standing just outside the cell door. Either the man was unnaturally quiet or Norwood had been so deeply engrossed in his own morbid thoughts that he hadn't heard him arrive.

"You got my message, Sergeant?"

"Yes, sir, I did. Did you get mine?"

"No." He turned to face the man, knowing what the message must be. Tamir had been charged with protecting the two nobles scheduled for assassination this night. "Tell me."

"They're fine, sir," he said, his mouth trying to smile while his face tried not to.

"Fine?" Norwood's bushy eyebrows shot up. He advanced on the man, demanding clarification. "What do you mean, fine? Did you kill the bastard?"

"No, sir. I mean they're fine because nobody *tried* to kill them." He gestured down the hall where two maintenance workers were scrubbing the blood stains from the floor. "All this must have distracted him."

"Well, I'll be damned!" He looked back at the cell, wondering. "Maybe she..." He let the thought remain unsaid. It was best not to question such a fateful event, lest the gods reverse their judgment.

"I've got four squads ready, sir," Tamir said, interrupting him yet again.

"Oh, yes. Well, let's be at it then. I want to find out everything that innkeeper knows, Tamir, but I don't want him hurt." He headed for the stairs, grateful for the comforting presence of the sergeant behind him. "We'll take that inn apart if we have to, and we'll leave as big a force as necessary behind to ensure that he doesn't disappear, too."

"You're not going to arrest him?"

"I don't think so, Sergeant. It didn't protect his daughter; that's evident, and it might put more pressure on him to let him stew. Now that she's vanished, the truth is the only thing that's going to help us find her."

"Whatever you say, sir," the sergeant said in a tone that clearly stated that Tamir wasn't happy with the captain's plan. Norwood didn't particularly care if his sergeants were happy; all he cared about was that they followed his orders.

Mya knew something was wrong long before she rounded the corner onto Old Fort Street. There were more than the usual number of guards making their presence known in the quarter. When she made the turn onto the street, she almost stopped in her tracks and went back home. She hadn't seen this many constables and Royal Guard since the duke's most recent wedding. They were milling around the front of the barracks like bees before a hive, and at the center of the throng stood an undertaker's wagon. For her to walk right into their midst, disguise or no, took as much courage as she could muster.

She steeled her nerves, checked her disguise, and walked into the proverbial lion's den.

"You there, lass! What's your business here?"

"Why, I'm just headin' home, Captain sir," she said to the corporal she'd been counting on to stop her. She stumbled a bit, making sure her words weren't entirely crisp, trying for half-drunk and tired.

"This time of the morning?" He took in her unsteady stance, her slightly disheveled appearance, and the low cut of her dress. His eyes lingered in all the places she intended. "A little early for the likes of you on this side of the river, isn't it?"

She smiled the girlish smile that always worked on men like

this, and traced a finger down the guard's armored chest. "I had a bit of a late night at the magistrate's party, but I don't mind helpin' you greet the day right if you can break away from your duties, Captain."

"Not this morning, I'm afraid. We've got some dire business here. You'll have to be off."

"Dire business?" She looked at the crowd of guardsmen and constables all talking and bustling about. "Somebody die in their sleep?"

"That's no business of yours, lass," he said, grabbing her arm and steering her away from the crowd.

"It *could* be my business, Captain, if you'd just let it be." She turned in his grasp until her plunging neckline was pressed against his chest. "The news hawkers pay good money for the latest bits of who died and who did the killin'."

"This is an affair of the Royal Guard, and not for you." He pushed her away, but she felt his hand linger where no lady would let it. It was as much of an invitation as she needed.

"Oh, come now, Captain. Someone's gonna find out sooner or later." She pressed against him again, letting her hands wander. "You might as well be the one who *profits* by it."

"I'm on duty!" he said, lowering his voice and pushing her back again.

"Well, when do you get *off* duty?" She grabbed the hand he used to push her, clutching it to her bosom. She used the distraction to glance past him at the group of guards and saw a number of draped litters being carried from the door to the wagon. She counted five before he commanded her full attention.

"Mid-morning," he said, not withdrawing his hand. He glanced at the lightening sky. The sun would be fully up in less than an hour. "Four glasses or so."

"Oh, the news will be out by then, Captain," she said, pulling away from him and taking a step back. She fiddled with the lacings of her bodice and watched his eyes. "But if you tell me what happened, I promise I'll be back at the end of your shift."

"And I should trust you?"

She pouted at his incredulous tone. "You'd trust me with more than a little information, I think." She let her hand slip down to indicate exactly what she meant.

"Here! Stop that!" He pushed her hand aside, glancing over his shoulder. "You're gonna get me in trouble!"

"Come on, then. Give me a little something I can sell to the news hawkers, and I won't cause you any more trouble." She smiled mischievously. "Then maybe later you can cause *me* some trouble."

"Fine then." He stepped closer, lowering his voice to a whisper. "The same dark wraith that's been killin' nobles for the last few nights finally got 'round to payin' us a visit here. We were holdin' a girl, supposed to be some sort of witness or somethin', and last night, in he came. Killed one short of a dozen guards slick as you please and took her out of here without a trace."

"Took her?"

"Yep. Snatched her up like a trinket and vanished."

"Why not just kill her?"

"Don't know. And ever'body's been askin' that very question." He shrugged, and then grinned. "That little tidbit should be worth somethin'."

"When did you say you're off duty?" She didn't want to spoil the ruse quite yet.

"Mid-morning. I'll just wait down at the corner café."

"They rent rooms over that café, don't they?"

"They just might."

"I'll see you around mid-morning then, Captain."

"See you."

Not likely, she thought, giving him one more smile and turning on her heel. It never failed to amaze her how easily men were swayed by a bit of flesh.

Well, most men.

She quickened her pace as soon as she was around the corner.

A shaft of morning sunlight crept across Wiggen's face. She squinted in her sleep when it finally reached her eyes, and sleep dissolved into wakefulness. She rolled over on the hard floor, struggling to get comfortable, and her eyes fluttered open long enough to bring her fully awake in a heartbeat.

Lad sat there in the position he'd called 'lotus,' legs crossed, each foot upon the thigh of the other leg, his hands upturned on each knee, forefinger and thumb touching in two perfect circles. His eyes were closed, his face serene. He was meditating, his mind and body relaxed and at peace.

She sat up slowly. Trying not to disturb him, she wrapped her blanket around herself and watched him. His breathing was rhythmic, the faint pulse at his neck slow and even. He wore only his black silk trousers, and again she looked at the rows of blistered symbols raised on his skin. She longed to ease the pain those wounds must be causing him, the wounds he had earned in gaining his freedom, the wounds her love had carved into his flesh.

"Love hurts," she whispered under her breath, remembering the words that had almost seemed funny at the time. Her hand unconsciously rose to her face, her fingertips tracing the scar that ran from her temple to her chin. It was so familiar, such a part of her now, that she really didn't mind it so much. The pain of it had left her…finally.

She wondered if the other pain would ever leave her.

She closed her eyes as tears welled into them with the memory of what they had done to her, of what they had done to Tam. The memories hurt much less now, and never invaded her sleep or her conscious thoughts as they had before Lad taught her to calm her mind. Now she remembered only when she wanted to, and now the pain was bearable, like the cleansing of a wound so it would heal properly. She wondered if she was really beginning to heal all that had been done to her.

"Love hurts, and love heals." She truly didn't know where the thought came from or why she had said it aloud. She opened her eyes, hoping that she hadn't disturbed Lad's meditation, and was instantly delighted to see him smiling at her.

"Good morning," he said, reaching out to brush her damp cheek with the back of his fingers. "I didn't mean to wake you, and

I *certainly* didn't mean to make you cry."

"You *have* changed," she said, leaning into his caress. His smile had given his words a certain humor, something she would never have expected of him before last night. "There are good tears and bad tears. These are good tears. Healing tears."

"You were injured?" His smile vanished like a snowflake on a hot skillet, his hand dropping away from her face. "I didn't see—"

"No, Lad. The old hurt; the one you helped me with before, when you taught me how to meditate. I'm still healing. Sometimes tears help."

"How?" he asked, his alarm melting into that honest, open curiosity she'd fallen in love with.

"How do tears help?" At his nod she shrugged. "I don't really know. It's like some of the bad feelings escape with the tears. When you cry, you release some of the pain, and after, sometimes, you feel better."

"Can you teach me?"

Now it was her turn to look curiously at him. "Teach you how to cry?"

"Teach me how to heal," he said, and she could hear the pain in his words. His gaze dropped to his lap, his features sagging, adding years he hadn't lived. "You were right, Wiggen. About me, I mean. You were right about why I was made."

"I know." His eyes rose to meet hers, and the pain in his words was mirrored there. "All the nobles who were killed. We thought it was you."

"I killed them."

"I know, Lad," she said, reaching out to grasp his hand, pleased that he didn't shy from her touch as he had so many times before. "It's not your fault. You didn't want to kill those people."

"It was the magic, Wiggen. I don't know..." He took a deep breath, and she could see him reining in the anguish. "I was made to kill, Wiggen. The magic, the training, the things they made me not feel, it was all just so they could tell me to kill people and I would do it."

"I know."

"And *I* know now, how *you* feel." The anguish in his eyes gripped her heart in talons of steel. "Memories plague my thoughts every moment, Wiggen. It's hard to meditate and harder to sleep." His eyes closed as he took another deep calming breath, grasping for control, but she knew that kind of control was just an illusion. "I see their faces every time I close my eyes."

"Then let it out, Lad." She squeezed his hand harder, commanding his attention. "Let yourself grieve, not for what you've done, but for those poor people your *master* killed!"

"My master?"

"Yes, Lad. Your master killed those people, not you. Like you told me, you were made to be a weapon, and a weapon you were. Is a sword to blame if an evil hand takes it up and kills an innocent person?"

"But I..." He tried again to hold his feelings in with a deep breath, but she grabbed his other hand and jerked both of them hard.

"No! Stop it! Don't do that! Don't hold it in!" She didn't know how to make him understand that if he didn't let his feelings out, they'd drive him mad. She watched his face transform from incomprehension to recognition. Then, in one horrible rush, the terrible anguish surfaced.

"I *killed* them, Wiggen!" he cried, his face contorting with pain. "Every one of them! I killed them all! They were afraid, and they died by my hand, and their blood is never going to wash away! All their friends and families, everyone who loved them will hate me. They'll want me dead, and they'll be *right* to want me dead."

"No, Lad," she said, pulling him closer, forcing him to look at her. "You were just the weapon. It wasn't you!"

"I'm *not* a weapon, Wiggen," he wailed, his voice cracking, his grip painful and urgent, "I'm a *murderer*!"

"No, Lad! You're not!" She pulled him close, wrapping him in a protective embrace, wanting only to take his pain away. "It wasn't you! It wasn't!"

"How could they make me do those things, Wiggen? How

could they?" She felt his shoulders shudder with a wracking sob, and felt his arms envelop her.

"I don't know, Lad. I don't know."

He cried into the blanket wrapping her shoulders, his tears wetting the nape of her neck, one wracking sob after another, until he finally calmed. His arms slackened their embrace and his head ducked away. She let him go, wanting nothing more than to keep holding him close a little longer.

"I'm sorry, Wiggen," he said, sniffing back the tears. "All these feelings..."

"Don't be. It's all new for you. I can't imagine what you're feeling."

"I'm *scared*." He met her eyes once more, and she could see the truth in them. "I'm scared for you and for Forbish and for myself. I've never felt this way before, and I don't *like* it. I don't know how I'm going to do *anything* feeling like this." He laughed shortly and pointed to a bundle propped against the bin. "I could barely get us new clothes and some food."

"But you did!" She grasped his chin and forced his eyes to meet hers. "You were afraid, but you did it. That's courage."

"Courage?"

His eyes told her that this was a word he had never heard before. At first, she was stunned by the irony—a warrior, an assassin, unfamiliar with the concept of courage—until she realized that Lad was unfamiliar with it simply because he had never needed it.

"Yes, courage," she said, grasping his hands once again. "Courage is when you overcome something that scares you because you know what you're doing is right. It's what brought us through that sewer, whether you know it or not. You have more courage than you know, Lad."

"Courage..." he said, as if trying on the word for the first time. "How do you get more of it?"

"Uh...I don't know. I never thought of it that way. I don't know if you can get more. Some people have more than others, and some just have it when they really need it, like Father. He's not very courageous, but he did what he had to do when you were taken away."

"And what was that?"

"Oh, he asked some old friends of his if they knew anything about you, and he found out that they were just as afraid as he was." She laughed shortly. "I think that surprised him more than a little."

"What were they afraid of?"

"The people who took you, I guess. Father was scared of these old friends of his, but they were even more scared."

"They were right to be scared, Wiggen. The man who had me made, they call him the Grandfather. He's old, and he's evil. He was using me to put pressure on the duke for some reason. He wants something, but I'm not sure what. I think Mya knows, but she never told me."

"Mya?" Wiggen felt a tug at her stomach. "Who's that?"

"She's an assassin, a Hunter. She's the one who caught me." He looked at the palm of his hand as if it held some secret, and smiled thinly. "She's very treacherous and very smart." He looked back to her. "She was my keeper. She gave me orders, made sure I was fed, clothed, and healthy enough to keep killing for the Grandfather."

"She sounds terrible," she said, not liking the tone of Lad's voice when he spoke of this woman.

"I don't think she liked what she was being made to do, but she did it anyway. She was a slave, like me, but she wouldn't admit it." His short bark of laughter caught Wiggen off guard. "I was trying to convince her to help me kill the Grandfather, but she wouldn't do it, of course. She was probably smart not to. He would have killed her."

She didn't know what to say to that, so she just sat and watched him, trying to imagine all of the things that had happened to him and wondering if she really wanted to know.

"Are you hungry?" he asked suddenly, breaking the silent tension.

"Starving!" she admitted, pushing herself up as he vaulted to his feet and retrieved the bundle.

"Come eat then." He began laying out cheese, bread, and a link of hard sausage.

She joined him, and they ate together, the conversation lagging in favor of much-needed food. But while she ate, Wiggen wondered. She wondered at all the terrible things that had befallen Lad, at what they would do now that he was free, and she wondered most of all why he had so suddenly changed the subject.

# Chapter XXV

Mya walked unhindered through the gates of the Grandfather's estate just before the orb of the sun had risen over the high walls. The guards just nodded, letting her pass without a challenge. They knew her now; they knew she was the Grandfather's favorite and, regardless of her diminutive rank, they treated her with respect. That was one of the few advantages she'd gained with her position. On the walk from the gate to the estate steps, however, she realized that something was amiss. The stable boys raked dung and hauled hay, but without their usual banter. Twice as many guardsmen as usually manned the outer wall now walked in pairs at odd intervals around the lofty perimeter. They followed her progress across the courtyard, questions unasked hidden behind their narrowed gazes. The Grandfather's valet stood at the foyer, his arms folded, his face even more of a scowl than usual.

"What's wrong?" she asked without preamble.

His eyes flickered to hers with open annoyance before he gave a short shrug and said, "He's gone."

"Who?"

"Who do you think?"

With all she'd been through in the last few days, the valet's insolence grated on her like a dull blade on bone. Without thought, she produced a dagger from the folds of her dress. One step and a truncated thrust brought the tip of her blade to rest under the point of his chin.

"I asked who had gone missing! I already know one person is missing, I wish to know if there's another. If this is too much for your menial little mind to grasp, I'll ask someone else," she twitched the tip of the dagger just enough to break the skin, "right after I have your *kidneys* on *toast* for my breakfast! Now *answer* me!"

"The Grandfather is missing," he said without moving his jaw in the slightest. "He hasn't been seen since you left earlier this morning."

She withdrew the dagger, wiped its tip on her dress, and sheathed it. "And he didn't say where he was going?"

"If he said where he was going, he wouldn't be missing, now, would he?" The valet wiped the blood from his chin with the back of his hand and looked at the red smear disdainfully.

She ignored him and walked away, wondering if insolence to the point of stupidity was a prerequisite for the position of guildmaster's valet. She had little doubt that he'd looked in all the likely places, so she resigned herself to waiting for the Grandfather's return. In the meantime, she could do with a bath and some much-needed sleep.

Another advantage of her position was the use of the estate staff. Within minutes she had a huge copper tub full of steaming water in her chambers and an attendant waiting with soap, towels, and a warmed robe. In those few minutes she drafted a succinct account of her findings at the barracks and told one of the attendants to see that the Grandfather received it upon his return.

Submersed in hot water, a trained masseuse kneading the knots out of the muscles of her shoulders, she felt the tension begin to melt away.

Lad was gone, and now the Grandfather as well. There was relief and unease combined in both of their absences. She knew Lad wasn't dead; the guardsman she'd seduced would have spilled that much, she was sure. How he'd circumvented the magic was a mystery to her, but one she felt no compulsion to solve. He was free; she couldn't change that. What he would do with his newly won freedom was of much more concern.

Clean, dry, and enveloped in the robe's comforting folds, she began to feel somewhat human. As the servants cleared away the tub, Mya pulled the heavy drapes to block out the morning sun. She slipped out of the robe, climbed into the plush bed, drew up the covers and closed her eyes. But despite her exhaustion, her thoughts were a tumult of images, worries, and dangers. Death could come for her at any moment from either of two likely directions: the Grandfather, who might kill her for her failure to keep his weapon secure; or Lad, who, now that he was free from his magical bonds, would be out for blood.

And not just her blood.

That could work to her advantage, she thought, if Lad came for the Grandfather. Depending on how that encounter played out, she might come out of this with her skin intact. She rolled over and tried to relax, but sleep was a long time coming.

"Bloody Hells," Forbish muttered as the heavy bag of flour hit the floor and flames of pain coursed up his back. He straightened, grinding his knuckles into the spot that plagued him. The pain eased, and he bent again to pick up the bag.

"Here, now! Don't you lift that," Josie scolded, backing through the door to the main room, laden with a stack of cups and saucers. "You'll hurt yourself serious, and then what are you going to do?"

"Who else will do it?" he grumbled, dropping the bag onto the counter with a grimace. He stiffened his posture and ladled several cups of flower into his largest mixing bowl. "Until Wiggen's back, there's naught but me to do the lifting." He cracked six eggs, two at a time, with one hand while he poured fresh milk into the bowl with the other.

"Oh, and what am I?" Josie put the cups down and bustled over, glaring all the way. "I'm not just another pretty face, you know!" She lifted the flour off the counter and balanced it on her hip while she tied the bag closed and railed at him. "Which is another thing I been meanin' to tell you. You take too much onto yourself. Let someone else do some work around here. I've got two good-for-nothin' nephews who'd be tickled to death to come work for you, just until Wiggen gets back, you know. You needn't pay them much. They're better off here than rattin' around down by the docks where there's only trouble."

"I don't know, Josie," he said, adding the remaining ingredients for his oatcakes and beating the batter with a large spoon. "I've got to figure out a way to get Wiggen back, but all the work's piling up around here. It wouldn't feel right hiring strangers. Maybe I should close the inn for a few days."

"Here now, what kind of talk is that?" Josie heaved the bag of flour back into its protective bin and closed the lid tightly. "They wouldn't be strangers; they'd be my *nephews*. If they touch one thing they oughtn't, I'll whale 'em within an inch of their scrawny lives!"

Forbish opened his mouth to answer, but was interrupted by a booming call of, "INNKEEPER!" from the main room. His eyes widened in worry, and he dusted his hands on his apron.

"Oh, what now?"

Josie followed him through the door.

They were confronted by a contingent of royal guard that seemed to flood into the common room without end. A full troop of twenty had already startled the few patrons out of their seats and backed them up against the hearth, and more came through the doors with every passing second. None of the guardsmen had drawn weapons, but their mere presence was intimidating enough. Forbish and Josie found themselves backed into the corner by a gruff-looking sergeant and two nervous men-at-arms.

"What's this about?" Forbish managed to ask despite the sudden shock. "Who's in charge here?"

"Captain Norwood's in charge, innkeeper. Now you just keep your mouth shut until we got this place squared away." The sergeant glanced over his shoulder and snapped, "Corporal, secure the kitchen. Take a squad and sing out if you see so much as a mouse!"

"Aye, Sergeant!" The corporal gathered together five guardsmen and burst through the door into the kitchen, hands on their sword hilts.

"The rest of you quarter and search the upstairs. Don't take any chances! Any door that's locked gets the boot! Go!"

Sixteen guards thundered up the stairs to the second floor as Forbish's guests stared on in shock, taken aback by the invasion of their privacy, but too afraid to say anything. The guards' departure thinned the crowd in the common room enough for Forbish to finally spot the man in charge of this invasion.

"Captain Norwood!" he shouted, fear and anger vying to edge his words. "This is twice in as many days you've invaded the *Tap and Kettle*. Have you come to take the rest of us under custody for these murders we know nothing about?"

"Curb your indignity, Master Forbish, or at least save it for someone who gives a damn." The captain strode through the assembled guardsmen like a ship parting a choppy sea, and when he finally stood before Forbish, the innkeeper could tell he was very near the limit of his temper. "Your daughter is no longer in my custody. I've come here to make sure she hasn't returned home, and to try to find the murdering bastard who freed her."

"Wiggen's gone?" Forbish surged forward, ignoring guards. They held him back as his heart hammered in his chest. He felt it would surely break if Wiggen were dead. She was the last family he had. If she were gone… "What's happened to her? You said she'd be *safe*!"

"Eleven of my guardsmen *died* trying to protect your daughter, innkeeper," the captain said through grinding teeth, his hand clenched white on his sword's hilt. "We're going to search this inn for any sign of her. If I find so much as a scrap of bloodied cloth, I'm going to take you in and lock you in the deepest, darkest hole in the duke's dungeon. Is that perfectly clear?"

"Yes, Captain," he muttered, his thoughts whirling in an attempt to make sense of this. Clearly, Lad had taken Wiggen; no one else could wade through a dozen royal guardsmen and survive. But Lad couldn't have been acting on his own. Or could he? Stealing Wiggen away didn't make sense. If someone was controlling him, killing her would have been easier, and would have kept her quiet for good. That should have been enough. It made no sense, unless Lad had freed her on his own. Which would mean there was a chance she was still alive. Hope blossomed in him, but he was unsure exactly what to do with his newly found optimism.

To the sound of boots thundering around upstairs, Forbish realized that there was at least one thing he could do. He produced a ring of keys from his pocket and held them out to the captain.

"There's no need to go busting down doors, Captain. These open every door in the place from basement to rafters." The captain took them with a nod and handed them to another guardsman, who ran upstairs. "And you'll want to have a look at Wiggen's room. It's in the back, through there. I know you won't believe me, but I haven't seen her since you took her away."

"Actually, I do believe you, Mister Forbish." The officer's face softened a bit then, and Forbish could see the fatigue and pain beneath the iron facade. "I'm not trying to harass you or bully you into telling me anything new by coming here, but I had to search the inn, and I'm through losing guardsmen to this murderer. I need to know why your daughter was taken and not killed, and I need to know why the murders scheduled to occur last night didn't happen. Something has changed—I can feel it—but I don't know enough about this killer or his motives to make a decent guess."

"You look like you could use a cup of blackbrew, Captain," Forbish said, thinking that the captain would make a much better ally than an enemy. If the man was right, and something had changed, maybe it was time to tell him some of what he knew. "I was about to serve breakfast to my guests here when your men came in. If you let them sit back down, and take a seat yourself, I'd be willing to sit and have a chat with you."

"I could use a cup at that, thank you. Sergeant, have the men here go search the barn and the cow byre. Let the guests relax. When the search is finished, leave a squad and take the rest back to the barracks."

"Aye, Captain." The sergeant made a few gestures, and all but four guardsmen left for the barn. He then took up station next to the fireplace, arms folded, scowling at the entire room.

"Just have a seat over here, Captain," Forbish offered, guiding the man to the table nearest the kitchen door. "I've got a kettle on, and there'll be oat cakes with honey for you if you're hungry. Josie here will see to you until I finish cooking."

"Thank you." Captain Norwood took a seat and Josie set a place for him, casting curious glances over her shoulder at Forbish while she worked.

"I'll be out with blackbrew for you in a moment." He nodded to Norwood and winked at Josie, as he headed for the kitchen. "I'll bring out a cup for your sergeant, too, just to show there's no hard feelings."

He opened the damper to the stove and put the kettle over the firebox. Cooking was like meditation for Forbish; it calmed his nerves and helped him think. By the time he had a stack of steaming oatcakes on the sideboard and six cups of blackbrew on a tray for Josie to take out to the Captain and his men, he'd figured out just how much to tell Norwood. He only hoped it was enough to save his daughter, and maybe even enough to save Lad as well.

After their makeshift breakfast, Wiggen and Lad had both grown sleepy. At first, she closed her eyes contentedly and slipped off to a dreamless slumber, but exhaustion notwithstanding, the floor of an abandoned laundry is not a bed, and in a matter of hours she found herself tossing and turning. Finally, she opened her eyes in frustration.

Lad lay perfectly still, his eyes open and staring at the ceiling.

"You're awake," she said, pushing herself up. "You should be sleeping. You must be exhausted."

"I can't sleep," he said with a weak smile. He brushed the burns on his chest and winced. "These blisters won't let me rest, and my mind is full of thoughts that won't let sleep come to me." He rolled up to a sitting position, and she noticed the blanket beneath him was splotched with moisture. Many of the blisters on his back had burst.

"We should find some salve to put on those blisters," she said, gathering her blanket around herself. "If they go septic, you'll get sick."

"I've never been sick before." He shook his head, his smile faintly pinched. "I wouldn't know if I did get sick. What does sick feel like?"

"You feel weak, tired, nauseous. You'd know if you felt it."

"Maybe I'm already sick. I feel strange, like there's something in my mind that won't rest. I feel all these things, think all these things, and it won't stop."

"What do you think about?" she asked, hoping to bring his trouble out into the open. Perhaps it was something she could help him overcome. The gods knew he'd helped her enough; some reciprocity would make her feel less helpless.

"I should tell you what I *don't* think about, Wiggen," he said with a laugh. "It would be a shorter list!"

"Sounds to me like you're worrying too much." She reached out and rested her hand on his knee. "Tell me some of it. Maybe I can help."

"Very well. My foremost worry is what will become of us. Where will we go? How will we live?" He gestured to her, then to himself. "We are both easily recognizable, and the Grandfather has a very long reach. Eluding him will be very difficult."

"Well, we could ask my father for...uh." He was already shaking his head.

"The duke's Guard is also seeking us. The *Tap and Kettle* will be watched by both the duke's men and the Grandfather's."

"We could slip out of town on a barge, couldn't we? Head down the river to Southaven? The Grandfather can't reach *that* far."

"I don't know how far Southaven is, but getting out of the city on a barge would be dangerous. The Grandfather has men on the docks. He's deeply involved in trade. I think that might have been part of the reason he was pressuring the duke. Something to do with trade on the river."

"Well, there are other ways out of the city. He can't watch every gate all the time."

"Yes, he can, Wiggen, and he will. We might be able to spot his watchers, but the only way to keep them from telling the Grandfather of our passage would be to kill them." His expression grew grave. "I don't want to kill anyone I don't have to."

"I don't want you to kill anyone at all," she agreed, but she could see that there was more to what he'd said. The muscles of his jaw clenched and relaxed rhythmically, as if he were chewing on an idea that had formed and couldn't be swallowed.

Then, as if a light had been kindled in her mind, she knew what he was thinking.

"You want to kill him...the Grandfather. Lad, I don't think—"

"It may be the only way we can stay alive and free, Wiggen."

"It's more than that," she said flatly, seeing something in his eyes that she had hoped never to see. "You hate him."

"I...don't know." His brow furrowed in thought. "I don't know what hate feels like."

"Hate feels like..." She struggled for an analogy. "If you feel angry whenever you think of someone, like you want to hurt them, that's hate."

"Then yes, Wiggen. For what he did to me, that he had me made, and what he made me do, I hate him, but that is not the only reason I want him dead."

"It's revenge, Lad. I understand you want to get back at him for hurting you, but—"

"No. Not for hurting me. Not just that." He stopped then, and his gaze slid away from hers, down to the floor between them. "It's...more than that."

"What, Lad? What more?" she pleaded, wanting more than anything to understand him.

"He *made* me, Wiggen. You must understand how that makes me feel, now that I *can* feel."

"No, I don't understand. I can't imagine it. But I *do* know what it's like to be helpless and tortured and left for dead. Killing him won't make that feeling go away, Lad."

"I was told my whole life that all my work, all my training, was for one purpose. I was told that I had a destiny, a reason for living. You can understand that, can't you Wiggen?"

"I suppose," she said, trying to imagine it. "You only knew what they told you, so you believed it."

"Yes, and it was the truth, Wiggen. I *did* have a destiny: I was destined to be the perfect killer: unthinking, unfeeling, without any reason to believe that what I was doing was wrong. I would have been content, except..."

"Except for me," she finished for him. "I told you killing was bad."

"Yes, Wiggen, and for that I owe you more than I can ever give you back. You opened my eyes before I was made into something evil. You saved me from it."

"Yes! And now we're free!" She didn't understand the conflict in him. It was all behind them. All they had to do was escape.

"And the Grandfather is free to have another such as me...constructed."

"But that would take years, Lad. He couldn't wait that long."

"It took years to have *me* made. I don't think time is something that the Grandfather worries about. He's old, but he's not aged. His skin is wrinkled, but his body moves with more grace and power than anyone I've ever seen. Even the trainers my master paid to instruct me didn't have his..." She could see him searching vainly for the word, the one term that really described the Grandfather. He failed. "I think he would wait another twenty years for the perfect weapon."

"And we'll be far away and have children of our own by then, Lad," she said, pleading with him not to take such a dangerous course. "Why risk it?"

"How could I *not* risk it, Wiggen?" he asked, his eyes searching her face, his mouth quirking into that innocent smile she loved more every time she saw it. He reached out to her, the tips of his fingers brushing aside a lock of hair that had fallen across her face. "How could I live, and love, and feel all these things, knowing that another like me was being made, blind to the evil he was being made for?"

"But they're *killers*, Lad!" She shook her head in denial,

pushing his hand away, angry that he would risk all they had gained for something so intangible. "How can you even think it?"

"I can think it because I'm a killer, too, Wiggen."

His voice changed with that, it had become dangerous and cold. She shivered beneath her blanket despite the day's warmth.

"I'll remain a killer until the Grandfather of Assassins is dead. He holds the secret to what I am. He holds a power over me, even without the magic." Lad held up one hand; all but the palm was pocked with rows of blisters. "I can't allow him to do this to someone else, even someone I don't know. His evil will go on forever if someone doesn't stop it."

"But why you? Why do you have to be the one? Why not tell the guard? Tell the duke! Let *them* kill him!"

"Would they believe me, Wiggen, after all the things I've done?" He shook his head and reached out to brush away a tear that had found its way to her chin. "No one believes a murderer."

"But it's not *fair*!" she cried, clutching his hand and pressing her lips to his palm. "I just got you back, and now you're leaving me! They'll kill you, and I'll be alone, and I won't even be able to go home!"

"They won't kill me, Wiggen," he assured her, taking her face in his hands and forcing her to look him in the eye. "I was made to be better than they are. I've bested their best before."

"They *caught* you before!"

"Yes, by treachery, after I had beaten them. That was Mya. I know her now, and I'll be ready for her tricks. Only the Grandfather poses a real threat. I mustn't give him the opportunity to fight."

She didn't like any of it, least of all this treacherous woman whom Lad thought he knew. This Mya didn't sound the type who could be second-guessed so easily. No, it was far too dangerous. He'd been stolen from her once. Now she had him back, and he was going off to risk his life. She couldn't lose him again. She glared at him, angry and hurt, but also knowing that he was right. Whether she liked it or not, he had to do it…for himself. He had to do it to be free.

"Do you have to go now?" she asked, grasping at his wrists, trying in vain to hold back her tears.

"No. Not until dark."

"Until dark, then," she said, pulling him to her until their lips met, the salt of her tears mingling with the kiss. "You're *mine* until dark."

Mya woke to the aroma of eggs, sausage, fresh bread, and blackbrew. At first, she thought it was a wonderfully vivid dream, but when her eyes opened and spied the full tray inches from her nose, she bolted upright in surprise.

"Careful," the Grandfather said, holding the tray perfectly balanced before her, "you'll spill the blackbrew."

She stared at him in shock. He sat on the edge of her bed, black robes clean and pressed, his wizened features calm and faintly amused. He held the tray an inch above the bed so that her sudden awakening hadn't tossed the whole thing onto the floor.

"Grandfather!" She sat back against the headboard, trying to banish the sleep from her mind while clutching the covers to her breast. His mild manner unnerved her more than if he'd woken her with the tip of one of his daggers at her throat. "You're back!"

"Yes, Mya. I am back." He put the tray down carefully on her lap and poured blackbrew for her. It was already lightened exactly the way she liked it. "I didn't know how lengthy my little fact-finding mission would be. I had thought to be back in but a few hours."

She accepted the cup from his rock-steady hand, still trying to blink the sleep from her eyes. The sun was coming through a slit in the drapes at a very steep angle; it was close to noon. "What facts did you seek to find?" she asked, sipping the blackbrew carefully.

"I must admit that I suspected you had betrayed me."

Mya ran the warm blackbrew over her tongue, wondering if some subtle poison lurked there for her to swallow. But he could have killed her easily enough as she slept.

"The sudden and seemingly inexplicable disappearance of my weapon, the fact that his other targets weren't eliminated, and my belief that the magic that bound him was inviolate, led me to conclude that you had altered my commands and told the weapon to take the girl and flee." He inclined his head in a stiff bow, a gesture she could tell he was unaccustomed to performing. "I erred in my judgment of you, Mya. You have my sincerest apologies."

He was apologizing to *her*? Now she was *really* unnerved.

Mya had absolutely no idea how to respond. There was more to this than a simple 'sorry for thinking you had betrayed me.' He had no reason to apologize for judging her harshly or falsely; her life was his to spend. He would only put himself in this position if he needed something from her, something that she could provide only if she trusted that he wouldn't betray her loyalty. But what? She had very little doubt that her belated breakfast wouldn't be finished before she knew exactly what he wanted from her.

"I live to serve you, Grandfather," she said with a minute shrug. "You may judge me as you wish. It's not my place to forgive the actions of one such as yourself."

"Very politic, as always, Mya," he said with a tight smile, one that didn't match his apologetic manner. "That, I believe, is why I've come to find you so valuable. You never stop thinking, even when you know your life is in danger."

"Thank you, Grandfather."

"In answer to your original query, I sought magical assistance in divining the circumstances of my weapon's disappearance." He gave a shrug, as if he had finally decided just how much to tell her. "As I said, I thought you had betrayed me. I found this not to be the case, which meant the weapon's magical bonds had been circumvented some other way. I'd been told that the magic that bound my weapon was inviolate. It would appear that Corillian exaggerated the potency of his own enchantments. An expert in this area of magic has informed me that any binding magic may be broken given the correct circumstances and a sufficiently strong force of will."

"So you believe that the spells that held your weapon have been broken?" Mya had very little doubt of it, having seen the power of Lad's will first hand.

"That's what I believe. My weapon is free. Exactly how many of the other enchantments that infused his body failed when the binding spell was broken, we can't know until he's captured. Then the wizard I have contracted can—"

"You think to get him *back*?" she asked incredulously, spilling hot blackbrew on the tray.

"That's my wish, Mya," the Grandfather said after a short, strained pause. "Once he's in my possession, the spells of binding can be recast. I believe you're the one with the proper talents to capture him for me."

"Excuse my frankness, Grandfather, but why do you think Lad will come within twenty leagues of here?" The luscious breakfast that had been so mouthwatering moments ago had lost its enticement. Her appetite was gone.

"Oh come now, Mya, be truthful with me. You know my weapon far better than I, and even I know that he hates me more than he loves his own life, even if he is too emotionally crippled to understand it." He stole a piece of sausage from the tray in Mya's lap and bit off a quarter of its length. "He'll come for me, and soon, if I'm any judge of human character. You think he won't?"

"I think he'll come for the both of us, Grandfather," she admitted, pushing the tray away a few inches. "He may despise me even more than you. I also think there's precious little either you or I can do to keep him from killing us if he's set his mind to do so."

"I beg to differ on that point, my dear," he said, taking another bite of sausage and smiling at her as he chewed and swallowed. "I think you underestimate both your *and* my capabilities. You defeated him before—not with brawn, but with cunning deception. That, coupled with my own talents for stealth and martial conflict, should be sufficient for the task. All we need do is devise a trap that will render him unconscious without damaging him."

"He won't be fooled so easily this time, Grandfather. He learns very quickly. I didn't tell you of the fighting forms I commanded him to show me. He took six of the classic martial styles and melded them into one. It is the most complete form of martial combat I've ever seen." She paused, fixing his ancient eyes with her own. "He did this on his *own*, sir, without instruction, without being taught how. He's more than a weapon, Grandfather; he's a thinking, analyzing, learning weapon."

"Which is all the more reason to get him back under my control." The guildmaster stood from the bed and reached into the folds of his robe. "I'm unused to asking for help, Mya. I am used to commanding it. Yet I know you'll serve me better if you trust that I no longer doubt your loyalty. To that end, I have a gift for you."

He withdrew his hand from his robes and held it out to her. On his palm was a ring of purest obsidian, as black as the depths of the Abyss. Mya knew what it was. She had coveted it for most of her life. It was a master's ring.

"Take it," he said, his voice like bloodstained silk.

Desire for power was something that had driven Mya since the day she'd left home. More than half her life had been spent in the pursuit of this single token, this one symbol that would give her all the power she'd ever longed for. To have it bestowed upon her at such a tender age was unprecedented. The guild would never allow it.

But the Grandfather *was* the guild. His word was law.

She just stared at it.

"Grandfather, I—"

"Take it!"

She lifted the tiny thing from his palm. It felt heavy, more of a burden than it should have been for its size. She looked at it closely, having seen only one before. There were five of the rings in existence, which meant...

"It belonged to your erstwhile master, Targus. Put it on."

Targus... Visions of his death swam in the ring's burnished surface.

Now, as her life's goal rested in her palm, she thought it more akin to a link of black chain than a vaunted symbol of power. It would bind her to the Grandfather forever, but she had seen how loyalty had been repaid. The Grandfather could have saved Targus with a single word, but that word had been withheld on a sadistic whim. She knew she'd fare no better in the end.

The power she'd sought was an illusion, a lure, a seduction into slavery.

"Put it on!"

The lure had worked. She was trapped. She'd come too far to refuse the last link in the chain that would bind her forever.

She slipped the ring onto the third finger of her left hand and felt it size itself to fit her. It could never be removed, lest her heart ceased to beat. The rings of the master assassins were said to have other powers as well. She knew some of the rumors, and hoped most of them were only that.

The Grandfather held up his left hand, showing her his own ring. His was obsidian woven with gold. "We are now bonded, Mya; I to you, and you to me. Loyalty will be repaid with trust, service with reward, and folly with death. I've already informed the guild of your new position. You are now Master Hunter Mya. Anyone who flouts your authority will answer to me, and that will be a very brief conversation indeed." He bowed to her then, and turned to go.

"Grandfather," she said, stopping him in his tracks. He turned and regarded her with veiled amusement.

"Yes?"

"It will be tonight. Lad will come for us tonight."

"So soon?" One snowy eyebrow cocked at her, questioning.

"I know him. He'll come tonight."

"Then we must be ready for him, don't you think?"

"We'll be ready, Grandfather."

"Good." He left her room, the door closing with a definitive click.

"Or we'll be dead by morning," she finished, leaving the comforting folds of her bed to face the task she knew in her heart would end in her own death, one way or the other.

Chapter XXVI

$\int$he woke to the feather-light touch of his fingers running through her hair and the whisper of her name from his lips.

"Wiggen..."

For a moment she thought it a dream, the sound and touch mixing with the sweet memory of their lovemaking. She was warm and comfortable lying like this, his body curled against her back, fitting like two spoons in a velvet case. She didn't want to wake up, didn't want the dream to end, but she knew it must.

"Wiggen." Lad's fingers brushed through her hair again, soft and tender. "It's time."

"No," she mumbled, snuggling back against his warmth. His skin was like a furnace against her back.

"Yes, Wiggen. I have to go."

"I don't want you to go." She clenched her eyes closed, wishing she were dreaming.

"I know. I don't want to go, but..."

"But you have to." She turned until she could see Lad's face in the dim light, inches from her own. She could see the battle raging behind those luminous eyes, and she knew there was only one way for that conflict to end. "I know."

He kissed her and rose from their bed, the fading light of dusk from the high windows playing over his form as he donned his black silks. She sat up as he finished, knowing this could be the last time she ever saw him, and wondering if there was anything she could say to make him stay. She knew there wasn't.

"When will you be back?" she asked, pulling her blankets closer. This wasn't an attempt at modesty, for they knew every inch of one another now; she was already feeling alone, and the blanket still smelled of him and held his warmth. The closer she held it, the longer she could stave off the feeling of being left alone.

"I should be back by morning. Midmorning at the latest." He cinched the drawstring of his trousers tight and looked around. He was taking nothing with him; he needed nothing.

"What should I do if you don't come back?" Saying it almost broke her heart, but she wanted to know what he wanted. If Lad died, there was nothing left for her. She wanted to do as he wished; nothing else would matter.

"If I don't come back before highsun tomorrow, go to the inn. The duke will have men there, and you should be safe." He shrugged, smiled, and added, "Tell them everything I've told you about the Grandfather. His estate is near the river in the north of Barleycorn Heights. It's walled and has a single tower higher than any in the district. It's easy to find."

"Should I tell them about you?"

"It won't matter. If you want to tell them, then yes, but the Grandfather is the one who controls the Assassins Guild. I never knew why he wanted those nobles dead, but he's the one they want. If they kill him, there will be no more nobles murdered."

"I'll tell them," she said, pushing herself to her feet. "Now, let me hold you one more time before you go."

"Come here." He took her in his arms then, burying his face in the nape of her neck. They stood clutching one another for a long time, neither wanting to let go. Then, finally, he whispered, "Wiggen..."

"I know."

"I love you."

"I know. I love you, too." She released him then, and wiped the tears from her eyes with the corner of her blanket. "Please promise me, Lad. Be careful. Come back to me."

"There's nothing I want more in the world than to be with you,

Wiggen. I'll come back to you if I can. I promise."

That was all she could ask of him.

She pulled him close one last time and kissed him. When their lips parted, she said, "Go now, before I do something silly like break down bawling and beg you to stay."

"I *will* come back to you, Wiggen," he said, squeezing her hands once more before turning to dash down the steps.

Wiggen sat down in her blankets, pulling them close. She listened for his passage through the furnace and the vent, but she heard nothing. He was already moving as if his life depended on it, utterly silent, invisible, and lethal as death itself.

"Good," she said to herself, drawing the blankets closer and breathing deeply of his scent. "Maybe he *will* come back to me."

Captain Norwood leaned back in the chair, his feet on the wide stone hearth, the warmth of the fire baking through the hard leather soles of his boots. The tankard in his lap was almost empty, and it was not his first. Forbish's tale had taken more than one tankard of ale to swallow, and he still was having trouble believing it.

"And you say the boy knew nothing of why he'd been given this magic." He'd heard the same story a dozen times, but he kept repeating it, hoping for some clue.

"He was as witless to his own purpose as he was to everything else, Captain, I swear it." The innkeeper sipped his own tankard. "Whoever made him the way he was wanted him ignorant. He didn't even know what a family was. He asked Wiggen if her being my daughter was the same as two people being friends. If he didn't know right from wrong, he'd follow orders without question, kill anyone they wanted."

"And when he fought, when those thugs threatened you, you said you saw him heal a wound that would have killed a man." Once again, it wasn't a question as much as a statement waiting for corroboration.

"He had a knife through his back and almost out his stomach, and all he did was pull it out, without so much as a twitch, mind you, and slit the bastard's throat with it." Forbish drained his tankard and reached for the pitcher. That also had not been their first. "In less time than it takes one side of an oat cake to brown, he was healed."

"Incredible." Norwood finished his tankard and held it out to be filled again.

"I wouldn't have believed it myself if I hadn't seen it." He poured the Captain's tankard full, and then emptied the pitcher into his own. "There's more magic than flesh to that boy, I tell you, but he saved Wiggen and me from those thugs."

"And you're sure he's the one committing these murders."

"From what you described, how these people were killed and how nobody could stand against him...it's got to be Lad. That and the timing. I mean, the first murder was right after he vanished."

"It does sound like too much to be coincidence." He paused, sipped and stared into the flames for a while before he said, "Magic... It had to be. Why didn't I trust my instincts?"

"I'm no wizard, but I've never heard of magic being used like that. That's probably exactly why they had Lad made the way he is. I mean, you could look at him, see him walking right down the street, and he just looks like a scrawny kid. But the way he moved...so fast you couldn't see it. Whoever made him sure knew what they were doing." He leaned forward and looked at the captain until the man met his eyes. "That's the person you want, Captain. Lad was just the weapon, the killer's the one who's controlling him. *If* he's still controlling him."

"That's not likely to go very far with the duke, Forbish. He wants the killer, not some wizard. If this boy killed my men and those nobles, he's the one who's got to answer for it."

"But he's spelled! It'd be like...like a man puts a viper in another man's bed, and the snake bites this fellow and he dies. You don't arrest the *snake*, do you?"

"Just because the boy didn't know right from wrong doesn't make him innocent."

"He *knew* killing was wrong, Captain! He knew because my Wiggen *told* him it was wrong. Wiggen's the only reason those last two nobles aren't dead. Whatever happened when he took Wiggen out of that cell must have set him free. Lad wouldn't have killed on his own, not if someone just told him to. There *had* to be some kind of a charm or spell that made him do it."

"Or a threat," Norwood suggested with a raised eyebrow. "You say your daughter and this boy were involved. Well, whoever stole him away could have held the threat of harming her over his head if he didn't do as they said."

"I suppose that could be, but what would have prevented him from running straight here and telling us the first time he was out on his own?" Forbish shook his head. They'd been over it dozens of times, and every idea for why Lad would kill fell flat except one: magic.

Norwood sipped his ale, unsure of what to do with all the information Forbish had revealed. He still had no specifics on how to find this boy, let alone who was controlling him, but he felt that Forbish was telling him the truth.

"I can't keep the boy from being punished, Forbish," he said finally, putting his tankard down and pushing himself to his feet. "He's killed too many of my men and too many high-ranking nobles. The duke won't allow justice not to fall on the murderer of his kinsmen, not even if the boy is guiltless."

Forbish nodded, seeing the logic of it, though not liking it one bit. Even if Lad walked through the door of the *Tap and Kettle* this instant, Norwood would be bound by his oath to the duke to arrest him. With so much evidence against him, and now Forbish's own word that Lad was the killer, the boy would be on the guillotine in a week.

He knows, Lad thought to himself as he scanned the Grandfather's estate from hiding. Guards patrolled the walls in pairs, walking at irregular intervals, never out of sight of one another, and the gate guard had been doubled. Half of the guards carried crossbows loaded and ready. Additional guards were posted at the five corners of the outer wall, and watched both the courtyard and the street. *He knows I'm coming for him, and he's afraid.*

That makes us even.

He moved through the shadows cast by street lamps, invisible as a ghost and as silent as a falling feather. He circled the entire estate twice, analyzing the security, looking for an opening. It was not a fortress; there were no crenellations, no towers to support flanking fire. The wall was simply a sheer twenty-foot-high expanse of fitted stone, the top flat and featureless and about the width of a wagon. He'd gone over it many times—once with an arrow in his chest—so it didn't present much of a barrier. The real barrier was the additional force of guards. If just one of them saw him, a single shout of alarm would bring them all down on him. He couldn't fight them all, nor did he want to. The guards weren't his enemies; they just worked for the Grandfather. They didn't even belong to the guild. He didn't want to kill anyone he didn't have to.

So, the problem was not getting in, but doing so without being seen, just as when he'd killed for the Grandfather. The necessary similarity in tactics made him smile thinly; if Mya only knew...

Mya...

That was a problem. She was the one element of the Grandfather's security that he couldn't predict. Strangely, the security measures he could see bore none of her distinctive brand of deception. Simply adding more guards was a typically brute-force tactic, and if Mya was anything, it was subtle and deceitful, which led him to question whether she was part of the security he would be facing this night. Did the Grandfather still trust her? Had she left after he disappeared? Was she still a slave? Was she even alive?

Too many unanswered questions.

He could only proceed with all these possibilities in mind and be ready for every eventuality.

Like a courtyard full of bowmen ready to fill me full of arrows, he thought, pushing the fear down.

That was the other problem. He'd never had to deal with fear before; he'd never *had* fear before. Now it gnawed at his every step, set his heart pounding and his ears ringing with surging adrenaline. His senses sang with an acuity he'd never felt, but he had to keep reminding his hands not to shake. Fear, it seemed, was a double-edged sword.

He picked a spot midpoint on the longest segment of wall, and so, as far as possible from the corner posts. The walking patrols passed one another at this point occasionally, and when they passed, for a very short moment, their backs would be to one another and their positions would obscure the view of the other watchers. There would be a dead zone, a patch of wall that wasn't being watched at all. Maybe.

He waited, crouched in the shadows across the narrow street, watching and listening.

The moment came.

The guards approached, their hard boots clicking on the stone in a staccato rhythm. They passed without a word and walked on. Lad crossed the street with three running steps, the last of which changed his horizontal momentum to vertical. One foot touched the wall on the way up, and his fingertips clutched the edge. He twisted in a spiral flip as he cleared the wall, taking note of the guards in passing. Their backs remained to him, their steps relaxed. He dropped to the courtyard, landing in a crouch, eyes and ears straining for signs that he'd been seen. He vanished into the shadows against the wall and waited, calming his hammering heart with several deep breaths. No shouts rang out, no running footfalls echoed against the stone, and no bowmen waited in the courtyard ready to fill him full of arrows.

Well, that's good, he thought, moving along the wall to a spot where he could cross the courtyard without being observed. There was a service entrance near the stables that he had used once before. It led past the kitchens, which should be quiet this late at night. The door was never locked since the kitchen staff were in and out so often, and it had never been guarded.

Not until tonight.

As Lad slipped through the door, he found himself standing less than a foot from two sleepy guards. Their eyes widened to the point that he thought they might pop out as both guards drew breath to shout an alarm. All they managed were truncated gasps, since Lad hit each one with a careful blow just below the larynx. Neither was a killing stroke, but both men were effectively deprived of the ability to speak. In the confusing melee that followed, Lad discovered that not killing was much more difficult than killing. In the end, however, one guard lay unconscious and the other lay moaning weakly, clutching his manhood. Two minutes later, both lay gagged and bound in the kitchen pantry. He knew they'd be missed eventually, but he didn't know how long it would be.

Time was now a factor.

He had to find the Grandfather quickly, and there was just one person who always knew exactly where to find the guildmaster. Fortunately, he also knew exactly where to find the Grandfather's valet.

The valet stood at the base of the main stair, patiently awaiting his master's call. He would stand here until summoned or informed of his master's wish that he retire. He didn't expect to sleep this night, but that wasn't unusual. He would wait and watch and listen; such were his duties.

He also didn't expect to live through the night.

But if it was required that he die, that also was his duty.

He waited, watched, and listened.

The first indication that the time had come for him to serve his master came with the pressure of two fingers upon either side of his throat. He started to take a breath. There were six guards just on the other side of the main door. He knew they were too far to save his life, but if he raised an alarm...

"I can feel it if you try to speak," a voice whispered in his ear. "If you do, I'll crush your throat before a sound escapes your lips. Nod if you understand me."

The valet nodded. He thought of the daggers at his belt; if he could twist and strike quickly enough...

"If you do as I say, you'll live. If you try for a dagger, you'll be dead before it clears the sheath." There was a pause, and the pressure on his throat increased until it was uncomfortable.

Chris A. Jackson

"Decide which it will be, but do so quickly."

He lifted his hands away from his body and his weapons. There was no profit in dying when he could serve his master just as well by living.

"Good. Now, tell me, very quietly, where is the Grandfather?"

The pressure eased until he felt he could speak.

"He's in the interrogation room," he whispered, then added, "entertaining someone."

"You mean the room where I was kept?"

He nodded.

"Now, where is Mya?"

The valet couldn't help but smile as he said, "She's being entertained."

The grip on his throat shifted, and the pressure increased sharply. His vision dimmed, and darkness welled up and overcame him.

He had no idea how much time had passed when he woke, bound and gagged in a closet, wondering why he was still alive.

Lad's senses were stretched to a fever pitch as he crept down the hall from the sparring room toward the stairs. Fear had become a part of him now, familiar and welcome, like the pain of his blisters. Fear and pain; the two things he hadn't felt until the previous night had become his allies, companions that kept him alive and reminded him that he wasn't invulnerable.

The only thing that hadn't changed in him was his curiosity. The valet's words rang in his mind, and he wondered at their meaning. He knew there was no love lost between the valet and Mya, and he knew he'd interpreted the amusement in the valet's voice correctly. This didn't bode well for Mya, but he couldn't be sure his surmise was correct until he reached the interrogation chamber.

He listened at the top of the stairs for as long as he dared, knowing the longer he took, the greater the chance that either the guards' or the valet's absences would be discovered. If that happened, he was dead.

303

Lad descended ten steps, paused to listen for a few breaths, and then continued for ten more. He paused and listened after each ten, before continuing. Finally, more than two-thirds of the way to the bottom, he heard something. Someone was breathing, quick and shallow from exertion, fear, or pain. Ten more steps and he could see the door and the sliver of white lamplight seeping from under it. Then he smelled something that stopped him in his tracks. It was familiar, and stimulated a cascade of memories. He'd smelled it many times before.

It was blood.

He reached the door and rested a hand on the latch, listening yet again. Only one person's breathing reached his ears, but he knew the Grandfather could remain silent if he so chose, just as Lad was doing now. This reeked of a trap, but he wouldn't know unless he opened the door. He pressed the latch carefully, feeling and listening for anything that wasn't right. The simple mechanism worked freely, and he felt the latch click with the faintest tap of metal on wood. He pushed ever so gently, straining to detect the slightest resistance. The door swung easily on its hinges. When there was a wide-enough gap, Lad held the door steady and ran one finger along the edge, feeling for wires or trip strings. There was nothing. He opened the door further, inch by careful inch, until he could slip through the gap.

He knew the inside of this room like he knew the roof of his own mouth. It had been his prison for many days. There were no shadows with the overhead lamps lit. There was nowhere for him to hide near the door, and several places within where someone might lie in wait undetected. Once inside, he would be exposed. He catalogued in his mind the best places an assailant could hide and edged through, scanning for danger

The room was silent; the Grandfather wasn't there.

Mya was.

The blood he'd smelled was hers. She lay upon the slab that once held him; the same bindings that had restrained him now held her. The injuries that marred her flesh from head to toe bore the mark of careful infliction; flesh had been surgically parted and nerves carefully dissected, but the bleeding was minimal. Blood vessels had been avoided to prolong her torment.

Of all the possible things he thought he might find, this had not been one of them.

Why would the Grandfather torture Mya?

Two possible answers clicked into his mind: First, Lad's sudden and unexplained disappearance led the Grandfather to believe that Mya had betrayed him. She could have orchestrated his disappearance simply by altering her master's orders. In retribution, or perhaps to find out if Mya had indeed been disloyal, the Grandfather had used pain as either punishment or an inducement to confession.

The other possibility was that this was a very elaborate trap.

In Lad's mind, the former seemed infinitely more likely, simply because he couldn't imagine Mya agreeing to such mutilation. The wounds were real; of that he was positive. She had been flayed very carefully and very precisely to inflict pain. And even now, as he listened to her rapid, rasping breath, he knew she was in agony.

If this were a trap, what was the worst that would befall him if he ventured into the chamber? He could make sure no one lay hidden quickly enough. There was only one entrance to the room, and he would know well in advance of any surprise attack unless the Grandfather chose to follow him down and attack while Lad tried to free Mya. If that happened, Lad would be only slightly worse off, for he was ready for such an attack. He had to fight the Grandfather regardless, so what would be the advantage to this?

No, the advantage was only in position, not surprise, and Mya would never have agreed to it.

The torture was real. She was in pain. And he was the cause of it.

He moved into the room, every step calculated, every breath held for a heartbeat while he listened and looked for any clue of attack. All was quiet save for Mya's labored breathing. No one hid in the twisted machinery.

He moved to the slab where she lay.

She was splayed like a sacrificial lamb, stripped and bound at elbow, wrist, knee, and ankle with padded iron. Unfortunately for Mya, she and he were about the same size; the bonds fit her very well indeed. There was no room to struggle, and she hadn't the immunity to pain that had allowed him to wrench free of the restraints.

He stood less than a step from her and took a moment to examine both her condition and the iron bands that held her. The restraining bands were held in place with black iron pins, not locks. He could free her in seconds. The wounds were quite real, and a tray bearing the implements that had inflicted them lay nearby. The blood on the tools was dry, but just barely. Where it had pooled beneath her was still moist to the touch. Scarcely a finger could he have placed upon her without touching some type of injury. Her face, neck and arms were lined with parallel grooves, her legs cut in patterns that followed the lines of the muscles. One cut had been cauterized when it bled too freely. Breathing itself was a torture, he could see, for both her abdomen and torso were crisscrossed with shallow trenches of crimson. Her chest fluttered with every breath, the muscles between each rib having been teased apart to expose the nerves. The Grandfather was very skilled to have inflicted so much damage and not killed her.

Despite the restraints, her clenched hands strained, struggling for freedom. He knew that feeling, that helplessness.

"Mya," he whispered, laying a hand over her mouth to prevent any noise.

Her eyes flung open, then widened even further as she recognized that he was not the Grandfather. She jerked away from him, fighting the bonds, her cries of fear muffled against his palm.

"Mya, be still! You must be quiet! I'm not here for you, just the Grandfather." She seemed to calm at this, which honestly surprised him. Did she fear him so much? "Quietly now. He may be listening from another room. You must tell me where he is; then I'll release you. Do you understand?"

She nodded frantically, and he eased his hand away.

"Why? Why come here? He'll kill you!" Her voice was

strange, husky, probably hoarse from screaming.

"You know why. I'm here to kill him, and he knows it." He placed a hand on her brow, trying to avoid the cuts. "Now, where is he?"

"I don't know. I passed out. When I came to, he was gone." Her eyes flickered to the door, pupils wide with fear. "He could come back any second!"

"I'm here for him, Mya. I'm going to kill him. When I do, we'll both be free."

"No, Lad. We won't be free." Her eyes were strange, the lids lolling closed whenever she wasn't looking right at him. Her pupils weren't tracking his movements. "I'm sorry, Lad. He won't let me go. He made me..."

"What, Mya? He made you what?"

"He made me put it on. I thought I wanted it, but I don't. Now I'm trapped, and he'll never let me go."

"What? Put what on? What are you talking about, Mya?" She was acting strangely, even for one who had been tortured. It was almost as if...

He gripped her face, forcing her mouth open. One sniff told him she'd taken opium, a strong narcotic that would dull even the most intense pain. That meant...

He leapt back from her and scanned the room quickly, but there was still no one there. It was a trap, but how...?

"The ring," Mya said as both of her hands opened wide, releasing two small glass spheres to fall to the hard stone floor.

He saw the motion out of the corner of his eye and dove to catch one of the spheres, but the other struck the floor and shattered. He sprang away, sprinting for the door, but it was already closing. It slammed well before he reached it, and a silvery light shimmered around its perimeter. Magic. He was trapped.

Heedless, he slammed into the door as hard as he could. The room reverberated with the impact and pain lanced through his shoulder, but the magically bound door held. It was useless. Escape was impossible.

He turned back to Mya, but her form was already obscured by

a billowing cloud of vapor released by the shattered sphere. The cloud would expand to fill the entire room, and he could already tell from Mya's slow, steady breathing that the gas would render him unconscious.

He had to think of something. There *had* to be a way out.

Lad looked at the door, then at the advancing cloud of vapor. He had about ten more breaths before he'd be engulfed by the narcotic gas. He sat down, struggling through the fear to calm his mind. He breathed as deeply and as rapidly as he could for nine breaths, then held it. He let the cloud engulf him while he slipped into a meditative trance. He slowed his heart, slowed his blood in his veins, slowed his mind...

The vapor tingled on his skin as the cloud swallowed him up. Lad struggled to fight the effect, struggled to shunt blood away from his skin where the narcotic was invading him. Slowly, he began to lose the battle. Numbness invaded his limbs, then his mind, and finally darkness engulfed him.

Chapter XXVII

Wiggen watched the sliver of sunlight migrate across the floor, just as she had watched the moonlight hours before. She'd not slept. Instead, she sat wrapped in her blankets, thinking of the one she loved and trying to keep hope alive in her heart. It almost struck her as funny that one such as she, scarred and tainted by violence, should be in such a position. How could she fall in love? And even more a mystery, how could someone love her?

But she knew it was real. She could feel it. It was different than anything she'd ever experienced. It made her want to laugh and cry at the same time; it was like beautiful music and a pain deep within, like a song and salt in a wound. She knew that the pain was simply Lad's absence, and that he hadn't come back to her yet.

As the patch of light moved inch by relentless inch, and she remained alone, the pain began to overwhelm the joy; the music began to fade behind the ache.

She recalled the first time she saw him, standing in the kitchen, filthy and skinny as a starved rat with a whole side of beef balanced on his shoulder. And there was that quizzical look on his face, all curiosity, not a malicious thought in him. That, she realized, was what she'd fallen in love with, not the strength or that he had saved her from those thugs. It was his innocence, the honesty that comes only with frank curiosity bereft of avarice or any hidden motive. He was the first person she'd ever met who wanted to know her for who she was, good and bad, strengths and flaws. He didn't want to change her, didn't want to make her something more or take something from her that she didn't have to give. And he'd helped her with her own pain, not because he expected something back, some payment for his effort, but because he could. Lad was an honest and good soul, and she loved him for that.

The wedge of sunlight became thinner and thinner as it approached the wall into which the window was set, much as her hope became slimmer with every passing minute. She willed it to stop, wished time would halt in wait for his return. But time and love and pain do not wait, it seemed. Then the wedge of sunlight vanished completely. It was highsun. It was time.

He wasn't coming back.

She found herself standing without remembering having stood. The meager pile of belongings—the food, a skin of water, the blankets and her dress—looked alien to her. She wasn't hungry. After drinking some water, more because she knew she should rather than from thirst, she got dressed. Two of the blankets she folded neatly and draped over her arm. The rest she piled back in the trunk.

It was more difficult than she remembered, crawling through the furnace vent to the damper that led to the alley and outside, but she made it after resting only twice. There were people about, but the alley was not well traveled, and her egress from the furnace vent went unseen. She tucked her bundle over her arm, draped her hair down over her distinctive scar, and started walking north toward the more familiar neighborhoods of Eastmarket and the *Tap and Kettle*.

At least she'd see her father again before they arrested her, though it really didn't matter anymore.

Nothing really mattered anymore.

Lad awakened as he never had before in his life—in pain.

It pierced through the haze that fogged his mind and numbed his limbs, bringing him to a groggy wakefulness that allowed him to perceive his surroundings as if through a thick, smothering blanket. The pain was sharp but not deep, a recurrent prick upon his chest. It wasn't the ache of his burns, to which he'd grown accustomed; in fact, that discomfort was much less than it had been. His head hurt somewhat as well, but that really didn't bother him as much as the continuous stabbing on his chest.

He rolled his head to the side, weak against the lingering fingers of numbing narcotic, and tried to brush away the bothersome pain. He couldn't lift his arm. He tried the other, but it, too, wouldn't answer his commands. He tried to sit up, but that action was denied him as well by a restraining pressure on his arms and legs. Then the pain suddenly stopped.

"He's moving too much. I can't work with him moving like this."

The voice was unfamiliar, but as Lad struggled to open his eyes, he heard another that was all too easy to recognize.

"The drug is wearing off."

He forced his eyes open and redoubled his struggles. The Grandfather simply smiled down at him and chuckled in cold amusement. The bearded man standing next to him was unfamiliar; rings glittered on each finger, and he wore elaborate robes of purple satin embroidered with golden symbols along the collar and cuffs. He held a small pot and a needle in his ink-stained hands. This left little doubt in Lad's mind as to what the pain had been.

"He should calm down when he realizes he can't break free."

Lad glared at the Grandfather and surged up against his bonds. They were the same that had recently bound Mya, and he could still smell the sweet tang of her blood in the air. The bands of iron on his arms and legs were as tight as ever and, unfortunately, he no longer possessed the immunity to pain that had allowed him to wrench free. As he pulled against the bands, pain lanced through his wrist and shoulder. His struggles subsided.

"See? He can't escape. You may resume, Master Vonlith."

"Very well." The wizard moved forward, dipping his needle into the pot of ink. But as he leaned forward to press the needle into Lad's flesh, his robe draped over Lad's bound wrist. Lad deftly grabbed a handful of the thick material and lurched up, aiming a vicious bite at the wizard's wrist.

"Gaa!" Vonlith cried out, jerking away just enough that Lad's teeth clamped down on his sleeve instead of his flesh. Ink spilled from the pot, spattering both the robes and Lad's torso. "Get this filthy beast off me!"

The Grandfather snatched a handful of Lad's hair and jerked the wizard's sleeve out of his mouth, tearing off a sizable patch of velvet, which Lad promptly spat out. He retained a grip upon the robes with his hand, however, regardless of how the wizard strained to free himself.

"Make him let go of me!" the man squawked, tugging at the fabric.

The Grandfather slammed Lad's head back down onto the stone slab, and pain lanced through his skull. He bit back a cry of shock.

"Let him go, boy!" the Grandfather growled, cuffing him hard across the face. His ears rang with the blow. "Now!"

"I won't be your slave again!" Lad yelled in his face, true hatred edging his words. The Grandfather just sneered down at him.

"Yes. You. Will!" the ancient assassin growled through a rictus grin of triumph, slamming Lad's head back against the unyielding stone with every word. At the second impact, Lad's grip slackened involuntarily. At the third, darkness welled up and dimmed his vision.

When Lad came to next, he felt something cold against his neck. It was iron. A new restraint had been added. He also felt the continuous punctuating pinpricks of the wizard's needle etching magic into his flesh. He rolled his head from side to side, trying to clear the haze of pain and nausea.

"Don't...please..." he mumbled, struggling to open his eyes. The pricks of the needle stopped. When he finally managed to regain his senses and opened his eyes, the wizard Vonlith was watching him with some trepidation. He had replaced his damaged robes with new ones, slightly less elaborate, but the same shade of purple. He placed the needle in the pot of ink and looked across the table, past Lad.

"I can't work if he won't hold still. He should either be drugged or otherwise rendered motionless."

"I'll see to it."

Lad turned groggily toward the new voice. It was another he recognized, but looking at her told him that something in his erstwhile adversary had changed drastically. She wore a dark robe of crimson silk edged with black. Her hair flowed down her shoulders freely, where it was usually tied back out of the way. Thin pink scars crisscrossed her skin wherever it showed. The wounds that had so effectively fooled Lad into thinking the Grandfather had tortured her had been healed. He wondered how such grievous cuts had been healed so quickly until he remembered his own lost ability. It must have been magic.

"Mya..." he said, his throat dry as old parchment. His head still swam with pain where it had been slammed against the stone. "I...won't..."

"Be quiet." She held a small green crystal vial before his eyes. Or were there two of them? He was having trouble focusing. "I'm going to pour this into your mouth, and you're going to swallow it. It will heal your injuries. If you don't swallow it, I'll call the Grandfather, and he'll make you drink it. Do you understand?"

He nodded.

"Will you drink it?"

"Why would I? It will only keep me alive longer."

Mya leaned forward until her face was close to his. Her hair fell forward to tickle his bare skin as she said, "Think, Lad. There is much life between your current condition and death, and it could be filled with more pain than you can imagine. It's no longer your choice whether you live or die, but how much misery you endure while you live *is* your choice. You don't want to go through what I've gone through. Trust me."

"Trust you?" He tried to laugh at her, but found he couldn't muster the strength through the pounding in his skull. "How can I trust you, Mya? All you know is deceit."

"I know the Grandfather." In that one admission he could hear how she had changed. There was something more and something less to her voice. "I've lain on that table and felt his blades part my flesh while he laughed, and even through the opium, I screamed. If you want to experience the same without the benefit of having the pain blunted by drugs, then refuse to swallow this potion one more time. I won't ask again. Now open your mouth."

Even through the fog of his injury he could hear the truth and the terror in her words.

Lad opened his mouth and swallowed the bitter liquid.

The rush of healing magic swept through him like a cleansing tide, washing away the nausea, blurred vision, and pain. His shoulder popped, and he felt the sinews knitting where he hadn't even known they'd been torn. His view of Mya sprang to crystal clarity, and he could see even more changes etched on her face.

"There. That wasn't so hard, was it?"

"No." He looked her over, and she watched him do so. There was something missing in her; something had been torn away or lost. Though her stance and body language were as arrogant and self-assured as ever, her eyes showed a vacancy. But this wasn't just the result of lying under the Grandfather's knives; he knew her better than that. There was something else that had caused her to give up hope on herself. Then he saw the black ring on her finger, and he remembered her words as she lay flayed upon the table he now occupied.

"Becoming a slave isn't hard," he said, meeting her slack gaze. "Living with it...that's something else."

"Irony? From you?" She let out a bark of scornful laughter. "I don't know what breaking those spells did for you, Lad, but I never expected it to turn you into a philosopher."

"I *feel* now," he said, letting his gaze slip off her. He stared blankly at the domed ceiling. "I love, I hate, I fear, and I feel shame for the pain I've caused. I don't know how I lived not feeling these things, but now that I do, I don't want to let them go." He nodded to the wizard. "That's what he's here for, isn't it? He's going to take all that away from me."

"He's going to put what spells he can back in place. The

bonding spells will be first, of course. That will eliminate the need for these." She tapped the iron band around his neck with a fingernail. "Then the healing, the pain block, and the emotional block." She had a strange look on her face that told him there was more.

"What else?" he asked, directing the question to the wizard. "What else are you going to do to me?"

"I was told to remove certain of your memories, young man," he said, moving forward again, stirring the pot of ink with his needle. "They're the source of this pain you're feeling, am I not correct? You're better off without them."

"It won't matter," Lad said, turning his head away from both of them. He knew from experience that it would take days, if not weeks, to complete even one of the spells. He also knew Wiggen would divulge everything he'd told her to the captain of the Royal Guard when Lad didn't return. He had no idea the time of day, but he imagined it couldn't be much past midday. The Royal Guard would storm the building, and everyone here would be killed. "Nothing matters anymore."

He heard Mya turn and walk away, then felt the painful press of the needle and the familiar rush as ink and magic infused him.

Wiggen walked into the courtyard of the *Tap and Kettle* like she'd done a thousand times before. Two guardsmen stationed in the courtyard gaped at her, but she ignored them. As she passed, they fell in behind her, their hard boots scuffing the cobbles with every step. She went to the kitchen door out of habit and entered. The guards were through the door behind her before it could close.

"Good gods! Wiggen!" Forbish dropped a tin of scones and rushed to smother her in his beefy embrace. "Gods, girl, but you gave me a scare. I was beside myself!" He pushed her to arm's length, his hands enveloping her shoulders in a grip that was so desperate it was painful.

She tried to smile, but couldn't. "I'm sorry," she said, forcing down the wailing cry of anguish that had been building in her all morning.

Then another hand enveloped her arm, and she heard the guardsman say, "And I'm sorry, miss, but we've got to take you in."

"Like hell you will!" Forbish snapped, releasing her and slapping the guard's hand away. He stepped between his daughter and the two guards with a quickness that she didn't think his bulk could have managed.

"Sir, please. We've got our orders. She's to be taken in for questioning."

"I know you've got your damned orders, and I know who gave them to you!" Forbish folded his arms and glared at the armed men, defying them with sheer determination. "You try to take my daughter from me again, and there's gonna be a fight, boy! You can just send a runner to get Captain Norwood and bring him here."

"Father, I—"

"No, Wiggen," he said firmly, keeping his eyes on the two guardsmen, who were now exchanging dubious glances. "You're staying here."

They'd been ordered to take her in, but they looked reluctant to do so by main force. They appeared confident that they, perhaps with some aid from the four additional guardsmen stationed in the inn's common room, could overcome one plump innkeeper, but they also knew that their captain had spent a good bit of time sitting and drinking ale with this same innkeeper. Harming a friend of Captain Norwood's, even in the act of carrying out one of his orders, was not a good idea.

"We'll have to call the sergeant," the senior of the two said, turning to his companion. "Go get him."

"That'll be fine," Forbish said. "He's right out in the common room having a nice hot lunch."

The other guard left, while Forbish and the first one stared at one another, both refusing to move. After all Wiggen had been through, the confrontation seemed utterly silly. She couldn't care less whether they took her in and questioned her or questioned her here. It didn't matter.

316

Nothing mattered.

She turned away from the two stubborn men and bent to pick up the dropped tin of scones. Two had rolled off the sheet and would have to be thrown out, but the others were fine. She gripped the hot metal using the blankets in her hands as a hot mitt and dumped the rest of the scones onto the cooling rack with a practiced flip. Then she put the blankets aside, greased the sheet with a bit of butter and started dolloping batter into neat rows. She worked mechanically, without thought, without concern for what was happening right behind her, even though it concerned her directly.

When she had put the tray in the oven and moved the one that was half done to the upper rack, four more guardsmen entered the kitchen, along with Josie and two young boys about twelve years old looking as eager as spring colts. She ignored them all, a formidable task, since the kitchen was now full to bursting.

"Now, Master Forbish," the sergeant began, placing his huge fists on his hips and glaring his worst. "You know we've got to take the girl in. Captain Norwood's given his orders, and we've got to see to 'em. He's got more'n a few questions for her, and we've got to have answers."

"Norwood can get his answers here," Forbish fired back, not budging an inch.

Wiggen scooped up the two fallen scones and tossed them in the bin, stirred the soup to keep it from scorching, and began cleaning up the kneading board.

"She's not safe here! That killer could slip in here come night and—"

"She's as safe here as she was in your barracks, Sergeant!"

Wiggen scoured the board with boiling water from the kettle and dried it with a towel, then measured and poured flour and milk into the mixing bowl.

"Near a dozen of the duke's finest guardsmen died tryin' to protect her, innkeeper," the sergeant growled, wagging a finger under Forbish's nose. "A little more respect from you, if you please!"

"It's not disrespect, man, it's a question of whether or not she *needed* protection!" He waved a hand at his daughter without taking his eyes off the guardsman. "Here she stands, safe and sound, and your friends lie dead in their graves. And for what?"

Wiggen cracked three eggs into the bowl and threw in a dash of soda. Then she grabbed the big spoon and started stirring the mix, adding a spoonful of molasses and a handful of raisins. She lifted the heavy bowl and stirred the thick mix with a steady *whop whop whop* of the spoon.

"They were following orders. Just like I'm following orders, innkeeper!"

"I *know* you're following orders! Stop for just a heartbeat and use your brain, man! She's no safer with you than with me!"

"She's coming along with us, Master Forbish, and that's my final word!"

Whop whop whop went the spoon in the batter.

"She's staying here!"

"Stand between me and my duty, innkeeper, and you'll find yourself clapped in irons!"

"Oh, then maybe both of us will be safer. Is that the idea, Sergeant?"

"Oh, stop it! Both of you!" The last was Josie. She stepped between the two parties like she was breaking up a scrap between her two nephews. "Would you maybe both just stop and look at her for half a breath? She's not even payin' attention, and here you are ready to come to blows."

"Wiggen?" Forbish said, turning for the first time from the burly sergeant. "Honey, what's wrong?"

Wiggen didn't answer, she just put down the big bowl and went back to the oven. She opened it and took out the top tin of scones, flipped them off onto the cooling rack and began spooning more batter onto the hot sheet.

"She's spelled!" hissed one of the guardsmen.

"Oh, shut up!" Josie spat, stepping past them all to Wiggen's side as the girl finished filling the pan with fresh dough. "Wiggen, you don't have to do that, dear. We've got enough, and these men,

318

they're here to take you to see the captain of the guard."

"It doesn't matter," she said, moving the lower tray to the top rack and putting the new one on the bottom.

"What doesn't matter, dear?" Josie asked as Wiggen put the scones from the previous batch into a serving basket.

"Anything." She handed the basket to Josie and stepped past her to the mixing bowl. The batter didn't need more stirring, but she did it anyway, steady strong strokes, the spoon going *whop whop whop*.

"Something *is* wrong," Forbish said, moving to his daughter's side. "What is it, honey?"

"It doesn't matter, Father. It's done. We can go back to doing what we were doing before."

Forbish watched his daughter stir the batter for several breaths, then his face changed, as if a sudden realization struck him. He put his hand on his daughter's shoulder and said, "It's all right, honey. You don't have to do that."

"Somebody's got to do it."

"Wiggen." He put a hand on her arm, stilling the steady motion of the spoon. "What happened, honey? Where's Lad? How did you get here?

"He didn't come back," she said, staring down at the bowl. "He left me, and he didn't come back."

"Why didn't he come back, Wiggen?"

"Because he's dead," she whispered, barely audible.

"What? What happened, honey?"

"He's DEAD!" She stepped away from him, letting the heavy bowl fall. It struck the floor and shattered, but everyone was looking at Wiggen. Her eyes were wide with horror, and she was looking right through them all as if at a distant horizon, her face set in a grimace of sheer anguish.

"He went to kill the Grandfather, but he didn't come back!" she shrieked, fists clenched at her sides, retreating until she was against the wash pot in the corner. "He didn't come back because they killed him! He promised me, but he didn't come back!"

"Oh, dear," Josie said, stepping past Forbish to take the girl in her arms.

Wiggen collapsed into the embrace as if she were a marionette whose strings had just been cut. Tears finally began to flow, and between the sobs she cried, "He didn't come back to me. He didn't come back to me."

"Send a runner for Captain Norwood, Sergeant," Forbish said, his voice shaking with unspent anguish. "My daughter's in no condition to go anywhere."

"I'll send a messenger," Sergeant Tamir said with a nod. He ushered his men out of the kitchen, barking orders as he went. "You there! Private! Grab a horse and…" But Wiggen heard none of it over her own wailing sobs and the numbing pain of her shattered heart.

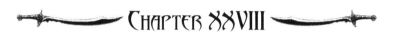

CHAPTER XXVIII

Wiggen sat upon the hearth with the heat of the banked fire warming her back. She held a cup of hot hard cider in her hands, and half of its contents warmed her from the inside out. She almost felt like herself.

She'd cried until she thought she could cry no longer, and then cried some more. Josie had taken her to her room and helped her change into cleaner clothes. She hadn't commented on the scrapes and bruises Wiggen had received in the sewers, and hadn't asked about the two blankets that Wiggen refused to let out of her sight. When she was clean, dressed and fed, Captain Norwood arrived.

He surprised her.

Without so much as a raised voice, he'd beckoned her to sit and make herself comfortable. He'd not asked a single question, but simply asked her to give an accounting of what had happened to her from the time two nights ago when she'd been freed from the barracks to the moment she'd walked back into the courtyard of the *Tap and Kettle*.

She had simply sat comfortably by the fire and talked. He didn't pressure her at all, except to ask for clarification on a few points. When her story was done, he asked for it again from the beginning, and she'd told it again, without a single fault. She knew she wasn't lying. She'd lived it.

Now he sat in one of the big chairs, a tankard on his knee, though he'd barely sipped from it, asking a few more gentle questions while Forbish and Josie sat nearby and listened.

"After the magic was broken," Norwood said, directing his question once more to that moment in the cell when Lad had freed himself from the binding spells, "when you crept through the sewers, did you notice anything different about him?"

"Yes, Captain. He was very different." She sipped her cup and even smiled at the memory. "He talked differently, acted differently. He even said things that were funny. He'd never done that before. Not intentionally anyway. He was scared, too, though he didn't tell me that until later."

"Scared? What scared him?"

"Oh, lots of things, I guess. He said he was scared for me, for my father, for all the people who he knew hated him for killing those people. He never wanted to kill anyone, Captain. It was the magic that made him do it."

"Yes, so you've said. I'll have to take your word on that account, since we're just a little bit short on evidence to that effect."

"Yes, you will, Captain," she said, more disappointed than angry. It didn't really matter what he thought of her, after all. If he thought she was lying, well, fine. He could arrest her.

"And this, uh, Grandfather fellow. I'd like to know more about him. You said he was the one who put the magic on the boy..."

"Lad."

"Oh, yes. I'm sorry, on Lad."

"No, he wasn't the one who put the magic on Lad. A wizard did that, and I only ever heard Lad call him 'Master.' He died when they were attacked by brigands on the way here."

"Not much of a wizard if he was killed by simple brigands, I should think."

"I wouldn't know about that, Captain."

"Mmm, yes. But this Grandfather fellow. He was the one responsible for the murders, you say."

"Yes," she said, swallowing more cider to calm her nerves. It seemed to her that the questions had suddenly become more pointed. "Lad said that the Grandfather had had him made. I think he must have paid the wizard to make Lad as he was."

"Must have been a tidy price for that many years' work." She heard the doubt in his voice, and couldn't refute it. It was all too incredible. She wouldn't have believed it herself, if not for Lad. He'd made her believe.

"And did this boy, Lad, tell you why he was made the way he was? I mean, to invest that much in something, a man must have something specific in mind."

"He didn't say, sir. I don't think he was ever really told why. They just told him when and who to kill. Every night there was one or two more, some just children." She paused, her eyes going slightly vacant as she remembered Lad recounting each one of those murders, each innocent who had died by his hand. "He told me about them. All of them. He mourned each and every one of them."

"He mourned them? A trained killer?"

She fixed him with eyes that gauged the depths of his disbelief. It is one thing to enlighten someone who is ignorant, quite something else to try to convince someone who chooses to remain ignorant because it better suits his convenience.

"He wasn't made to mourn, Captain, the magic kept that from him, but he knew killing was wrong. That was what bothered him. He knew he was hurting people. Not the people he killed, but all those who loved them. He knew how I felt, having lost a brother and a mother. Then, when the magic was broken, it all came crashing down on him."

"And that's why he went to kill this Grandfather fellow. Well, that I can understand, at least. I'd certainly want revenge on someone who'd done all that to me."

"It wasn't revenge, Captain," she said, shaking her head at his continued inability or refusal to understand. "He went to kill the Grandfather to make sure the same thing didn't happen to others. If it worked once, it might work again. He couldn't let that happen."

"Well, if this Grandfather fellow is as old as you say, he'd likely not live long enough to have another boy such as Lad made. I mean, sixteen years would put him in his grave."

"Lad said he didn't think the Grandfather aged. He was old, but not aged, is what he said. Maybe he had some magic, too."

"No doubt."

Wiggen just stared into the depths of her cup. There was nothing she could say to corroborate her story.

"And Lad said he'd come back to you, but he hasn't. Is that right?"

"That's right." She knew what he was thinking, and she knew he was wrong, but there was no way to convince him that Lad would never abandon her. "He must have underestimated the Grandfather."

"And he told you where this Grandfather lives, didn't he? You mentioned it, but it slipped my mind. Someplace in Barleycorn Heights?"

"Yes. The north end, near the river. It's a walled estate with a single tall tower. It's taller than any other around. He said it would be easy to find."

"Yes, I know the estate, and I know the man who owns it." The captain straightened in his chair and set his tankard of ale aside. "It might surprise you to know his name is Saliez, and that he's a very wealthy businessman. He runs an import-export business and is well established in the Teamsters Guild."

She didn't like the tone he was taking; his disbelief was edging toward insolence. That, if nothing else, piqued her ire. "If that's true, then *you* may be surprised to know that he is also the master of the Assassins Guild."

"I'm sorry, Wiggen, but I can't bash down the door of such a prominent man on hearsay. The duke would have my head."

"Then don't." Wiggen shrugged, gulped the last of her cider and stood. "The man I love is dead, Captain. I couldn't care less what you do." She hadn't bothered to keep the bitterness out of her voice, and saw the astonishment on the captain's face as she turned away.

She wasn't really surprised when he said, "Even if that includes arresting you?"

She stopped and turned back, stopping her father with a glance.

"Yes, Captain, including that. But if you don't do anything about the Grandfather, even though Lad is dead, nobles are going to start dying again soon, and the duke will come to you for answers." She turned and walked to her room without another thought concerning Captain Norwood.

"You heard her, Tamir," Norwood said, stepping off the porch of the *Tap and Kettle* and starting across the courtyard. "What do you think about her story?"

"It is a mite hard to swallow, sir, I'll give you that. But I don't think she was lying. And she's right about one thing; it don't pay to just say she's crazy as a bedbug and leave it at that." The sergeant cracked his knuckles loudly as they reached the street and the waiting imperial carriage. "Might not hurt to have a little talk with Master Saliez tonight, just to check her story."

"And if she *is* right about all this, it might hurt a great deal," Norwood countered, turning to face his subordinate with a knitted brow. "If we walk in there and start asking questions of the good Master Saliez and he *does* have something to do with this mess, we can kiss goodbye any chance we ever had of finding out the truth." He scratched the stubble on his chin and grimaced at the thought of the choice he had to make.

"I got a man in my squad what used to hunt quail, sir."

"What's that got to do with anything, Sergeant?" the captain asked, taken aback by the apparent non sequitur.

"Well, sir, you gotta be real quiet and real steady to get close enough to a covey of quail to cast your net with any hopes of gettin' any birds. Strikes me that we're tryin' to do just about the same thing here, get close enough to have a look without spookin' the quarry."

"He'd never be able to get inside the estate, but it might be useful to have a look. If there's more to this fellow than those high-priced trinkets he imports, it might be worth the nine shades of hell I'll get for bursting in there with sword in hand." Norwood nodded and mounted his carriage. "Have him look around, Sergeant, but make damn sure he knows he's not to be seen. The last thing we need is to tip our hand."

"Aye, sir," the sergeant said, saluting as his commander climbed into the carriage. He stepped back as it rolled away, then turned and walked back to the inn to carry out his orders. He didn't notice the patch of shadow that moved away down the street toward the affluent neighborhood of Barleycorn Heights.

Lad heard the door open. He hadn't been able to sleep, and his attempts at meditation had failed miserably, largely due to his recurrent recriminations for his utter failure. He had failed Wiggen, he had failed himself, and he had failed every other soul who would be tormented by the Grandfather's cruelty in the future.

He kept his eyes closed, not really feigning sleep, but not wanting to open them, though he didn't know why. Whoever had entered the interrogation chamber approached with footfalls that were virtually silent. That ruled out the Grandfather, for he was utterly silent, and the mage Vonlith, for he bore no semblance of stealth in any of his movements. That left a very short list of who would be creeping into this room so late at night.

Mya wasn't the type to gloat. If she was here, she was here for a reason, but he wasn't in the mood to talk.

Especially with her.

He doubted if she'd give him the option, so, when she was close, he said, "What do you want, Mya?"

"I'm curious," she said, coming to stand right beside him.

He finally opened his eyes. She wore the same crimson robe; her hair was pinned back this time, but still draped to her shoulders. The last remnants of her torment under the Grandfather's hands had vanished, at least those on the surface. She was looking down at him, her eyes traveling up and down his torso as if scanning him for flaws. Her curiosity for some reason annoyed him, but there seemed to be no advantage to antagonizing her, so he said, "About what?"

"About these." She ran a finger down the newest row of tattoos that lay livid upon his chest. The ink was as black as night and would never fade; the invisible ink had been a trick of his former

326

master, Corillian. Vonlith hadn't the same subtlety, but the runes, and the magic in them, were the same. The new tattoos were also quite tender, and her touch elicited a flinch of pain. "Do they hurt much?"

"Only when someone touches them," he admitted, not bothering to keep the annoyance from his voice.

"Sorry, I didn't mean to—"

"Didn't mean to hurt me?" he asked incredulously. "You trick me into a lifetime of slavery with your own torment as the price, and you expect me to believe that you give a good gods' damn about my pain? Go away, Mya. Go sit and stare at that ring on your finger that you bought with your soul. See how many friends, how much love and devotion, your new power grants you."

"I didn't want it," she said, her voice far too calm, too resigned to her fate.

"Then why accept it? Why ever step into the position in the first place? Why not just disappear? Your skills are *that* good, if not good enough to deserve the title of Master. You could have walked away, Mya, but you decided to serve him. *Him*! Why, Mya? Why would you *ever* do what you've done, not only to me, but to yourself?"

"Simple," she said, meeting his eyes for the first time since she'd arrived. "I'm a slave. Slaves don't have choices."

"You had a choice."

"Maybe." She held up her hand and looked at the band of polished obsidian that encircled her finger. "No longer. I must follow his orders."

"The ring compels you?"

"No, but if I fail to serve him, he'll kill me, and the ring does prevent me from raising a hand against him, even to save myself. The rings of the masters assure that those who are most skilled within the guild don't practice their trade upon their own master." She dropped her hand to her side and tried to smile, managing only a weak grimace. "I must serve him or die."

"To what end?"

"Whatever end he sees fit for me, I suppose."

"Death?"

"Eventually, but death takes us all in the end anyway."

"It's not that we die, Mya, but *how* we die that matters."

"I imagine I'll die by treachery then."

"And how we live. That matters."

"Does it?"

"Yes."

"Why? And don't give me that flap about the gods' judgment."

"How we live defines us, Mya. I'm a killer, but not willingly. I'm also someone's friend and someone's lover. That's who I am. You can make me a slave, and even take away my memories with magic, but you can't change what I am."

"You're also quite a philosopher. I never would have expected it from you."

"Maybe we're more than others expect from us. What are you?"

"I told you, I'm a slave."

"Only because you choose to be."

"I told you, slaves have no choices."

"You're wrong, Mya. You have the power to free yourself, just as you have the power to free me."

"I can't harm my master, Lad," she said holding up her hand, the ring dark on her pale flesh. "I'm bound to serve him."

"But I'm not." Her eyes widened a trifle with that, just enough to let him know his point had scored. "At least not yet. I can free you from him."

She looked down at him a long time, thinking. Her eyes moved to the iron straps that bound his neck, arms, and legs. There were nine in all, each held in place with iron pins. He could see her thinking of a way, the plan taking shape in her mind.

"There would be only one chance. You'd have to kill him instantly or he'll kill us both."

He could hear the fear in her, and strangely felt the lack of it in himself. "Now or later, it doesn't matter, Mya. What does matter is time. What time is it?"

"About half between dusk and midnight. Why?"

"If I'm to do it, it must be soon, or we'll *all* die." He was taking a horrible risk telling her, but it was the only chance he had.

"What?" Her eyes widened again, this time in astonishment.

"I haven't returned in time. Everything I know, the captain of the Royal Guard now knows."

"By the gods! They'll overrun the place."

"Yes."

She cast around the room and left his side. He watched her rummage among the wizard's things; she returned with a long black candle. "You have to wait for the right moment, Lad. It'll be soon; Vonlith is resting, but will resume his work shortly. I'll bring the Grandfather, but you have to wait."

"I'll wait." He watched her set to work, steeling his nerves against the task that lay before him. She finished her work and left without another word, her steps as soft going as they had been coming.

Lad lay there, thinking, preparing himself. One by one he flexed and relaxed every muscle from his scalp to his toes, willing them to lie quiescent until he called upon them. He set his mind into a careful light meditation, one that would be broken by the slightest sound, scent, or tremor in the stone beneath him. And most of all, he nurtured the fear, the pain, and yes, even the hatred that lay deep within him for the thing that was called the Grandfather of Assassins.

The man who stood before Captain Norwood's desk wore not the uniform of a Royal Guardsman, but dark leathers and the soft boots of a woodsman. He was tall and lanky and moved with a certain grace that the captain found somewhat unsoldierly. He would have thought him a liability without Sergeant Tamir's recommendation. Now what this dubious example of a man would tell him was to guide his career.

The thought made Norwood shiver with distaste.

"Well, let's have it. You found the place readily enough, I guess."

"Oh, aye, sir. I'd seen it before, so that weren't no fuss."

"And did you notice anything peculiar?"

"Oh, aye. The place is set up like a fortress, sir. There's more guards walkin' the walls than there are at the duke's palace, and I'm not exaggeratin' one bit! Six on the main gate, and pairs walkin' at odd intervals around the walls. Mercenaries, I'd guess. At least, they don't wear no livery. The place is sewn up tighter than a merchant's purse."

"Seems quite a lot of security for a businessman," Norwood said, clenching his jaw. There was still precious little evidence that the girl Wiggen's story was accurate. The master of the Assassins Guild, if there really were such a guild, would hardly be likely to live in such an ostentatious estate.

"Oh, aye, sir. Looked like he was preparin' for a siege."

"Was there anything else peculiar?"

"Well, there was quite a bit of traffic goin' in and out for this time of night. There was even a wagon parked in the courtyard, and not just a coach, but a big ornate thing with gold and silver writin' all over it. I couldn't read none of it. It seemed a bit flashy, even for the likes of some rich merchant."

"Gold and silver writing on a wagon?" Norwood hated mysteries worse than toothaches, and this one was killing him.

"Sounds like a wizard's wagon," Tamir offered. "I've seen some like that come and go out of Northgate. Tells everyone not to mess with 'em, I guess."

"A wizard?" He rubbed his tired eyes and swore under his breath. "What the hell would an assassin want with a...magic... Holy Gods of Light and Darkness!" Norwood gasped, lurching to his feet. "He's got him! He's got him back and he's having a mage put the spells back in place. That's got to be it!"

"The boy?"

"That's right, Tamir. It's the only thing that makes sense! If they'd killed him, why the wizard? But if they captured him... A shrewd man, one who'd put years and thousands in gold into an investment that had yet to pay off, might try one last time to make it work."

"But if they do put the magic back on him..."

"Then Wiggen's prophesy will come true. Nobles will start dying again."

"What do we do, Captain?"

"We go in there and make sure it doesn't come true."

"When?"

"First light, Tamir. We'll have an advantage in the daylight." He stood up and retrieved a clean roll of parchment from his shelf. "But we're not taking any chances on this one." He pushed his inkwell and quill across the desk toward the lanky guardsman whose importance had suddenly transcended his captain's original estimation. "I want an accurate rendering of the estate, where every guard was, what perimeter defenses they have, and anything else you can remember."

"Aye, sir!"

As the man set to work, Norwood turned to his sergeant. "Tamir, our only hope on this is to get through the front gate before they can close it. We can't besiege the place; we're not equipped, and the losses would be too high. We've got to figure out a way to get inside fast, without giving them a chance to react."

"And without gettin' ourselves killed, I suppose."

"Yes, and that. Especially that."

Chapter XXIX

Mya was prowling. That was the only way you could describe it.

She had no quarry, she wasn't hunting, but she was restless. She knew that what was to come would end with her either dead or free, and the anticipation of that moment had her nerves singing like violin strings.

There were so many things that could go wrong. The timing had to be perfect: the wizard Vonlith had to remain ignorant of the plot up to the culminating moment; Lad could strike too soon or too late; or he could have already betrayed her, as she had betrayed him more than once. But she knew in her gut that he wouldn't. He would play this out, even at the risk of his own life. That was where the two of them differed, not in some ephemeral judgment of what was good and what was evil, but in their priorities. Mya's priority was Mya, as it always had been, and as it always would be. As it had to be for her to survive.

The story she'd concocted to bring the Grandfather to the interrogation chamber was paper thin and would bear no scrutiny. One question at the wrong time would mean her death. But planning and preparing were her forte; she had laid out all possible contingencies in her mind and planned responses should any of them occur. Unfortunately, too many of these responses involved her defending herself against the Grandfather, which would be difficult, for she couldn't injure him due to the bonds of the ring. The best she could do in that instance was defend herself.

So she prowled and thought and planned.

And as if the gods had decided to prove to her that one can't prepare for every eventuality, she was utterly astounded when she heard a familiar voice ask the Grandfather's valet for an audience.

"Jax!" she said, descending the main stair with all the bravado she could muster. "What are you doing here? You were ordered to watch the *Tap and Kettle*!" Her mind raced ahead to all the reasons Jax would leave his post. All of them were bad.

"Mistress Mya. I didn't think you'd be awake at this hour." He bowed to her, having been informed of her new position, and having learned what happened to subordinates who didn't show proper respect for their superiors. The rumors of Targus' death were many, and had grown in the telling.

"Answer my question!" she snapped, dismissing the valet with a flick of her hand. "Why are you here?"

"Something has happened at the *Tap and Kettle* that the Grandfather needs to know about," he said. She could have thanked him for being such an evasive bastard. If he'd spilled something important in front of the valet, her whole plan would have collapsed.

"Well, it better be important or we're both going to regret it!" She turned her back and ascended the stairs. "Come on, Jax. Dragging your feet won't make it easier."

She heard him fall in behind her, and the middle of her back began to itch where she imagined he would put a dagger. The two of them had never really gotten along, and her meteoric rise to power had thrown a log on the fire of his animosity. He answered to her because he was required to, and that was all.

"So what's happened that you think the Grandfather needs so desperately to know that you planned on telling him without first coming to me?" She looked over her shoulder at him as they topped the first flight of stairs and started down the hall toward the second. The Grandfather's chamber was on the third level, occupying the entire west wing. She had to have a plan for dealing with this by the time they reached the top of the stairs. "You do know you're supposed to bring all matters to me, your direct superior, don't you?"

"Yes, Mistress. As I said, I thought you'd be asleep." The muscles of his jaw bunched and relaxed, lending little credence to the lie. "I sought only to ease your rest."

"Very thoughtful of you." Mya rounded the corner and started up the stair, letting her steps slow slightly as they ascended. "Now, answer the question. What happened at the *Tap and Kettle*?"

"The innkeeper's daughter returned. The captain of the Royal Guard knows who's orchestrated the recent murders of the duke's kinsmen."

Mya stopped in her tracks, two steps from the top of the stairs. As she turned to face him, she let her face register all the pent-up fear she'd been harboring since her conversation with Lad. She hoped it was convincing.

"The captain of the guard knows who the Grandfather really is?"

"He suspects. He is sending someone to investigate."

"This could be disastrous! You were right to come so quickly. We've got to stop up that leak first, then get this place looking like a merchant's estate instead of a military camp!" She began ticking off her fingers as she gave him his orders. "Go to Jingles and get two good Blades. The inn is still being watched by the guard, so you'll have to be careful, but we need that girl and her fat father dead by morning. You understand?"

"Yes, Mistress!" He seemed a bit taken aback by her prompt and direct response.

"Good! We shouldn't have to deal with that blockhead Captain Norwood if we get this place squared away before his goons show up. Now go!"

"Yes, Mistress!" He turned to go.

There's a spot at the base of the skull where the spinal cord enters, no larger than the tip of a man's finger. A tiny target, and so not often used. But it affords the advantage, when penetrated by a thin blade, of severing virtually every nerve in the body in a single stroke. The victim doesn't cry out, as death is instantaneous.

Mya's aim was perfect.

The thin stiletto snicked through Jax's gray matter with a quick flip of her wrist. His body crumpled, and she pulled him backward into her arms without a sound, lest he tumble down the stairs. His body twitched spasmodically as she rolled him over, obsolete nerve impulses dying without reaching their appointed destinations. She left the stiletto in place, for that was another disadvantage to this method; the heart, bereft of direction from the brain, would continue beating until it died for lack of oxygen. If she removed her blade, blood would drench her, the stairs, and everything else. As it was, she only got a bit on her hand. Now her only problem was to hide the body.

She felt for a pulse at his neck, and when it faded to nothing she made sure there was no bleeding around the blade, rolled him back onto his back and pulled him into a sitting position. This was the dangerous part; she had to pull him up and over her shoulder in order to carry him to her chamber, but he weighed a good bit more than she. Every apprentice assassin was trained in the technique, since carrying the fruits of their labors was a common task of the profession. Jax wasn't a particularly large or heavy man, but Mya was more than a hand shorter and several stones lighter. She could lift the weight, she was sure, but the danger lay in the uneven footing. If she fell on the stairs...

Mya locked his knees straight, braced his feet, and pulled him up. As Jax teetered forward, she ascended two steps, ducking under his lolling torso. His weight came down on her shoulder perfectly, and she kept her balance. Now all she had to do was to walk down the stairs and to her chambers without leaving a trail of blood or falling to her death.

"Easy," she muttered, turning and taking the first step down. It was harder than she thought it would be, and by the time she got to the landing, her knees were trembling and her heart was pounding. It was just a hundred feet to her door, but it felt like a league. The latch of her door worked easily and she entered, thankful that simple locks were superfluous in this place. She used her burden to nudge the door closed behind her, and took the four steps to her bed. She let herself fall forward; Jax landed on the thick mattress with an audible thump. She collapsed next to the corpse, heaving breath after breath to calm her hammering heart.

"Well, I never thought we'd end up in bed together, Jax," she said between breaths, forcing herself to sit up. She surveyed her handiwork. Her stiletto was still in place, but there was a red stain marring her bedspread. A quick check confirmed that there was no trail of blood on the floor. Dropping him to the bed must have knocked something loose.

"Now look what you've done! You've stained the coverlet!" She grabbed one arm and flipped Jax onto his stomach. She wrapped a kerchief around the knife where the blade met the crosspiece and withdrew it from its warm sheath, wiping it clean and stopping up the hole in the process. "Leave it to a man to make a mess on a lady's bed and then make her clean it up!"

Mya flipped the corpse onto the floor on the far side of the bed and pushed it underneath, then removed the coverlet from the bed and flipped it over. The red stain hadn't soaked through the thickly feathered spread, so the reverse side was still clean. She wiped her hand clean on a towel from the nightstand and tossed that under the bed as well. What did she care? She'd never be sleeping in this bed again, however the night played out.

She straightened her robe, finger-combed her hair, and repinned it, then exited her room just in time to see the wizard Vonlith vanishing down the stairs. He was through resting, and was going back down to resume his labors. It was just about midnight. She would wait about a quarter hour, then bring the Grandfather down.

Mya spent that time prowling as before, checking to make sure there was no blood on the stairs, checking her weapons, checking their escape route, checking and rechecking her plan for flaws.

Then it was time.

She knocked firmly on the Grandfather's door, forcing down her fear lest it betray her. If he suspected for a moment, she'd never feel the stroke that took her life.

She waited. She was considering knocking again when the door opened. The Grandfather stood in his black robes, glaring at her, the weariness of recent sleep still evident in his eyes.

"This better be good, Mya."

"My apologies, Grandfather." She bowed shortly, exposing her neck for the perfect killing blow for the barest instant. "The wizard instructed me to fetch you. He has a question regarding the boy's memories. He says it's time to begin destroying the memories that caused him to want to break the original magical bonds, but he doesn't want to obliterate any of the boy's training. He needs exact times or days you want him to destroy."

"Tell him to destroy everything after the day the boy arrived in the city." The door started to close.

"I thought to suggest that, but I wondered if he had any experiences on the road that might have caused him to distrust us. Also, I didn't know if you wanted the memories of any of the successful assassinations destroyed. He also has a remarkable knowledge of the city. It would cost a lot of time to wipe that out, then have to retrain him."

"Right you are, dear Mya," he said, raising an eyebrow at her with a wry smile. "Always thinking ahead. Very good." He whirled back into his chamber and recovered a few items from his desk that Mya didn't see before they vanished into his robes. "Keep this up and I shall shortly find you indispensable!"

"You've discovered my ulterior motive, Grandfather," she said. She heard metal click on metal and the creak of leather. *Weapons*, she supposed, *the suspicious bastard*.

"*No* one is indispensable, Mya," he said, turning back to her with the same wry smile. "But keep trying. Come on then." He strode past her and she followed, the two descending the stairs in swirling cloaks of black and crimson.

Lad heard their approach long before they entered the interrogation chamber. The Grandfather's voice continued a light banter, almost casually discussing the future murders his weapon would commit once the magical bonds were reestablished. Such calm and calculated cruelty disgusted Lad. He slowed his fluttering heart and eased his breathing; if he appeared agitated, the

Grandfather might suspect something.

He lay there, enduring the pain of the wizard's needle as he readied himself. All the years of training, all the countless hours of instruction and preparation would come to play in this one moment. His destiny. Not exactly the destiny his creators had planned, but the one he had chosen for himself. His single purpose in life now was to kill one man, to end the evil that had caused so many so much anguish. Whatever else happened, however he was injured, whoever else died, that was his only goal.

No pain...

No fear...

No mercy...

"I think your suggestion to slow the pace of the assassinations is wise, Mya," the Grandfather said as they entered the room and approached the table where Lad lay prone. "The prior incident when the weapon was injured during the first, then nearly killed during the second assassination the same night, demonstrates his vulnerability. The inflexibility of his obedience puts much more focus upon the care we must exert when giving him his orders."

"Such was my thought, Grandfather," Mya agreed, following a step behind and to the Grandfather's right, wisely out of the line Lad's attack would take. "Your original timetable is ruined, so changing it now shouldn't incur additional cost."

"True, though modifying it has cost me a small fortune in bribes." He was close now, just steps away.

No pain...

"Well, the investment will yield tenfold in time. We'll sit down today and analyze the schedule, you and I." The master assassin stopped a step away from the table. Still too far.

No fear...

"Come to my chambers at highsun. I'll have a meal prepared on the balcony and we'll discuss it."

"I'd be honored, Grandfather," Mya said. Lad heard her move to his side, felt the movement of air of her robes fluttering as she waved her arm, gesturing her master forward. "Now, Master Vonlith..."

"Ah, yes, the good Master Vonlith." The Grandfather took one step forward. "What exactly seems to be the—"

No mercy...

Lad exploded from the table, flinging off the iron bindings that were held in place by false black-wax pins. He vaulted into a rolling spin, two lightning kicks crashing into the Grandfather before the other could even raise a hand in defense. He felt bone break under his first blow—a collarbone. The second snapped the Grandfather's head to the side. Blood and broken teeth sprayed as the man spun with the blow, but it hadn't been hard enough to break his neck. The third kick missed as the ancient assassin twisted and flipped backward in a swirl of black cloaks, landing in a protective crouch, guarding his injured side, eyes wide with surprise and shock.

Lad barely touched the floor before he leapt after his target, three snap kicks pounding the Grandfather's blocking arm. The hand on his opponent's guarded side flicked, and Lad caught the glitter of flying metal in time to turn his head. Sharpened steel cut a furrow from the corner of his right eye to his ear. The dagger lopped the top off of his ear and clattered to the floor behind him.

Lad pressed the attack, pounding kicks, sweeping trips, and triphammer punches into his opponent faster than the eye could follow. The Grandfather blocked and dodged, rolled and spun, a swirl of black and steel, for two daggers now filled his hands, and Lad's punches and kicks were often met with the edge or point of a blade. Cuts grazed his knuckles and shins where he had narrowly averted disaster. He heard a scuffle and some hissed words from behind him, but could spare no moment to glance.

Then came his opening; a fold of the Grandfather's billowing cloak snagged on a sharpened bit of metal protruding from one of his machines of torture. The master of assassins missed a critical block, and Lad's foot smashed into his ribs. Lad felt the bones shatter under the sole of his foot; breath left the Grandfather's lungs in a bloody spray. The Grandfather was knocked cleanly off of his feet, his daggers flung away into the tangle of twisted machinery. It was a telling blow; the shattered ribs had ruptured lungs. He'd be unable to breathe and his lungs would fill with blood. Lad's opponent would be dead in moments.

As he watched the elder assassin crash into a heavy rack and rebound, a wave of relief swept through Lad that almost brought him to his knees. So much pain suffered, so much heartache and loss, all caused by one man, all now ended. He thought it unfair that such evil should meet such a relatively easy end, but he wasn't one to cause pain unnecessarily, even to one such as the Grandfather. The reign of torture, murder, and brutality was ended; that was enough. Lad was no longer a murderer. He was the master of his *own* destiny now.

And yet, the Grandfather remained standing.

Hate radiated from the ancient assassin's eyes in a palpable wave, his broken teeth clenched in a rictus grimace of rage. He wrenched himself upright and stood there, glaring at Lad, blood dripping from his chin. He turned his head and spat, then flexed his shoulders, which should have been impossible with as many broken bones and other injuries as Lad had inflicted. The man shouldn't even be alive...

"Oh, come now. You can't think I could have lived so long if I was *that* easy to kill," the master assassin asked venomously, reaching up to the clasp of his dark robes. The dark garment fell to the floor.

And Lad understood.

Above the hem of his dark silk pants, the Grandfather's blood-streaked torso was covered with a tapestry of tattooed runes. They were identical to the ones that Lad bore on his own chest, and as the bones beneath that parchment skin writhed and knitted back together, the runes shimmered with power. The Grandfather of Assassins flexed his shoulders again and took a step forward, drawing two more daggers from the leather sheathes strapped to his forearms.

"Now, boy," the ancient assassin hissed, "do you see how truly akin we are, you and I? We share the same magic, the same sweet curse." He drew one of his blades across his own chest, leaving a line of blood that vanished as he laughed.

340

Lad understood, finally, what he was up against. He understood his origin, the impetus for his creation. And he also understood that he would die before he became a shadow of the once-human thing who had created him. This would be the fight of his life, the focal point of all his training, all his preparation. Lad took the stance of the first form in his daily ritual dance of death, and waited for the Grandfather of Assassins to try to take his life. It would not be given freely.

The wizard stood like a block of wood in Mya's hands, so stiff she thought he might keel over from fright. She couldn't blame him. After watching the Grandfather heal a mortal wound, then seeing the tattoos that had been hidden under his robes, she understood that they would all die here.

At Lad's first blurred tumble from the table Mya had lunged away, her first concern being to stay as far out of the fight as possible. Her second concern had been the wizard. She didn't know what magic Vonlith could conjure to aid the Grandfather, but she knew how to prevent it. The blade tucked under his beard and her threatening whispers in his ear kept him utterly silent. And if the Grandfather chose to send sharpened steel flying her way, his plump body would offer formidable protection.

As the runic tattoos on the Grandfather's chest glowed in the wake of his own dagger's bloody trail, the peal of his evil laughter turned May's grip on the wizard to water. Lad took the stance that began his morning exercises, and she realized that he was overmatched. Lad was as quick and agile as ever, perhaps even a touch quicker than his opponent, but his ability to heal and his imperviousness to pain had been burned away—every nick, every cut and bruise, would sap his strength. The Grandfather need only defend himself against lethal attacks to win.

Her plans for power were foiled; her death lay before her, cold and hard, utterly barren. Pointless. Her mind whirled with unanswered questions.

"And you, my traitorous apprentice." The Grandfather's voice snapped her wandering attention into focus as he strutted back and forth, brandishing his daggers. "Do you see what immortality is, Mya, what you could have become?" He twirled the daggers defiantly. "Do you see the power you gave up by betraying me? We could have ruled this city together, the three of us. With your ambition, Mya, and my gift, and the perfect weapon to share between us. No one could have *touched* us."

"I would *never* become like you!" she said between clenched teeth, pleased that her voice didn't quaver with her fear. She gripped her dagger more tightly.

The Grandfather strode around Lad in a broad circle, daggers flashing in his hands, totally confident of the outcome of this confrontation.

Mya considered her pending death. *It's not death, but how we die that matters...*

Lad stood perfectly still, waiting, even when the Grandfather walked directly behind him. He would wait for the attack and use it, Mya knew, but she also knew his response would be futile.

Her whole life she'd wanted only power—now she had it, and it was useless. What power was there in killing? The power of fear only.

The Grandfather cursed and spat as he moved, showing his contempt for her and her would-be accomplice, but his barbs and insults slipped away without stinging. He promised a thousand deaths, each a thousand times more painful than the torment she had already felt under his touch, but his threats were impotent. The dagger in her hand would pierce her own heart before she'd allow him to touch her again.

What victory was there for her after all the horrors she'd lived through as a child?

The Grandfather struck.

His attack came in the middle of one of his tirades, cursing her deceitful ways. Lad responded before the attack was even fully launched, moving through the first forms of his dance... *block, twist, sweep, strike....* His movements, the dance she'd learned, fit perfectly into the interplay of steel and flesh. It was happening a hundred times faster than she'd learned it, but his dance was flawless. Maybe...a chance to live…

How we live defines us.

What had she done with this life? If living defined her, who was she? Living...deciding how to define herself, that was the victory.

Each of the Grandfather's attacks met a perfect parry, each thrust a block, each block a counter thrust, each step a sweep... It was all so fast she could barely follow the movements, but she could see the frustration on the Grandfather's face. And with each failed attack, with each blocked thrust or thwarted parry, his temper swelled to rage. His daggers cut only air, and she could see their tiny weight dragging at his lightning movements. And with his hands filled, he could not block, grasp and strike as freely as Lad.

The Grandfather's weapons were a hindrance; Lad *was* a weapon. But the pace of the fight was unrelenting, and both of them were beginning to tire.

Unless...

"If that boy dies, I die," she whispered harshly into Vonlith's ear, pressing the blade against his neck until it threatened to cut, "but not before I kill you first!"

"What? I don't—"

"Help him or die! The choice is that simple, wizard! Do it!"

"Do *what*?" the man gasped, straining against her grip as the two assassins battled before them. In the span of a single sentence dozens of blows and kicks were blocked, parried, or avoided. "How could I intervene in that?"

"With magic, for the gods' sake! Cast a damned spell or something! Blast that sadistic bastard to cinders!" Her dagger twitched with her demands, drawing a line of blood at his throat.

"I don't *do* spells like that!" Vonlith complained. "The only spells I know are runes. My magic is cast with pen and ink, not by wiggling my gods-damned fingers!"

Lad slipped past the Grandfather's guard, his fist smashing into the older man's jaw, shattering the joint, but he paid for the strike with a deep gash to his forearm. The Grandfather spat broken teeth in Lad's face and grinned, his jaw crackling and knitting as he did.

The exchange had been a net loss for Lad, for his arm bled freely, and with each drop of blood he weakened minutely.

"Then you better figure out a way to make your pen and ink mightier than a sword very quickly," Mya hissed in the wizard's ear. "Now!" She turned and pushed him toward his workbench of inks, needles, and quills. She took a step and placed the point of her dagger at his back.

Vonlith cast about the littered table, eyes wide with panic. There was no way out for him except to help Lad and Mya defeat the Grandfather, but if he tried and failed, he'd be killed for his betrayal. He snapped a glance at Mya, then another at the two combatants, biting his knuckles in frustration. He was trapped and he knew it; Mya could see it in his eyes.

Then an idea struck his features as plainly as if it were written there for all to read.

"Maybe..."

He snatched up a bottle of ink and a quill. He dipped the quill in the bottle and scrawled several magical letters on the side of the vessel itself, murmuring under his breath as he did so. The bottle suddenly flared to light in his hand, and he turned to Mya and grinned in wide-eyed triumph.

"This *may* work!" He looked at the glowing bottle, then at the embattled pair of men. "Or it may kill us all. But even if it does work, it will last only moments."

"What is it?"

"A negation. It will arrest the magic of all runes in this room, but only for a very short while."

Her agile mind clicked to the effect the spell would have. Without the magic, Lad would still be a healthy young man in peak condition; the Grandfather would be a healthy *old* man in peak condition. It was a slim difference, but it was an advantage.

"Do it!"

Vonlith nodded, raised the bottle of magically imbued ink before him, and poured it in a shimmering arc. The ink fell to form glittering runes of energy that hung in the air. And when the last drop of ink left the bottle and the last letter formed, they exploded into blinding radiance.

Both Lad and the Grandfather screamed in pain.

A wave of agony coursed through Lad as the spells that had been a part of his being for most of his life were suddenly inactive. His vision dimmed, his hearing dampened, and his strength melted away like a snowflake on a hot skillet. But the pain passed, and with it his vision cleared. Before him, the Grandfather had fallen to his knees, similarly afflicted.

"Kill him, Lad! Now!"

He glanced at Mya, and the blinding light of the glowing runes floating in the air told him what had happened. He flexed his hands, watching his fingers open and close; he felt weak and slow. Then he looked to the Grandfather struggling to his feet, and he could see weakness and more in his opponent's face. The Grandfather felt *old!*

Lad sprang to the attack, his movements a syrupy shadow of his former lightning speed, but he was faster than the Grandfather could counter. The kick struck, not with bone-shattering force as it would have moments before, but hard enough to drive the air from his opponent's lungs and send him sprawling.

The Grandfather rolled up, grimacing in shock and pain, something he hadn't felt in a lifetime. He swept his daggers menacingly, but his slashes were slow and ill-timed. Lad smacked them aside and struck again, a spinning back-kick that drove his opponent to the floor and sent one dagger clattering away. He pursued with another vicious kick, but the Grandfather rolled with the blow and slashed Lad's shin. Lad should have dodged such a clumsy cut easily, but without the magic, both of them were moving as if something intangible dragged at every effort. The bone-deep cut hurt horribly, but the Grandfather was struggling just to get to his feet. Lad was winning…

He advanced again, pushing down the pain, intending to end it quickly, but the Grandfather drew the dagger back and threw, not at Lad, but past him, at the wizard. If Vonlith died, the spell would dissipate and…

Lad turned in time to see Mya step in front of the wizard, her shape dark against the blinding light of the runes. She took the dagger meant for the wizard. He squinted against the glare as she crumpled to the floor, but he couldn't tell where the dagger had struck. And he was short on time; the blinding glow of the runes was beginning to dim.

Lad turned and lunged at the Grandfather, thinking only to end it as quickly as possible. He took a hard blow to his cheekbone, but was inside the older man's guard now, his fingers clenched around the Grandfather's throat. Lad's ears rang with two more hard punches, but he retained his grip. The light from behind him dimmed further, and he could feel the strength seeping back into him. The runes covering his opponent's skin shimmered as well, but with Lad's hands around his throat, the Grandfather couldn't breathe.

Lad pushed him backward until he sat on the man's heaving chest, his arms locked, his fingers tightening with every ounce of strength that returned to him. The Grandfather's blows became frantic, then weak, and finally stopped. The glow from behind him faded completely, and Lad exerted all the force he could muster into his grip until bone cracked and splintered under his grasp. And still he didn't let go, fearing that the Grandfather's magic would heal even a broken neck. He maintained the hold, squeezing every last vestige of life out of the man who had tortured him.

"Die..." he growled between clenched and bloody teeth. "Die...die...die..."

Finally, when the flesh split beneath his grasp, and shards of broken bone pierced his straining palms, he relented.

Lad stood and stumbled back from the corpse of the Grandfather of Assassins. The evil was at an end, it was truly and finally over. But Lad felt as if he had simply committed one more murder.

"No more killing," he muttered to himself, looking down at the blood on his hands. He shook his head and turned his back on his former life, on the destiny that would have destroyed him. It was time to make his own destiny.

"Boy!"

Lad's attention snapped up at the wizard's call, and he ran to Mya's side. She lay on the floor, the hilt of the Grandfather's dagger protruding from just below her sternum. Her hands were wrapped around the bloody weapon, her face painted with shocked agony.

"She stepped right in front of the dagger," Vonlith muttered. "First she threatens to kill me, then…"

"Lie still, Mya." Lad forced her hands away and tore open her cloak, exposing the dire wound. He looked to the wizard. "Can you heal this?"

"I'm no healer! The spells I know of healing would take a *week* to transcribe."

"My…po—" Mya gasped, trying to speak through the blood that welled up in her throat.

"Quiet, Mya. I've got to find a way to heal you before I take the dagger out. It's in your liver and stomach. You'll bleed to death if I take it out without healing!"

"My…pocket…"

"What?" Lad rifled through her robes with all the skill of a master pickpocket. He came up with several weapons, a strip of worn red ribbon, twelve pieces of silver, and a small glass vial. He held up the vial; it was the same she'd forced him to drink from only hours ago. "Yes!"

He pulled the stopper and held the rim to her bloody lips.

"You'll have to swallow it as I pull the dagger out, Mya. Can you do that? It will hurt."

"Do…you…*think*?" she asked, opening her mouth for him to pour in the potion.

"Okay. Ready?"

She nodded.

He poured the potion into her mouth and nodded. "Swallow it!"

As she did, he slipped the blade from her viscera. Mya screamed through clenched lips, but forced the bitter liquid down. Dark blood welled from the gaping wound, but then quickly slowed, and finally stopped. The wound closed completely, leaving a wide pink scar. She gasped a deep breath and coughed.

"How do you feel?" He realized it was a foolish question as soon as he asked it.

"Like I've been knifed in the gut," she said, forcing herself up to a sitting position. "But better than dead, which is what I *would* have been. Thank you, Lad. You saved my life."

"Thank me by getting us the hell out of here!" he barked, standing and retrieving a towel, a pair of trousers, and a shirt from the shelf that held neatly folded stacks of the black garments he'd come to loathe. "We've got about an hour before this place is surrounded by guardsmen, and even though we just did them a favor, I don't think they'll be inclined to give us a pardon for it." He began tearing the towel into strips and binding his bleeding shin and forearm.

"We can get out in Master Vonlith's wagon," she said, pushing herself slowly to her feet.

"You can?" the wizard asked incredulously. "What makes you think I'll help you escape after this?" He waved a hand at the Grandfather's corpse in emphasis. "You've just killed my employer and cost me a fortune, besides threatening my life!"

He seemed to have suddenly forgotten that she also just saved his life.

"Because if you don't," she growled through clenched teeth, "I'll tell the entire Assassins Guild that *you* killed their guildmaster!"

"You wouldn't!"

"Try me!"

"What do you mean, 'tell the guild?'" Lad asked, pulling a shirt over his head as he rejoined the others. "There isn't a guild anymore. The Grandfather's dead!"

"You thought that would destroy the *guild*?" Mya laughed shortly, shaking her head as she retrieved the items Lad had taken from her pockets. "You're still a little naive if you did, Lad. The guild will live on, and they'll appoint another guildmaster. Though this estate will never be used again, now that the duke's guard knows who lived here."

Lad stopped tying his bandages and stared once again at the blood on his hands. He felt as if they would never come clean. "So all this was for nothing."

"Not for nothing, Lad," Mya countered, moving to the Grandfather's body and removing the black and gold ring from his lifeless finger. "In fact, as we're getting the hell out of here, let me pitch a little something to you that I've been planning for a while."

"What plan?" Lad asked, suspicious of her motives.

"Something that will suit us both, and something that *might* suit the guild as well."

"I won't help you become an even more cruel guildmaster than he was, Mya."

"You couldn't pay me enough for the job, honestly. No, I've got something else in mind. The guard's looking for you a lot more than they're looking for me. I'd think you'd be a little more receptive to a proposition that will let you stay in Twailin where you'll be close to Wiggen and have some influence in changing the guild into something a little less brutal."

"I won't kill for you," he stated flatly, folding his arms across his chest in defiance.

"If things go as I plan, you'll never have to kill again. I promise."

"Your promises have the tendency to leave me manacled to that slab," he said.

"Excuse me for interrupting," Vonlith put in, frowning at them both, "but aren't we in a hurry to, how did you put it, 'get the hell out of here'?"

"Right you are, my good wizard. Right you are." Mya pulled her cloak tight around herself and said to Lad, "I'll explain my plan when were safe. You can take it or leave it."

"Fine," he said, motioning the two of them toward the door. "But know that I don't trust you, Mya. I never will. And while I don't *like* to kill, I will if I have to."

"Then we have something in common. Now come on."

The three left the interrogation chamber without looking back.

Chapter XXX

Mya nodded to Paxal as she strode into the back room of the *Golden Cockerel* and smiled to the assembly she had summoned.

"The news that the Grandfather has been killed has undoubtedly reached all of you by now," she said, making herself comfortable at the large table where her four peers were already seated. She sipped from the glass of blood-red wine that was set before her, exchanging glances with each of the other masters in turn: Inquisitor, Blade, Alchemist, and Enforcer. She was the youngest of the five by a score of years, and she could see the animosity in their eyes.

"You may have also heard a rumor that I had something to do with his death." She swirled the wine within her glass, enjoying the play of crimson on crystal, and put it down. She smiled, spreading her hands wide in supplication. "I won't corroborate or deny that rumor, other than to say that I still wear this." She held up the hand bearing the onyx ring of the Master Hunter. "And that I was present when Saliez met his end."

With that she placed a ring of black and gold in the center of the table before her. The eyes of the four other master assassins were drawn to it like moths to a flame, and she could see the avarice in them.

"And you fancy yourself his successor. Is that why you've

called us here?" That was Master Youtrin, head of the guild Enforcers. He flexed his broad, scarred hands, his knuckles popping like corn on the fire.

"Please don't be ridiculous, Master Youtrin. I'm far too young to be the guildmaster." Mya sighed dramatically. "And, in fact, I'm probably too young to be Master Hunter. But I *am*." The last she directed with a flat, hard tone that told them all she expected to keep her vaunted position.

"So why exactly *did* you call us here, *Mistress* Mya?" Mistress Alchemist Neera asked, tapping her long yellowed nails on the table. "Do you wish to nominate one of us for the position?"

"No. I called you here to propose that we do away with the position of guildmaster, at least for a while." There was some murmuring, and a few exchanged glances and raised eyebrows. "I believe this would not only be good for us, but for the guild. Saliez squandered the guild's wealth on personal extravagance, he used the guild's power to further his own ends, and he delighted in directed cruelty that did nothing to advance the standing, position, or power of the guild as a whole. As you may or may not know, Saliez's grand plan was to pressure Duke Mir into relaxing the trade restrictions with the southern kingdoms. The river trade from Southaven to Twailin would have multiplied tenfold, and with it, the ability of the duke's agents to thoroughly inspect cargos would have plummeted."

"Smuggling? Is that what this was all about?" Mistress Inquisitor Calmarel asked incredulously, sweeping her ebony hair back in a dramatic arc. "That seems so...trite."

"No," Mya said, sipping her wine again while ignoring the woman's penchant for the dramatic. "Saliez was prepared to ship tons of high-quality black lotus into the Empire through this city. He had suppliers, distributors, and traffickers all lined up. It would have brought in tens of thousands in gold every month."

"And would have started a war with the Thieves Guild," Neera stated flatly. "They've always controlled the lotus trade within the empire. Was he prepared for that?"

Mya looked to the slim figure standing at her elbow and let a predatory smile grace her sensuous lips. "Yes, he was."

"Regardless of his plans, proceeding without a leader..." Master Blade Horice shrugged noncommittally, steepling his long, graceful fingers before him. "It seems dangerous. No?"

"*We* will lead the guild. We are, together, more powerful, smarter, and more able to govern our own actions and serve the guild than *any* one man or woman," Mya said, steel edging her voice. "We would vote on any action that requires the resources of more than our own areas of expertise, or anything that might affect the guild as a whole. We take a simple vow not to contract without at least one other master's agreement to do so, and we take another not to contract one another. This wouldn't be a vow bound by magic, but one backed by common interest." She smiled thinly and sipped her wine.

Horice frowned. "Breaking these vows would naturally have to carry a *significant* penalty."

"Is that what *he's* for?" Mistress Calmarel asked accusatively, flicking a manicured nail at the slim figure standing at Mya's elbow. "To keep us in line?"

There were more murmurs around the room, some between the masters, and some between the comparably large number of bodyguards each master or mistress boasted. Lad was Mya's only companion in the room, and she felt utterly safe. The rumors of exactly how the Grandfather died *had* reached them, just as she intended.

"No. He's here to keep daggers from sprouting from between my shoulder blades." She turned and patted Lad's arm affectionately. He stood rock still, eyes staring forward at nothing, impassive as a statue. "That's all."

"And what of that?" Youtrin growled, gesturing toward the lonely ring lying in the middle of the table. "What do we do with that?"

There was an extended silence, all of them considering the fact that the wearer of that ring could not be harmed by any of the five masters seated at the table.

"Personally, I think it should be melted down." Calmarel flexed her own left hand and the polished ring of obsidian on her finger glittered in the lamplight. "It poses too great a risk for the rest of us."

"I agree," Mya said evenly, smiling at them all. "But it's obvious that none of us trusts the others enough to delegate the task. Keep in mind that while we all can't harm the bearer, others may. If one of us were to suddenly be seen wearing the ring of the guildmaster..."

"Fine then. Who do we trust to have it destroyed?" Youtrin glared around the room, his broad brow furrowing.

"I trust him," Neera said finally, pointing one ancient crooked finger toward Lad. "There's no deceit in his face. Give him the ring and tell him to destroy it, Mya. He's bound by your command. He'll see it done."

"Is that acceptable to everyone?" Mya asked, keeping her tone calm despite her racing heart. They still thought Lad was under her control, just as she had hoped.

They all nodded their ascent, so she said, "Lad, take the ring, and tomorrow morning take it to a blacksmith and have it melted down. Bring the lump of gold back to me so the others can see it upon our next meeting."

"Yes, Mya," he said, his tone perfectly obedient. He took the ring and tucked it into his black silk tunic.

"I can't say that your proposal doesn't sound good to me, Mya," Horice said with a pensive wag of a finger. "The agreement between the masters would have to be drawn up and signed by all of us, of course. Transgressions by any one of us would be dealt with by the rest of us directly. As you say, much effort was wasted under the leadership of the late Saliez."

"I just happen to have such an agreement drawn up already, if you please." Mya withdrew four ribbon-bound scrolls from the satchel at her feet and passed them around. "This is just a rough draft, of course. We can discuss any changes, additions, or deletions as a group and vote on them right here and now. Or, if you prefer time to study the document, we can reconvene in, say, three days?"

"Agreed," three of her four peers said in unison. Youtrin simply grabbed the scroll and handed it to one of his men.

"Very good!" Mya stood and raised her glass to the others. "In parting, I'd like to offer this toast: To the *new* Assassins Guild!"

The others repeated her toast and touched the rims of their fine crystal glasses together. The sound rang in Mya's ears like music as she drank.

The masters shared a few parting false pleasantries and gathered their entourages. Mya bid them all good evening and finished her wine as the door closed behind the last of them.

"Paxal, you've once again served me well," Mya said as the innkeeper moved about the room, clearing the glasses and small plates of tidbits that had gone largely untouched. She tossed a small pouch on the table. It landed heavily. Thick gold coins rattled inside as it vanished into the innkeeper's hand. "I'll require the room in three days. Until then, please see that my presence in your establishment remains a secret."

"My pleasure, Mistress Mya," he said with a bow, turning to leave.

"And you, Lad," she said, turning to her silent partner in this dangerous gambit. "Thank you. *Your* presence is the only reason I'm still breathing." She withdrew another pouch from a pocket and held it out before her. "I don't suppose you'd consider trading that ring in your pocket for this?"

"No, I wouldn't, Mya." He narrowed those luminous eyes at her.

"Oh, fine. You really need to learn some humor, Lad. Take the money. You've earned it. Go spend it on that innkeeper's daughter of yours." She thrust the pouch at him.

Slowly, almost reluctantly, he took it.

"I *still* won't kill for you, Mya," he said, tucking the pouch into the belt of his trousers. "Not now, not ever."

"And I won't ask you to, unless it's to defend me from those jackals." She moved to the rack in the corner and removed a heavy cloak of crimson-dyed wool. She drew it over her shoulders and tied the clasp with a smile. "Our partnership is simple, Lad. Don't read more into it than is really there. You protect me and help me change the guild into something slightly less brutal, and I keep you safe from the Royal Guard and keep Youtrin's racketeers out of the *Tap and Kettle*." She paused and checked the weapons hidden inside the heavy cloak. "Personally, I think you're getting the better end of the deal."

"Where are you going?" he asked, his eyes raking over her and, she knew, cataloging every one of her hidden surprises.

"Out." He didn't need to know anything more.

"Should I accompany you?" He nodded to the back door. "The others could have someone waiting for you."

"No, Lad. Not tonight. I'm...meeting someone."

"Who?"

He was still so naive that she had to smile. "A *friend*, Lad. That's all you need to know."

"Good." Lad smiled and nodded at her, his strangely honest features relaxing somewhat. "It's good that you have a friend, Mya."

"Yes." She had to smile again. "Yes, it *is* good. And thank you, if I didn't tell you before. I owe you a lot."

Mya held out her hand to Lad then, and he took it, though she did notice that he checked to make sure that she wasn't wearing a ring on that hand before he carefully matched grips with her.

"You're welcome, Mya," he said as their hands parted. "I still don't trust you, you know, but.... Well, I suppose there's no harm in trying."

"No, Lad. No harm at all."

"Goodnight, Mya," he said, heading for the door. She knew where he was going, so there was no need to ask. She thought, not for the first time, that Lad was wasting his time with that innkeeper's daughter, but it really wasn't her business. The door closed, and she waited a few moments before following.

The night was cool, and a light rain fell, dampening the air and her high spirits. She had never liked the rain, especially the cool rains of winter. She could never get warm enough, and always felt like her feet would stay wet forever.

Mya stayed to the shadows, more from habit than from any need for concealment, and made her way a few blocks north and east. She made sure that her enthusiastic bodyguard was not following her by doubling back a few times, ducking into a couple of pubs and exiting through different doors than she entered. Lad could have followed her through the open streets without her knowing, she knew, but she doubted he could manage to keep track of her through the noisy public houses.

Finally, she entered the stately inn that was her destination. She passed through the common room without a nod to anyone; the room had been reserved in advance. Besides, the proprietor knew her and knew what she was; he wouldn't have interfered with her if she'd walked in without a penny in her pocket and claimed the finest suite. When the landing of the third floor was finally beneath her boots and the noise of the rowdy common room was dampened and distant, she felt sure that she had reached her goal without being observed. The proprietor of the inn was the only person who knew who she was meeting here, and he knew equally well that he'd be dead by morning if he betrayed that trust.

The key in her pocket worked the latch without a hitch, and she slipped into the room without any more sound than the click of it locking behind her.

"Hello, my dear," her clandestine associate said in a soothing, even tone. He knew she was uncomfortable with this, and his calming manner was to set her at ease. He almost accomplished it.

"Hello," she said, releasing the clasp on her cloak and hanging it on one of the pegs behind the door. "Are you ready for me?"

"Presently, my dear. Just make yourself comfortable."

She knew what he meant, so she hung her sword belt on another peg and slipped off her high, soft boots. The hard mattress creaked as she sat and loosened her tunic lacings. She watched him covertly as she drew it over her head and folded it neatly, but he kept his attention on his work. The light chemise came over her head and was folded atop her tunic on the small night table. She stood, removed her trousers and added them to the pile. Her thin scanties and socks, she kept, the former for some modicum of modesty, the latter because her feet got cold.

Next was the hardest part, as far as she was concerned; she lay on the bed and tried to relax, tried to think of something else, tried not think at all. She tried not to listen to the tick, tick, tick of metal against porcelain, tried not to hear the droning of his voice, tried not to wonder about the words she could never understand. As with so many things she tried, she failed.

"Ready, my dear?

Mya forced herself to answer, willing her voice to radiate the calm that she didn't feel. "Ready, Vonlith."

"Very good." Mya closed her eyes and felt him move to the side of the bed. "Now, just try to relax, my dear."

"Just shut up and do it," she snapped, steeling her nerves for that first prick of the needle and the overwhelming rush of the magic.

EPILOGUE

I t's late, Wiggen," Forbish said, taking the mop from her weary
grasp and resting a comforting hand on her drooping shoulder.

"Is it?" She looked around the common room, brushing a
lock of hair back from her face. All the guests had gone to bed.
The fire was burning low, and the lamps had been turned down.
"I hadn't noticed."

"You should go to bed. We can finish up here."

"I'm fine, father." Wiggen wiped her hands on her apron and
sniffed, blinking away unshed tears. She'd been thinking while
she mopped, and time had fled. "I'll get the dinner dishes, and
then go to bed."

"The dishes are done, honey. Josie did 'em, and those two
rascal nephews of hers have the kitchen clean as a whistle."
Forbish leaned back and stuck his thumbs in the tie of his apron.
"Never thought those two would take to work like fish to water."

"It's because you pay them too much, Father," Wiggen said
humorlessly, loosening her apron's strings and drawing it over
her head. "I am a little tired. If you're sure you don't need me,
I'll see you in the morning."

"Everything's fine, honey. You just get some sleep. You've
been looking far too tired lately. You need your rest."

Wiggen could hear the concern in his voice and felt guilty
for it. "I...don't sleep much, Father. I know I should, but

something keeps me awake." She rubbed her eyes with her apron and shrugged, trying to smile. "I'll be fine."

"Well, you just don't worry about anything, and try to think of happy things. That always works for me." He wrapped a massive arm around her shoulder and guided her down the hall to her room. "We've got our health, business has picked up, and we're not bothered by those blasted ruffians anymore. There's nothing to keep you awake but what's in the past, honey. Let it go and you'll sleep."

"I know, Father," she said, nodding to his wisdom. "I know he's gone, but sometimes it's like he visits me in my dreams, but I'm not dreaming, not even sleeping."

"It'll ease in time, Wiggen. Just think of the life that's ahead of you. That's what's important now."

They stopped at her door, and she turned and embraced him heartily, though her hands still wouldn't touch around his substantial girth.

"I will, father." Wiggen squeezed as hard as she could, and felt him sigh in contentment. It was all she could give him. "I love you, father."

"And I you, Wiggen. More than life itself." His thick arms enfolded her, and she felt utterly safe and at home. "Now get some sleep."

"I'll try." She opened her door and stepped through, smiling back at him as she turned up the lamp. "Goodnight, father."

"Goodnight, Wiggen." The door clicked closed, and she wished not for the first time that there were a lock.

Before she could even turn, hands slipped around her waist, quiet as a breath of midnight shadow, soft as a feather in the wind, and warm. Oh, they were so warm.

"You're becoming quite an actress, but that was a little too close to the truth, love," Lad breathed into her ear. "Something keeps you awake, does it?"

"Something *does* keep me awake," she said, turning in his embrace until their faces were a hair's breadth apart, his breath warm on her cheek. "It's been keeping me awake almost every night for weeks, and I just *don't* know what to *do* about it." She let her hands explore under his silken shirt and suppressed a giggle. Their lips met and his warmth invaded her, leaving her breathless and hungry.

When their lips parted he said, "I've brought you a present."

"A present?" She smiled at him and ran her fingers through her hair. "For me?"

"Yes." Lad held up before her eyes a ring of braided obsidian and gold. "It's very important, Wiggen. It's a secret, and you must promise me never to put it on. If you do, it will never ever come off. You've got to keep it safe, just in case..."

"In case what?" She took it from him and looked at it. It wasn't particularly pretty, and she felt no desire to slip it on her finger.

"In case I have to kill someone," he said, shaking his head slowly.

"I'll keep it safe, Lad. Don't worry." Wiggen dropped the ring into the pocket of her dress and forgot about it. She wouldn't let such a trifle ruin their evening.

"I'm sorry about this, Wiggen. Having to sneak in here like this." His face drew serious, his eyes longing. "Asking you to lie to Forbish. Keeping our love a secret. We should be able to be together all the time, day and night, forever."

"We will be, Lad," she said, drawing him to her once again. "One day, when they aren't looking for you any longer."

"But that could be years, Wiggen."

"I don't care," she breathed into the hollow of his neck, relishing his scent. She walked him backward until his legs struck the edge of her bed and they tumbled onto the thick coverlet together. "Because, until dawn, you're *mine*."

About The Author

From the sea to the stars, Chris A. Jackson's stories take you to the far reaches of the imagination. Raised on the deck of a fishing boat and trained as a marine biologist, he became sidetracked by a career in biomedical research, but regained his heart and soul in 2009 when he and his wife Anne left the dock aboard the 45-foot sailboat *Mr Mac* to cruise the Caribbean and write fulltime.

With his nautical background, writing sea stories seemed inevitable. The acclaimed Scimitar Seas nautical fantasies won three consecutive Gold Medals in the *ForeWord Reviews* Book of the Year Awards. His Pathfinders Tales from Paizo Publishing combine high-seas combat and romance set in the award-winning world of the Pathfinder Roleplaying Game. Not to be outdone, Privateer Press released *Blood & Iron*, and *Watery Graves*, swashbuckling tales set in the Iron Kingdoms role-playing game universe. Chris' latest venture is a contemporary fantasy, *Hellmaw: Dragon Dreams*, and the high fantasy Stormtalons novel, *The Queen's Scourge*, from The Ed Greenwood Group.

Chris' repertoire also includes the award-winning and Kindle best-selling Weapon of Flesh Series, as well as additional fantasy novels, the humorous sci fi Cheese Runners trilogy of novellas, and short stories.

Preview Chris' novels, download audiobooks, and read his writing blog at jaxbooks.com. Follow Chris' sailing adventures at www.sailmrmac.blogspot.com

Other Fantasy Novels by Chris A. Jackson

From Jaxbooks
A Soul for Tsing
Deathmask

Weapon of Flesh Series
Weapon of Flesh
Weapon of Blood
Weapon of Vengeance
Weapon of Fear*
Weapon of Pain*
Weapon of Mercy*
(* with Anne L. McMillen-Jackson)

The Cornerstones Trilogy
(with Anne L. McMillen-Jackson)
Zellohar
Nekdukarr
Jundag

The Cheese Runners Trilogy
(novellas – also on Audible)
Cheese Runners
Cheese Rustlers
Cheese Lords

From Dragon Moon Press
Scimitar Moon
Scimitar Sun
Scimitar's Heir
Scimitar War

From Paizo Publishing
Pirate's Honor
Pirate's Promise
Pirate's Prophecy

From Privateer Press
Blood & Iron (ebook novella)
Watery Graves

From The Ed Greenwood Group
Hellmaw: Dragon Dreams
Stormtalons: The Queen's Scourge

Check out these and more at
JAXBOOKS☐COM
Want to get an email about my next book release?
Sign up at: http://eepurl.com/xnrUL

Made in the USA
Columbia, SC
16 August 2019